WHERE DO YOU GO TO

Jean Cerfontaine

Inspired by "Where do you go to (my lovely)?"
Peter Sarstedt (1969)

Cover designed by Marki Fourie

Jean Cerfontaine
Visit my website www.jeancerfontaine.com
Follow me on Twitter @CerfontaineJean

Printed in the United States of America

First Print Edition: January 2019
Independently published

ISBN-13 978-1-7908001-3-1

To my wife Natasja

COLD AND DARKNESS, 1948

The night was cold and dark, midnight long since passed. A battered blue truck lumbered down the unlit city street, light fog parting in its wake. As it slowed down, a small form emerged from beneath the tarpaulin covering the back. The young girl clung to the rear of the truck, preparing to leap off. A sudden burst of acceleration caught her unaware, her tenuous grip lost. She hit the roadway in a mad tumble, her momentum finally arrested by the raised curb. Her lifeless body settled on the sidewalk, unmoving in the cold.

When she awoke, all memories were absent, an opaque veil hung over everything prior to this moment. She didn't know how long she had been out, but now faced the prospect of an unknown city in the grim, dark time just before dawn. Even though it was late March, the night was freezing and the local populace knew better than to be outside. She was a young girl of perhaps eight years of age, her clothing totally out of place in the dark streets, dressed only in a tattered yellow summer dress and a soiled cardigan. The cold and darkness consumed the lost child, having already spread to her very bones. Somewhere a shoe had gone astray, her progress hampered by the loss.

She was running from something. She knew that much. But the memory *of what*, eluded her. Her name escaped her as well. Certain things were still present in her memory- she could read the street signs and she could count her steps. Who she was and where she came from, however, had eluded her mind, a black hole consuming her memories of self. A splitting headache left her feeling nauseous. If she tried to think too hard, it ached even more. The pain was a reminder she must have injured herself earlier in the night. *Perhaps that is why she cannot remember anything? How hard did she hit her head? And while doing what?* She had touched the part of her scalp which was the most painful and her fingers came back, covered in drying, dark blood. *At least she was not bleeding at the moment.*

Plodding along, the cold pavers of the street stung the sole of her bare foot. She passed a road sign, pointing in the direction she came from. It read *Pomezia/Napoli. Perhaps I came from one of those two places*, she thought. In her confused state, she could not place the towns in any country. She was in an unknown city, in a strange country, in a foreign world. And she was cold. The cold was the only thing she knew with certainty and it concerned her that if she were to stop and sit down, she would die.

A chilly breeze cut through her flimsy dress and cardigan as if they were absent altogether. She looked forward to the coming dawn, because with it, the sun would bring a little warmth. Somewhere in the next block a dog barked woefully, *she was not completely alone outside in the cold.* In the distance was another sign, an arrow pointing ahead. She had heard of the *Colosseum*, but could still not figure out where she could be, based on this knowledge. A road branching off to the left seemed more inviting than the one she was on. *In the absence of a destination, any road would do.* The new road was lined with shop windows, dark displays peering out at her from the inside. The roadside shops evolved into a suburban neighbourhood, houses now flanking the street on both sides. *Should I knock on one of the doors? Would they open up? Would they be friendly?* There was too much uncertainty behind the closed doors and dark windows of the houses. She rather kept moving along.

The distance she had travelled to get here was unknown, but her strength was waning. The part she remembered walking was already quite a journey for someone of her age, in the dark of night, all alone. For one so young to have gone so far on her own, demonstrated persistence and grit far beyond her years.

She was driven by the courageous feeling that she should keep going and carry on.

As the skyline on her right started showing shades of red, the promising prospect of a little heat was now in the near future. The outlines of buildings became visible and birds started waking up in the trees lining the road. Ahead, she saw a small square in the road, a fountain proudly standing in the centre of it. She had not realised how parched she was until she saw the water and ran forward to quench her thirst from one of the fountain spouts. The freezing cold water burned her hands and her throat, but helped settle her severe dehydration. She washed her arms; the water stinging the cuts and grazes. Standing by the fountain, she could see a large building behind it, a tall, pointed tower raising skywards with a cross on top. Although she could not remember ever having been to a church, the building looked familiar, giving rise to feelings of comfort and maybe even a sense of hope. Warmth and safety emanated from the tall stone structure. She somehow knew safety must lie within its walls. Going with her gut instinct, she investigated the building, sensing that staying outside in the cold was slowly killing her.

She approached the entrance stealthily, still hesitant of the chosen course and of what lay within. The front door was a massive, wooden thing, with elaborate carvings on the surface. She was able to discern some of these in the light of the rising sun. Some of the carvings gave her hope, but some were eerily frightening. She pulled on the wrought iron handle to try opening the huge door. It did not budge. In her weakened state, she could not move it, even if it had not been locked. She gave another desperate tug, all in vain. The door remained an immovable barrier between her and the imagined warmth on the other side.

Walking back to the square, for a moment, she considered lying down next to the fountain and dozing off, never to wake up again. *No! You must persist. Find another way!* An inner voice prompted her. She investigated the side of the building, the early sunlight reflecting off a hundred stained glass windows set in the wall of the church. It would have been beautiful under normal circumstances, but now it was only creating distance between herself and her last hope of staying alive at the back of the building, where an alcove with another door was visible. As she walked past the church, her cold mind wandered and a red pool suddenly spread on the cobblestones, a human form floating to the surface. She shook her head and the frightening vision was gone as quickly is as it came.

Tugging on the handle, she expected the side entrance to be locked, as the front one had been. The door creaked and opened slightly. A ray of light escaped from inside the church, giving rise to a sliver of hope. She entered and was greeted by a candle-lit interior filled with wooden benches. It was warm and welcoming. The ceiling was ornately painted with multiple frescos, depicting biblical scenes of inspiration and fellowship. In the dim light, the people in the paintings stared at her with kind eyes, and she felt safe in their presence.

She looked at the bench next to her. Someone had left a prayer pillow on it. After her exhausting journey, even the hard wooden seating appeared inviting. She sat down on the bench, swung her legs up and rested her head on the solitary red pillow. Her eyes closed and she drifted off to sleep. Sister Agnes found her passed out on the church pew, cold but breathing, when she came into the church for morning prayers an hour later.

A NEW BEGINNING IN
MARCIGLIANA, 1948

T he little girl woke up in strange surroundings, for the second time in as many days. She knew she was no longer in the church where she fell asleep. Everything was different. The bed was soft and the ceiling was bland, no sign of the expected church frescoes. She pushed up on her elbows and looked at her surroundings. The walls were whitewashed, as far as she could discern in the dim light from the bulbs spread out in a row across the room. There were no stained glass windows here. Her head throbbed to the rhythm of her heartbeat and when she reached up to touch it, her fingers felt a bandage wrapped tightly around her hair.

An olive green metal trolley stood next to her bed, with a jug and a glass, tidily placed on a tray. She was terribly thirsty and helped herself to some water. The bed was made with white linen, faded yellow with the relentless passing of time. Worn tiling covered floor, the repetitive pattern leading off into infinity. At the end of the row of beds was a recessed door set in the centre of the far wall. Next to it was a table, a neatly dressed nun sitting behind it. She was reading in the light of a desk lamp.

Memories of any sort before her cold night time journey still eluded her, but somehow, she recognised the clothing and demeanour of the woman at the desk as that of a nun. It was an ingrained type of memory, like knowing the sky was blue, or that water was wet. One of the beds opposite her was occupied. In the fading daylight, she could discern a black-haired girl lying under the sheets. What little was visible of her face, did not reflect contentment. The girl opposite was suddenly racked by a coughing fit, the concerned nun getting up to see to her. She noticed that her other patient was awake as well and staring at her. 'How are you feeling this evening, young one?' she asked from across the room as she felt the forehead of the coughing girl.

'My head hurts and I'm hungry,' was the curt response, quickly followed by some questions. 'Where am I? How did I get here? Do you know my name?' She was desperate for answers to a great many things. The nun, satisfied with the temperature of the second girl, walked over to her bed. 'I am Sister Cecile and you are in the orphanage of *Marcigliana*. I do not know who you are my child, they only brought you here this morning. You must have hit your head quite hard, as you have been asleep for most of the day,' the nun continued, 'Do not fret, you are safe here and we will look after you. I will go to fetch you some supper from the kitchens so that we can ease your hunger.' The nun left the two girls alone in the sick-bay.

'Hello. What is your name?' she asked the black-haired girl across the aisle.
'I am Arianna,' the second girl responded in a weak voice, hoarse from days of coughing. 'Do you really not know what your name is? How strange...'
'Arianna? That's a pretty name! Yes, it is rather strange. I do hope I get my memory back soon. It feels like I was born yesterday. But I do know *some* things, at least. Where is this place?' she asked waving her arm around in a vague circle.
'The orphanage is in the hills, just outside Rome,' Arianna responded. She coughed again.
'How long have you been here? Do you know if the *Colosseum* is in Rome?' she asked Arianna, who was a bit surprised at the second question.
'I've been here most of the week and... uhm, yes, the *Colosseum* is in Rome. I caught a terrible cold and I just hope it clears up soon.'

So then I was in Rome yesterday, she realised. Not that it helped her memory at all. She responded to Arianna. 'No silly, how long have you been at the orphanage?'

'Ooh,' Arianna gave a feeble laugh, 'I've been here for three years, since I was seven. My aunt got very sick and died in the hospital. I didn't have any other family left to take care of me. Then the nuns brought me here. They looked after me ever since. What about you?'

'I have no idea! I arrived in Rome during the night, only I didn't know it was Rome. I can't remember how I got there and I lost my shoe. Then I luckily ended up in a church and fell asleep on one of the benches. When I woke up, I was here. Did you see what time they brought me in at all? I do hope the food comes soon, I'm awfully hungry.'

'I think you came in around 10 o'clock this morning. I usually get my medicine then and you arrived just after. Ghastly stuff, that medicine. I hope you are not too hungry. The food here is not a lot you know, but at least we have three meals a day,' Arianna replied. 'The cook is from France, I suppose she might have been a chef before. She can make magic in the kitchen! There's also a herb garden behind the building and a chicken coop.'

The girl continued quizzing Arianna. 'How many children live here?' Before there was a chance to respond, Sister Cecile returned with a tray. The serving dish contained a bowl of pasta, with some tomatoes and a glass of milk. The food was a welcome relief and she devoured it and gulped down the milk. The pasta was actually quite tasty, more so than she was expecting. Sister Cecile gave her some more medication and she took the pills with the water on the bedside table. Very soon, she was feeling drowsy again and drifted off to sleep.

The following morning, the girl with the bandage was woken up by the bright sunlight streaming in through the windows. Sister Cecile was nowhere to be seen and was ostensibly replaced by a different nun, continuing the vigil in the infirmary. Arianna was still asleep in the bed opposite, softly snoring. She got out of bed and slowly walked over to the nun, her bare feet noiselessly traversing the floor. *At least my head is feeling a bit better*, she thought.

Her sudden appearance at the desk startled the nun out of a light doze. 'What!? Who.!? Oh, hello. How are you feeling my child?'

'Much better, thank you. My head is only aching slightly now. Where is Sister Cecile this morning?'

'Oh bless your heart, my girl. Sister Cecile is at prayers in the Chapel. I am Sister Rosa.' She looked at the time. 'Breakfast should be here soon, then we can take you to see the Mother Superior. Can you remember your name yet, child?'

'I'm afraid not. It's all fuzzy. I can't remember anything,' was the dejected response from the little girl.

'That's fine, my child. We'll get Holy Mother to remedy that with a temporary name, to use as you please until you can remember your own.'

The breakfast arrived and she enjoyed the meal sitting over the side of the bed. The rations were meagre, but very tasty. The breakfast of soup and bread, was well received by the hungry youngster. Feeling invigorated after the night's rest and the morning meal, the young girl was now ready to accompany Sister Rosa to see the Mother Superior. She had not seen anything but the sick-bay and was curious about the rest of the building. It seemed to be a large structure with several floors. On the way, they passed some winding staircases and a courtyard could be seen through the windows in the passages. The building was painted a pale shade of yellow, faded and cracked by years in the sun. There was a noteworthy absence of any other children in the passages. *Perhaps they are all having breakfast somewhere in a dining hall at this time of the morning*, it occurred to her. The nun's footsteps echoed down the corridors in the deserted building. Her own feet were still bare and did not make a sound on the linoleum floors. They arrived at a faded blue door, knocked and went inside.

The office on the other side housed the Head Nun of the orphanage and was rather threadbare, or humble, far removed from the grandiose offices often associated with senior clergy. There was a very functional, stout wooden desk, with little aesthetic value. It served its intended purpose of being a work surface and was filled with papers and books. The floor was bare, except for a stained area rug in front of the desk. It offered the barefoot orphan a brief respite from the cold floors in the rest of the building. There was a picture of the Holy Madonna against the wall behind the nun. Her arms were outstretched in the portrait, a much needed welcoming figure. One wall had a bookshelf against it, filled with religious writings and other books. Two wooden chairs in front of the desk completed the furnishings in the room, the feet wedged into the carpet. The woman behind the desk was an imposing figure, ample in size filling and the chair beyond its capacity. She had a friendly face, though, and the youngster felt at ease in her presence.

Behind the friendly face, was a contradictory commanding voice- 'You may excuse yourself, Sister Rosa. I am sure you have other patients to tend to in the infirmary.' The obedient nun turned and left, leaving the girl alone with her stately elder, who cast a scrutinising eye over the bedraggled little girl in front of her. She was wearing one of the green infirmary gowns, made from a donation of old theatre scrubs by a local hospital. Her dark brown hair was covered with a bandage which still looked brand new. She had a cute face with a little button nose. Her eyes were an azure shade of blue, with an intelligent look behind them and every indication that her spirit had not been broken yet. 'What is your name my girl, and how did you get here?'

The girl regaled the nun with her story of memory loss and the little she could remember of her night-time journey through Rome. The elderly nun was saddened by the tale, short as it may have been. She was a compassionate and caring authority figure in the orphanage and was still filled with empathy for fellow human beings, even after many years of exposure to human suffering in her cloister during the war. 'We shall have to name you something, you cannot wander around here nameless. However will we call you for dinner??' The young girl giggled at the nun's humour.

9

The nun pointed to the bookshelf. 'There is a thick green volume on there, called *Names in Europe*. Please bring it over so that we can start remedying your unwanted anonymity.' The girl complied and placed the large volume on the only open space on the table, in front of the nun. 'Now come stand here next to me behind the desk, little one.' The nun closed her eyes and muttered a short prayer. With her eyes still closed, she opened the book at a random page. She then opened her eyes. 'Now close your eyes and drop your finger on this page, little one.' This had been the naming ritual at *Marcigliana* for countless years.

There were many nameless orphans after the war and many fatherless babies being left at churches, mostly anonymously. The nun firmly believed the Lord would guide her hand and the hand of the child to the appropriate name. The girl opened her eyes and looked at her finger. It was positioned in the "M" section of French names, on the name *Marie-Claire*. 'Well there you are. *Marie-Claire*! A beautiful name even though a pretty girl like you could do with any old one.' The young girl was pleased as she thought it was a pretty name too and it seemed a good fit. 'We will call you that until your memory returns and you remember your own name.'

'Let me tell you a bit about the orphanage, so you know your place in the greater scheme of things.' The nun launched into an oft repeated description of the orphanage and its hierarchy. 'We are located about 15 miles from Rome and if you take one of the round corner staircases to the roof and look to the South West, you can see the city. You'll have to take my word for that, as you are never allowed to be on the roof!' She said the last bit with a forbidding smile. 'The orphanage has been running since the 30s and during the war we had an influx of orphans from all over Italy. There are around 150 orphans here, almost equal numbers of boys and girls. At least we are not as crowded as some of the facilities in Rome itself. You will see that the orphanage is arranged in a square around the central courtyard. You are allowed to be there any time of day. You are not allowed outside of the walls of the building at night! The outbuildings contain the laundry and garden shed, which is adjacent to the herb and vegetable garden. You should also take heed to care for the garden properly when called upon, this is an important supplement for the rations delivered by the government every week. We don't want you getting scurvy!' There was an accentuating wink.

Marie-Claire now had an idea of her surroundings in *Marcigliana*. She felt like having a name was the first step of a new life. *Knowing oneself.* Or at least knowing which name to use when creating memories of oneself. The nun escorted her back to the infirmary to recover from her ordeals for another day before joining the rest of the orphans in their daily programme. She arrived at the sick-bay, ready to start the rest of her life journey. Unlike most other journeys, hers started by getting back *into* bed, if only until the next morning. The sense of bewilderment and confusion that had plagued her earlier in the day had started abating slowly. Marie-Claire experienced the first flickers of dim hope that originated from having absolutely nothing in life and then being given a gift to call her own. The simple gift of a name. A name handed out by a kind, wise old nun in rural Italy.

SPRINGTIME IN PARIS, 1965

The City of Lights had a magical quality in the springtime. From the manicured emerald lawns of the *Eiffel Tower*, packed with picnic blankets and couples young and old, to the lush greenery of the *Parc de Buttes-Chaumont* in the North East of the city, there was no shortage of romance in Paris. The city appeared dressed in a corsage of flowers, bright colours permeating the daily lives of every Parisian, as the trees blossomed and the ladies bloomed. The *Boulevard Saint Michel* cleft the Latin Quarter in two before it crossed the *Seine* and the *Île de la Cité*, finally running to its conclusion at the *Gare de L'Est*, the railroad gateway to Eastern France.

On the left bank, close to the *Pont Saint Michel*, was a narrow cobbled thoroughfare to the *Place Saint André des Arts*. At the corner of this nondescript intersection stood *La Bouffe*, a charming brasserie. *La Bouffe* was popular amongst the local student population and was often crowded with a veritable throng of patrons in the late afternoon, until early into the morning hours. The upper floors of the building contained residences, the very top floor playing host to Marie-Claire's Penthouse. Her residence, spacious by Parisian standards, seemed much larger than one would have expected a single student to occupy.

The front door opened up to the living area, tastefully decorated in modern furniture, with a hint of Provençal charm added in. A record player in the corner was playing something by Yves Montand, a live recording from a show in Russia. This particular album's cover was signed to Marie-Claire with a personal message. The remainder of the record collection had the newest Rolling Stones albums, mixed with more traditional French music by Serge Gainsbourg, Sacha Distel and Édith Piaf. In the other corner of the living room was a large fireplace, the wall above it accentuated by a deep burgundy wall paper, on which hung an unfinished nude artwork. It was reminiscent of the earlier works by Picasso. Although the flat fell short of luxurious, the dark wooden floors and stylish furnishings created an elegant living space. There were some items that seemed out of place in the room, not matching the rest of the decorations- a battered copy of *20 000 Leagues under the Sea* by Jules Verne and an old leather satchel hanging on a coat hook, amongst these.

The main bedroom had an *en suite* bathroom and an abundance of closet space, filled to capacity. Above the bed hung a beautiful oil painting depicting *The Creation of Adam*. The dressing table had a collection of cosmetics, arranged in baskets and a bejewelled Madonna figurine. The second bedroom was used as a guest room, also containing a large writing desk. Next to the lounge, the dining room was re-purposed as an art studio. Stained sheeting covering the floor under an easel, containing a work in progress, prominently featuring cobble stones, some stained dark red. Art supplies were neatly arranged on a table and other artworks stacked in haphazard fashion against the walls. The kitchen had clean lines and modern appliances, which did not reflect regular use. A doorway by the stove led to a second bathroom.

A set of French doors in the dining room opened up to a balcony, wrapping around the corner of the building. The spires of the *Notre Dame Cathedral* were visible over the adjacent rooftops. Marie-Claire sat on the balcony enjoying her breakfast- a croissant with strong, local coffee. Flower boxes added some colour to the peaceful rooftop, which created a scene worthy of an impressionist painting. After sunset, this was one of her favourite times of the day. Marie-Claire stared at the cathedral and contemplated her programme for the rest of the day.

This evening, she would be attending a party with her father at the Soviet Embassy, by invitation of his long-time friend, Valerian Zorin. Zorin had quite recently been appointed as ambassador to France. His diplomatic duties had introduced Marie-Claire's father to many fellow diplomats over the years and Zorin was one of these. They had met while the Frenchman served as the ambassador in Moscow in the 50s. Marie-Claire had considered the Russian an honorary uncle. The party inadvertently gave rise to a packed schedule for the day. She had both a dress fitting at the House of Balmain and a hair appointment to attend, all before lunch. Balmain had been designing dresses for her for many years now and her closet brimmed with his creations.

She checked her wristwatch. *I need to leave. Now.* Having a last sip of coffee, she grabbed a bag and ventured out into the city. A floral summer dress gave her a fashionably chic appearance, perfect for the balmy spring weather. Marie-Claire took the Metro to *Châtelet,* where a quick change routed her to *Franklin D Roosevelt* station. Exiting the metro station, she strolled up the *Champs-Élysées.* The wide avenue was lined with designer brand boutiques, fulfilling anyone's wildest shopping dreams. She turned into the *Rue Marbeuf,* continuing her stroll past the multi-coloured café awnings covering Parisians, enjoying their coffee and breakfast while observing the passing world.

Marie-Claire turned into *Rue François 1er* and arrived at the headquarters of the House of Balmain. The drab exterior of the building totally belied the creative genius harboured therein. A friendly doorman greeted her with a touch of his hat as she swept past. 'Good morning *Mademoiselle.* Welcome the House of Balmain.' She crossed the lavish foyer and reported to the desk. A fashionably dressed young woman greeted her.

'I have an appointment with Erik Mortensen at 10 o'clock. Marie-Claire le Blanc. I am a little early, so I am happy to wait for him.'

'You may take a seat miss. Could I offer you some refreshments while you wait?'

'No thank you, I just had some breakfast coffee.' Mortensen did not leave her waiting for too long. He was a tall gentleman in his early forties with dark, wavy hair.

'Marie-Claire, delighted to see you again! You look positively radiant this morning. Such a chic outfit, you have to tell me who dresses you,' he joked as he kissed her on the cheeks. 'I think you will be extremely pleased with the design for this evening, Pierre did a marvellous job.'

'Thanks Eric, I can't wait to see what he has in store for me.' They entered a change room upstairs, a covered mannequin standing in the centre of the mirrored room. An assistant was waiting for them. Eric pulled the sheet off the mannequin with a flourish, revealing a dark grey, sleeveless evening gown with finely embroidered obsidian flower patterns. 'Oh Eric, that is absolutely gorgeous,' Marie-Claire said, once she had caught her breath.

'I will step outside and Janine can assist you with trying it on.'

The dress slipped over her head and fell down her shapely body until it was perfectly positioned, clearly designed to hug her flawless figure. After giving them ample time to adjust the dress, Mortensen re-entered the room. 'Simply magnificent!' he praised the outfit and its wearer. 'Fit for royalty. You will be the belle of the ball, my darling.'

As Marie-Claire observed the beautiful dress from all angles, Pierre Balmain himself walked into the dressing room. The balding couturier kissed Marie-Claire on each cheek. 'You are an absolute vision, my dear!' She walked around the small room, turning and bowing, observing the flow of the dress. *A work of art.* 'I love it Pierre! You are a genius. I do hope you're never planning on retiring!' Balmain blushed. 'Can we make the usual arrangements for payment?'

'Certainly!' Balmain responded. 'We will add the invoice to your father's account, as normal. I have to take my leave. It was wonderful to see you again and I think you look spectacular in the dress. Janine, could you please arrange to have the dress delivered to Ms Le Blanc's residence this afternoon?'

'Certainly, Mr Balmain, I will make all the necessary arrangements.'

15

'Oh Marie-Claire, one more thing... We are having the launch of our new spring collection in two weeks. I would be most honoured if you could join us as a guest? I will include some tickets in the delivery to your apartment. Of course, I will reserve you a front-row seat!'

'Thank you Pierre. I would be my pleasure to be your guest. Thank you again for the gorgeous dress.' She changed back into her own clothing after the two designers stepped out, arm in arm. *What a delightful pair of gentlemen*, she thought.

Once again, her pressing schedule left her short of time as she left the change room. 'Could you please hail me a taxi?' she asked the doorman politely. He complied with practised professionalism and soon she found herself seated in a yellow Peugeot, en route to her next appointment.

Alexandre de Paris was widely hailed as the master of hairstyling in Paris and Marie-Claire would not want anyone else to do her hair for the evening. He had promised her a very special design and she couldn't wait to see what he had in mind. The taxi ride to his salon, just off the *Place Vendôme,* was a brief one, passing by some of the famous landmarks in the area. The discreet salon proved a humble veneer for all the remarkable exploits of the owner. She arrived just in time for her appointment.

The Maestro's salon was chic and contemporary with artful touches of décor, reflecting the unique style of the proprietor. Alexandre himself greeted her when she entered the salon. 'Marie-Claire! Fabulous to see you! Welcome, welcome! Jo, please take *Mademoiselle* Le Blanc to the back and wash her hair without delay.' There were four other clients in the salon, in various creative stages of hair design by the master stylist. Ten more junior staff members were looking after the various needs of the guests during the process. Coffee, *Petit fours* and snacks were on offer, while reading of glamour magazines accompanied the multiple stages of styling.

Marie-Claire was escorted to a basin at the back of the salon where her hair was washed with Alexandre's own secret shampoo and conditioner. He had discovered early in his career that commercially available hair products simply did not meet his exacting standards and he started experimenting with his own mixture, which he has now perfected. Her styling would be broken up into two sittings today. The current session would be a wash and style, while Alexandre would be adding the final touches this evening at her apartment, complementing the design with a selection of additional hair jewels to complete his artistic work. While she waited on him, two assistants started tending to a manicure and pedicure. They worked with efficiency and professionalism borne from years of training and mentoring by Alexandre. His salon offered a complete service and no element of styling and pampering could detract from any of the others. *Simply divine*, Marie-Claire thought as she lay back in the chair.

Halfway through her manicure, Alexandre joined the fray and began drying and styling her hair. He added his unique touch to the style, with elaborate brush strokes in-between the blow-drying and curling of her shiny brown locks. His face was a portrait of concentration as he plied his trade. Shortly after one o'clock, the work was completed. 'There you go, Marie-Claire. Wonderful, wonderful. Perfection! I am pleased with the outcome. Are you happy?'

She admired the design in the mirror. 'I am delighted, Alexandre! A marvellous creation. Thank you so much!'

'Giselle, flag down a taxi for *Mademoiselle* Le Blanc,' he commanded one of his staff. 'I will see you later in the afternoon, Marie-Claire. Good day.'

'Later, Alexandre!'

The trip home proved pleasantly atypical. A shiny blue Citroen picked her up, driven by a middle aged Albanian that smelled vaguely of garlic and onions. He commented non-stop about museums, monuments and which seating at the *Palais Garnier* opera house had the best acoustics, as the taxi headed south towards her neighbourhood on the left bank. It was a fascinating trip. Marie-Claire paid him his dues and a handsome tip and he sped off to his next fare, now entering a heated political debate with the radio announcer. The extended nature of her morning programme had left her both exhausted and ravenous, so she decided to stop by *La Bouffe* for lunch, before returning to her apartment.

Some residual patrons were still present after the lunchtime rush, the stragglers mostly students from the nearby *Sorbonne,* getting inadvertently waylaid and missing their afternoon lectures. The *Maître'd* acknowledged her instantly and came straight over with a menu and a warm smile. 'Good afternoon, Marie-Claire. You are looking lovely as always!'

'Hello Peter. How are you? Are the locals keeping you busy and out of trouble?'

She had been staying in the apartment for several years and was a regular at *La Bouffe*. All the staff at the restaurant adored her, as she had been a consistent fixture in the establishment. Peter was a little older than her, but had started off as a busboy shortly after she relocated to the area to begin her studies. One could say they almost matured together in Paris over the years. The two shared some wine and conversations when it had been quiet and he was often the last one to leave the premises in the evening. He was well acquainted with her dining and drinking proclivities. Peter was taller than the average Frenchman and his accent did not quite sound Parisian. Marie-Claire suspected he hailed from somewhere else originally, but had never come as far as to ask where that may be. He had a scar on his left temple, which was slightly lighter than the rest of his face.

'We always enjoy serving the locals, Marie-Claire. You know that better than most. One of these days summer will arrive and the only French we will be able to speak will be swearing under our breaths at the tourists.' Marie-Claire knew he was in the restaurant business for a living, but that his passion had always been writing poetry and prose. She laughed at his remark. 'That's why I don't spend my summers in Paris. I tend to speak my mind and sometimes, some unfortunate local gets called upon to translate. Frightfully embarrassing for everyone involved. I'll have my normal baguette please, Peter,' she requested '… and a glass of white?'

18

Peter walked off in the direction of the kitchen, shouting instructions to the barman when he passed, and picking up some dirty dishes as he skirted a freshly vacated table. Five minutes later, a waiter came with her drink and shortly thereafter, lunch arrived. It looked fresh and scrumptious, with Camembert cheese, fresh tomatoes and lettuce filling the bread. Marie-Claire was looking forward to a reclining nap on her sofa upstairs after lunch. Feeling freshly revived for the party this evening was very important, she would not want to disappoint her father by leaving early. Her mother had been recovering from a bout of illness and she would officially accompany the ageing diplomat to the function as his consort for the evening.

She sat under the green awnings, watching Paris pass by and enjoying lunch. Serge Gainsbourg strode past the restaurant, heading towards the adjacent square. She waved at him. 'Hi Serge! How are you?'

'Marie-Claire, so good to see you again!' the singer greeted Marie-Claire warmly when he spotted her. He had known her for several years and they often spent time together at social functions. 'How are you?' he continued unabated, without waiting for an answer, 'Lovely weather we are having. I see you're making the best of it out here. I'm actually glad I ran in to you. I am hosting a dinner party for some friends on Friday evening. Sacha and France will both be in attendance and it would be fantastic if you could join us?'

'Thank you Serge, that sounds lovely. I would be happy to come. It has been too long since I last saw Sacha and I am thrilled at the prospect of catching up. Do save me a seat next to him?'

'Great! I will do so. It promises to be a lively affair. Here is my new address, I have moved since you last attended my birthday party,' he wrote it down on a napkin for her. After exchanging some pleasantries, Serge continued on his way. 'I'll see you at eight on Friday,' he said as they parted company.

'I look forward to it. Say hello to Béatrice!' she half shouted after him as he walked off.

When the meal was done, Marie-Claire was feeling satiated, but still desperately craving some rest before the evening. She settled her bill, bid the waiter goodbye and left the restaurant. Peter was busy chastising a new delivery boy that brought a crate of vegetables in the front door of the restaurant. This was an error he was unlikely to repeat in any future deliveries, anywhere. 'Bye Peter,' she waved at him as she strolled away and he gave her a wink.

Marie-Claire unlocked the adjacent green door which led to the residence lobby, taking the elevator up to her apartment on the top floor. She sat down on the couch, kicked off her shoes and put her tired legs up. *Wow, what a morning.* Her eyelids were heavy, partly due to exhaustion and partly the meal. She dozed off on the couch, her head resting on the armrest. At four o'clock, the doorbell rang, and she was startled awake from a dream, the content of which she was unable to recall. There were tears on her cheeks and, as on so many other occasions, their emotional origins eluded her.

LIFE IN MARCIGLIANA, 1950

The young orphan Marie-Claire had been a resident at *Marcigliana* for two years now. She fit in as best as one could expect to fit into circumstances such as these. She was a quick study and seemed to have understood the institutional environment straight away, as if she had been exposed to such hardships before. Her memory had failed to return and her life story still started on that cold morning in Rome, two years prior.

Marie-Claire had spent a further two days in the infirmary after her initial arrival. A doctor Gardi tended to her on the second day, and being pleased with her progress, recommending her discharge. Marie-Claire and Arianna were the only occupants in the infirmary and they formed a strong bond during the time spent together in recovery. The two were soon the best of friends. Arianna remained behind in the sick-bay when Marie-Claire was discharged and subsequently, the daily visits continued until Arianna was well again, and discharged herself. The nuns at *Marcigliana* were compassionate and understanding of the plight of newly arrived orphans and seeing the friendship between the two girls develop, the decision was made to place Marie-Claire in the same dormitory room as Arianna. There were normally only four girls to a room, but they squeezed Marie-Claire in, nonetheless.

The room they shared was on the second floor, overlooking the inner gardens in the courtyard. There were only four standing cupboards in the room, so Marie-Claire was provided with an old chest at the bottom end of her cot as storage space for her meagre belongings. When she arrived, the chest was empty, except for a brown teddy-bear with a missing eye. The five cots were lined up in a row against the wall. Marie-Claire was assigned the middle one. Several windows in the wall above the row of beds provided ample natural light. The room decorations left much to be desired, with little else beside the furnishings to add to the décor. The other three occupants already living in the room were Katharina, Karin and Sofia.

Katharina, the eldest, had recently celebrated her fourteenth birthday in a muted ceremony, attended only by her roommates. She was a tall girl with blond hair and had a friendly demeanour. Born in the Soviet Union, she somehow ended up in an Italian orphanage at age seven and have been there ever since. As with many of the other children, she did not like discussing her history. Karin was the same age as Marie-Claire. The ginger's parents had been German scientists in Rome when the war broke out. When Italy surrendered to the Allied forces, Germans became very unpopular almost overnight. Even though they had been in the country for many years, the unfortunate couple were not spared the reprisal of an angry mob.

Sofia was ten, the same as Arianna. She was an unkind, unhappy person and would prove to be thoroughly nasty to Marie-Claire on every occasion that presented itself. Her black hair and dark brown eyes, which sometimes almost seemed to have a red undertone while she taunted Marie-Claire, gave her an ominous, brooding appearance. She did not take kindly to Arianna's friendship with the new girl and her actions spoke of deep betrayal by the easy acceptance of the newcomer.

The children at the orphanage were all assigned to chores. The nature of these varied between the ages of the children, but the underlying need to develop skills and a sense of responsibility prompted the arrangement. In an environment such as this, learning the virtue of hard work proved very important, as nothing in life would come easy for the orphans. Familiarity with performing menial labour was also an apt preparation for the standing they could expect to gain in life. Assignments rotated between the kitchens, laundry and gardens. The nuns expected everyone to clean after themselves, despite a number of permanent custodial staff employed by the orphanage. The laundry had some full-time staff and a kindly groundsman looked after the gardens. *Marcigliana* was run with a firm disciplinary undertone and orphans knew better than to bend the rules. The kitchen staff were the only ones recruited from amongst the ranks of the nuns at the convent.

Marie-Claire's first assignment came to be in the kitchen. Experience had shown that small hands found it easy to wash the insides of cups and jars, and so, she found herself in the scullery. This was often the entry level chore in the kitchen and applying oneself with enough enthusiasm and efficiency meant promotion to other, less greasy tasks. Sister Marcelle was in charge of the large kitchen and the ten children helping out the permanent culinary staff. A few of the older girls were taught how to cook and assisted by chopping vegetables and preparing, and dishing up all manner of meals which featured on the limited menu.

The kitchen could not be confused for a gourmet quality establishment, but Sister Marcelle had the gift of being able to coax wonderful flavours out of any foodstuff with the skilful addition of herbs and spices from the vegetable garden. She had a history of culinary training in Paris, but personal tragedy had changed her life path- first to an exploratory one through Italy, and finally ending at a convent door. The divine intervention leading to her arrival there had inspired her to submit to a life of service to church. After many years of service, she was assigned to the kitchens of *Marcigliana*, skills from her previous life now becoming once more useful.

On the day of Marie-Claire's first shift, Sister Marcelle gave her the less-than-grand tour of the kitchen. 'This is the scullery, my child, you will probably spend most of your time in here until you show us you are ready for higher levels of responsibility.' She continued the introduction to the rest of the kitchen environment. They spent some time in the pantry as Sister Marcelle explained her storage system for foodstuffs and dried goods. Everything in the pantry had its place and a reason for being where it was. 'Do you understand why it is so?'

'Yes, ma'am,' was the simple, unassuming response. The system made perfect sense, even to an eight-year-old.

They moved on to the rest of the cupboards, where the crockery was kept in neat stacks. There were masses of plates and bowls, for there were a great many mouths to feed at *Marcigliana*. The tour finally concluded in the vegetable garden. The nun explained in great detail the various herbs which were grown and what they could be used for. It was an important lesson to remember, as Marie-Claire could be called upon to fetch any number of herbs, if required for meal preparation.

'Any other questions?' the nun asked, after finishing the tour.

'Sister Marcelle, could you teach me to talk like you? I like the way the words sound when you say them,' came the innocent response from the child. The nun laughed. 'I'll have to teach you French first, then the accent will follow after.' Marie-Claire seemed excited at the prospect. 'I'd like that very much,' she said while clapping her hands in delight. Their French lessons started on the first day in the kitchen and continued every day thereafter. Initially, Sister Marcelle focused on vocabulary in and around the kitchen and later progressed to grammar and conversation in other environments. Marie-Claire seemed to have a natural ear for languages and was a fast study. After her first month, she had been almost fully conversant. The two woman, separated by decades in age, enjoyed speaking together in French, as it was almost as though they shared a secret bond of sisterhood.

When the time came to rotate her duties, Marie-Claire was almost a fluent conversationalist and returned to the kitchen daily to practise with Sister Marcelle. They eventually even progressed to writing the language, and the nun shared some of her French literature with Marie-Claire, to assist with her reading. What started off as only reading magazines, soon turned to being enthralled by Esméralda in *Hunchback of Notre Dame*, dreaming of riches described in *The Count of Monte Cristo* and wonderment at the fantastical settings sketched in the writing of Jules Verne. In an imperfect world, Marie-Claire had found a perfect escape in French literature and language.

Under ideal circumstances, Marie-Claire would not have been in need of this escape route from her surroundings, as although the nuns and staff at the orphanage were kind, all her fellow orphans were not. Sofia's cruelty seemed to have increased over time and she despised Marie-Claire for reasons known only to herself. One day, as they had been tending to their newly assigned garden chores, Sofia shoved her off her feet between the flower beds. The older girl had been behaving oddly for most of the day, talking to herself incessantly. This cruel act was the culmination of her abnormal conduct.

There was no-one else around in the immediate vicinity and as Marie-Claire sat on the gravel path, nursing her bruised knee, Sofia overturned an adjacent wheel barrow and spilled its contents on the already sobbing youngster. The contents, dry fertilising manure, covered Marie-Claire from head to toe in a dusty avalanche. Sofia pointed a finger at her, laughed maliciously and ran away, leaving the miserable girl crying in a pile of filth. Her tears made streaks in the grime on her face.

Mr Antonio, the groundsman, found the despondent girl in this state when he walked past a few minutes later. The sympathetic old man helped to dust her off and suggested that they rinse her off under the sprinkler. It was a warm day, so the cool water was not unpleasant. Getting wet brought out the terrible stench of the manure, making her gag as it washed off her clothes and out of her hair. This was but one of many unpleasant encounters with Sofia in her time at the orphanage.

On a morning like any other, Marie-Claire had breakfast with her fellow orphans in the large dining-hall of *Marcigliana*. Unknown to her, she was about to have an epiphany. The meal reflected the monotony of the meals at the orphanage, soup and bread served at the start of every day. Sofia entered late and was walking between the rows of tables, apparently arguing with herself. As she passed Karin, she yanked on one of her pig tails with distressing force. In response, Karin screamed at Sofia in German. Marie-Claire was astounded and gasped with wonder. She had often found herself thinking in this foreign language, but this was the first time she had heard it out loud and could understand it perfectly! Karin was hurling obscenities at Sofia and Marie-Claire hoped none of the nuns spoke the language, as the punishment for the foul language used in this tirade would be much worse than the act leading to it. She spoke to Karin in German, much to the surprise of everyone at the table. 'It's okay Karin, she's not worth it. Don't let it get to you.' Karin calmed down as suddenly as the outburst started and stared at Marie-Claire, equally amazed by this turn of events. Sofia had simply continued walking on and sat down at an empty seat several tables away.

Karin spoke to Marie-Claire. 'You speak German? Why didn't you ever tell me?'

'I didn't know I speak German! I often had thoughts in the language, but I didn't know *which* language it was. I didn't even know it was real. I've never heard anyone speak it, until today!' As amazing as this new discovery was, it created a social challenge for Marie-Claire. Karin was now much closer to her and the two were able to have secret conversations, most of the other orphans, however, started keeping their distance, as they disliked Germans. Due to the circumstances surrounding her parents' passing, Karin did not have a particular liking of Italians either, so the arrangement suited her rather well.

Arianna was not perturbed by the discovery that Marie-Claire had German origins. She was still her friendly self and spent most of her spare time in the company of Marie-Claire and sometimes Karin as well. The two girls did not speak German in front of Arianna, as they did not consider it polite. The chore rotations continued unabated and life carried on at the orphanage. Some days, a lucky orphan would be adopted by couples that came to visit and other days, new faces would arrive. It was the ebb and flow of life at *Marcigliana*.

One fateful day, Marie-Claire was walking through the garden towards the laundry with a basket of clothes. As she rounded the tower, she suddenly came across a lifeless form lying next to the base of it on the pathway. The girl's head was twisted at an unnatural angle and blood was beginning to seep out from underneath the body. Marie-Claire was shocked by the inhumanity of the scene she was witnessing. When she got close enough, she recognised the body as that of Sofia, her room-mate. Seeing the blood pooling on the gravel pathway, Marie-Claire had a sudden flashback. *There was a body in the moonlight, with blood pouring from the side of a boy's head, staining his dark hair and the cobblestones underneath it with a growing pool of dark blood.* The stark vision was only there for a moment and then the recollection disappeared from her thoughts again. Marie-Claire screamed for help at the top of her lungs.

DEPARTING MARCIGLIANA, 1950

The frantic cries for help in the quiet of the afternoon siesta soon led to two of the nuns arriving on the scene. It only took a moment to surmise what had happened. Their expressions reflected the horrific sight of the dead girl. One of the nuns kneeled next to the body and started reciting the last rite prayers, hoping that there was still an opportunity to save the soul of the departed child. The other nun hurried back into the building, to report the unfortunate turn of events to Mother Superior.

Marie-Claire observed the nun performing the prayer ritual. She appeared shocked by the solemnity of the situation, but did not feel deep feelings of regret or sadness. Although she had shared a room with Sofia, the girl's animosity towards her had grown increasingly intense of late, with continuous outbursts of anger and erratic behaviour. Marie-Claire had to start looking out to actively avoid Sofia in her daily programme at the orphanage. She felt that Sofia must be in a better place and said a silent prayer for the deceased girl.

A further group of nuns and Mr Antonio arrived hurriedly, with the Holy Mother in the lead. Sister Rosa came with a sheet she had brought from the infirmary. Once the kneeling nun had concluded her rituals, they covered the body with the sheet, obscuring the distressing sight. They would have to wait for the police to arrive before the body could be moved into the building. 'What happened?' the Holy Mother asked Marie-Claire, once arrangements had been made to contact the police.

'I was walking to the laundry and I thought I heard an odd sound. When I rounded the building, I found her here.'

'Did you see anyone else when you arrived?' the nun probed further.

'No, Reverend Mother. It was only her. I arrived quite quickly after hearing the sound, so I would have seen if anyone else was leaving the area.' The nun, satisfied with the explanation, would wait on the police to confirm the cause of this horrible event. She had experienced suicidal teenagers before and recognised the signs of a fall from height. There remained little doubt in her mind as to what had transpired.

Two police cars arrived about half an hour later, the coroner's van completing the procession. Three uniformed police officers and a detective descended on the macabre scene, trailed by the coroner and his assistant. Detective Mazelli, a portly balding gentleman in a black pin-stripe suit, introduced the policemen to the gathered nuns. He questioned everyone and then spoke to Marie-Claire at great length, as the first person on the scene. She described the event as she had done before, while the detective took notes in a leather-bound notebook. One of the uniformed policemen took photographs of the body, after the coroner removed the sheet.

The gravel was undisturbed around the body, showing no apparent signs of struggle. Detective Mazelli and the coroner examined the body, using a magnifying glass, while taking copious notes. The detective noted a small frayed tear with a piece of missing material in the hem of the girl's blue dress. When they were done photographing the scene, the body was partially covered with the sheet again. The detective asked one of the nuns to escort him up to the roof, while two of the officers stayed behind to guard the body, which was still being further examined by the coroner.

Detective Mazelli arrived at the top of the tower, out of breath from ascending the circular staircase. The upper end of the tower was not visited very often and a thin layer of dust covered the floor. A single set of footprints were visible in the dust on the floor, leading to the window. There was a dustless section between the window and the roof door. It seemed she was pacing back and forth, probably building up the courage for what was to follow. The police officer took photographs of the floor before the detective crossed it to the open window. As he leaned out the window to look down at the body and the small gathering of nuns holding vigil, he noticed a piece of blue material stuck to a protruding screw in the window frame. Mazelli collected the sample using a tweezer and placed it in a small plastic bag. He walked around the perimeter of the tower and onto the roof, checking for any other clues. After he was satisfied that he has covered all areas in the tower and the roof, he concluded his investigation and went downstairs. His final act was to match the piece of material from the tower to the rip in the dress. He stepped away with the coroner and had a muted discussion. After reaching a consensus, they returned to the gathered group. 'Upon careful consideration of all the corroborating evidence, I must conclude that the poor girl leapt to her death from the tower. There is no evidence of foul play,' the detective stated in summation of his findings.

Detective Mazelli bid everyone farewell, leaving his card with Mother Superior before departing the orphanage. The coroner and his assistant placed the body onto a gurney and covered it, before wheeling it to the waiting van. Sofia's abnormal behaviour in the preceding period had been an advanced sign of mental instability which had grown increasingly worse as time passed. The untrained nuns could not recognise the unfortunate girl's Schizophrenia for what it truly was and her worsening state of mind eventually led Sofia to leap off the tower to her untimely demise. It seemed that the voices in her head had finally driven her to take this drastic step. It proved but another senseless tragedy in the history of the *Marcigliana* orphanage.

The event haunted Marie-Claire for several weeks, even though Sofia had been callous and cruel to her at every possible opportunity. She was reminded that death came easily and the impersonal nature thereof in the orphanage. The young girl was more determined than ever to find an escape from her unfortunate circumstances. She did not want to end up like Sofia, a simple plaque somewhere on a stone wall her only proof of ever having existed. Marie-Claire spent many hours with Sister Marcelle, confiding in her the fears of her situation and her hopes for a better life, somewhere away from the oppressing routine of the institution and the terrible memories. Her French had really progressed remarkably and she was now able to even express abstract concepts and deep emotions in the language. There came a period where her conscience bothered her about the whole event. Marcelle gathered that Marie-Claire somehow felt responsible for the tragedy. She tried her best to make the young girl understand that death is a natural part of life, even if it sometimes happened prematurely. The nun knew the only viable chance of getting out of the orphanage was to get adopted and that mental well-being was an important factor in successful adoptions. She counselled the young girl as best she could and encouraged Marie-Claire as much as possible to carry on with her normal life and routine. Unstable children did not cope in new families and eventually, instability led to conclusions such as the case of Sofia, even if the nuns were aware of the problems and tried their best.

Marcelle had counselled Marie-Claire back to a level of normalcy and by the time she had rotated back to kitchen duty, she was coping with the events and with her life at the orphanage. The girl was 10 years old now and assigned more complex chores in the kitchen. In the normal world, ten-year-old children would be playing outside in the park, but in *Marcigliana* they were already seasoned kitchen hands. She was chopping vegetables on the day that her life changed forever, without any advance knowledge of the magnitude of the events that were about to transpire.

Childless couples often approached the orphanage of *Marcigliana* with the aim of making a better life for one of the orphans at the institution. Sometimes, couples that lost children in the war also came to try and mend their broken homes with the help of the nuns. The reasons for today's visitors were no different from previous ones. What was dissimilar from the norm, had been the stature of the pair. The Ambassador and his wife were sitting in Mother Superior's office, having tea with the elderly nun. 'I am unable to impregnate my wife,' the Ambassador confided in the nun. This was not an easy confession for most men to make, as pride often forced them away from the truth in the matter. But, the Ambassador was a noble man. He would not wish to cast aspersion on his wife's ability to bear children. The diplomat bore the shame silently, and his wife loved him for this. He was also an honest man, and sincere. Ambassador Henri Le Blanc was forty-one while his wife, Josephine, was younger, at thirty five. He had never had want of anything in his life, as his father had been a successful industrialist in Paris. The surroundings and circumstances of the orphanage touched him and he could empathise with the nuns and the unfortunate children in their care.

'I am about to leave Italy in the next couple of days, as I have been posted to Greece by the French Diplomatic Corps,' Mr Le Blanc started explaining. 'We would like to adopt one of your children and take them out of the country with us. We feel we could give them a better life and that we owe it to ourselves and to your beautiful country to help someone in this way.' The nun nodded. *She could understand this sentiment.*

'I can appreciate your situation, Ambassador. I am also appreciative of your willingness to assist a child at our facility, by providing them a chance at a better life. Do you know whether you want to adopt a boy or a girl?'

'We would like to adopt a girl,' the couple responded. 'I have many nephews to carry on the family name, so we would rather try to assist a girl out of these circumstances, as we think they will have a harder life here than any of the boys,' the Ambassador elaborated. The nun nodded her head again.

'Have you got any idea about the age of the girl you would want to adopt?' the nun enquired.

'We would hope for someone younger than a teenager,' Mrs Le Blanc responded. The couple had discussed this at length. They did not want a baby, or someone too young to understand that they were being taken away, but also did not want someone that have been exposed to the harshness of this lifestyle for too long. They felt that someone like that was bound to have grown apart from the joys of life and would have a heart which was difficult to open to a loving family. The nun nodded in understanding. 'I will take you on a tour of the facility and you can meet some of the children.'

It was early afternoon and most of the children were confined to their quarters, busy with their school homework. The nun took the couple from room to room and introduced the girls to them. They spent some time with the girls falling in the right age group and enquired about their circumstances. By late afternoon, they had met most of the girls, their tour ending in the kitchen. Marie-Claire was busy chopping carrots as the couple came in and spoke to Sister Marcelle. The youngster was focused on the sharp knife and was not paying much attention to the strangers in the kitchen. The couple requested Mother Superior to excuse them, as they wanted to have a private discussion. They left the kitchen through the back door and stood outside, discussing the girls they had met this afternoon and the decision they would have to make.

Marie-Claire had to empty the kitchen bin in the larger garbage can outside, as it was now full of carrot shavings and potato peels. As she approached the rear screen door, she heard the couple outside the door having a discussion in French. *They were talking about Karin!* Marie-Claire was surprised and stood still to listen. '... she seems like a nice girl, even if she is German. She is also likely to have a much harder time here, not being Italian. These are prejudiced times we find ourselves in,' the woman said to her husband. The husband nodded in agreement.

'Yes, that may well be the case. And she is ten, which is a good age.'

Marie-Claire opened the screen door. She looked at the couple and said in French 'I'm sorry, I overheard your conversation. You should take Karin away from here. She is my best friend on earth, but if you take her, I won't blame you.

She deserves better than this and you seem like nice people.' The couple was dumbstruck by the unexpected appearance of a French speaking girl.

'What is your name?' the lady asked.

'I am Marie-Claire,' was the response. 'Pleased to meet you.' The couple was still somewhat flustered. 'How did you end up here, so far away from France?'

'Oh no, I'm not French. I learnt the language from Sister Marcelle. She had such a lovely accent, that I wanted to learn it from her and ended up learning French. She is a great teacher.'

'But where are you from originally then, Marie-Claire?'

'I don't know. The memory always escapes me. I arrived here when I was eight, but can still not remember anything from before that day. I took a knock to my head. Ever since then, I've been trying to remember, but it has been three years and I am still no closer to an answer,' she explained to them, as she shrugged her shoulders.

'And your parents?'

'I can't remember them either. But they must have been German, because I realised I can speak that too.'

The couple was intrigued by the ten-year-old girl, who could apparently speak flawless French, German and Italian. 'How do you feel about living here, Marie-Claire?'

'I'm okay with it now. I was really sad about being here after Sofia died, but Sister Marcelle helped me understand that it was not all bad. There are people worse off than us. Someday I will leave here and go to a better place, whether it be on earth or in heaven. I hope it's someplace on earth, first.'

The lady laughed and dabbed at a tear that had escaped her one eye with a handkerchief. *What a lovely, innocent child*, she thought. The couple gave each other a knowing look. Sister Marcel popped her head out the door to inform them that the Reverend Mother had gone back to her office to complete some paperwork.

'Would you come with us to see Mother Superior?' the gentleman asked.

The girl seemed alarmed.

'Don't worry, you did not do anything wrong.'

Marie-Claire seemed relieved at the response and followed them to the Holy Mother's office.

The nun was surprised to see the couple returning to her office with Marie-Claire. She had not been in her room when they had visited earlier. 'Holy Mother, we came across this fine young lady behind the kitchen and if she would be willing, we would like to take her home with us.' Marie-Claire was astounded at what she had just heard. The nun smiled. 'Well child, would you be happy for these people to adopt you?'

Marie-Claire gave it the briefest moment of thought. 'I think I would like that very much!'

The nun gave her a brown leather satchel and sent her to her room to pack, while she completed the necessary paperwork with the couple. Marie-Claire broke the exciting news to Arianna, Katharina and Karin. She packed her meagre belongings from the chest into the satchel. While Karin and Arianne were sad to say goodbye to their friend, they were also happy for her having an opportunity at a better life. It did not happen to everyone at the orphanage and the orphans never resented anyone for being adopted and taken away. The three girls hugged each other. 'I'll promise to write you whenever I can,' Marie-Claire said, with a lump in her throat. Katharina gave her a hug and said goodbye to her in Russian. She responded in kind. She had learnt many things from the older girl, including basic Russian.

As she walked back to the office, she thought back on the time she spent at *Marcigliana*. She had endured many things and made a few good friends and she was now both excited and scared at moving on. She went past the kitchen to say goodbye to Sister Marcelle. The nun gave her a copy of the book, *20 000 Leagues Under the Sea* as a parting gift. Marie-Claire was very sad to leave the nun who had played such an important part in her life. 'I'll always remember you Marie-Claire, you are destined for great things,' the nun bid her farewell.

'Goodbye Sister Marcelle, thank you for being my teacher, my counsel and my friend. I shall miss you.'

The nun escorted her to the office where the couple was waiting with the Holy Mother. They all walked out of the building together, to a black car parked in the drive-way. Marie-Claire greeted the elderly nun. 'Goodbye Reverend Mother. Thank you for giving me shelter and a name.' The nun hugged her.

'Keep well my child. May you have a long, blessed life.'

As the car drove away, Marie-Claire looked back at the two nuns standing in front of the old building. She knew she would probably never see them again and was saddened by the thought. They were good people and they cared for her deeply, as they did for every other child at *Marcigliana*. She turned around and looked ahead as the headlights lit up the roadway in the dusk and shone brightly into her future with her new parents.

AN AFTERNOON IN PARIS, 1965

Marie-Claire took a moment to find her bearings after being woken from her slumber so abruptly by the doorbell. She wiped her cheeks with a sleeve and walked to the door. Looking through the peep-hole, she recognised the elongated form outside. She opened the door for Jeanne-Pierre, one of the delivery boys from Balmain, who had a large box in his arms. 'Good afternoon J-P,' she greeted him, a long-standing customer of the young man's employer.

'Thank you very much. I trust traffic was not too bad?'

'Oh no Miss, my scooter makes easy work of any traffic.' He placed the box on the coffee table. He dawdled as much as he could on the way to the door, expressing appreciation for her stylish couch, in the interest of wasting time and adding some further small-talk on his way out, all the while taking in the beauty that was Marie-Claire. Young men will be young men, and a beautiful woman will always make them fawn. He bid her farewell at the door and boarded the lift, which was still waiting on the floor. The doors closed and he disappeared from view, still gazing at the closing apartment door.

She checked the time. It was just after five o'clock. She was expecting Alexandre at half past 6 to complete her hair styling. Marie-Claire realised she would have to hurry and started drawing a bath. She took the dress from the box and laid it out on her bed. *Magnificent!* she thought, as she poured over the finely embroidered detail of the elaborate creation. The man was undoubtedly a virtuoso and he never failed to delight her. The doorbell rang again. She wondered who the unexpected visitor could be. She looked though the peep-hole and opened the door, her eyebrows arching into question marks. 'I'm sorry Miss, I forgot to give you your tickets for the fashion show,' the apologetic delivery boy stammered. Balmain would have been quite upset at his oversight in this regard.

'Its fine, Jeanne-Pierre. Thank you and have a good evening.'

This time she really did not have time for further small-talk and closed the door, leaving the smitten young man with only a whiff of her perfume to accompany him down the passage. She dropped the tickets on the coffee table and rushed to close the taps in the bathroom, just in time to stop the rising foam from spilling onto the floor.

Marie-Claire finished her bath, not having as much time as she would have preferred to pamper herself with the various imported oils and scrubs in her collection. She took great care not to disturb her hair in the process. After drying off with her Egyptian cotton bath sheet, she donned the intricate dark grey gown, checking the fit in her mirror. She sat at her dressing table and finished doing her make-up. It was understated, yet elegant with bright red lipstick, to contrast the dark dress. Dark mascara drew attention to her radiant blue eyes. She finished up, just as the doorbell rang. *That must be Alexandre*, she thought as she walked to the door on her stockinged feet.

Marie-Claire opened the door to let the stylist in and he mock kissed her. He knew better than to smudge the freshly applied make-up. 'You look marvellous, my dear!' he complimented her. 'What a wonderful dress! Pierre has outdone himself again.'

'Thank you Alexandre. Come in, come in. We don't have a lot of time.' He entered the apartment and pulled a chair from under the small dining table, which she sat on. The stylist put his case on the floor and started styling her hair, using a selection of hair products and a comb. When it was to his exacting standards, he pulled a complex string of pearls from a hidden pocket inside his jacket.

The pearls were strung in a mesh-like pattern, which he applied to her hair and attached with various pins he took from the case. He used the comb to straighten up some of the hair elements and then finished off the dazzling coiffure with a diamond studded silver brooch, which he took from a false bottom in the suitcase and attached on the one side. All of this took the stylist a mere thirty minutes. Alexandre stood back and surveyed his work. *A masterpiece!*

'There you go. Perfection.' Marie-Claire got up and glided to the bedroom mirror to view his work, as the stylist watched her with his hands on his hips.

'Oh Alexandre, it is gorgeous!' she exclaimed from the bedroom, highly impressed with his artistic creation. She used a hand mirror to get several different views of the mesmerising design. This, once again, affirmed his status in her mind as *the* creative genius of hair. Alexandre gathered the tools of his trade into the case, in preparation to leave.

'I am off, princess. You enjoy your evening. You are sure to make every girl jealous and every man want to profess his undying love.'

She said goodbye and let him out of the apartment. He meandered to the lift as her gaze followed him through the half-open door. He appeared deep in thought. *Was he imagining his next creation, perhaps?* Marie-Claire had a moment to spare before her father would arrive to pick her up for the party. High-heeled shoes and a black evening bag were added to complete her ensemble. Admiring herself in the full-length mirror, she was extremely pleased with the completed look. She poured herself a small measure of *Rémy Martin* brandy in a glass and sipped the drink while waiting on her father to arrive. Marie-Claire had developed an appreciation for Napoleon brandy in recent years and it was now one of her preferred beverages, if Champagne was not available. It had certainly proved a life saver on many cold occasions one winter in *St Moritz*. There was yet another ring of the doorbell, this time announcing her father's arrival. She opened the door and warmly greeted the ageing diplomat, who looked quite taken out himself.

RETURNING TO ROME, 1950

Marie-Claire woke up in the home of her adopted parents the next morning. Her cheeks were wet after a night filled with dreamy memories she could not recall, try as she might. They had arrived in the dark the previous evening and she had not seen her surroundings in the light of day. She got out of bed and walked over to the window, pulling open the heavy green drapes. Once her eyes adjusted to the sunlight streaming in, she looked down onto the square, two stories below.

Marie-Claire's window overlooked a large piazza with two ornate fountains. The top portion of both fountains appeared to be shaped like stone bathtubs, seemingly floating on the water of the bottom half. *How peculiar*, she thought, as she imagined a giant person taking a bath in the square. The rest of the piazza was surrounded by multi-coloured buildings, their windows facing inwards on the large square. The view from above was beautiful and she stood admiring it. The bright umbrellas around the edges of the square contrasted the dark cobblestones. The piazza was mostly empty, as it was still early.

She shifted her attention back to the room she had woken up in. It made her feel like a princess in a fairy tale. The canopied bed faced the windows and was surrounded by large paintings on the walls, showing varied scenery. A wooden table with a pot of flowers on had two chairs next to it, one of them holding her satchel.

The young Marie-Claire was a little perplexed as to her next course of action. *Should she go out the door and explore the house, or would that be considered rude? Should she just wait around until someone came for her..?* The latter seemed like the prudent choice, for now. After washing her face in the lavish *en-suite* bathroom, she went back to the window and continued staring at the people in the square.

The previous evening had passed in a blur. She had been introduced to a handful of evening staff at the Embassy and joined the Ambassador and his wife for dinner in a dining room on the third floor of the house. The table had twenty chairs and the three of them sat at the one end of it. The dim light of the candles failed to illuminate the whole room and Marie-Claire could only vaguely discern the painted shapes on the ceiling. They sat quietly eating their meal. The young orphan was too overwhelmed to speak much and the two adults, on their part, did not want to ask her too many questions on her first night there. She was very tired. 'May I be excused to go to bed?' Marie-Claire enquired after everyone finished their food.

The kind couple took her down a corridor to the, now familiar, bedroom she had woken in this morning. She noticed the size of the house, with more staircases visible in the distances, descending to the floors below. There were plush carpets on the floors and marvellous paintings on all the walls. She had only read of museums, but this was what she imaged one would look like inside. 'You have a lovely house,' she remarked.

'Thank you very much, Marie-Claire,' Mrs Le Blanc responded, the couple sharing a smile. They showed her the room and the adjoining bathroom. 'Our room is right next door, if you need anything. You don't have to be up early tomorrow, sleep as late as you want.' They tucked her in under the covers. 'Goodnight, little one.'

'Goodnight. Thank you very much for everything,' she gave them each a hug, before falling asleep, exhausted.

She was still staring at the ever-increasing levels of activity in the square when there came a soft knock on the door. It was Mrs Le Blanc, bringing her a breakfast tray. The Ambassador's wife wore a floral print dress this morning. Her brown hair hung in loose curls on her shoulders. She was a beautiful woman. 'Did you sleep well, Marie-Claire?'

'Yes, Ma'am,' was the slightly awkward reply. Marie-Claire was not quite sure how to address the couple that adopted her. Mrs Le Blanc took a seat at the table and Marie-Claire joined her.

'Have some breakfast, child.' The girl started slowly picking at the breakfast, not wanting to appear famished. The pastry was fresh and crispy and the yogurt delightful. She had never had either before. 'Thank you very much. The food is delicious.'

'Marie-Claire, I want to welcome you to our home and our lives. We have not been able to have children of our own and we hoped that we could make a difference for someone at the orphanage, by being a family for them.' There was a sad expression in her eyes. 'You are welcome to call us Mr and Mrs Le Blanc, until you feel more comfortable, or decide otherwise. My husband has been transferred to Greece and we will be leaving here next week. Things are a little frantic for him at the moment, with a number of projects needing to be finalised or prepared for hand-over. Henri apologises for not being able to join us for breakfast this morning. He has promised to meet us for lunch, though. Our first order of business today is to help you pass for a young lady, which will start with a bath.'

Mrs Le Blanc was chattering away while helping Marie-Claire wash. They trimmed her nails and shampooed her hair. She enjoyed the attention and felt refreshed afterwards. They dressed her in an outfit she had brought along from the orphanage. 'Oh, dear! This simply won't do, princess,' Mrs Le Blanc said kindly as she regarded the old dress, tugging at it. 'We will have to get you some pretty new things.' Marie-Claire was excited at the prospect.

'Oh, thank you! I have never had any pretty new things.'

'Well, come along dear, we have a full day ahead.'

They went downstairs into the Embassy, which was now bustling with staff carrying around boxes, packing and tending to all manner of administrative duties. Mrs Le Blanc led her down a second set of stairs to the ground floor and entered an office from the courtyard. A neatly dressed man in a dark suit was seated at the desk, tending to paperwork. He appeared to be in his mid-fifties, with regal looking silver hair. 'Jacques, I'd like to introduce you to Marie-Claire. She has joined our family from the orphanage.' She turned to the girl. 'Jacques is our chauffeur and personal aide.'

'Pleased to make your acquaintance, Miss.'

'Likewise, Sir.' she responded, adding a curtsy for good measure. The adults laughed.

'We need to take Marie-Claire shopping this morning. She does not have a thing to wear. Then we will meet up with the Ambassador for lunch,' Mrs Le Blanc informed the aide.

'Right away, *Madame*,' he said as he grabbed his hat and keys. Jacques carefully shepherded the two ladies into the rear of a black sedan, one of a number of cars parked in the open space, surrounded on all sides by the magnificent building. They drove through a vestibule running under the structure, which exited into the square Marie-Claire had seen earlier through her window. 'This is the *Piazza Farnese*,' Mrs Le Blanc explained to the wide-eyed Marie-Claire, as she pointed to the square surrounding them. 'It is named after the *Palazzo Farnese*, which was built in the 1500s. Michelangelo even worked on the building in his heyday.'

'Which one is the *Palazzo*?' Marie-Claire asked.

Mrs Le Blanc laughed. 'The one we live in. It has been the French Embassy since 1874.' Marie-Claire was very impressed. *It was a palace after all, so that did make her a princess!*

'Take us to *Via Condotti*, Jacques. We need to get this young lady a new wardrobe,' Mrs Le Blanc instructed the chauffeur. Jacques headed out towards the River *Tiber* and followed its banks, passing the *Castel Sant' Angelo* on the opposite side, before turning towards the city centre. Marie-Claire gaped at the surrounding scenery and discovered new wonders at almost every turn. She had not seen the city before, outside of the small part she saw on the ill-fated night three years ago when she wandered through the streets before dawn. Having spent her last years at the orphanage, the bustle of the city was something she was not accustomed to. It did not take her long to start enjoying the hubbub and the new exciting sights. 'I think I like Rome a lot more than the countryside around *Marcigliana,*' she remarked.

The trio arrived at the northern end of the *Piazza di Spagna* and parked the Embassy vehicle. Jacques, escorting the two ladies, led them over the piazza on foot, towards the fountain at the bottom end of the famous Spanish steps.

'What a beautiful fountain!' Marie-Claire exclaimed as they approached the boat shaped water feature. 'What is it called?'

'*Fontana della Barcaccia,*' Mrs Le Blanc responded. Marie-Claire laughed at the irony. 'It must have been a blind person that decided to call this the fountain of the ugly boat!' Jacques bought each of the ladies a gelato cone from one of the vendors and they took a respite on the steps, which were already crowded. Like countless tourists before and after them, they lounged on the Spanish steps, while enjoying their Italian treat. Marie-Claire gawked at her surroundings. She had never imagined there could be such magnificence in the world. The buildings, the square, the fountain, the steps, everything astonished her.

Once they were done snacking, they strolled down *Via Condotti.* It was every shopper's dream paradise. Luxury stores lined the street as far as the eye could see. On the first corner was *Bellini,* with a beautiful display of exclusive blouses and skirts. They followed the crowds for a while, Marie-Claire ogling all the window displays they passed. She found the jewellery display at Bulgari especially riveting, with the diamonds sparkling like shiny stars. When they passed *Cucci,* she admired the displayed ties, silk dressing gowns and custom-made shirts. Halfway down the street, they came across a children's boutique store called *Neuber* and Mrs Le Blanc entered the shop with the youngster in tow. An eager sales assistant hurried over. 'How may I assist you, *Signora?*'

'We need a new wardrobe for the young lady. Shoes, socks, dresses, the whole works. Let's do ten outfits with shoes and accessories.' The assistant gave a broad smile.

'Certainly *Signora*. What colours do the young lady like?'

'I don't know. Anything will be fine, I like all colours equally,' Marie-Claire responded.

They spent the next two hours fitting numerous outfits and accessories. Marie-Claire really enjoyed herself, modelling each ensemble for Mrs Le Blanc and Jacques, who applauded each new appearance. She would twirl and bow before returning to the change room. By the end, they left with twelve outfits, which included an evening dress and a sleep gown. Marie-Claire wore one of her new outfits from the store and did not feel any remorse when her old dress was resigned to the shop dustbin. She was now in an adorable floral print dress with white shoes. The assistant had also tied a bow in her hair. Jacques was carrying the seven bags of shopping as they headed back to the car for their lunch date with Mr Le Blanc.

They sauntered back towards the square, Jacques trailing slightly behind with the bags. It was easier to follow Mrs Le Blanc and Marie-Claire than having to carve a path through the tourists while carrying the load of shopping. It also allowed him to keep an eye on them and their surroundings, without having to turn around. The crowds in the streets seemed to naturally part for the ladies, as they made their way towards the fountain. They reached the *Piazza* and Marie-Claire took a last longing gaze up the Spanish steps to the church at the top, before they crossed the plaza to the car. The vehicle was sweltering hot inside, forcing them to crank open the windows as they drove in the direction of *Via Veneto*, where they would meet up with the Ambassador.

Jacques skirted the *Piazza Barberini* and its fantastic fountain, paying homage to the god Triton. Marie-Claire was fascinated by the scenery as they travelled along, the one fountain, plaza, and building simply more extravagant than the next. They found Mr Le Blanc already seated at a table outside Café Rossini. He was in meetings all morning at the US Embassy, just up the road. The two countries and their respective diplomats had good relations and it was to be their final meeting before his imminent transfer to Greece.

Mr Le Blanc was sipping iced tea from a tall glass. He was in a linen suit and his brown fedora was on the table. His light brown eyes were gazing unfocused into the distance. Jacques, Marie-Claire and Mrs Le Blanc entered the restaurant and approached the Ambassador. Jacques settled at the *café* counter. He could keep an eye on the family from here, but would not intrude on their private lunch. Marie-Claire greeted Mr Le Blanc with a slightly stiff hug and Mrs Le Blanc kissed her husband, before being seated at the table by the waiter. 'May I take your drinks order, ladies?' the young man enquired. Marie-Claire was overwhelmed by the variety of drink choices on the menu, as she had not really encountered any of them before. She stared at the menu with a confused frown on her face and Mrs Le Blanc intervened on her behalf. 'The young lady will have the lemonade and I would like a Bellini.' The waiter scuttled off to place their order. 'How was your morning, my darling?' Mr Le Blanc enquired of his wife.

'Oh, we had a fabulous time! Marie-Claire needed clothes, so we shopped up a storm. Now she can look like a true lady. See her lovely new outfit?'

'What a beautiful dress, Marie-Claire. You are so pretty! Did you enjoy your morning? What else did you see?'

'I enjoyed it very much! I like shopping.' The two adults laughed at Marie-Claire. 'We also saw some gorgeous stairs and a pretty fountain. Then we had gelato and there was sparkling jewellery and never ending rows of clothing stores.'

'Ah, *Via Condotti*! That street is going to encounter another great depression when we leave this country. Oh Josephine, it only took you one morning to corrupt young Marie-Claire into a total shopaholic,' Mr Le Blanc said in jest. They laughed again. The waiter arrived with their drinks. Marie-Claire sipped the lemonade, which was cool and refreshing. She hadn't realised how thirsty she was. A few minutes later, the server was back to take their lunch order. Marie-Claire had given up on choosing something to eat, the options were just too many and she had trouble recognising most of the menu items. They ordered her some *Pasta Carbonara*, while Mr Le Blanc went with the *Ossobucco* and Mrs Le Blanc the *Truffle Risotto*.

'My meetings are done for the day, so I will be able to join you for the afternoon. What do you feel like doing, Marie-Claire?' They looked at her enquiringly. 'Sister Marcelle once told me about her visit to the Vatican and how splendid it was. Could we go see that?'

'Most certainly. What an inspired idea!' Their food arrived. Marie-Claire loved her pasta and also tasted some of the adults' food. They were happy to share with her, so she could be exposed to different flavours and develop an idea of what she liked. It was an unusual situation, with Marie-Claire never having encountered restaurant cuisine previously in her life. She seemed to have a fairly educated palate, despite this lack of fine dining. For dessert, Marie-Claire had chocolate fondant, while the couple shared a *crème brûlée*. Their meal was perfectly rounded off with a serving of coffee. Now they were prepared for their afternoon expedition to the Sistine Chapel and the other sights in Vatican City. Jacques returned to the Embassy with the one vehicle, while Mr Le Blanc drove the ladies to the Vatican in his own car.

FAREWELL TO ROME, 1950

The trip to the Vatican took them past some of the sights Marie-Claire had seen earlier in the day. Mr Le Blanc took a detour, so she could get her first sight of the *Trevi* fountain. Marie-Claire was astonished by the beauty of the marvellous water-feature. The area surrounding the fountain was filled with a crowd of people, all admiring the pristine waters and awe-inspiring sculptures.

They stopped the car for a moment so the youngster could appreciate the fountain, leading to love at first sight for Marie-Claire. The wondrous façade with its carved figures of gods and sea-horses appealed to her at an almost primal level. *What a glorious fountain*, she thought as she looked longingly back when it disappeared from view. They crossed the *Tiber* River at the Supreme Court and drove around the *Castel Sant'Angelo*. Mr Le Blanc parked the car and they completed the journey by foot, walking towards St Peter's Square.

The couple and Marie-Claire crossed the world famous piazza in the Vatican. 'Oh wow, look at the size of the plaza!' Maria-Claire said in awe. The square was growing less crowded as the afternoon wore on. They strolled across it to St Peter's Basilica. Mr Le Blanc paid the entrance fee and they entered the Basilica through the massive, wooden doors. Marie-Claire's mouth dropped open as they entered the basilica. *It was astonishing!* The size and grandiosity of it all was beyond words. She stood silently, gazing at the golden ceiling panels and the marble inlays adorning the floors and walls. *What a sight to behold!*

Mr Le Blanc provided some information as they entered the massive cathedral. 'This is considered the largest cathedral in the world and it is believed that St Peter himself is buried below it. There are, of course, many popes buried below the building as well.' He turned right and led them into the chapel of *Pietà*. Marie-Claire was astounded by the sculpture at the far end. 'This was one of the earliest works by Michelangelo, coincidentally also the only work he ever signed,' Mr Le Blanc narrated. They stood in front of the marble statue of the Virgin Mary holding the body of Jesus, silently bearing witness to its magnificence. Marie-Claire could see the peaceful look on the statue's face, but didn't think to question the absence of grief, as she had never known a mother's love or lost a loved one. After some time adoring the work of art, they strolled back into the main nave of the cathedral, moving in the direction of the large dome.

'This was another piece of design by Michelangelo and was only completed after his death. It was the second largest dome in the world for a very long time,' Mr Le Blanc explained. The sheer size of the dome was hard to comprehend, as it dwarfed the altar, which was ten stories high itself. She experienced the whole building as one awe-inspiring sight after another, having never experienced anything of such a scale. *The chapel in Marcigliana is miniscule compared to this,* Marie-Claire though, almost overwhelmed by it all. She took a respite on one of the pews, sitting down to give herself time to digest what she had experienced in such a short space of time. Mr and Mrs Le Blanc sat quietly next to her, taking in the interior of the building one last time, before they would leave the country for the shores of Greece.

After a period of quiet reflection, having dealt with the multitude of sensory inputs, Marie-Claire rose from her seat. 'I am really tired after all this walking. Can we please leave now?' The two adults stood up and made their way towards the massive doors, entering the square again. It was now after four o'clock and they would not be able to enter the Vatican Museum. 'We'll come back for the rest later in the week,' Mrs Le Blanc promised Marie-Claire. The youngster did not appear overly disappointed, as she had clearly encountered enough stimulus for one day. The threesome walked across the square, which was now much less crowded than when they first arrived.

They found the car where they had left it and Mr Le Blanc opened the doors for the two ladies. Leaving the plaza behind, they crossed the river, driving back towards the French Embassy in *Piazza Farnese*. Traffic was picking up as the work day finished on their short drive to reach the Embassy. There was now a different set of guards at the entrance, who opened the outer doors for the ambassadorial family with courteous greetings, before returning to their surveillance post in the square.

'Mr Le Blanc, would you mind showing me the rest of the building? I would really like to see it all.' Mr Le Blanc gladly agreed and they took the opportunity to escort her on a tour of the *Palazzo Farnese*, which still housed many statues, paintings and tapestries from its days when occupied by Cardinal Farnese in the 15th century. They took the stairs from the ground floor and entered a large, double volume, room, painted bright white. There was a huge statue of Zeus and a beautiful fireplace. In one corner was a janitor, busy mopping a part of the ornate floor. 'This is the ballroom. We host social events here from time to time.' He looked perplexed. 'Giuseppe, what are you still doing here, it is after five already?'

The janitor looked at his watch. 'Oh, sweet Mary. My watch stopped two hours ago! I thought it was taking me a lot longer than usual to mop this darn floor today. Have a good evening, Ambassador!' He scurried off the way they had come, his cart in tow.

Marie-Claire was amazed at the craftsmanship of the ceiling and the fireplace. She could imagine a hundred children running around playing in the room, but perhaps only after the floor dried. The salon next door had deep red damask wall coverings, with an ornate candelabra adorning another intricate wooden ceiling, this time in a lighter shade of wood. Marie-Claire stroked one of the colourful tapestries covering a wall, it was soft and velvety. They went out one of the French doors and stood on a small balcony, overlooking the Piazza. Marie-Claire was amazed at the rooms she has seen in the building. 'This must be the most beautiful Embassy in the world,' she reflected. 'I am sure if you had tours, people would circle around the block to see it!' The adults laughed.

'Maybe one of the future ambassadors would consider that,' Mr Le Blanc said thoughtfully, never having considered that the world might be interested in sharing in the splendour of the building. Room after room displayed the same grandeur and opulence that every other room exhibited. In the library, a wall of books faced several tables in the middle of the room, used by the Embassy staff for research purposes. Marie-Claire was both excited and saddened by the large volume of books, as she knew she would not be able to read them in the short time they had left in Rome.

The wide inside corridors all overlooked the internal courtyard. They entered a sitting room with extraordinary painted murals and walked through it to a terrace overlooking the back garden. Marie-Claire admired the view over the city. There was patio furniture with umbrellas, as the Embassy staff also enjoyed the scenery when taking their coffee breaks. The sun was starting to set over Rome. Suddenly, Marie-Claire felt anxious. *What if this was all a dream? What if she woke up and found herself back in Marcigliana, the whole day one cruel joke? What if she broke something and they took her back to the orphanage?* She started crying.

Mrs Le Blanc hugged the little girl. 'What's wrong, my dear?'
'It's all so beautiful. I'm afraid I'll break something and you'll send me back to the orphanage,' she sobbed.
'We will do no such thing!' Mrs Le Blanc exclaimed in horror. 'You are not some object we can simply discard when it displeases us. You are a person, Marie-Claire, and you have more worth than any piece of art or pottery. Never

forget that! You will always be welcome in our home, even if you break everything we have.' Marie-Claire felt relieved. *The Le Blanc's were kind people.*

The living quarters on the top floor had several bedrooms, a private kitchen, dining room, two salons, a billiard room and a private study, also adorned with row upon row of books in stacked wooden bookcases. All the luxury felt foreign to the youngster. *It will take a while to get used to all of this. At least the people are nice.* They sat in the salon and ruminated on the day that passed, enjoying tea and macarons. Marie-Claire was feeling slightly peckish and found the cookies a delightful treat. 'What was your favourite part of the day, Marie-Claire?' Mrs Le Blanc asked. With all they had seen and experienced during the day, the response was most unexpected. 'Coming home. My favourite part was coming home with you.' Mr and Mrs Le Blanc looked at each other with astonishment and a certain sense of satisfaction. *Marie-Claire was indeed a very special girl.* The conversation continued, but the day had exhausted the youngster and she soon started dozing off on the couch, the cares of the world left behind.

Marie-Claire woke up the next morning, her pillow wet. Her unwelcome dreams were now forgotten. She was wearing the new nightgown, but could not remember donning it the night before. The familiar surroundings of her room greeted her. Opening the curtains, she admired the piazza and the fountains for a moment, before going to find company. She came upon Mrs Le Blanc in the dining room, having coffee and a croissant. She was reading a Parisian newspaper, which had come overnight in the diplomatic bag from Paris. 'Good morning, angel. Did you sleep well?'

'Yes, thank you. Although I don't remember going to bed.'

'Oh, yes. You were almost passed out on the couch, so Mr Le Blanc carried you to your room and I dressed you in your new pyjamas. They are very fetching. Would you like some breakfast?'

'Thank you. That would be lovely.' They ordered food for the youngster, which arrived on a tray, complete with a little flower in a vase. 'Let's decide what we want to do today...'

The last few days in Rome flew by, Marie-Claire hardly being able to remember half of all the wonderful things they saw and did. Each day would start with breakfast, but would then diverge into a myriad of different experiences of all that Rome had to offer. They visited the *Colosseum*, several incredible museums, further extended Marie-Claire's wardrobe, and finally finished their tour of the Vatican. The young girl always remembered the ceiling of the Sistine chapel quite vividly. Her neck had eventually started aching from the odd angle of looking up at the magnificent frescos for such an extended period. Of all the sights in Rome, this one was burned into her memory forever. 'What do you like most about the ceiling?' Mrs Le Blanc asked her.

'The touch. I think it is lovely that one can reach out to God, even if your fingers never quite meet. I think Man was never meant to touch God, but that doesn't mean one can't reach out.'

Although spending time in the parks and carousels was enjoyable, Marie-Claire enjoyed the visits to the various museums and galleries the most. She took an instant liking to art and sculpture and could spend hours looking at a beautiful painting, trying to imagine what the artist was thinking while they painted. Without even knowing what the word meant, the young girl had grown into an *Aesthete* by the time she left Rome.

Marie-Claire also enjoyed exploring the rest of the Embassy and playing in the lush gardens. One whole afternoon was spent in a game of hide and seek with some of the Embassy staff. When the time finally came to go, Marie-Claire was very sad to leave the Embassy, which was the only real home she had ever known, brief as her stay may have been.

The day of the departure from Rome had arrived. It was late morning as the Embassy staff lined up in the courtyard to bid the Ambassador and his family farewell. He walked down the line of staff as he took his leave, trading goodbyes with a few personal words of thanks. Most of the staff would stay behind to serve with the next ambassador, but some of the personal aides were travelling with the family to Greece. It had always been the way of the French Foreign Service- some served the Embassy and some served the ambassador. All served France.

The last person in the line was his replacement, Gerard du Pont. Du Pont had arrived during the past week and had been acquainting himself with the politics of Rome, under the tutelage of Mr Le Blanc. When they greeted, Mr Le Blanc handed over the ceremonial keys to the Embassy, another long-standing tradition of the Diplomatic Corps. The group left the Embassy in two cars. Their luggage and personal effects had been sent ahead already to the port city of *Bari*, where they would board a ferry to Greece. Rome was left behind as they drove towards the east coast town of *Pescara*.

The trip was an extended one, but Marie-Claire enjoyed the passing Italian countryside. Some three hours later, they could see the ocean in the distance. The young girl had never seen this much water and she was astounded by the size of it, an azure blanket stretching endlessly to the horizon. When they reached *Pescara*, they took a rest break, Marie-Claire admiring the view over the Mediterranean. After a late lunch overlooking the boats in the harbour, they left *Pescara* behind.

Initially, the road south ran close to the coast, with splendid, scenic views over the vast blue expanse of water. Occasionally, the road would run at the top of cliffs, which would drop down dizzying heights to the rocky beaches far below, while other times it was almost on the beach. When they reached the town of *Lesina*, their route turned inland, cutting across the *Gargano* peninsula and leaving the coastline behind. The city of *Foggia* was visible in the distance as the road turned in an easterly direction, back towards the coast. Marie-Claire enjoyed the journey, as each turn exposed her to new breathtaking views and unexpected scenery. She wondered whether she had ever seen any of this before she arrived in Rome. She doubted that she did. *Who could ever forget such wonderful scenery?* 'They have such lovely villages here by the coast.'

'Yes, the Italian coastline is quite beautiful,' Mr Le Blanc responded. 'We shall miss that, the countryside and the people equally, when we leave.' Marie-Claire, with her limited exposure to the coastlines and the people, would miss the kind nuns at *Marcigliana*, especially Sister Marcelle and the views of the countryside around Rome would always form part of her first living memories of the country she had called *home* all her life.

They finally reached their destination, the port city of *Bari*. The ferry port served a number of routes crossing the Mediterranean to Albania, Montenegro, Croatia and Greece. Their ferry would depart in an hour and would reach *Patras* the next morning. Jacques helped to unload the luggage onto a cart, which was wheeled to the terminal building. Mr Le Blanc said goodbye to Remi and Gaston, who would drive the Embassy vehicles back to Rome. He had known them both for five years and they were good friends. Diplomatic staff tended to be close-knit groups, often with only their fellow countrymen to rely on in foreign soil. Marie-Claire waved as they departed, both having proved worthy adversaries in games of hide and seek at the Embassy.

Mr Le Blanc and his personal secretary, Jean-Pierre, managed the necessary check in at the ferry desk, while Jacques supervised the luggage being taken to their rooms below the aft deck. The group passed through customs and they crossed the gangplank to board the ferry. Trucks and cars were being loaded on in a steady stream. The ferry whistle started intermittently reminding people of the imminent departure and with the last frantic blow, the gangplanks were raised and the two great diesel engines started labouring. They exited the harbour and turned south towards Greece. The Le Blancs stood at the railing, each caught up in their own thoughts, watching the coastline fade in the distance. Marie-Claire shed a tear as the sun finally set over Italy, the only country she had ever known as home.

SUNSET IN PARIS, 1965

Mr Le Blanc kissed his daughter on each cheek and stepped inside the penthouse apartment, placing his top hat on the coat rack by the entrance. He was smartly dressed in a tuxedo with a white jacket and a black tie. Polished black shoes completed the ensemble. 'My darling daughter, you look enchanting! How are you?'

'I am well, father, how have you been? Enjoying your retirement?'

'I am excellent. I find my new pursuits utterly fascinating. Politics can be just as challenging as a good game of chess.'

Mr Le Blanc was recently appointed as a Member of Parliament by President De Gaulle, to fill in for a dismissed MP whose love-life had become too scandalous, even by French standards. He would serve until the elections in December. His years of service in the Diplomatic Corps meant that he was a well-respected diplomat and knew the political nuances of the French Parliament all too well.

'How is Mother doing?'

'She is still a little weak, but is improving. She's seeing the physician again next week for her follow-up, but all the interventions seemed to have done the trick. The preliminary results all seem positive.'

He entered the apartment and Marie-Claire poured him a measure of cognac. 'That is a marvellous dress. Balmain I presume? Pierre is such an artist!'

'Thanks, Father. Yes indeed, it is gorgeous. His genius truly knows no bounds.' They sat down on the couch, sipping their drinks. 'Is there a specific reason for the frivolities this evening?'

'Oh yes, they are celebrating Cosmonautics day. It promises to be a party out of this world,' Mr Le Blanc said in jest.

Marie-Claire laughed. It would undoubtedly have been, even if it wasn't celebrating the first man in space. The first social function by a new ambassador was always a major affair and would set the tone for every other function to follow. 'I look forward to seeing Uncle Valerian again. Do you think it will be the usual crowd at the gathering?'

'Of course! I am sure we'll know almost everyone there. You know how these things are... The circles are small and the players all move around fighting for occupation of the different squares in the board, a never ending game of musical chairs. Unless someone is lying dead when the music ends, or really embarrasses their country and gets posted to the Arctic. Valerian mentioned inviting several young gentlemen, they might prove interesting company.'

'Oh, Father. These diplomat's children can be such a bore sometimes. They were all born with a silver spoon up their backsides. I'd much rather spend my time with someone that worked to earn their place in society. No offence meant to present company.' Mr Le Blanc gave a laugh. Marie-Claire had always been humble and never let his wealth or standing go to her head. He had inherited a small fortune from his father and although he supported her whenever needed, she had always strived to be independent and not rely on his handouts. He took joy in still being able to settle her bills at Pierre Balmain, even though she didn't require it anymore, these days.

Mr Le Blanc looked at his daughter. She had grown into a fine young woman. Her radiant skin was flawless and her bright blue eyes shone with intelligence, but also hid an occasional hint of sadness, which would disappear as fast as it sometimes appeared. And then there were instances when he saw something completely different in her eyes. Something deeper. Something else.

Something that almost scared him. He could never quite place it and he could never explain it. She was tall and with her heels on, she outranked him in height. Years of ballet training gave her a perfect posture and he looked forward to seeing her on the dancefloor later. He still believed she had what it took to dance in the Bolshoi, but unfortunate circumstances had prevented him from finding out.

Marie-Claire had developed a unique artistic flair over the years and had been quite successful in her art studies at the Sorbonne. There had also been success in many of her other endeavours. Mr Le Blanc could not account for most of the items in the apartment, Marie-Claire had decorated it herself and did not require any contributions on his part. Despite a large collection of his art being in storage and available for use, she had not requested access to any of it. He was very proud of the woman she had become.

'Have you met any interesting gentlemen of late?' he enquired, as most fathers would.

'I always meet interesting people. If you choose your circle of friends wisely, it is inevitable. But no-one special, to answer your actual question.'

'Oh well, I can only remain hopeful that someone will come along to meet your exacting standards.'

'Oh, Father! I just don't want to marry the first rich philistine that comes along, simply because he asks me. I want someone appealing, with charisma but without an ego; someone who knows how to treat a lady with respect and someone I can truly love.'

'Well, let me refrain from being the Spanish inquisition then, you seem to know what you are looking for. I'm sure you'll find such a man. I eventually found your mother and she still makes me happy, after all these years. Enjoy your life and in the meantime, I'll always be around to share a drink and a laugh with you.'

Marie-Claire's thoughts wandered to her parents and their love for each other. They sipped their drinks in silence for a few moments, Mr Le Blanc staring into the cold fireplace. She had quietly observed their passion for each other first-hand over the years. She thought about their love for her and then, randomly, the incident popped into her mind which cemented them as her parents. Until then, they had only been Mr and Mrs Le Blanc.

Several months after their arrival in Athens, they took a day trip to ancient Delphi. Although Stavros had driven them to the archaeological site, Mr Le Blanc declined for him to accompany them into the ruins. They wanted to spend some time on their own. The security man positioned himself in the shade of a restaurant by the entrance, where he could observe the people entering and avoid the heat. Delphi was brimming with late summer tourists and local police, so it was quite safe. The family followed the sacred way towards the temple of Apollo, winding through the ruined buildings. Marie-Claire stopped to look at a particularly beautiful mosaic next to the path. Her parents continued with the throng of people up the hill, not noticing her absence. Five minutes later, she had finished her examination of the intricate tiling and looked up. Mr and Mrs Le Blanc were gone!

She looked around through the crowd of people and could not see them. She ran up the hill, trying to spot Mr Le Blanc's hat in the gathered masses. It was not there. When she reached the temple of Apollo, she ran around the columns, frantically looking for any sight of the adults. She kept running up the hill, eventually reaching the amphitheatre, now beyond worry. She sat down on the theatre steps with her face in her hands. They were missing. She was alone in the world, all by herself. They found her there thirty minutes later, staring unseeing into the distance, almost in a trance-like state. 'Marie-Claire...' she looked up to see them standing over her.

"Father! Mother!" she exclaimed, hugging them. 'I thought I had lost you forever. Don't ever leave me again!' she gave a sob, clinging to them. Stavros was standing behind them. Mrs Le Blanc wiped away her tears and kissed her. 'Don't fret little one. You are safe now,' she lulled the young girl. When she had calmed down, they each took a hand and led her out of the theatre, safely tucked between the two of them. The family Le Blanc, walking as one, down the hill of Delphi.

Marie-Claire snapped out of the memory, back to the present in her Parisian penthouse. 'How is the apartment hunt going, Father?' Although he officially retired to his estate near *Chantilly*, his recent appointment to Parliament had necessitated consideration of an abode in the city. A regular commute from that far north of the city was not something he had considered doing for any extended period of time again. They have been actively looking for a suitable investment property around the parliamentary district. 'It is progressing well. We have seen a couple of promising residences in the 7th *arrondissement*, so we should probably sign the paperwork any day now. Your mother just has to decide which of the three places she prefers.'

'It will be nice to have you close-by in the city again, it was a bit taxing to travel up north regularly to visit, even though *Chantilly* itself is quite relaxing.'

'Indeed. I should have probably insisted on it earlier, when your mother had to come through for her treatments regularly, but she was adamant she wanted to live in the countryside. The peace and quiet, bracing air and all that…'

The duo finished the last of their drinks and stood up from the couch. Mr Le Blanc did a cursory inspection of a half-finished painting on the easel through the arch in the dining room, before heading to the door. It had a dark tone about it and seemed to show a blood red puddle of spilt wine on a cobblestoned street. *Odd…* he thought to himself. *The girl was immensely talented, but the strangest subject matter, sometimes.* He grabbed his hat from the stand, as he exited the apartment. They spent a moment waiting for the elevator, which transported them to the ground floor.

The sun was starting to set as they left the building, walking past *La Bouffe* towards a car parked in the adjacent boulevard. In the swiftly approaching dusk, the brasserie had a large gathering of rowdy patrons, all partaking in a variety of drinks. The general frivolity was on the rise, reflecting the ascension of the moon over a neighbouring building. Emile, the stout, newly appointed young parliamentary security detail to Mr Le Blanc, smartly opened the door of a dark coloured Citroen for the pair. They left the Latin Quarter behind, the car following the *Quai des Grands Augustins*. The spotlights on the Notre Dame were starting to light up across the water, illuminating a thousand years of French history. Their course ran parallel to the river Seine, heading towards the Eiffel Tower in the distance. The evening out was about to commence.

ARRIVING IN ATHENS, 1950

Marie-Claire and the Le Blancs shared a cabin aboard the ferry to Greece for the overnight trip. The first class accommodation had a double bed with a single sleeper bunkbed above it. They had packed overnight bags for this leg of the journey, the contents of which were packed into a small closet in the one wall. There was a tiny bathroom attached to the suite, which contained a shower, toilet and a small basin. Through the porthole in the wall, the twinkling lights of the Albanian coastline were visible in the far distance. The porthole was slightly open and a pleasant sea-breeze wafted into the cabin, cooling it down. Everyone settled in for the evening. 'Good night, Marie-Claire. Sleep well.'

'Goodnight.'

In the morning, Marie-Claire woke up with a start. The Le Blancs were standing next to her bunk, looking at her with concerned expressions on their faces. 'What is wrong dear? You were crying.'

'I don't know. I can't remember. I can never remember. I have a sad dream every night, but I can never recall it in the morning. Don't worry about it,' the little girl explained. The concern did not abate from their faces. 'How long has this been going on?' Mrs Le Blanc enquired.

'It has been happening for as long as I can remember. I wake up crying. But it's okay, I'm not sad now.'

The Le Blancs were worried about Marie-Claire. *The poor child. What had happened to her? What horrible nightmare drove her to tears every morning, only to be forgotten until the following night's sleep?* She needed their love and support, that much was clear. She must have been traumatised in the orphanage, how horrible!

'Did something happen to you in the orphanage?' Mr Le Blanc asked.

'One of the girls, Sofia, jumped off the tower. She died. But I was waking up crying long before that. I just thought that's how it is.'

Concern was visible on the faces of the two adults. 'Oh no, my dear,' Mrs Le Blanc said. 'That's not the case. Something terrible must have happened to you. Can you not recall anything it might have been?'

'No, my first memories were when I arrived in Rome one night. I can't remember how I got there, but I must have hit my head very hard in the process. I spent a couple of days in the infirmary with a bandage. It started then already.' Mrs Le Blanc hugged the young girl, holding her tight.

'We'll arrange for a Psychiatrist when we arrive in Athens. Perhaps some ongoing psychotherapy will help get to the bottom of this,' Mr Le Blanc offered as a solution.

'Thank you. I'll try it out for you. Maybe it will help,' Marie-Claire responded, now fully awake and out of bed.

The three stood in silence for a while, not quite sure what to do next. 'Can we go have breakfast now?' Marie-Claire finally asked, breaking the ice.

'What a splendid idea,' a slightly relieved Mr Le Blanc responded. The young lady seemed to have an enormous well-spring of untapped resilience inside her. *Maybe she is fine after all,* he thought. But they would get her analysed in Athens by the Psychiatrist, just to be safe. The couple got dressed while Marie-Claire finished up in the bathroom. Once they were all looking fresh and dapper, they made their way to the restaurant for breakfast.

The restaurant was on the upper deck of the ferry, giving magnificent views of the surrounding ocean and the passing Greek landmasses. The ferry passed between the islands of *Kefalonia* and *Lefkada* as the Le Blanc family were having their breakfast. In the far distance, the green outcroppings of the islands ended in yellow sandy beaches or dark rocky shorelines, shaking hands with the turquoise waters of the Mediterranean, a beautiful meeting of everlasting friendship. The views were breath-taking and more than made up for the mediocre, buffet style meal which was dished from lukewarm bay-marine serving stations. Breakfast proved a stark contrast to the dinner from the previous evening, which was top notch. The singular saving grace for the morning meal was the coffee, which was strong and flavourful, providing a feisty kick-start to the day. Marie-Claire found the breakfast much better than those she was used to in *Marcigliana*, but was unaccustomed to the strong coffee. She kept tasting a sip and then adding more milk to her cup, until it eventually turned into a pale looking excuse for a brew, more akin in colour to tea. The adults were used to drinking strong Italian espresso and chose to drink the proffered coffee black. 'How far is Athens from the port?' Marie-Claire enquired.

'It should take us about three hours by car, once we have cleared through customs,' Mr Le Blanc responded. 'The Diplomatic Service will ensure there are some personnel to drive us to the Embassy.'

Once they were done with breakfast, they quickly returned to the cabin to pack their luggage for departure, which Jacques came to collect. 'Good morning. I trust everyone rested well?' he asked, wearing a dark suit and red tie. He looked quite officious, clearly feeling the requirement for presenting a formal façade upon their arrival in their new country. Mr Le Blanc donned a linen suit without a tie, while the two ladies wore bright skirts. Jean-Pierre was waiting for them on deck, also dressed formally, as the ferry steamed into the port of *Patras*.

The arrival of the ferry was earmarked by organised chaos, as passengers and cars disembarked after the long voyage. The diplomatic group could skip the queue at passport control and was met by a trio of smartly dressed Embassy employees, with three shiny cars awaiting their arrival. 'I am Patrice Marceau, *Chargé d'affaires* at the Embassy,' the leader of the group introduced himself in French. 'And this is Louis Benoud and Stavros Nicolides,' he indicated to his two colleagues. While Stavros had the dark Mediterranean complexion common amongst Greeks, Louis was a large, blond man with a rugged face. Patrice appeared to be in his late thirties, with a dark beard and hair. 'Louis is the head of security at the Embassy,' Patrice continued, 'and Stavros is the head of your personal protection detail.' Mr Le Blanc was surprised by the youthful appearance of Stavros, looking more like a local intern, brought along to do the heavy lifting. He introduced his family and the rest of the party to the second-in-charge at the Embassy and the security officers. From what he remembered in their files, Stavros had Special Forces training, while Louis came from a background in the French foreign legion.

Stavros assisted Jacques to load the luggage into the three cars. He opened the door of the middle car for Mr Le Blanc and the two ladies, while Patrice was joined in the first car by Jacques and Jean-Pierre. Louis found himself alone in the last car, making up the rear of the procession. The convoy left the harbour and headed for the capital city, some 200km away. The road curved north east and then followed the *Peloponnese* coast towards Athens. It was a beautiful day and the scenery was spectacular. The road had remarkable views over the Gulf of *Corinth* with the far shoreline sometimes visible on the horizon. They passed several coastal villages, all of which appeared quaint and alluring, often leading to the procession coming to a halt for some appreciation of the architecture or scenery in a town they were driving through. When they reached the town of *Corinth*, they decided to stop for lunch.

The trip had taken longer than anticipated, due to the many stops along the way. Louis found a restaurant overlooking the beach, where the whole party settled at a long wooden table for a late lunch. Patrice excused himself to call the Embassy, as they were already an hour behind the expected arrival schedule. The restaurant owner graciously allowed him to use the house phone to make the call. They ordered several platters for the table, containing a variety of different Greek *mezze* dishes. Some local wine completed the order for Mr and Mrs Le Blanc. The Embassy staff stuck to drinking coffee, while Marie-Claire had a milkshake. The spread was not fancy, but delicious and she took an instant liking to Greek food. While the adults were discussing dessert options, Marie-Claire asked if she could go walk on the beach. Stavros accompanied her as she took off her shoes and went running to the surf. She had never been on a beach before and she enjoyed the sensation of the sand between her toes.

She played in the shallow water, running in an out of the surf to the rhythm of the small lapping waves. The shallow water was crystal clear and she could see tiny fish swimming around her feet. A Greek couple came walking past with a small furry dog on a leash. Marie-Claire bent down and stroked the dog tentatively, careful to keep her fingers away from its mouth. She had never encountered a dog before. It licked her hand and she laughed at the sensation, wet and pleasurable. The dog followed its owners as they continued their stroll down the shoreline and Marie-Claire hoped she would see another one soon. She decided she liked dogs.

When they had finished their dessert, Mr Le Blanc called Marie-Claire back to the table. She reluctantly returned, none too happy with having to leave her beach adventure behind. The young Greek security officer was busy shaking the sand out of his dress shoes, as he didn't have time to take them off when following Marie-Claire on her outing. Everyone got back into the cars and the journey continued eastwards. They crossed the Corinth Canal, which separated the *Peloponnese* from the Greek mainland. The man-made gorge had sheer limestone walls and the watery connection between the Gulf of Corinth and Aegean Sea was visible far below the bridge as they passed over it. It would take another hour to reach their destination in Athens from here. The sea now lay on the right-hand side of the convoy, a beautiful blue expanse, as far as the eye could see. The trip had been a long one and Marie-Claire was looking forward to finally arriving at their destination. She nodded off in the afternoon heat of the car.

When she woke up, they were in the bustle of the city, surrounded by other cars and stuck in, what appeared to be, the afternoon rush hour traffic. They puttered along slowly, still in convey with the two other Embassy cars in front and behind them. It was an impressive feat, taking the traffic volume into consideration. They rounded a corner and Marie-Claire saw a massive park on the right side of the street up ahead, with traffic a little lighter in the road they found themselves in. Suddenly, she saw the French flag on the left, blowing in the afternoon breeze. It was atop a yellow, four-storey building opposite the park. Like a chequered flag signals the end of a race, the Red, White and Blue standard of France signalled the end of their journey. They had finally arrived.

The convoy turned in a side road and drove around the side of the Embassy, entering a black motor gate and parking behind the building. As the cars stopped, a horn and trumpet duo started playing *La Marseillaise*, in welcome of the new ambassador. A row of ceremonial sentries were smartly dressed in uniform and formed a guard of honour, leading to the door of the Embassy. Marie-Claire was very impressed by the pomp and ceremony and it was the first time she had heard the French National Anthem. She absolutely loved it!

They entered the rear entrance of the Embassy, leading into the private residence of the ambassador. Twenty-odd Embassy staff members were neatly lined up, all wearing formal dress of some kind. Patrice went down the row of staff members, introducing the Le Blancs to each in turn and giving a short overview of their duties in the building. Marie-Claire was struggling to remember all the names, but being new to the ranks of the French Diplomatic corps, and only ten years old, she could be forgiven. There would be plenty of time later to acquaint herself with all the new faces. She looked around the room. It was nowhere near as grand as the Embassy in Rome, but it felt homely, with a lovely black and white tiled floor and a wide staircase leading up to the second floor. Several rooms led off to the sides of the large entrance hall they found themselves in with the assembled Embassy staff.

Patrice welcomed the family to the Embassy, and the country, on behalf of the Diplomatic Staff. Mr Le Blanc in return, gave a short speech of his own. The length of the speech was limited by the extent of the travel weariness experienced by the ambassador. To the one side of the stairs stood a table with a spread of snacks and drinks and after his address, everyone helped themselves to refreshments while the newly arrived family mingled with the locals. Several of the staff members spoke to Marie-Claire, telling her of their own children and asking if she enjoyed the trip. The chef, Auguste, asked her about her tastes in food. His white jacket was crisp and clean and he was wearing his chef's hat. He was a large, jovial fellow and she liked him immediately. She told him about the food they had at the beach restaurant in Corinth.

'Ah yes, my *dolmades* are the best. I will treat you to them often. You are always welcome in the kitchen to come and see me prepare meals.' He pointed her to one of the side doors, through which a large table was visible. 'The kitchen entrance is through the dining room. There is also a well-stocked herb garden in the back. I like to use fresh herbs for my cooking.'

Marie-Claire was glad to hear there was a herb garden. It made her feel a little more at home. 'May I come see you tomorrow, then you can show me the garden and the kitchen?' she enquired.

'Oh yes, I'd be happy to do so!' the portly chef responded. He excused himself to tend to the dwindling contents of the snack table. She wandered around, helping herself to some lemonade.

The reception was starting to wind down and Patrice excused the staff to their various duties. He took the family on a brief tour of the Embassy. The personal quarters were located at the back of the building and upstairs. To the left of the grand staircase was an elevator, with a passage to the right of it connecting the living quarters with the official administrative spaces in the Embassy. The door at the end of the passage had a coded lock, to control public access to the private residence. Upstairs, the apartment had a comfortable lounge, dining room, a small kitchen, four bedrooms and a private study for the ambassador. There was also a private library, much to Marie-Claire's delight. It had a wide variety of reading material, including fiction, history and reference works. The wooden shelves stood wall-to-ceiling, with reading chairs and tables spaced around the room. Despite its size, the library was a cosy, welcoming space.

Marie-Claire's room had two single beds, the bedspreads covered in a bright flower motive. Wondrous paintings in the room showed various artfully done scenes from a circus, and a dancer. There was a desk positioned in front of the one window, while the second window had a chest below it, filled with toys and dolls. Marie-Claire instantly loved her room. She had never had a room to call her own. The room she occupied in the Embassy in Rome was more of a visitor's room, but this room was all hers. She was happy and probably for the first time in her life, felt a sense of belonging. She stared longingly at the Edgar Degas print of a ballerina above the one bed, forever frozen in an *arabesque* pose. The painting moved her. She wanted to *be* the ballerina. 'Welcome to Athens, Marie-Claire,' said Patrice.

LETTERS FROM GREECE

Embassy of France
Leoforos Vasilissis Sofias 7
Athina
Greece
8 June 1952

My dearest Sister Marcel

I trust you are well and that you are still blessing everyone in *Marcigliana* with your excellent meals. It has been two years since my arrival in Athens. How time flies when you stop paying attention to it for even the briefest of moments…

My life here has been really busy. Every day is an adventure filled with new things to learn, to love or to discover. Athens is a wonderful city, rich in history, culture, and fine food. You would love it! The Embassy is located in *Vasilissis Sofias* avenue in the capital. Both the American and British embassies are just down the road from us, and some nice museums also border the street. The Embassy itself is a distinctly French looking yellow building with four floors. The mansion used to belong to the Psicha family in the old days. My room is on the top floor and I have a lovely view of the Royal gardens and the adjacent Greek parliament from the window. It seems that the Embassy is in a really nice part of Athens and I enjoy living here. We often stroll in the gardens at sunset and if you walk south in the park and reach the *Zappeion* terrace, there are beautiful views of the *Acropolis* and the columns of the temple of Zeus. I am very happy to be living across the street from such a marvellous park and watching the sun set over the ancient Greek temples is a sight to behold.

The food in Greece is really delicious and the chef at the Embassy, Auguste, really makes a lovely meze spread. He is actually French, but has been in Greece long enough to master their food too. I am also a big fan of his Lamb *Kleftiko*, which he does really well. He also does French dishes, which father and mother really enjoy. I think it reminds them of being back in their country of origin. Although I have never been to France, I hope to go there someday and Father said he will take me to Paris when he next has to travel there. I have only ever known *Marcigliana* and a little piece of Rome, so Athens is really home for me now.

Besides Auguste, the Embassy has quite a number of staff members. There is Jacques, who does most of the driving for father. He came with us from Rome and also takes care of most of father's day-to-day chores. Then there is Jean-Pierre, who also came with us from Rome. He is father's personal secretary and tends to most of the administrative duties that helps father do his job. He is about the same age as father and seems to be quite good at what he does, as father seems happy with his work. Initially, he bumped heads a bit with Patrice, who is second in charge in the Embassy. I think it just took them a while to make Jean-Pierre understand how things ran at the Embassy in Athens, which is a bit different from Rome. Now everyone gets along splendidly!

Stavros Nicolides serves as personal security for Father, Mother and myself. I don't know who we upset that we need personal protection, but it apparently comes with the territory. He is not an old man, but he has old eyes. I think he has seen many things, as he was in the army during the Greek civil war. Stavros always accompanies Father everywhere he goes. He has also been giving Jacques some training, so that they can function as a "well-oiled machine" when they take Father out for his work. Jacques has been tending to Father's security for some time, so he is quite adept at looking after him and it didn't take long before they were that oily machine Stavros was hoping for. Louis Benoud is the head of the Embassy Security. I don't think he knows how to smile. I have often tried to amuse him, but it is an impossible task. He is an enormous, muscular man, with short blond hair. I think he is older than father, although, it might only be in appearance. I heard that he was in the French Foreign Legion before. He must have spent a lot of time on the beach without wearing a hat when he was with the Legion, as his face is all leathery and rugged. The rest of the Embassy staff are all very friendly. Some of them I don't see too often, as they work in the front offices, being all diplomatic with the Greeks. The ones that work in the residential part of the Embassy I see every day, as they are always around.

Greece is so rich in history! I really enjoy seeing all the ancient temples and ruins dotting the countryside. There is never a dull moment when we travel outside Athens, although the natural colour scheme can be a bit drab in the dry summers. At least the sparkling blue waters of the Aegean sea gives a bit of colour to the landscape and is excellent to cool down in when it gets really hot. There are such lovely beaches here! We occasionally travel to some of the surrounding islands for weekend getaways and it is truly spectacular to see.

I am doing well in school here. Father enrolled me in the international school. It was difficult at first, because I had to learn English to go there. I had about four months here before the school classes started and I had tutoring in English for four hours every day. Luckily father could also speak English, so it helped to speak to him in English as well, to practise. By the time school started in September, I could manage to get by and I understood everyone there. By December, my English classes were done. Mother then decided that I should also learn Greek and arranged for a Greek tutor to give me classes after school every day. We had Greek as a subject in school as well, so that helped me a bit. A lot of the staff at the Embassy can speak Greek and Stavros also helped by talking nice and slow to me, so I could follow his words. By the end of that year,

I was fairly fluent in Greek too. This was rather funny, because I could now speak better Greek than Father. I guess children learn language faster than adults.

My Greek tutor was Iana. She had lovely green eyes and dark hair. What a beautiful woman! She worked part-time as a Greek/French translator at the Embassy and then also assisted us with our Greek lessons. I am surprised that Father took such a long time to learn Greek, as he often had long tutoring sessions with Iana in the afternoons in his private study, especially when mother was out of the Embassy playing tennis with her friends. They were very diligent and he sometimes even locked the doors so that people would not disturb them during their lessons. Once my Greek language classes were finished, Iana stopped working at the Embassy and I haven't seen her since. She was rather friendly and Father seemed to like her, but Mother not so much. When Iana left, the translator that replaced her was a big lady with some hair on her chin. Mother appeared to like her a lot more. I think she was an excellent tutor, because Father's Greek skills improved a lot quicker once she took over his lessons. Mother also seemed pleased with his progress and she was a lot happier now.

I have really grown to love my adopted parents. They are really wonderful people. My mother is a kind and gentle woman and has a deep love for nature and animals. She installed some bird feeders at the Embassy shortly after our arrival and was logging all the different types of birds she saw. She also got me a kitten for my birthday! I called him Salvador, because he had black hair and funny looking, curled whiskers. Mother seems happy with the circumstances of living outside France, although she sometimes gets sad and refers to Father as a "typical Frenchman", whatever that may mean. She likes to play tennis at the club with her friends and she also has them over to play bridge on Thursday mornings. We still visit museums together and she enjoys showing me all the different types of art that one can see in Athens. It is not often that a week passes without us going to shop for a new outfit for either her, or me. Luckily, all the nice shops are located in the areas around the Embassy, so we are always spoilt for choice.

Mother's parents had died when she was in her late twenties, so she is also an orphan now. I feel that is why we get along so well. I think she misses them sometimes and often tells me stories about them and when she was a girl before I go to bed. It makes me that glad she is in my life and I hope I bring her joy too. I try to please her and I like doing little things that make her happy, as she does for me too.

Father works long hours. He is always busy reading and writing papers for work and I think the French government is lucky to have him in their service. He makes time to spend with myself and Mother and takes us on outings whenever he can. His parents were very strict when he was a young boy, so he tries to not be too hard on me. I try to be good, so he does not need to get upset with me. He is a patient man and does not lose his temper easily. Father never seems to get angry with Mother and myself either. He is also gentle and Salvador loves sitting on his lap as he works, gently purring as his ears get scratched every so often. I have noticed that he is excellent at spotting lies. One can clearly notice his right eyebrow arching up when he does not believe what he is hearing. It is funny, because the speakers who do not know him well, mistakenly think it is because he is interested in what they are telling him. His hair seems to be getting slightly lighter with all the sun here in Greece. Or maybe he is just getting old?

I have a lovely painting in my room. It is of a ballet dancer and is a print of something by *Degas*. I can stare at it for hours on end. The dancer is striking an elegant pose and looks very regal. It has inspired me to become a ballerina! Shortly after we moved in, I asked Mother if she can arrange for me to have ballet classes, as I would like to learn. She was quite excited for me and found a ballet studio not too far from where we live. The teacher is a lovely lady called Mrs Antonides. She is a retired ballerina herself and is still an excellent dancer.

Her posture is so perfect and it looks like she glides when she demonstrates any movements. Such grace!

I take classes with her three days a week. I started in the beginner's class, but I have now moved up to join some of the older girls in an advanced class. I find that I am really doing well. The poses and movements seem to come naturally, as if they have always been buried deep inside me, just looking for an opportunity to bloom. After classes we always go to the coffee shop below the studio and mother buys me a milkshake. In the first year, we did a performance of Swan Lake. I got to play the part of the Swan Princess! Everyone was impressed with my performance after the show and I even got a bouquet of flowers thrown on stage for me. I dried the flowers and hung them on my wall. It is still very pretty. I got to play the sugarplum fairy when we performed the Nutcracker the following year. By then I was in the advanced class, so the older girls with more experience played the more important parts. Father has converted one of the bedrooms in the Embassy into a dance studio and has installed a bar and mirrors. Now I get to practice even when I am at home. He is really encouraging me, as I am enjoying the dancing very much. I still practice three afternoons a week with the company, but Father has arranged for Mrs Antonides to come to the Embassy for a private lesson twice a week as well.

She is highly impressed with my progress. She seems to think that I might be able to become a professional dancer someday. They say I have lots of natural, raw talent, which she is busy moulding into shape. I just enjoy the dancing, I don't want to worry too much about where it may take me someday, even if my parents do seem to have their own ideas on the subject. Mrs Antonides has a son called Andros. It is short for Androsthasiou, but luckily we don't have to call him that. He is also in the ballet class. It doesn't seem to be too popular amongst the boys, as there are only three of them in the class. I think Andros would have done it even if his mother wasn't the teacher. He seems to like wearing the ballet tights to class. He played the Nutcracker Prince in the show and did so very well. Next year they are talking about performing Peter and the

Wolf. I don't know whether he would play Peter or the wolf, but he is bound to be one of the two.

I have also started playing with Andros outside of ballet class and he is now my best friend. We often host tea parties for all my dolls and then he would do the voice of a butler when serving them. It is rather funny. We often go play across the street in the park. Usually mother comes along and then she sits on a bench and reads, with Jacques monitoring our movements like a hawk, while other times only Stavros would come along and keep an eye on us. I think that Father's work as a diplomat actually makes enemies for him, it is rather ironic. He takes our safety quite seriously and is always looking after myself and Mother with a bit more caution than one would presume is necessary. There is always someone from the security staff not too far away when we are outside the Embassy grounds. I also learnt that we are not allowed to play hide and seek when we are in the park. Being skilled at the game seemed to cause some consternation amongst the security staff and I once had ten of them quite frantically looking for my hiding place. After that, I wasn't permitted to play the game anymore.

Andros' father is in the olive oil business. His father owns several olive groves and also buy up olives from surrounding farms to produce their oil. The family has been doing it for many generations. He always brings us some olive oil when he comes over to visit. Auguste is a huge fan of his and considers Andros' family almost like Greek royalty. He always makes Andros extra special dishes when he is around for lunch. Andros is probably a bit small for his age, but all the ballet has made him strong as an ox. I think his father makes him pick olives in the autumn, which also helps his upper body strength. I don't see as much of him during November, besides in ballet class and even those he sometimes misses during the harvest. He is a good friend to me, although I still miss Arianna and Karin sometimes.

Our quarters in the Embassy are filled with the most magnificent paintings. I was really curious about what it took to paint something like that. Mother bought me some art supplies and I tried my hand at painting. I seemed to have a bit of a knack for it and Father decided I should attend some art classes as a hobby. We also have art at the school, so my parents arranged for me to take it as a subject. Learning something at school sometimes takes the fun out of it. They have the most boring art history classes on occasion, which is a terrible way to spend an hour. I just want to learn how to make the different colours and how some of the paintings were done, I don't care if the artist went mad and cut off his ear in the process. It would just cause a terrible mess if that was to happen to me and I am sure mother would scold me if I soiled the nice carpets in the Embassy by doing that.

My parents were very concerned when we first arrived in Athens, because I was crying in my sleep. I had to see a Psychiatrist for some sessions. He was a nice old gentlemen with a great, big, bushy beard. We played a lot of word games and he showed me some nice symmetrical ink blotches and asked me to describe what I saw. All of them had the most interesting shapes. There were trees and animals and even one that looked like Father. The one card was a bit worrying to me, as it looked like a puddle of blood. Who would put something like that in a nice stack of cards? I saw him for about two months and we talked about my life a lot. He seemed incredibly interested in what I remembered from the orphanage and also what I remembered from the day I had arrived there. He tried all kinds of tricks to get me to remember how I ended up in Rome that day, but without success.

Dr Kauffman could also speak German and he told me he would have loved for me to have spoken to one of his friends who was a professor in Vienna, to hear what his opinion was of my situation. Unfortunately his friend had passed away just before the war, so it was not to be. They even tried putting me on some pills to help with the crying. They made me feel sleepy all the time and my mouth was terribly dry. Mother eventually put a stop to it after the first week, as it was not helping and she was concerned that I was so tired and didn't want to do anything but stare at the fireplace. After those two months, my parents decided that I should stop seeing the doctor. Besides waking up in tears some mornings, I was a happy girl and enjoyed my life. At least we made sure I wasn't crazy and in any danger of cutting off one of my ears. The crying did not seem to affect the rest of my life in a bad way and they decided to leave it be, an unanswered question of where I came from.

I want to thank you for your friendship and guidance when I was at *Marcigliana*. I will always remember you and I will always remember the lessons you taught me. I will try and make you proud. I hope you are at peace with yourself as well. Are Karin and Arianna still there at the orphanage? Send my love and regards to everyone at *Marcigliana*.

Best wishes,
Marie-Claire

SNOWFALL IN ST MORITZ, 1953

arie-Claire woke up and wiped the tears from her eyes. She had been roused by her mother with a gentle shake. The teenager bound out of bed, disrupting the peaceful slumber of Salvador, who was curled up besides her legs. The cat was not happy. 'Morning, Mother!' she exclaimed excitedly. *It was finally 20 December!* The sky was still dark outside in the early hours of the morning. She had been eagerly looking forward to this day since June, when her father announced they would be travelling to *St Moritz* in Switzerland for Christmas this year. She had not heard of it before, but it did not take her long to find the little town in the atlas in her Father's study, and once she read up on the Swiss Alps and the *St Moritz* Winter Olympics in the encyclopaedia set, she was instantly excited. Marie-Claire had never seen snow before and now she would finally experience a white Christmas. The remainder of the year had dragged by, with her routine of school, ballet classes, art class and weekend excursions to elsewhere in Greece. It is difficult to think that travels through Greece would be considered dull routine, but she had worked herself up for the trip to Switzerland and everything else paled in comparison.

Her bags had been packed and ready for weeks, as far as preparation went. The contents mostly consisted of undergarments, as they were going to be shopping in *St Moritz* for the required cold weather gear, which was not readily available in Athens. They were leaving for the airport soon and would be flying to Zurich at 6:00. They planned to pick up travel clothing at the airport for their train trip into the Alps. Marie-Claire had never flown before and she was a little scared at the prospect.

Their trip to the Athens airport proved uneventful, while the check-in went like clockwork. Jacques assisted with their luggage, while Stavros had flown through to Zurich the previous day already for advance preparations. The family walked across the runway to the Douglas DC-6 aircraft. Marie-Claire wondered how it would ever get off the ground and hoped the signature white cross on the tail would provide the necessary divine intervention to get them airborne. 'Don't worry my dear, everything will be fine,' Mr Le Blanc said as he gently took her hand and led her up the stairway, into the gaping door of the metal beast.

Once inside, Marie-Claire saw that it was not so scary. She sat across the aisle from her mother, with her father and Jacques flanking the two ladies at the window seats. She grabbed Mr Le Blanc's hand as the plane sped down the runway and took off with a couple of bumps, heading north over Greece. Once she got used to the sensation and her stomach settled, Marie-Claire leaned over her father to look at the passing scenery far below. Soon, the Italian coast was visible through the window. Three hours later, the plane crossed the Italian Alps as they neared Switzerland. The plane shook in the turbulent mountain air and Marie-Claire grabbed her father's hand again. Seeing the mountains from the plane was a spectacular sight, with the early morning sunlight reflecting off the snow-capped peaks below. The view was lost on the youngster, who was quite distressed, only focusing on her prayers and the hand she was holding.

The landing in *Zurich* went smoothly, but Marie-Claire was still happy to get out of the flying tin-can. She could understand the advantages of travelling at such speed, but it would take a while before she would get used to the sensations. The cold air hit everyone like an arctic gale as they exited the plane. It felt considerably colder here than when they had left Athens. They rushed to the warmth of the terminal building, where Stavros waited with their cold weather travel gear. Everyone received a warm coat, mittens, scarf and a hat. It was a lot more comfortable when they exited the terminal building in more appropriate clothing and walked to the waiting cars. The trip to the station was short, but scenic, and twenty minutes later the party arrived at the *Zurich Hauptbahnhof*. The historic station building with its many arches was different from anything Marie-Claire had experienced before and she stood gawking at the number of railway tracks leading out of the building into the unknown. Cream and red trains left the station exactly as scheduled on the big board, Swiss precision at its finest.

The family and their entourage boarded the train on the South track to *Landquart* station, where they would change trains for the final leg of the journey to *St Moritz*. They had acquired a private, First-Class cabin for the trip. Marie-Claire was excited and sat next to the window, staring at the passing crowds on the platform. The cabin could easily fit eight people, so the five of them sat quite comfortably. Mr Le Blanc read a newspaper while they waited for the train to depart. After what felt like an eternity for Marie-Claire, the train whistle blew and they left *Zurich*.

The railway line ran in a valley, with the hills on either side already displaying a scattering of snow. The surrounding scenery was breath-taking and all the mountains had snow on them. There was now also a light snow covering of everything around the line. It was a winter wonderland and Marie-Claire thought that she had never seen anything as beautiful. 'Is *St Moritz* as pretty as this, Father?'

'Oh, yes. Even prettier, actually,' Mr Le Blanc responded.

They arrived at the *Landquart* station two hours after having left *Zurich* and they departed the train. They walked a short distance to the adjacent platform. 'Mind the gap,' Mr Le Blanc warned as they boarded the train following the *Rhaetian* narrow-gauge rail-line, which would eventually bring them to their final destination. The surrounding peaks towered above the tiny town, a quaint little hamlet in the snow. The journey continued onward and two hours later, they finally arrived in *St Moritz*. It was beautiful. The railway station stood on the edge of Lake *St Moritz*, which was one solid sheet of ice, almost as far as the eye could see. Interestingly, there appeared to be a racecourse of some sort set out on the ice. The panoramic views of the mountains and lake, all covered in crisp, white snow was a feast for the eyes. A crowd of fellow tourists also departed the train, many had skis and other equipment with them.

The Le Blanc party exited through the station, to find a hotel shuttle waiting for them in the street. The driver held up an identifying sign, neatly written in large lettering on hotel stationery. It must have been a common occurrence to meet hotel guests at the station. The large black Rolls Royce headed up the hill and trough the town centre. It was mid-afternoon and the town was abuzz with activity, warmly dressed tourists filling the sidewalks. Luxury shops lined the streets, their wares elaborately displayed in the windows. They went around a traffic circle in the centre of town with a huge, ornately decorated Christmas tree set up on it. This area served as the town square. Marie-Claire looked forward to walking around town, as it was very pretty and the tree completed the picture of a Christmas wonderland. The driver parked in front of the Hotel Kulm, their journey finally concluded.

The hotel manager waited for them on the steps as the car approached the entrance. He opened the doors for the family. 'Welcome to the Hotel Kulm, Mr Le Blanc, Mrs Le Blanc, young lady,' he said with a curt bow. 'I am Anton Badrutt, the general manager. If there is anything we can do to make your stay more enjoyable, do not hesitate to bring it to my attention. Kurt here will take your luggage to your suits,' he said indicating a smartly dressed bell-hop. 'We rent out a variety of winter sports equipment at our club house, should you wish to ski, ice skate or take the cresta run down to the lake with a toboggan,' he said with a wry smile, knowing that the Olympic bob-sled run was not for the faint of heart.

The hotel itself was a wondrous facility. The lobby had a large chandelier in the middle of the ceiling, with stairs leading up to all manner of lounges and restaurants at the back of the hotel. Jacques went to complete the paperwork at a wooden desk on the right side of the lobby, leaving Marie-Claire standing between her parents, craning her neck to see all the corners of the elaborate room. 'It's beautiful father. So grand! I can't wait to see the rest of it,' the excited youngster exclaimed.

'Don't worry my dear, there will be plenty of time to see it all. You have two weeks to explore it to your heart's content,' the diplomat responded. They were escorted to a suite on the third floor, with Jacques and Stavros sharing a room across the passage. It had lovely Italian furnishings and two rooms leading off the central lounge. The suite had scenic views of the Kulm sports-park below and Lake *St Moritz* in the distance. Marie-Claire observed a crowd gathered at the top of the bob-sled run, mostly young men trying to impress their companions by braving a run down the icy chute to the lake. The ice-rink was filled with revellers, sliding about with varying degrees of success. It looked like ballet on ice and she was immediately keen to give it a try. 'All right, let's go and get our winter gear, so we can start enjoying ourselves,' Mr Le Blanc said as he walked to the door.

'Speak for yourself, Father. I have been enjoying myself for quite a while already,' Marie-Claire said with a smile.

They walked down the hill towards town. There were a number of high end boutique stores to choose from for their vacation wardrobe, but they opted for a ski shop. Their visit required more pragmatic clothing. Once they each got a practical outfit, they requested the shop to deliver the rest of the clothes to the hotel. The shop assistant, a sprightly young blond, was very pleased with their choices and the number of outfits they bought, as she was also paid a commission on sales. It was to be quite a Christmas bonus. 'Where would you like to go first, Marie-Claire?' Mrs Le Blanc enquired of the youngster.

'Let's go see the ice-rink,' she responded excitedly. She couldn't wait to try her hand at the ice bound ballet.

They ambled to the winter sports-club below the hotel. Some skates were charged to the hotel-room and they made for the ice-rink. There was a beginner's class on the ice and Marie-Claire observed the teacher, showing the students how to move across the ice. The sun started to set over the Alpine resort town and the floodlights went on above the ice rink, bathing it in a yellow curtain of light, drawn from all sides. They took to the ice, Marie-Claire for the first time and her parents with some previous experience from their youth. The youngster caught on very quickly. Her ballet training served her well on the ice and she displayed poise and balance in her movements. As soon as she got used to propelling herself forward, she tried an *arabesque* pose. Her first attempt ended in disaster. She raised her back leg and then out of habit tried to get up on her leading toe. The tip of the skate got caught in the ice and she tumbled full length and slid over the ice. Mr Le Blanc was there to give her a hand to get up. 'Careful princess, you're only just starting.' Marie-Claire shrugged, 'I'll be fine Father, don't worry. My outfit luckily has a lot of padding!' Only slightly winded from the fall, she tried again, this time with more success.

Marie-Claire managed to hold the ballet pose on the ice. First left, then right. She continued experimenting, by adding rotation to the poses. The movements came quite naturally to the young girl. Mr and Mrs Le Blanc stopped skating and observed the youngster, who was busy putting together quite a routine of ballet poses on the ice. 'She's a natural, our little Marie-Claire,' Mrs Le Blanc observed. She felt pride for the teenage girl, who showed glimpses of maturing into a young woman.

Mr Le Blanc held his wife's gloved hand. 'Indeed. She's taken to it like a duck to water. Seems all the ballet training will come in very handy during this vacation.' They laughed, good-naturedly.

As she was gliding along the ice on one leg, a portly boy of about her own age careened out of control and skidded into her, both of them toppling down in a tangle of limbs. Mr Le Blanc was about to skate over to check on her, but the girl had stood up and was chatting to the boy, shaking his hand. No harm seems to have been done and soon Marie-Claire was back to her routine of turns and poses. Eventually, they almost had to drag her off the ice, as supper time at the hotel was approaching.

Dinner at the Kulm hotel was a stately occasion. Everyone was dressed formally for the meal in the ballroom, overlooking the frozen lake. The surface of the lake shimmered in the moonlight, creating a fairy-tale landscape. The services of Jacques and Stavros were not required for the evening meal and they went off, gallivanting about town. 'Did you have fun on the ice today, Marie-Claire?' Mrs Le Blanc enquired.

'Oh yes, Mother, it was very enjoyable. I met a boy called Gunter on the ice, he crashed into me. It was very funny for him! I hope I get to skate every day. It's like ballet on ice.'

Their main courses arrived, a tasty sea bass imported from Italy. Afterwards, a band played some music and people took to the dancefloor. Mr Le Blanc got up, bowed and extended a hand to his wife, 'Would the Madam care to dance?' he asked in a formal voice. As they were about to leave, Marie-Claire asked if she could go to the room, as she was very tired from the day. 'Will you be all right on your own?' Mr Le Blanc enquired.

'Yes Father, it's just up the stairs, don't worry about me. I'll be fine. Enjoy yourselves!' They gave her the room key and she put on her coat and headed out of the ballroom. The couple walked onto the dance floor, hand-in-hand and joined the throng of couples waltzing away to the music. When they returned to the room an hour later, they found Marie-Claire fast asleep in her bed. Her face was cold when Mrs Le Blanc kissed her on the forehead, so they added another blanket to the bed before turning in for the evening.

The next morning, as they were crossing the lobby for breakfast, there seemed to be an anxious flurry of activity in the hotel. Bell-hops ran around and the hotel manager was standing next to a map of the hotel with what appeared to be the local police chief. 'What is going on?' Mr Le Blanc asked their waiter in the breakfast room. 'Everyone seems to be very busy this morning?'

'A boy went missing last night! He left his parents at dinner time and it appeared that his bed was not slept in when they checked on him this morning. Everyone is now searching the hotel grounds for him. The police chief is helping to organise the effort.'

The sad news created a muted atmosphere in the restaurant. By the end of the meal, even more disturbing news had reached those gathered for breakfast. They had found the missing boy's body on the lake! It seems he had fallen into the bobsled track after dinner and had slid all the way to the bottom of the run. With the high speeds of the icy track, his body was thrown around as he descended and he had fractured his neck. The whole hotel was in a sombre mood because of the tragedy. Mr Le Blanc gave Marie-Claire a stern lecture about keeping away from the bobsled run and not venturing out on her own, especially not after dark. 'Yes Father, I promise I'll be careful,' she responded politely. Mrs Le Blanc proposed that they rent a car for the day and drive around to some of the surrounding towns, to get away from the hotel and the veil of melancholy covering it after the accident.

The scenery on the journey was even more beautiful than the valley surrounding *St Moritz* and they had soon almost forgotten about the tragic events at the hotel. It was a crisp, clear day, with not a cloud in the sky. The panoramic drive lifted their spirits and the snow-capped mountains and frozen lakes cleared their minds, to mirror the bright blue heavens above. They passed through the towns of *Silvaplana*, *Bivio* and *Cunter*. Each town was prettier and more charming than the last. Little town squares were surrounded by old school craft shops and family-run businesses, with the locals waving at them as they passed. The mountains towered over the towns, snow-covered stone fortresses protecting them from an invading modern world. They finally stopped in the bustling ski resort town of *Lenzerheide* for a meal. The Grand Hotel Schweizerhof, served as their lunch venue. The hotel was steeped in history, having been open since 1904. It had a jovial atmosphere and was filled with tourists in ski apparel, taking a deserved break from enjoying the various ski runs the area offered. The food was wholesome and tasty and filled the void left by an interrupted breakfast. 'Are you all right, Marie-Claire?' Mrs Le Blanc asked with concern, worried about the effect the boy's death could have on their daughter's psyche.

'Yes, Mother. I am fine. Don't fret. I am sure Gunter must be in a more deserved place now. The nuns at the orphanage always said that innocent children who died went straight to heaven.' Her answer seemed to please the adults, as they were visibly more relaxed. The harsh life the young girl had to contend with previously always made them concerned about her mental state and they were thankful that religion played such a positive role in her life. She seemed resilient, bouncing back almost effortlessly from disappointments and taking challenges in her stride. They felt lucky to have such a well-adjusted young girl in their lives. 'I look forward to the rest of our vacation. I am sure it can only get better from here,' Marie-Claire excitedly announced as they left the hotel to continue their journey.

A WHITE CHRISTMAS, 1953

The Le Blancs departed *Lenzerheide* shortly after lunch, as the locals returned to their various activities on the slopes. Their next port of call was the town of *Chur*, where they decided to stretch their legs and see the sights of the ancient village. The cobblestoned streets reminded them of the older sections of Rome and the town, being one of the oldest in Switzerland, was steeped in history. They explored the St Lucius Cathedral, which, despite lacking the colourful frescos they were used to seeing in the churches of Rome, was still beautiful.

The town itself, in contrast, was brightly coloured, with houses displaying almost artful paint schemes. This created a marvellous contrast to the white snow on the rooftops and the surrounding mountains. The streets were lined with the waving multi coloured standards, reflective of the town's history and the typical white cross on a red background of Swiss flags, creating interesting thoroughfares all around the old town. The squares in the oldest section of town were crowded with tourists, weathering the cold to enjoy the outdoors, before the next snow storm came around. A huge Christmas tree adorned one of the fountains which had been emptied out for winter. Twinkling strings of lights crossed the square, creating a wonderful, festive atmosphere.

Marie-Claire could pick up snatches of German conversations from the locals as they moved about town. '… and then Joseph said that the pig was not big enough yet and would have to wait until next Christmas. I only hope I'm still alive then to enjoy it,' she overheard an old man say to another. It was not always exciting, local people were just getting along with their lives in rural Switzerland.

They passed a house where a crying woman was being consoled by her neighbour. Apparently her father had passed away this morning in a nearby town. Sometimes everyday life was also harsh and unforgiving. It reminded Marie-Claire of the boy who had died at the hotel, where they would have to go back soon. Their escape would be at an end and they would have to face the grieving parents in the restaurant, or the lobby, or in town. She hoped they would choose to grieve at home, leaving the other guests to enjoy their vacations in peace, unburdened by the constant reminder of the life that ended somewhere in the curving path of the downhill sled run. She thought of a Shakespeare poem they had covered in school. *Out, out, brief candle...* The boy's life was similarly snuffed out before his time. Such a striking display of higher power over someone's destiny, who would have thought... Mr Le Blanc interrupted her train of thought with a suggestion 'Let's go have some coffee.'

The three entered a quaint little local restaurant and found a table inside, close to the fireplace. A variety of German beer on offer was cheaper than the coffee, but was not well supported in the cold. The warm, mulled wine proved extremely popular with everyone of legal drinking age, which was a great many of the patrons. Mr Le Blanc ordered a coffee, while Mrs Le Blanc opted for a glass of the warm, spicy wine, which was a speciality of the establishment. Marie-Claire asked for hot chocolate, which proved rich and creamy and simply delicious. 'It seems there's a storm brewing,' Mrs Le Blanc expressed, looking out the window towards the clouds gathering in the west over the mountains with some concern.

'Indeed,' Mr Le Blanc responded. 'We shouldn't dawdle too much longer. One does not want to get caught out in a snow storm in these mountain passes.'

'Such a pity,' Marie-Claire said. 'I would have loved to spend more time here. The town is so remarkable! Perhaps we could come back again some other time?'

'That would be terrific!' Mrs Le Blanc exclaimed, her demeanour now less inhibited than before the wine.

The walk to the car took longer than expected, the maze of small streets causing some confusion, initially. Once they re-discovered the car where they left it, they followed the road south out of town, the same direction they came from earlier. Their plan of a longer circle route back to *St Moritz* was now unrealistic, in light of the approaching inclement weather. In the end, their journey to the hotel turned into a frantic race against the approaching storm. It reminded of the carriage racing the sunset towards Castle Dracula in Bram Stoker's novel, the hackman desperately trying to avoid the night terrors in Transylvania. Two hours later, they arrived at the hotel in unison with the howling blizzard, only just managing to make a safe return. The Transylvanian carriage driver would have approved of their efforts. Crackling fires greeted them in the lobby of the Hotel Kulm. It was a welcome sight, warm and hospitable compared to the fast freezing landscape outside.

The mood in the hotel was still far from upbeat, with people having whispered conversations about the events of the morning. The boy's parents had checked out of the hotel, opting to relocate to one of the surrounding towns, while the police finalised all the administrative formalities. Dinner was not announced with much fanfare. The tables were arranged in rows across the ballroom floor, there would be no dancing this evening. Musical entertainment for dinner was limited to only the pianist, playing a collection of soft compositions, merely to break the silence. It was clear the hotel management had made a decision to show respect to the family of the departed youngster, by curtailing any frivolity in the establishment, at least for the foreseeable future.

The dinner conversations were muted and everyone left soon after finishing their meals. Subdued discussions continued in the salon and the smoking room after dinner, far removed from the festive atmosphere of previous evenings, filled with laughter and jest. Mr Le Blanc was nursing a glass of brandy by the fireplace in one of the lounges, Mrs Le Blanc joining him. Marie-Claire was sitting between them staring into the fire, mesmerised by the dancing flames. Outside, the storm raged unabated, with the snow bucketing down. The Le Blancs eventually retired upstairs from the glum affair in the lounge, hoping the new day will bring with it better prospects.

This did not prove to be the case. The inclement weather continued for three whole days, with everyone confined to the shelter of the hotel. All ski slopes were closed and outdoor activities mostly avoided, both due to the risk, but also the sheer unpleasantness of being outside in the storm. The days dragged by and Marie-Claire spent many hours exploring the hotel buildings on her own, having promised her parents not to go outside. There were many passages and staircases, each leading to new areas to discover. She came across some other children doing the same thing, which quickly led to the establishment of the KEG, or the Kulm Exploration Group. The half-dozen intrepid young explorers designed a flag, mapped the hotel corridors and eventually, resorted to a spirited game of treasure hunt which was enjoyed by all involved as a welcome respite from the boredom.

There was also a wonderful games room which all the young guests in the hotel frequented. After two days, the terrible accident had been mostly forgotten and the play area had turned into a hive of activity with table tennis, snooker, shoots and ladders, chess, and other board games keeping the children gainfully occupied. Marie-Claire preferred solitude and was delighted at the selection of books offered in the hotel reading room.

The small library had many interesting volumes and she was quite comfortable in a chair by the fireplace enjoying some of them. She could see out the window and between chapters, she would stare at the falling snow outside. Sometimes she would see patterns in the wind, forming shapes in the darkness. She had always been alone and keeping herself busy on her own in the hotel did not prove difficult. At mealtimes, Marie-Claire would talk with her parents, reporting on her activities since she last saw them. Stavros and Jacques were also enjoying the time off. Everyone being confined to the hotel gave them an opportunity to relax and let their guard down.

Mrs Le Blanc found her reading in a chair on the one afternoon and ordered two hot chocolates from one of the staff. 'How are you doing my dear? Keeping busy?'

'I am fine, Mother. They have plenty of interesting reading here. It's a nice library. So I'm keeping out of trouble.'

Mrs Le Blanc nodded, sipping her hot chocolate. 'You know, I used to work in a library when I was younger. It was an enormous one. It took forever to sort all the books. Sometimes it took all day to return a single trolley of books to their places. But it is important that things are in the places they belong. You will see that it applies in life as well. Everyone has a place where they belong.'

Marie-Claire looked concerned. 'But Mother, can one not change your place? My place was once at an orphanage and yet, here I am, sitting in this wonderful five-star hotel with you.'

'Yes, dear. Never resign yourself to anything. Never let anyone tell you what you cannot do. If you make up your mind to do something, you can do it. And that includes changing your fortune in life. Always remember that.'

'Thanks, Mother. I will remember. Thanks for the hot chocolate. We should go, it is almost dinner time.'

At Christmas Eve dinner, there were a group of carollers gathered in the ballroom, giving a performance for the guests. It was a tradition for these locals to do the rounds at many of the hotels and they also collected funds for the town church as they moved about town. Getting around tonight between venues was harder than usual, with the snowdrifts in the village almost reaching waist height in places. They sang mostly in German and Marie-Claire recognised many of the carols, from having heard them in Italian before.

The atmosphere differed greatly from the past Christmases she had experienced in the orphanage. There was a sense of wonderment and hope filling the room, something that was always conspicuously absent at *Marcigliana*. Christmas always served as a stark reminder to the orphans of their plight in the world. Now, even the tragedy four days ago was long forgotten in the festive atmosphere at the hotel. The room was bedecked with strings of lights and ornaments hanging from the ceiling and a large, elaborately decorated tree stood in the corner of the ballroom, complementing the two trees on either side of the steps in the hotel lobby. Undoubtedly, the Kulm hotel knew how to do a classic, white Christmas.

The food was festive, with a spread of cooked ham, some kind of scrumptious pork pie, goose and even imported turkey, catering for American visitors. There was also a whole table of desserts to follow the main course. It was a feast that few eateries in the world could emulate. 'Are you enjoying yourself, Marie-Claire?' Mrs Le Blanc asked, taking another sip of wine.

'Yes, Mother. The food is delicious! And everything is so cheerful. Look how beautiful the Christmas tree is!' The white landscape was visible outside the arched windows, as the full moon finally broke through the clouds for the first time in days, reflecting off the snowy blanket covering the countryside. With their stomachs full to the point of discomfort, the Le Blancs retired for the evening, a happy, close-knit family.

Christmas morning arrived and the weather was perfect. A cloudless sky greeted them, everyone only too happy at the prospect of finally being able to enjoy the outdoors again. Marie-Claire, still dressed in her pyjamas, eagerly unwrapped the present her parents gave her in the lounge of their suite. The excitement was almost too much for her. She opened the small, oblong box to reveal a beautiful *Jaeger LeCoultre* watch. The golden timepiece was exquisite and had the appearance of a bracelet, with a clock face set into it. The winding mechanism was atypically located on the back surface of the watch, further adding to the illusion of a bracelet. 'Thank you very much! It is beautiful!' she exclaimed excitedly, admiring the gift from all angles, after having given each parent a hug and a kiss. 'Now you will always be expected to be on time for things,' Mr Le Blanc said in jest. 'No more excuses of not knowing what the time is, or where it went.'

After breakfast they walked to the ice-rink, Marie-Claire adorned in a bright red ski suit she had specially selected for the occasion. The resort staff had been busy from dawn and the ice-rink was open and ready for use, despite the early hour. Piles of snow removed from the surface encircled the one side of the arena. In the distance, the downhill bob-sled track was still closed for use and would probably remain so for the rest of the week. There were already a dozen people skating on the ice, enjoying the freedom of being outside for the first time in days. Marie-Claire took to the ice, continuing her skating routines where she left off four days prior. She now added little jumps as well. The consequences were disastrous at first, with the girl spending lots of time flat on the ice. After another hopeless landing, she ended up sliding into one of the piles of snow next to the rink. 'Land on the tip of the skate,' a friendly old man sitting on a bench next to the ice offered.

'I beg your pardon?' she asked as she dusted the snow off and got up. 'Land on the front tip of skate, then you can control the landing,' he offered again. 'You are very talented, I would hate to see you falling on your pretty face and breaking your nose if you keep this up.'

'Thank you, sir. I appreciate the advice,' she said as she slid back onto the ice. *Land on the tip?* She hadn't thought of that. She gave a small jump and landed perfectly controlled on the front tip, as suggested.

Marie-Claire was now really excited about the skating and added all kinds of jump variations to her routine on the rink. She enjoyed the freedom of gliding along the ice, it was almost more fun than ballet, as it didn't take us much energy. When lunch time arrived, she found Stavros standing next to the ice rink, observing her routine. Her parents had left earlier, they could not manage such long hours on the ice. 'That was very good, Marie-Claire. You really seem to have a knack for it,' he commented.

'Thanks, Stavros. I really enjoy myself out there. One can almost slide away from all your troubles, leaving them behind.'

The next morning was another gorgeous, sunny one and they rented some ski equipment and went up the mountain to try their hand at downhill skiing. The concierge at the hotel had suggested where they could take some beginners lessons. Stavros escorted them up the mountain, but did not join them in the class. He seems to have had advanced ski training previously, as he took the ski lift all the way to the top and barrelled down the run at great speed, never seeming to be in danger of losing control. The fresh powder from four days of snow made for wonderful skiing. By the end of the class, the Le Blancs could safely navigate the children's slope. 'I still prefer ice-skating over skiing,' Marie-Claire remarked, despite having caught on to the skiing much quicker than her parents. Once again, her agility and balance was of great assistance. 'Can I go up to the medium slope?' she asked her father hopefully.

'Only if you take Stavros along to keep an eye on you.' Stavros was quite happy to accompany her on the ski lift up to the medium slope. She glided down the hill, making lazy s-shaped curves, almost like a giant slalom down the mountain. Stavros copied her run, but always stayed on her outside and slightly above her, his advanced skills making this complex manoeuvre look mundane. They arrived at the bottom of the slope together and she sprayed her parents with some snow powder as she turned sideways to stop next to them. Stavros did not copy her audacious manoeuvre. He knew better. 'Well done my darling! That was an impressive run,' Mrs Le Blanc praised her daughter. They decided to call it a day as the sun started setting and took the shuttle down to the Hotel Kulm.

They spent the rest of their two week vacation on the ski slopes, the ice-rink and exploring several more of the surrounding towns. The area was beautiful and every town had unique sights and sounds to enthral the visitor. They also found the hot water of the hotel spa invigorating. On New Year's Eve, the Hotel had one of its legendary parties and the frivolities carried on well past the early hours of the morning. Marie-Claire had managed to stay awake until after 12 o'clock and joined everyone for the customary rendition of *Auld Lang Syne* as the new year started. She somehow knew the words to the song in German, despite not remembering ever having learnt it. Her parent sang the French version. 'Happy New Year, Marie-Claire. We hope you have a glorious year, filled with only the best of everything,' the Le Blancs expressed their blessing to her.

'Thank you very much! I hope you have a wonderful year too,' she responded, hugging each of them in turn. 'Thank you for accepting me into your lives and providing for me with such abundance.' It was a lovely end to a beautiful evening, with hope that the coming year will be equally blessed.

On the eve of their departure, they shared a dinner table with a writer from Paris. He was celebrating his birthday with his beautiful wife at the hotel and bought a bottle of Dom Perignon Champagne for the table. 'So early in the year to celebrate a birthday already, we've only just started the new year yesterday,' Marie-Claire remarked to the amusement of everyone in the group. 'I am glad you are around to share it with me, I owe you my gratitude for your delightful company,' the writer responded.

The next morning their journey home commenced. Their time at the hotel in *St Moritz* had run out and although Marie-Claire thoroughly enjoyed the vacation, she was happy to return to the Embassy in Athens. It was the only real home she had ever known and as the old adage goes, 'There's no place like home.'

AN ITALIAN AFFAIR IN ATHENS, 1954

Springtime arrived in Athens, with the weather drying up and the pleasant smell of a thousand flowering Jasmine plants filling the air of the city, like the perfume of the Athena rolling down into the surrounds from the Parthenon. The French Embassy was abuzz with activity, as those planning to visit France in the coming summer started their never-ending slew of inquiries at the diplomatic offices.

Marie-Claire had gone back into her routine of ballet training three times a week. She was also progressing well with her art classes and proved quite the artistic talent. Mr Le Blanc found her in the ballet studio training with Mrs Antonides, when he popped in to give her some exciting news. 'My darling daughter, I think you are now old enough to behave yourself properly in public and as such, I would like to take this opportunity to invite you to accompany your mother and I to a grand ball at the Italian Embassy.' He said all this with a pompous flourish and a bow. She gave a little shriek of excitement.

'Oh Father, that sounds lovely! What is the occasion?' she exclaimed gleefully, leaping over on her toes to give him a hug.

'It is the Italian Day of Liberation on 25 April, so they are hosting a special gala to celebrate the event. A messenger just came to drop off the invitation.' Mr Le Blanc was quite used to attending these type of events, so it was no longer such a momentous occasion to him. It would be Marie-Claire's first attendance of an Embassy party and she was justifiably enthusiastic at the prospect of joining a grand party at the Italian Embassy.

She had often passed the Embassy building, which was just two blocks further down *Vassilis Sofias* avenue, as one was passing the national gardens. The mansion looked very similar to the one that housed the French Embassy, with the only difference being the peach colouring of the walls. She had often thought the two embassies could pass for brother and sister. Not having ever been inside, she wondered if the interior was as pretty as that of their own house. 'What will I wear to the ball father? Can I get a new dress to go in? Pretty please?' She begged her father, who was clearly not going to endure much more of this arm twisting without conceding defeat and agreeing to a new dress. 'Yes darling, we can have something made for you. I have heard of a marvellous Design House in Paris, called Balmain. They can design a dress off your measurements. Apparently, they are all the rage in the Paris social circles. We'll have them design something for you and Mother.'

'Thank you Father, that sounds like an inspired idea!'

She could hardly contain herself and Mrs Antonides eventually called off the class early, as she was simply not able to concentrate on her exercises or her dance routine.

The following afternoon, a local seamstress and her assistant visited the private residence of the Embassy to take the two ladies' measurements. Mr Le Blanc had arranged a phone call to Mr Pierre Balmain, so she could ascertain exactly which measurements he required. Armed with the necessary information, she measured the young lady for her dress. Marie-Claire was busy flowering into a beautiful young woman. With puberty, her previously boyish body had started developing curves and suddenly, all the boys in school took notice of her. The seamstress went about her business, rattling down a series of measurements, which the assistant jotted down in a notebook. Marie-Claire giggled as the tape measure tickled her while the seamstress finished the assignment. Once done, it was the turn of Mrs Le Blanc to be measured for size.

An hour later, the whole process was completed and the measurements were handed to Mr Le Blanc, who would send them to Paris in the next diplomatic bag. This abuse of the diplomatic mail system was frowned upon by the Foreign Service, but Mr Le Blanc did not make a habit of such transgressions of etiquette. It was, after all, quite important that the dresses arrive in time for the official event on 25 April and was not simply done on a whim. He expected having all his days trying to contain Marie-Claire in anticipation of the arriving dress, so any delay would simply not do.

Marie-Claire ran into Mr Le Blanc's office every day after school to enquire whether the dress had arrived. 'Father, has my dress arrived?' only to be let down by the answer, leaving the office sad and disappointed. Two weeks later the dresses arrived, with a week to spare before the party. As had been the case the last two weeks, she ran into her father's office again after school. 'Father, has my dress arrived?' The question had lost some of its enthusiasm as the days had passed and she was almost half turned and on her way out again when Mr Le Blanc said 'You should go check your bedroom…' Now the young girl was beyond excitement. She ran down the stairs and through the public foyer, past a disgruntled Greek having words with the receptionist, to the connecting passage, before bolting up the stairs to the private residence on the top floor.

The dress hung in a bag on her cupboard door. She unzipped the garment bag, taking a moment to calm herself and do it slowly, lest she accidentally catch the fabric in the zipper. The gown was beautiful! It was a lovely, dark green velvet creation, with marvellous embroidered patterns on the bodice, leading to wide skirt flowing down to the floor in layers. She loved it! Without any delay, she started putting on the dress, to see what she would look like in it. She was very satisfied with the result. The dress fit her perfectly. The top part hugged her body, accentuating her developing bosom, while the layered skirt cascaded down her legs to the floor. She gave the accompanying clutch purse a cursory inspection, before running out of the room to find her mother. 'Mother! Mother! Where are you? Come see my dress!' She found her mother in her bedroom, busy twirling in front of the mirror in her own new outfit. The design was similar to Marie-Claire's but different. One could see the designer went to great lengths to have the dresses match, without simply being different coloured copies of the same design. It spoke of pure mastery of the art. The yellow skirt twirled as she rotated. Marie-Claire laughed and joined her mother by the mirror. 'You look marvellous, Marie-Claire!' Mrs Le Blanc exclaimed. 'The dress is so beautiful. And it fits you perfectly. You are going to be the belle of the ball!'

'Thank you, Mother. Your dress is really pretty too. Father will be very happy. Two such lovelies at his side. Everyone will envy him!' She hugged her mother and they stood side by side, admiring themselves in the full-length mirror. 'Now we only need to go shop for shoes!' Mrs Le Blanc said excitedly. Undeniably, shopping for shoes was amongst her favourite pastimes. Of course, Marie-Claire would never let an opportunity pass to join one of her mother's shopping excursions in *Ermou* Street, only a couple of blocks away. The Embassy really was in a glorious part of Athens!

Upon returning from their excursion to *Ermou* Street the following afternoon, they found Mr Le Blanc in his private study upstairs. 'Father, look at the magnificent shoes we got! They match our dresses to perfection.'

'Those are lovely,' Mr Le Blanc ventured with as much enthusiasm as he could muster.

'Aren't they, just!' his wife responded, as pleased with the purchases as Marie-Claire.

Sunday evening arrived in a flash and with it, the promise of an extravagant Italian *soirée*. Mrs Le Blanc approached Marie-Claire in her bedroom, for some motherly advice. 'Remember my angel, you must be on your best behaviour. Do not let any of the men at the party try to take advantage of you. You are now a beautiful young woman and men are going to fawn over you. If they want to dance, refer them to your father to request permission. But it would probably be best to stick with your father and myself.'

'Yes, Mother. I will be sure to behave. And not wander off on my own, I promise.'

Despite the proximity of the Embassy, two blocks in high-heeled shoes was simply not a prospect that either of the two ladies was willing to partake in. Mr Le Blanc capitulated and subsequently, Jacques opened the car door for them, as they left the French Embassy through the back entrance. Mr Le Blanc looked suave in a black tuxedo with his wife and daughter wearing their Pierre Balmain creations and newly acquired matching designer footwear. The three of them were an awe-inspiring sight and they would do their country proud at the event.

Jacques drove them the two short blocks to the Italian Embassy. Its brightly lit façade welcomed the arriving party-goers to the little piece of Italian soil in Athens. He passed through security at the main gate with minimal fuss and dropped them at the stairs leading to the main entrance. The Italian ambassador, Luigi Caravaggio, met them on the steps and officially welcomed the Le Blancs to the event. He was a short, squat man with a bushy grey moustache, matched by a pair of bushy eyebrows. His tuxedo appeared one size too small, no doubt tailored when he was a little younger and leaner. Marie-Claire thought he looked like the Monopoly man in his tails and top hat. His wife, Leonora, was several years younger than him, an ageing Italian beauty in a flowing blue gown, accentuating her ample cleavage.

'Welcome Ambassador Le Blanc, Mrs Le Blanc and Young Lady. I trust you will enjoy this evening with us, where we will be celebrating the Italian Liberation from the occupying Nazi forces.' He waved them up the wide staircase, the two ladies ascending carefully in their high heels and long dresses. There was a large crowd milling around the Embassy lobby, all gathered in little conversational groupings. *A collection of human penguins and their colourfully dressed companions*, Marie-Claire thought, sniggering to herself. Waiters passed bearing plates of snacks and drinks. Mr Le Blanc grabbed two glasses of champagne from a tray for himself and his wife. When a waitress passed with grape juice in crystal flutes, he took one for Marie-Claire. 'To your first Embassy party! May you enjoy yourself, so that there may be many more to follow,' Mr Le Blanc toasted Marie-Claire as they clinked their glasses. The grape juice was not as sweet as she was used to, but still very tasty. 'These affairs can be so dull sometimes, so it would be good to have another interesting companion, besides your mother.'

'They have some beautiful pieces of art on the walls,' Marie-Claire noted.

'Yes, it is a marvellous collection. Worthy of accolades,' Mrs Le Blanc affirmed.

'Their government apparently owns so many treasures that they rotate the art through their official buildings. We might find a totally different set here next year.'

'Would you excuse me, please? I need to freshen my lipstick. Come along, Marie-Claire,' Mrs Le Blanc said, as she took the young lady by the arm and ambled to the powder room. It left Mr Le Blanc pondering the age-old unanswered question which has stumped men for decades: *Why do ladies always go the powder room in groups, and what they get up to in there?*

Even the washrooms were lavishly decorated with art and marble finishes. Marie-Claire looked around, wide-eyed. There was a beautiful little figurine of the Madonna on the counter. It had a jewelled robe, the arms folded into an endless prayer, the bright colours and craftsmanship intriguing the young girl. She used the loo while her mother amended her make-up back to the exacting standards demanded by the occasion. Mrs Le Blanc applied a smidge of lipstick for Marie-Claire as well. The red shade highlighted her lips and made her appear eighteen, when viewed with the rest of her ensemble. She was a dazzling beauty. 'You are going to be a man killer when you get older my darling. I pity the young men of today. You'll have them weeping themselves to sleep with unrequited love,' Mrs Le Blanc observed. 'Remember, never just settle for anyone because they show interest, you are better than that.' Sound motherly advice to the young lady. They left the ladies room. 'I forgot my bag,' Marie-

Claire said, hurrying back to the unoccupied ladies room to grab the truant purse. She re-joined her mother, as they walked back to the main reception area, where the noise of a hundred conversations filled the air, all now heading to the ballroom. Mr Le Blanc bent his elbows and Marie-Claire and Mr Le Blanc hooked their arms in his, as the three made their way to the seating chart.

The Italian Ambassador welcomed all the guests to the event officially from a podium, Marie-Claire still half-expecting him to break from his written speech to announce that King's Cross Station has just been sold and that the owner now owns all four stations and can collect quadruple rent. She giggled to herself. The speech was long and boring, filled with historic references and quotes and she took the time to gaze around the room and observe all the other guests. While she could comprehend and follow the speech, some of the guests could not understand Italian and had companions muttering translations to them as the speech continued. Then there were those whose companions were apparently not sticking to the script, leading to laugher and sometimes blushing amongst the young ladies, as who-knows-what was whispered in their ears. The speech finally ended and Marie-Claire clapped along belatedly with the rest of the attendees. Their starters arrived and accompanying it, an operatic performance. A decidedly plump couple in fancy dress took to the dancefloor and rendered an inspired performance of an Italian opera piece. Marie-Claire recognised the famous melody, but couldn't place a name to it. The audience was hushed as the pair of professionals sung, their strong voices filling the room. All the murmuring ceased and everyone was caught up in the inspirational aria. The night had turned into a Grand Italian Affair and Marie-Claire could see the appeal of attending these events. She would make a point of ensuring that her father invited her along all the time.

The end of the performance was greeted by thunderous applause. The Italian Ambassador looked decidedly pleased with the response from those he had gathered for the evening. Dinner proved a delight and Marie-Claire enjoyed the roast boar as her mains. The meat was soft and sweet and the roasted peppercorn and rosemary exterior cracked when she bit into it. Her parents had several glasses of wine through the dinner service and her mother seemed pleased with the way the evening was progressing. She could not hear what the gentleman sitting next to her mother was saying, but he must have been a comedic genius, judging from her persistent laughter.

The dessert comprised a marvellous *panna cotta* and also *tiramisu*. Marie-Claire loved the texture of the creamy desserts which were rich and tasty. The official programme for the evening seemed to have been concluded by a few parting words from Ambassador Caravaggio and the playing of the Italian National Anthem. Marie-Claire was always enthralled by the words of the Anthem and wondered whether the singing Italians still paid attention to *them*. 'We are ready to die. We are ready to die…' *Anthems were supposed to inspire people to greater deeds. The wording certainly implied as much. But it was not always the case any more in modern times. People take these things for granted*, she thought.

She wondered whether she still qualified as being Italian. She thought she was born there, although she could not remember as much. And then there was the fact that she could speak German. *Were her real parents German? Was she German? And now she had been adopted by French parents. Did that make her French??* She shelved this thought for a future discussion with her parents. Being Diplomats, they would certainly know the intricacies of citizenship. The music faded away and another round of applause followed.

'Let's call it a night,' Mr Le Blanc suggested, looking at his inebriated wife and his yawning daughter. They could both do with some sleep. *Oh what a night!* They arrived back at home just after 11 o'clock. Mr Le Blanc decided that Marie-Claire should skip school the next day. She was not going to cope after such a late night. They certainly wouldn't make a habit of it, but there was a first time for everything. 'Did you enjoy your first official party, my dear?' he enquired.

'Yes Father. Very much so! I definitely think I could get used to it and hope there will be many more such occasions.'

'Excellent. I could do with another dashing companion, in case your Mother ever wasn't available, for some reason. Now go straight to bed and don't worry about school tomorrow, we'll write a note to have you excused.'

'Excellent! What an inspired idea, father. Goodnight. Goodnight Mother,' she said as she walked down the passage to her bedroom. Just before she fell asleep, she reflected on the evening. There were a lot of firsts for her today. Drifting off to sleep, she thought she could get used to all of them…

EVENING IN PARIS, 1965

It was a beautiful evening as Mr Le Blanc and Marie-Claire were driven to the Soviet Embassy, following the left bank of the river *Seine*. Further along the river they passed the grand *Les Invalides* esplanade and building complex. The dome had been inspired by St Peter's Basilica in Rome and it served as a reminder to Marie-Claire of the time, all those years ago, when she visited St Peter's with her new parents the day after she was first adopted in Rome. They crossed the river, as brightly lit dinner cruise boats passed underneath the bridge, filled with early season tourists and young romantics. The bow cleft through the water, making white waves, which dissipated outwards.

Marie-Claire stared at the spreading wave and memories came floating to her like the white foam in the river. *It was Greece, 1950. She was lying on her stomach on a yacht in the Aegean, staring over the front of the boat as the bow cleft the water, white spray occasionally hitting her face. The water had been comfortably cool in the residual heat of autumn. Mr Le Blanc had rented a yacht for a weekend trip amongst the Greek Islands. It was the first time Marie-Claire was back on the water after the ferry trip from Italy. The small crew kept out of their way, going about their business of sailing the yacht from one island to the next. In another couple of weeks, the Aegean would cease to be calm enough to enjoy sailing. Mr Le Blanc was steering, while Mrs Le Blanc was down in the galley, busy with some surprise which Marie-Claire was not allowed to observe. After their last stop at Egina, her parents were very secretive and she was not allowed below decks.*

They would arrive back in Athens in some hours, the end of a lovely, relaxed weekend at sea. Finally, she was allowed below decks as the three sat down for an early dinner before arriving in port. The main course was fresh fish, grilled to perfection. So that's what was in the crate they loaded aboard in Egina, she thought to herself. Mystery solved. Sort of. Why all the secrecy for a meal? After the mains, they asked her to close her eyes before dessert was served. When she opened them, there was a cake on the table. With candles. And her name on it, in icing. Happy Birthday, Marie-Claire! She was caught by surprise. She had never celebrated a birthday before. It simply did not happen at Marcigliana. The orphanage had registered her with a random date as birthday, in the absence of any memory on her part. And this had proven to be that particular random day. Mr Le Blanc had seen it on the paperwork when they adopted her and registered a passport, but Marie-Claire herself had never paid it any attention. They gave her a basket, which was making meowing noises. She opened it up and took the kitten out. It was a cute little tortoise shell critter, with a black tuft of hair on its head. It had oddly shaped dark whiskers which immediately reminded Marie-Claire of the pictures she had seen of Salvador Dali. 'Can I call him Salvador?' she asked excitedly.

'Yes darling, you may name him anything you want,' was the response.

'Then Salvador it is!' she said hugging the tiny kitten, which was smuggled on board the boat in Egina. The crate had not been filled with fish after all! 'Thank you Mother. Thank you Father. Thanks for Salvador. Thanks for everything. Thanks for taking me from the orphanage and thanks for caring for me. I… I love you very much.' It was the first time she had said that to them.

'We love you too, little girl…' The little kitten had cemented their bond of love.

A bump in the road jerked her thoughts back to the car, on its way the Embassy. After a twisting route, they arrived at the *Bois de Boulogne*, the massive park which also bordered the locale of the Soviet Embassy enclave in Paris. The imposing, almost bunker-like, concrete structure towered over passers-by, always reminiscent that the might of the Soviet Union was not to be trifled with.

Guards in crisp, military uniforms stopped the car at the Embassy gate and demanded their reasons for being there. Emile handed them the official invitation, the guard slightly less cautious after confirming its authenticity. After some time studying the invitation and a clipboard with dignitaries, Marie-Claire, growing tired of the delay, leaned forward and spoke to the guard in perfect Russian. 'Good evening Sergeant. Is there a problem? We would not want to keep Uncle Valerian waiting, he can become quite agitated when people disrespect him by being late.' The guard was taken aback by both the fluent language and the apparent familiar knowledge the French lady had of Ambassador Zorin. They were on the list and had the correct paperwork, so he allowed them to pass. 'Have a lovely evening Miss, Sir. I hope you have enjoy the festivities,' he waved them inside with a sharp salute. They left France and entered the territorial soil of the Soviet Union.

Marie-Claire stared at the grim looking façade of the Embassy, thinking back on her years spent in Moscow, a stark reminder of everyday life behind the iron curtain. As they stopped at the entrance, the open doors revealed the brightly lit, colourful interior. It was in sharp contrast to the cold, unwelcoming exterior. Valerian Zorin himself waited on the Embassy steps and opened the door for Mr Le Blanc and Marie-Claire. 'Henri, old friend! Marie-Claire, so glad you could make it this evening. It's such a pleasure to see you again!' Zorin greeted them warmly, kissing her hand and giving her father a bear hug. 'Uncle Val, it has been ages! You look well,' she said as she poked a finger at his slightly protruding paunch. 'Yes, I have been fattening myself up in preparation for your atrocious French food,' he said with a rumbling laugh.

'We'll be sure to feed you powdered eggs and potato, so you can be reminded of the good old days in Moscow,' Mr Le Blanc responded. The banter was most politically incorrect, but the two men knew each other well and no-one felt in the least offended. 'Come inside and have a drink, we have some of your lovely French champagne. At least your countrymen know how to ferment a grape properly.'

'I trust you also have some quality fermented product from your own country to offer us?'

'My friend, we have several cases of *Stolichnaya* that found its way into the diplomatic pouch, so we are well prepared for a long evening, perhaps even an extended winter siege.'

They entered the Embassy foyer, enclosing an elaborately sculpted granite fountain. The three descended a wide set of steps into a reception lounge, Marie-Claire appreciating the lavishly decorated, double volume space. A pair of curved marble staircases ascended around the room. Underneath the mezzanine level were several sets French doors, leading to an outside patio area, overlooking the magnificent park. In the centre of the floor there was a large round table, filled with a variety of canapés, caviar and the various gold plated utensils required to enjoy these in style. The space above the table was filled with a dazzling crystal chandelier.

A waiter came over with a tray of champagne and they helped themselves to a glass. 'To Mother Russia and her son in space' Mr Le Blanc said, lifting his champagne flute.

'… and to Dom Pierre Pérignon and his wine-making experiments. May his legacy last forever,' Zorin responded. The ensuing conversation would be oddly difficult to follow for an outsider, as the Soviet Ambassador conversed in French, while the French diplomat and his daughter responded in Russian. Finally, Zorin had to excuse himself. 'Please forgive me, I need to tend to some of my other guests. We shall speak again later.'

The string quartet switched to Vivaldi's Four Seasons, when Mr Le Blanc spotted a familiar face across the crowded room. He crossed the reception hall with Marie-Claire accompanying him, their arms interlinked.

STEAMING OUT OF ATHENS, 1955

June 1955 had arrived and with it, the time to leave Athens. Mr Le Blanc had handled the posting in Greece with aplomb and consequently, President Coty had proclaimed that Henri Le Blanc was to be the man to improve relations with the USSR, mitigating the diplomatic fall-out over West-Germany's official recognition by France. Once again, Marie-Claire experienced the omnishambles of an Ambassador being relocated. When she had arrived in Rome, she only partially experienced the organised chaos, but now, she was right in the midst of it. She was upset when the news first broke.

'Why, father? Why? I like it here. My ballet lessons are going so well. I was going to be the lead in the new show when the school years starts!' she ran out of the room in tears. Mrs Le Blanc found her lying on her bed, crying into her pillow.

'I understand, my dear. I know it is hard for you to leave everything you know behind again. I have been through this many times. It goes with the nature of your father's work,' she said as she stroked Marie-Claire's hair. 'Moscow is well known for the Bolshoi and there are many great ballet schools. You will probably find that the teaching there is of much higher quality than you would ever find in Greece. I am sure we can enrol you in a top notch ballet school so you can continue your dancing.'

'And what about my art classes? And Andros? Will I ever see Andros again?' the distraught girl asked her mother.

'We will arrange a new art teacher for you there. Russia has always been well known for its famous artists. They have grand masters like Chagall and Kandinsky that came from there. While Greece might have a richer history, Russia has much richer art from modern days. I have no doubts we will be able to find you a good art teacher as well. You can write Andros as often as you like and I am sure you will see him again. Moscow is a marvellous city, with wonderful art and architecture. I know it is hard for you to move on. But your father and I will still be there with you.'

'Will we have to become communists when we live there? I don't want to share my things with everyone.'

'No my dear. We are French. We will remain French, wherever we may find ourselves,' Mrs Le Blanc responded with a laugh. Marie-Claire was less distraught after the talk with her mother, but still not happy about having to part with everything and almost everyone she knew again. She would have to prepare herself for sad goodbyes in the next few weeks and by mid-June, they would be off to another country.

Her farewell to Mrs Antonides was particularly sad for Marie-Claire. She had her final dance lesson at the Embassy and the ballet teacher had brought along a new set of ballet shoes for Marie-Claire as a gift. The former ballerina shed a tear as she hugged her *protégé* farewell. She had seen the young girl's dancing skills grow from that of a simple, inspired young enthusiast into a highly skilled, competent ballerina. There undoubtedly was an underlying talent, as the youngster took to dancing like a fish to water. With her orphaned lineage being unknown, one would never know where the talent came from. Marie-Claire had been lucky to avoid injury in her career and she had hoped this would continue for the girl. Some of her other students had not been so fortunate in the last couple of years.

'Goodbye, dear Marie-Claire. You are one of the most talented students I have ever taught and I am sure you will go far with your dancing. Moving to Moscow can only do your career good. I don't think I would have been able to teach you much more,' she said in a final farewell. Marie-Claire was very sad to see her leave, as she had grown fond of her dance teacher in the last five years. They spent many hours together and had shared in many successes, blood, sweat and tears. She would miss the time with her mentor immensely.

Parting with Andros was equally sad. She had invited her friend to the Embassy for tea on the day before leaving. She would miss his company. Andros was almost like a girl-pal to Marie-Claire and he could be trusted to give informed comment on fashion, art, music, and many other topics of interest. For a teenage boy, she was always astounded at how little interest he showed in the girls surrounding him in dance class. She often pointed out pretty girls to him in passing and he would just give a non-committal shrug. They kissed once, as an experiment, but the experience felt like kissing her brother. Not that she had a brother, but she could imagine that this would be what it felt like. It made her wonder what the big deal was with kissing. Andros didn't seem too interested in continuing the research project at a future date either. He had brought her a pink, fluffy teddy bear to take to Moscow, "Friends forever" emblazoned on its chest in blue stitching, an enduring memento of their friendship.

She had consulted with her father about what to give Andros as a parting gift. Mr Le Blanc suggested a top hat. 'A man never forgets his first top hat, it represents a turning point in his life. One can never revert back to a time prior to owning the hat, marking it a new beginning in gentlemanly style,' he elaborated on the suggestion. Mrs Le Blanc indulged Marie-Claire in her request to go hat shopping, strange as it was. They returned with a fine specimen from an expensive millinery, for which Mrs Le Blanc made sure to pay with a cheque from Mr Le Blanc. If the man was going to be silly at the girl's expense, he should bear the cost of it as punishment. Andros loved the hat. He placed it on his head at an angle and did a dapper walk around the room, stopped in front of Marie-Claire, lifted the hat in greeting and gave a formal bow. *I'll be damned! Sometimes the man amazes one with his uncanny insight,* Mrs Le Blanc thought. 'Thank you so much Marie-Claire. I will treasure it always. And I will treasure your friendship for as long as I live. Write me when you get to Moscow,' he said in parting. She watched him walk out the back gate of the Embassy, wearing the top hat and carrying the box under his arm. He looked back one last time, tilted his hat at her and disappeared around the corner. She stood watching the empty space where he had been for the longest time, reflecting on the sad emptiness his departure left in her heart.

Leaving the Embassy was an emotional affair. Jacques, who was one of the people she had known the longest in her life, was retiring and would not join them in Moscow. He had many years of Foreign Service behind him and had seen many cities and experienced many cultures. Now he would go live out his life in a little cottage in *Provence*, raising chickens and tending a tiny vineyard he had bought with part of his savings. The Le Blancs were all emotional at bidding Jacques farewell, overshadowing their feelings about leaving behind the rest of the staff at the Embassy. He served for many years under Mr Le Blanc and they had shared many adventures, and non-adventures, over the years. Jean-Pierre would accompany them on their trip to Moscow, continuing in his position of personal secretary to Mr Le Blanc. Stavros, Louis and Patrice would stay on at the Embassy, alongside the other staff, not rotating in their assignment. Some serve the Ambassador and some serve the Embassy. Such is the way.

With all greetings completed, formalities concluded and tears shed, the family left the French Embassy in Athens for the last time. The trip to the railway station was short, the train trip, in contrast, would be an extended one. It would take them three days to travel the 2000 miles to Moscow by rail. The Le Blancs occupied a sleeper cabin in one of the first-class carriages. Jean-Pierre was sitting with them in their compartment, his single overnight bunk located elsewhere in the train. The carriages were utilitarian in nature and were not excessively grandiose by any stretch of the imagination. This was not the Orient Express. Their first port of call would be Thessaloniki, which would also be the last stop before leaving the country.

The border crossing from Greece into Bulgaria was uneventful, despite the armed soldiers accompanying the staff tasked with stamping passports and interrogating the odd traveller. The train was halted on the tracks for a half hour while the border control procedures were finalised. There was always an apprehensive handling of single travellers, with Bulgaria often serving as a back door for those wishing to enter the USSR in a clandestine manner. The border control personnel respected the diplomatic passports presented by the family, politely wishing them well on their long journey to Moscow. Jean-Pierre received a little bit more scrutiny, but diplomatic papers also ensured his smooth passage into Bulgaria.

The family made their way the dining car for a dinner, darkness now having settled over the steady progress of the train. The food was pleasant and still had a Greek theme, despite having left the country behind. Afterwards, they retired to the lounge car where they sat on a pair of red velvet couches, a piano player providing background music. 'The French Embassy in Moscow is located in *Igumnov House*,' Mr Le Blanc lectured, '… which is apparently an exquisite building. It is close to *Gorky Park* and the *Moskva* River, so we should be able to have some nice walks in the afternoon by the riverside. The *Tretyakov* National Gallery is also located in the area, so I am sure you will be able to see plenty of wonderful art while we are there, Marie-Claire.'

'I still don't think any Embassy can be more beautiful than our one in Rome, Father. That was truly marvellous. But I'll reserve my judgement until I have actually seen the one in Moscow, just to be fair.' They all laughed at this. It had gotten late and the salon was busy emptying out as passengers retired for the evening to their compartments.

Jean-Pierre said goodnight and ambled off to his sleeping bunk, somewhere to the back of the train. Marie-Claire did not have a good night's rest. She woke up in the middle of the night with light streaming in through the windows, the train not moving. She peered out through the curtains and saw that they were in

115

a train station. *It must be Sofia*, she thought, before turning over and falling asleep again. Marie-Claire slept fitfully for the remainder of the night. She woke up in tears the next morning as a change in the motion of the train broke through her quickly forgotten dreams and brought her back to reality.

They had arrived at the Belgrade railway station in Yugoslavia. The sun was rising and Marie-Claire briefly stuck her head out the window to look at the faded yellow station building visible at the front of the train, past the locomotive. She was still trying to dispel the cobwebs and come to her senses when the train departed again, now heading for Hungary. They had a tolerable breakfast in the dining car, a mixture between the typical Greek breakfast and an English fry-up. Mr and Mrs Le Blanc loved the flavourful, strong coffee, but Marie-Claire rather opted for tea. Jean-Pierre was grumpily nursing a back which did not appreciate the bunk he had slept in, clearly designed for shorter folk. He drank three cups of coffee and an aspirin with his meal. After breakfast, Marie-Claire walked along the length of the train. Fourteen cars and a locomotive. She found a small library and a seating area and decided to settle there with a book from their collection.

Just before midday, the trained arrived at Keleti Station in Budapest. There was an hour lay-over before continuing the journey to Warsaw and the Le Blancs decided to leave the train and stretch their legs. The station had an A-frame roof, covering all the platforms and the stationary trains waiting patiently to depart. The side of the station facing the street had wrought iron window frames and glass windows, allowing the light to stream onto the waiting passengers, the sky and outside views filling the entire wall. A solitary clock set in the middle of the large windows announced the time to weary travellers. Outside, the traffic was bustling past the busy station. Marie-Claire looked back at the station façade- it was very pretty. They stood outside, enjoying the sunshine and the opportunity to be off the train for a short while. They wanted to buy sandwiches from a street vendor, but realised they did not have any local money. It was not a long respite before they boarded the train again and set off for Warsaw. They had to resign themselves to lunch on the train. There was still another 26 hours of rail travel ahead of them, before finally arriving in Moscow mid-afternoon the following day.

The remainder of the trip reminded Marie-Claire of being stuck in a smaller, less fancy and much warmer version of the Kulm hotel during the Christmas snowstorm two years ago. She alternated aimless wandering up and down the passages with reading books and chatting with her parents in the lounge car or their compartment. She came upon Jean-Pierre sitting with two women by the bar, deep in conversation over drinks as she passed through on her way to the other end of the train. The next morning at breakfast, he was looking much friendlier and his back seemed fine, so he must have arranged an alternative sleeping bunk the previous night.

The train steamed endlessly across the Soviet Union, wide expanses of open farmland interspersed with small towns, forests and hills. 'Will anyone understand Italian, or Greek, or French in Moscow?' Marie-Claire asked Mrs Le Blanc as they sat down for afternoon tea.

'I don't think so my dear. It would probably be wise not to speak German either. They have a bit of a gripe with the Germans. I am sure the Embassy will send a translator with us when we move around.'

'I learnt a bit of Russian when I was in the orphanage. One of the girls taught me. But it don't think it would get me too far.'

'You are a diamond with many hidden facets, Marie-Claire. We'll organise some lessons for you.'

Marie-Claire eventually stopped counting the bridges they crossed and the towns they passed through on their thousand-mile journey from Warsaw to Moscow. At ten past three, the train finally pulled into the *Leningradsky* railway terminal in Moscow. A pair of men were waiting for them as they exited the building, a neat, hand written sign announcing their surname.

Ivan and Claude were both stationed at the French Embassy. Ivan was the head of security, while Claude was the *Chargé d'affaires*. 'Welcome to Moscow, Ambassador. This is Ivan Petrov and I am Claude Menot. We will escort you to the Embassy. I understand it has been a long trip, so we have not arranged any formalities at the Embassy for today. There will be a formal welcome function tomorrow morning at 8 o'clock. We have already made arrangements for your luggage. Please allow us to escort you to your transport.' Marie-Claire could see that Claude was French and Ivan not. Ivan had a different look about him, blond and unrefined like a prize boxer, not appearing at home in the dark suit he was wearing. Their transport was a large, black car with two rows of facing seats in the back. There was another Frenchman sitting behind the steering wheel of the car who got out as they approached and opened the set of rear doors for them with practised ease. '*Bonjour Madame, Monsieurs, Mademoiselle*. I am Philippe. It is a pleasure to make your acquaintance. Feel free to call upon me day and night for your travel requirements.' The Le Blancs positioned themselves on the back seat, while Jean-Pierre and Claude sat facing them.

The weary travellers paid little attention to their surroundings as they were transported to the French Embassy in *Dimitrov* Boulevard. After a fifty hour journey, they finally reached their destination. *The Embassy building is indeed gorgeous*, Marie-Claire thought. *Her father had been right*. The French Foreign Service definitely had an eye for beautiful properties to house their missions across the world. The car entered the Embassy grounds, depositing the family safely on sovereign French soil.

DEBUT IN MOSCOW, 1955

The inside of the French Embassy was remarkable. Marie-Claire loved the elegant design of everything, the art, the furniture, the tapestries, the delightfully decorated ceilings and walls... *It was even more beautiful than the Palazzo Farnese in Rome.* Her room had a four-poster bed and wondrous golden designs on the ceiling and walls, the window overlooking the garden at the rear of the building. As a young woman, the room decorations were still a little mature for her taste, but the absolute grand opulence of everything made it bearable. The one non-personal effect she did bring from her room in Athens was the *Degas* print of the ballet dancer. She had begged her father to arrange that she could keep it. It was currently standing in the corner, the maintenance staff not having had time to hang it yet.

On their first morning they met the entire Embassy staff. There were very few locals working in the Embassy in any capacity. Ivan was one of a small number of Russians on the premises. Even the translators were all French men- and women who could speak Russian. Marie-Claire could still remember some of the basic Russian taught to her all those years ago by Katharina in *Marcigliana*. She briefly wondered where the Russian girl might be in the world, *she would be in her twenties by now.*

Mr Le Blanc launched into a speech to the assembled Embassy staff. It was a short introduction of everyone that came with him and an expression of his expectations of the current personnel at the Embassy in these trying times.

There were no snacks and drinks this time around. When the formalities were completed, everyone went back to their normal daily routine.

Ivan and Claude spent the morning with the Le Blancs. There was a tour of the Embassy, with every room being almost more magnificent than the last. It was truly a beautiful building.

The ballroom proved just as impressive as the rest of the Embassy, displaying ornately decorated ceilings and walls. There was a small raised stage on the one side of the room with a wooden lectern, adorned with the French coat of arms. Mr Le Blanc stared at it for a moment. 'Claude, I want to arrange an event for Bastille Day. It should be a grand event. An event showcasing everything that makes France great. A statement event. I also want a ballet routine by my daughter scheduled into the programme. I think she would be a suitably majestic addition to the proposed affair.' Claude's already raised eyebrow edged slightly higher at the last suggestion. 'Ambassador Le Blanc, Bastille Day is in three weeks, it would take a miracle to put together something that extravagant...' he diplomatically objected.

'Well, Claude, then I suggest you commence work on this immediately. I will provide the required budget and I have full faith in you and your staff to perform the necessary wonders, for the glorification of our great nation. *Vive la France!*' Mr Le Blanc retorted, raising his hand to the French coat of arms to emphasise the last sentence. Claude gave it a moment's thought. 'Please excuse me, Ambassador, I need to call a staff meeting.' The challenge was accepted. No Frenchman turned his back on a call by France, least of all those serving in the diplomatic corps. France had lost too many wars over the years, and if a victory could be achieved, then it would be! Ivan finished up the Le Blancs' tour of the building on his own. Fifteen minutes later, as he was showing them the library, staff members from all over the Embassy could be seen rushing to the meeting room. An hour later, as the Le Blancs were entering the building after surveying the garden, there was another rush of staff leaving the meeting, everyone now tending to their new assignments.

By the following afternoon, two hundred and fifty gilded invitations were printed, and a team of couriers dispatched to deliver them all over Moscow. The guest list was filled with prominent figures, including Premier Khrushchev. Once the Premier confirmed his attendance, this suddenly became *the* event to be seen at on 14 July. The sudden need for coordinated security created quite the headache for Ivan and his team, who now had to deal with State Security personnel as well.

The next three weeks went by in an absolute rush, everyone working extended shifts to finalise the event. Mr Le Blanc suggested that Marie-Claire perform one of the pieces from Swan Lake, which she had performed so admirably as a young dancer. She spent several hours a day preparing in the ballroom and on the occasions that Claude Menot was in the room tending to preparations, his mind was set at ease. *This would not prove to be a mistake or an embarrassment.* The girl had talent and the necessary skills to impress even the Premier. 'I know of a ballet costume shop run by the designer for the Bolshoi, Fyodor Fedorovsky. I will instruct Phillipe to take you there tomorrow with your mother, so that you can get suitable attire for your performance,' he suggested, now eager to make the event an unparalleled success.

The next morning, Philippe took Mrs Le Blanc and Marie-Claire to *The Golden Swan*, aiming to acquire a costume for the performance on Bastille Day. Upon their arrival in the district close to the Bolshoi theatre, Philippe parked the car in front of the shop, hidden away in a side street. A gold coloured swan was embossed on the side of the building above the display windows. They entered the shop and found row upon row of ballet outfits hanging in display racks. A shop assistant approached them, 'Good day. How may I assist you?' she enquired. From her posture, it was obvious that she was not a ballerina herself and probably spent a great many hours behind a sewing machine. 'We are interested in a special costume for a performance of Swan Lake,' Philippe broached the subject.

'Which role?' she enquired, almost snootily.

'The Black Swan, Odile,' Marie-Claire responded.

The assistant frowned. 'Such a dark role for such a bright young lady. We have several options. Follow me, please.' The assistant led them to the back of the shop, where a rack full of black costumes were hanging. Two of the costumes were too small for Marie-Claire. She fitted the rest, showing each off in turn to Philippe and her mother. The costumes were all adequate, but not as exceptional as she desired. 'Are these the only ones you have? We were hoping for something really special,' a disappointed Marie-Claire said.

'We have one more, but the Swarovski crystals used makes it too expensive for the average patron. They made it specifically for a performance by the Bolshoi, but the dancer had to be changed and it no longer fit. I will fetch it, anyway.' The assistant returned with a beautiful costume, richly embroidered and set with numerous shiny crystals and a matching tiara. It fit Marie-Claire perfectly. 'This is the one! It is magnificent. We will take it!' she announced with great excitement, showing no concern for what it might cost. Mrs Le Blanc thought the young lady looked stunning in the costume. On her part, she showed some concern at the cost, but not much, before happily writing one of Mr Le Blanc's cheques to cover the expense. They included a pair of matching ballet slippers in the deal. The shop assistant was excited at the huge sale and bid them farewell, now much friendlier than when they first arrived at the shop.

Marie-Claire was very pleased and excited with the costume. She would make her father and France proud while performing in it and she would now certainly look like the pride of the nation too. She almost skipped back to the car. Philippe suggested they make a detour past Red Square. Neither of the ladies had been there before and they were very impressed at the marvellous beauty of St Basil's Cathedral, the multi-coloured domed towers creating a spectacular image against the blue midday sky. They walked across the massive cobbled square and took a closer look at the basilica. Marie-Claire was surprised to recognise two gentlemen standing behind them admiring the church. She previously noticed the pair standing across the street from *The Golden Swan* when they exited the store earlier. One was a fat man with a moustache and the other a thin, bald one. *It's a small world*, she thought. The size of the square made for a stiff walk to get across the vast expanse and Mrs Le Blanc was quite relieved when they finally got back to the car and she could sit down. Philippe and Marie-Claire were younger and fitter and did not experience problems with the large distance covered. The trip back crossed the *Moskva* River and they passed Gorky Park before arriving at the Embassy.

Mr Le Blanc was very impressed with the ballet costume, despite the obscene amount of money he had to part with to acquire it. He was sure it would prove to be a worthy addition to the Bastille Day programme at the Embassy. It would be an imposing event, sure to create a liberal dose of jealousy amongst his fellow diplomats residing in Moscow.

Bastille Day finally arrived, much to the relief of the Embassy staff, who looked forward to returning to their normal diplomatic duties. There was palpable excitement in the air as everyone scurried around like worker ants. In the garden, a pyrotechnics expert was busy setting up for the fireworks show. Catering vans were parked in front of the building, trolleys full of food being carefully carted into the Embassy kitchens for final preparation. In the ballroom, the floor was in the process of being waxed to a brilliant sheen while the table settings were supervised by Mrs Le Blanc. She had attended enough of these parties to be a subject matter expert on the required crockery, cutlery and decorations. Marie-Claire sat in her bedroom performing a stretch regime, prior to the big event. She was sure she would make Mrs Antonides proud with her performance, shaped by years under her tutelage.

At 7 o'clock, the guests began arriving. The top of the social ladder in Moscow was generously represented, all wearing their most ostentatious outfits for the party. Glitz and glamour abounded, while French Champagne flowed smoothly down hundreds of throats, along with the best local caviar. The Premier arrived fashionably late, to roaring applause by everyone present. With the guest of honour having arrived, the assembly could make their way into the ballroom from the reception hall. Many of the guests had not seen the inside of the French Embassy before and the amazing décor had them all craning their necks to appreciate every corner of every room they passed through. The inlaid floors and multi-coloured walls and ceilings were a magnificent sight, even for the assembled elite, who were used to opulence as part of their daily lives. The Embassy photographer was making the most of the beautiful backgrounds and the lavish outfits, creating an artistic spread of pictures for the Embassy records.

When everyone was finally seated in the ballroom, the official programme for the evening commenced. Mr Le Blanc was positioned behind the podium, the French coat of arms also having been polished to a glittering sheen during the afternoon. In his fitted tuxedo, standing amongst the two French flags, the Ambassador could have passed for the president of France on the occasion. 'Premier Khrushchev, ladies and gentlemen, honoured guests. It is my great privilege to welcome you to this celebration of the glorious French nation. It is a celebration of glory, it is a celebration of victory and it is a celebration of all that makes France great. On this day, 166 years ago, our ancestors had the conviction of their ideals to stand up for change. To challenge the status quo and to say "No more!" No more would there be tyranny and no more would a citizen of France be stood upon by those of a higher class. Equality would prevail, and as the Russian nation stands for equality today, the French nation took a stand for equality in 1789...' He continued with the rousing address for another eight minutes, finally ending with a call of '*Vive la France!*' The speech was met with a standing ovation, led by Nikita Khrushchev, the Premier of the USSR. He could relate to the call for equality and he now had a newfound respect this new man the French had sent over.

Once the applause died down, Mr Le Blanc continued announcing the rest of the programme. 'I now have the pleasure of presenting to you my darling daughter, the lovely Marie-Claire. She will be performing a piece by one of the great sons of Mother Russia, for the enjoyment of all her other sons and daughters gathered here this evening. Ladies and gentlemen, I present Marie-

Claire le Blanc!' The lights on the ballroom dimmed and a spotlight appeared, focused on the Black Swan in the middle of the dancefloor. Her dress reflected like a thousand twinkling stars as she raised her arms above her head. The famous Tchaikovsky ballet composition began playing over the turntable speakers and with it, the dance started.

It was inspired. The young woman twirled and leapt, her movements graceful and fluid, taking the audience on a journey of discovery of human movement. On one occasion, the spotlight operator missed a beat, the dancer disappearing into the darkness. The mistake inadvertently turned into a triumph, as her sudden return to the light from the darkness created a dramatic effect which wowed the crowd, gasping with united approval. The dance ended, the young woman holding her pose as the spotlight dimmed and the house lights came on. There was a moment of silence, the audience stunned by the wondrous performance they had just witnessed. And then the applause came. It grew in waves, a roaring crescendo of appreciation for a magnificent piece of human art, which they had the privilege to experience. It continued for almost as long as the dance routine itself was and Marie-Claire could still hear the final claps as she entered her bedroom in the other wing of the Embassy.

The evening ended off with the crowd gathered on the outside patio, gazing into the night sky. As fireworks illuminated the upturned faces of the guests, the French national anthem started playing. The dying cords of music were accentuated with a perfectly timed explosion of lights, dwarfing all the fireworks which came before. When the echoes of light and music died away, silence and darkness descended on the patio, but only for a moment. Then followed the massive collective cheer.

The party was talked about for weeks in the Russian capital. Those who weren't invited, jealously soaked up the enchanting reports of those who were. The French Embassy had managed to produce a phenomenal success, which would only be surpassed decades later. While talk of the party eventually died down, the one thing that remained resolute in everyone's minds was the star of the affair, the young dancer, Marie-Claire.

THE AFTERGLOW IN MOSCOW, 1955

T he grandeur of the party the previous night was such that it even made the social pages in the newspaper the following afternoon. A brilliant half page image of Marie-Claire appeared on the last page of the daily, the photographer having timed it perfectly to catch her in mid-air during a *Grande Jeté*, her legs extended to the front and back and her arms above her head. Her form was perfect and the dress shimmered, even in the grainy newsprint. The picture overshadowed even that of the smiling Premier shaking hands with Mr Le Blanc, and a local beauty queen placed below it.

Mr Le Blanc brought in the afternoon newspaper, finding Marie-Claire in the library. He pointed her to the picture spread on the last page. The young woman was beyond excited at seeing herself on the back page. 'Well done my dear! You have made quite a splash in the social pages. Whatever will we do with you now? You're way too famous to stay in our humble abode...' Mr Le Blanc said, quite proud of his daughter. Mrs Le Blanc heard the excited chatter from the salon and poked her head in the library to see what the fuss was about. She was also extremely proud of Marie-Claire. 'We'll have to find you a local teacher, so you can continue with your ballet classes. I'm sure your father can make some enquiries?'

'I will do so in the morning. Someone around here must have an idea who we could contact,' Mr Le Blanc responded, still beaming with pride at his daughter's achievement.

As fate would have it, enquiries were not necessary. At 5 o'clock that afternoon, one of the diplomatic aides found the Le Blancs in the salon, having a late tea. 'Mr Le Blanc, there are two guests here to see you.'

'It's a little late, Fabrice. The Embassy is closed for the day. Can we arrange for them to come back in the morning?'

'Uhm, I think their visit is personal in nature, Sir. They wish to speak to you and Mrs Le Blanc about Marie-Claire.'

'Well, I'll be... Escort them in, Fabrice! Let's hear what they wish to discuss,' Mr Le Blanc responded, now quite intrigued by the unexpected visit.

Fabrice announced the two visitors, 'Ms Mariya Kozhukhova and Ms Marina Semyonova from the Bolshoi Ballet Academy.' The penny dropped.

'Pleased to meet you Ms Kozhukhova, Ms Semyonova. Welcome to our home,' he greeted them in English. 'To what do we owe the pleasure this afternoon? May we offer you some tea?' Mr Le Blanc almost fell over himself, as he pointed to the tray. He felt a little out of his depth with these two ladies, who carried with them an air of importance and purpose. Their postures were also noteworthy to the diplomat.

'Yes, thank you, we would like some tea,' Ms Semyonova responded in English. 'We are also pleased to make your acquaintance. And yours, Marie-Claire,' she said as she nodded in the young woman's direction. After some small-talk, she continued. 'We received a personal note this afternoon from Premier Khrushchev. He requested, no, recommended, that we make contact with you as soon as possible. He was immensely impressed with your performance last night and felt that a talent such as yours needed nurturing in a proper Russian institution. We are therefore here to officially invite you to the Bolshoi Ballet Academy, to attend our summer teaching programme which is starting in ten days' time.' There appeared to be a slight air of reluctance in the request. The Bolshoi staff did not take kindly to instructions on student selection, even from the Premier. They had regained a certain measure of control of the situation by limiting the invitation to the summer school. If the girl's presence was a mistake, at least it would be a short-lived one.

Marie-Claire could hardly contain her excitement, 'May I go Father, please?' she pleaded with her father.

Mr Le Blanc was similarly excited by the invitation, 'Of course you may attend. What a marvellous opportunity! Ms Semyonova, Ms Kozhukhova, we are honoured by your invitation and Marie-Claire gladly accepts.' It was agreed. The lecturers left an information pack and bid them farewell.

'Oh, Marie-Claire, this is such a wonderful breakthrough,' Mrs Le Blanc said excitedly as the ballet teachers departed in a little green car. The Le Blancs went back inside the Embassy building and scrutinised the information pack. Besides three ballet classes a day, there would also be visits to local museums and theatres, as well as Russian language classes included in the programme. It would afford Marie-Claire some structured learning for the summer, which Mrs Le Blanc was pleased by. It would also give the young woman an opportunity to meet some local girls in her own age group, providing a welcome reprieve from her limited socialising with the Embassy staff and her parents.

Marie-Claire struggled to fall asleep that night. Her mind was churning with the thoughts of joining the Bolshoi Academy. She eventually switched on her bedside lamp and sat staring at the Degas print of the ballet dancer on the wall facing her bed. It was somewhat concerning that the Premier had to recommend her for a place in the Academy, as she got the impression the teachers were not too keen on having a late addition to the summer programme. *Should she have rather declined and insisted on an audition?* She was mulling over the idea of auditioning, when it finally hit her. *She already had an audition, the teachers were simply not invited!* Always having been one to depend on her own hard work to achieve what she could, she was never one for handouts. The recital at the Embassy party required a lot of hard work on her part, and she had managed to impress both the papers and the Premier. As a regular patron of the Bolshoi theatre, at least he should know a good performance when he saw it. Her thoughts settled a bit, her invitation to the school now having been properly justified in her own mind. She finally drifted off to sleep.

The ten days preceding the start of the summer school passed in a flash. They paid another visit to *The Golden Swan*, expanding Marie-Claire's ballet wardrobe with several more costumes. Three practice sessions a day called for a bigger selection of ballet clothes than she currently had at her disposal. The shop assistant was much friendlier than the previous occasion, as she regularly read the society pages in the newspaper and had recognised the Black Swan costume originating from the shop immediately. She also knew the Bolshoi Academy summer programme was imminently starting and correctly assumed that the costumes were for that. As they left the store, laden with paper bags, Marie-Claire noticed the same two gentlemen standing across the street that were there when they had previously visited the shop. Fatty smoked and Baldy was facing the direction of the Ballet store, reading a paper. They must work in the vicinity, she thought, since she had always seen them hanging around the area. 'Odd. I saw those two in Red Square when we visited last time, after seeing them here as well,' she said to Philippe.

'Once can be chance and twice might be a fluke, but three times probably merits a report to Ivan,' Philippe responded, slightly concerned.

She informed Ivan of the sighting upon their return to the Embassy and he duly produced a picture book, which Marie-Claire had to go through to see if she could recognise the two men. They were both in there, although Baldy still had hair and Fatty was a lot thinner. 'KGB,' Ivan said to Mr Le Blanc after Marie-Claire had identified the pictures. 'They probably have agents watching the Embassy all the time, following our people when they leave the grounds. I would not be too concerned at this stage. Be sure to let us know whenever you see them, Marie-Claire, or anyone else you keep encountering in different places. Moscow is a large city and coming across the same people all the time is unlikely to be a coincidence.'

After this revelation, Marie-Claire paid more attention to her surroundings when she left the Embassy. She studied the faces of those surrounding her, making an effort to remember characteristics. Soon, she also discerned the familiar faces in the vicinity of *Igumnov House* on a daily basis. The loitering regulars with no conceivable business in the area, were presumed to be more KGB agents. She made a point of sitting by the front windows and keeping track of these individuals. By deductive reasoning, she concluded there must be a team of fourteen rotating agents observing the Embassy, now the unwitting participants of a war of mutual observation with the youngest member of the ambassadorial family. Fatty and Baldy were there, along with twelve others.

The mutual observation became a game of cat and mouse for the young woman when she left the Embassy and she took pride in occasionally being able to evade her followers and then popping up nonchalantly next to them in public. The reactions were priceless, as they had to keep calm and appear to go about their business, with their target now right beside them.

A week later, her lessons at the Bolshoi School begun in earnest and playing with the agents was soon left forgotten. She was now focused on her dancing, spending all day at the school. Her Russian improved remarkably with the daily tutoring sessions and her ballet skills followed suit, under the expert guidance of the many retired professional ballerinas on staff at the school. The class had forty pupils from all over the world, although not many were from the West. The daily drills proved tiring, but at least there was a greater variety than those Marie-Claire got used to in the studio in Greece. This was definitely a different level of teaching, altogether. Marie-Claire made friends with a girl called Ekaterina Maximova, who was a brilliant dancer. Try as she may, Marie-Claire could not match the skills and grace of Ekaterina. Her failure initially frustrated her, but she soon realised that becoming disheartened only inhibited her own progression further. One of the wonderful techniques she learned was to meditate, which helped to control breathing and she found had a serene calming effect on her. She added this to her daily routine at home and she found it a brilliant way to relax after a hectic day of lessons.

One afternoon, after returning home from the Ballet School, she found her father deep in conversation with a man she had not seen before. The older gentleman was nondescript, with grey hair and glasses. 'Marie-Claire, come meet Mr Valerian Zorin, Soviet Deputy Minister of Foreign Affairs,' Mr Le Blanc introduced the bureaucrat.

'Marie-Claire, it is such a delight to meet you! Your beautiful performance at the Bastille Day event was very impressive. I suggested to Premier Khrushchev that we should get you enrolled at the Bolshoi School without delay. I am very glad to hear that he acted upon it. How are your lessons going?' Marie-Claire was grateful for meeting the man responsible for her induction into the academy. 'It is lovely to meet you Mr Zorin. The lessons are going splendidly! Thank you very much for the good word with the Premier. I will do my best not to let you down.'

'Oh, I am sure you will do just fine. Someone with your talent will probably take to it like a swan to water, if you can excuse the pun.'

She liked Mr Zorin. He was unpretentious and seemed like an honest man. She didn't get the concerning sensation she sometimes experienced when meeting new people in Moscow. There were often ulterior motives to many of the people she met in her father's line of business, but Mr Zorin didn't appear to be one of them. She bade him goodbye as she headed upstairs to change. 'Goodbye Marie-Claire. I hope to see you again soon. We should have tea, so you can regale me with tales of your experience in class. I have always wondered what they get up to at that school. Some say the troops in Siberia have less rigour in their basic training programme. I would love a first-hand account.'

'I'd be delighted! Lovely to meet you, Minister,' she said, before walking off. *What a pleasant man*, Marie-Claire thought as she entered her bedroom to take a well-deserved shower.

The classes at the Bolshoi continued for the remainder of the summer. Sometimes the summer intake watched the senior Bolshoi dancers during their practice sessions, or some of their performances from backstage. The first time Marie-Claire entered the Bolshoi Theatre, she was astounded by the sight. She thought that the outside, with its tall Roman columns, looked like the Parthenon in Greece might have looked like in its hay-day a thousand years ago. The lush interior with its deep red carpeting and chairs was a glorious sight and she hoped one day she might make her debut on the stage, looking down at the hundreds of adoring ballet fans filling every seat in the house. Occasionally, the young dancers also received the privilege of performing on the stage, although there was no audience present in the house.

The lessons gained intensity as the summer course wore on and the strain showed on some of the dancers. Injuries grew more common and aching bodies displayed signs of overuse. Marie-Claire now understood the Minister's reference to Siberian army training. As preparation for their final dance recitals to the school staff was gaining momentum, one of the local girls, who displayed a remarkable amount of talent, had an unfortunate accident during a practice session. As she was completing a series of leaps across stage for the fifth repetition of her routine, she landed on a wet patch on the wooden flooring of the stage. Someone had carelessly knocked over a water bottle and the spilled liquid had created a slippery sheen to the floor. Her foot slid out under her, falling onto her buttocks and snapping her wrist in the process with an eerie, wet cracking sound. She gave a loud shriek and the teacher rushed onto the stage to examine the stricken dancer. She held her limp wrist and trembled with shock, tears streaming down her face. Further classes were called off for the day, as the unfortunate youngster was taken to a local hospital to have her injury tended to. She would take no further part in the summer programme. The mood was sombre as the rest of the class left the theatre building, everyone visibly upset by the accident.

The trip back to the Embassy with Phillipe was quiet, Marie-Claire deep in thought about the events earlier at the theatre. *What if something like that had happened to her?* The thought of a career-ending accident dwelt in her mind as they reached the Embassy. *Maybe putting all your eggs in one basket was not the ideal situation?* Developing other interests and skills were equally important and she decided that she would take up art again. She had enjoyed her classes in Greece and she had definitely shown artistic talent. Marie-Claire resolved to discuss this idea with her mother later.

Phillipe and Marie-Claire found Mr Le Blanc finishing up a meeting with Minister Zorin. They were having a hearty laugh as they exited the Ambassador's private office in the residence. 'Marie-Claire, we were just about to have tea. Do join us?' the invitation was extended by Zorin.

'Certainly, Minister. I'd be delighted,' was her polite response.
'You are home early today?' Mr Le Blanc noted with interest.

'There was an accident at practice. One of the girls fell and broke her arm. They gave us the rest of the afternoon off.'

'What a terrible thing to happen,' Zorin chimed in, sounding concerned. 'I always said they practise too hard there, young people need rest too.'

'No, it wasn't that. She slipped on some water on stage and fell. It was *definitely* not overworking,' Marie-Claire came to a fiery defence of the teachers.

They settled in the salon and one of the Embassy staff bought a tray with tea and French treats. Minister Zorin seemed pleased with the prospect of chocolate croissants and macarons. The French Embassy always seemed to be able to source these treats with ease, having developed a localised supply chain over time in Moscow. Marie-Claire recounted her summer at the Bolshoi, with Minister Zorin hanging on her every word. He had clearly not had the opportunity to establish first-hand what the teaching programme at the Bolshoi Academy entails and was pleased with the apparent high levels of the teaching provided by the school. 'That sounds wonderful Marie-Claire! Did you enjoy the experience?'

'Indeed, Minister. I found it thrilling, to say the least.' She continued the conversation in Russian. 'My language skills have improved remarkably and I am now able to hold my own in conversation. Perhaps we should send my father there next summer?' Zorin and Marie-Claire laughed at the statement, while Mr Le Blanc appeared thoroughly confused at the mirth, which lay beyond his basic comprehension of the language.

Tea concluded with a formal agreement to further engage on the subject of ballet, with future expansion of the dialogue to include other art forms and culture. Marie-Claire enjoyed the tea-time conversation with Mr Zorin. He was a pleasant man and she found him quite entertaining. Zorin parted their company cordially and resumed his daily duties in the service of Mother Russia, heading off to an early evening meeting with some other cabinet ministers.

The summer flew by and before she could come to her senses, it was September. The seasonal programme at the Bolshoi had reached its conclusion. With just a week remaining before school started again, Marie-Claire was making the most of the warm Moscow weather by reading a book in the garden in a halter neck top, soaking up the rays of the sun. Mrs Le Blanc found her after some effort and set down on the sun-lounger next to the slightly sunburnt youngster. She held out a letter addressed to Marie-Claire. The young woman recognised the seal on the back of the envelope and tore it open frantically. She quietly read the enclosed letter. 'And…?' Mrs Le Blanc enquired, raising her eyebrows.

'They invited me to join the Bolshoi School, Mother! Permanently!' she could hardly contain her excitement.

'Well done my darling! Congratulations. You deserved it!'

Marie-Claire was in seventh heaven. Gaining access to the summer programme might have been because of someone else's intervention, but staying in the programme was all due to her own efforts. She had rightfully earned her place in Moscow High Society.

ART, SPACE AND OLIVE OIL IN PARIS, 1965

The party was now almost in full swing as the last guests were arriving. Soon, the official programme and dinner service would begin. Mr Le Blanc and Marie-Claire made their way across the reception room to speak to a parliamentary colleague of his. Marie-Claire did not admire Louis Basquet and his politics and once she recognised him as the target of their current sashay across the room, she started looking for an escape. She found it from a most unexpected source. Andros Antonides, in a familiar looking top hat, was standing by the stairs, deep in conversation with another young gentleman. 'Father, would you excuse me please? I see someone I know.'

'Certainly dear, run along. Send my regards to Andros,' Mr Le Blanc said, having also spotted the Greek lad. He kissed her on her cheek and continued on his way towards Basquet.

'Andros, what a surprise to see you here!' Marie-Claire announced her arrival in prefect Greek, kissing the young man on each cheek and embracing him. 'Marie-Claire, so good to see you! May I introduce you to Georgiades Papoulias? His father is the Greek ambassador to France.'

She shook the hand of the ambassador's son. He was easily recognisable as being Greek, with a tanned skin and dark hair. He was a handsome man. 'Please, call me Georgi. It is always a pleasure to meet such a lovely friend of Andros'. How do you two know each other?' he enquired.

Andros was first to respond. 'We met in Athens some years ago when her father was the ambassador there. He was the first French ambassador after the Civil war and played an important part in getting Greece into NATO. Marie-Claire and I were in ballet class together. My mother was our ballet teacher and she was never going to allow me not to learn her craft and follow in her footsteps.' Georgi looked rather surprised. He obviously had not known of this side of Andros, as he was a recent acquaintance. Andros could finally give up dancing when he left school, as although he had talent, he had to go into the family business with his father and was shipped off to business school in London.

'How long are you here for, Andros?' Marie-Claire asked.

'Only two weeks. I'm actually in Paris on business with father, looking for some wholesalers for our olive oil. Georgi's father is assisting us, by hosting some introductory meetings. They organised us an invitation to the party.'

The waiter who had served her drink earlier was positioned close by and Marie-Claire beckoned him over to grab another glass of champagne. If there was to be an extended discussion on the olive oil import business, she needed another drink. Luckily, it proved not to be the case. The discussion turned towards Paris itself, a subject Marie-Claire felt quite passionate about. They talked about the culture, the museums and the nightlife, the discussion now in English, after another group of young gentlemen joined the conversation, when it had briefly switched to English earlier, just as they walked past. Marie-Claire gave a recounting of her student life at the Sorbonne, which had the gathered group of young men mesmerised. Her descriptions of the art classes on nude studies and the human form, were especially well received, the young men hanging on to her every word. From a distance, the scene almost looked like a conductor leading a silent orchestra, the noiseless musicians swaying to the rhythm of an unheard metronome. Marie-Claire finally excused herself from the group, the men longingly staring after her as she glided away to join her father, who had now moved on from the dreadful bore that was Louis Basquet.

Mr Le Blanc was standing at the centre table, sampling some of the fine caviar, a far-off look on his face. 'Father, where are you??' she enquired, snatching him swiftly back to the present reality. 'The caviar brings back such memories. Moscow always had the finest to offer, to those in power. Luckily, they were willing to share with us on occasion.'

Marie-Claire did not seem overly impressed with the sentiment. 'Besides fine caviar, I do not think they have made such a contribution to the rest of the world that we need to get nostalgic about the country. The squalor of some of those not in power did not bode well for the concept of perfect equality in society. And they only shared when they wanted something from us. It would have been more convenient to just buy our own, or go without, and not have to cater to their whims in return.' She was decidedly bitter, the origin of which would surely have to be rooted deeper than the presence of a mere dollop of fine fish eggs on a cracker. 'Let it be, Marie-Claire. What's done is done. Don't blacken your soul. Those times are past. You are a better person than that, and you're a better person because of that.'

She sighed. 'You are right, father. But I could never forgive them for what they tried to do to you.'

'My dear, it is for you to rather forget. That is much easier and the option that leaves you with your sanity intact. Grudges are so unbecoming of you. Grab a canapé, there are some delicious non-caviar ones over there. Eat. Enjoy the music, dance and laugh. Your life will never have more hours left than right now and it is too short to dwell on the injustices of the past.' Mr Le Blanc had succeeded in placating his daughter, as she calmed down and nibbled an *hors d'oeuvre*. It was scrumptious and she soon added two more to her constitution. 'Do you ever wonder what would have happened if you had gone along with them, Father?'

'I never really gave it any thought…'

'Do you think it would have been worth their while?'

'I don't doubt that for a second. We had our fair share of sensitive information in the Embassy safe.'

'And would it have been worth *your* while?'

'I don't doubt that either,' he said with a smile, kissing her on the forehead.

The string quartet came to a halt midway through a Beethoven composition. Ambassador Zorin was standing on the stairs and cleared his throat. 'Ladies and gentlemen, I wish to welcome you all to this glorious celebration of one of the crowning achievements of the Soviet empire. We are here today to celebrate the first human being to enter the unlimited expanse of space. Four years ago today, comrade Yuri Gagarin left the atmosphere and circumvented the globe, before safely returning to earth. May he enjoy a long, healthy life and may the Soviet Union have a never-ending dominion, without end, like the path of a satellite perpetually orbiting the earth, never to fall. Long live comrade Gagarin!' There was a brief applause from the assembled audience, impressed by the feat of putting a man in space, but not all sharing his enthusiasm for a never-ending Soviet empire.

'Ladies and gentlemen, I now invite you all to join us for dinner in the ballroom. There is a seating chart by the door. Please keep to your assigned table, or we shall be forced to exile you to hard labour in the kitchen.' The joke drew boisterous laughter, with some of the guests not having doubts about the plausibility of the threat. The crowd immediately began moving through the side door into the ballroom, everyone heading for their assigned seating, just in case...

WELCOME TO PARIS, 1956

The Moscow summer had arrived, bringing with it warmer weather and three months of rest for those enrolled at the Bolshoi Ballet School. Mr Le Blanc had been summoned to pay an official visit to Paris, to see Prime Minister Mollet. The ambassador decided that this was the perfect opportunity to extend the trip into a family vacation, after his official business in Paris concluded. The fortuitous situation would also give him a chance to introduce Marie-Claire to the City of Lights for the first time. She had never been in her adopted country, despite having been a French citizen for many years. A family decision was made that it was time to remedy this situation. From Paris, they would travel on to the French Riviera, where they would spend their vacation break in *Juan-les-Pins*.

Marie-Claire was ecstatic when her parents broke the news to her. She had been preparing herself mentally for a boring summer in Moscow and this proved a most unexpected change to her plans. 'Father, will we be able to buy some things to wear while we are in Paris? I would not want to look out of place when we get to the coast,' she pleaded with Mr Le Blanc. The young woman had a gift for wrapping her father around her little finger and the diplomat conceded that a shopping trip sounded like a splendid idea. With only a few days to prepare for the trip, she had excused herself promptly and started packing. Of course, she left plenty of space for the additional clothes she would buy in Paris. There was a shortage of commercial flights from Moscow to France and the

French government had subsequently sent a private plane to pick up the Ambassador and his family at *Vnukovo* Airport.

The silver Douglas DC2 aircraft with a French flag painted on the tail was waiting for the family on the runway, shining as it caught the first rays of the early morning sun. The black Embassy car drove onto the runway and came to a stop next to the French Government plane. Phillipe and a steward loaded their luggage into the plane, along with various other diplomatic satchels that needed to be transported to Paris. Jean-Pierre would also accompany them on the first leg of the trip. His tall frame had to fold awkwardly to enter the rear door of the plane. Inside, he had to hunch over when he moved around. The Le Blancs did not have such discomforts in their movement about the plane. The passenger compartment of the aircraft was modified by the French government and it only contained ten seats. Some of the seats faced each other, with a table in-between. The interior had wooden veneer finishes and luxury curtains and seating which could almost fold flat. Marie-Claire was very impressed by the finery of it all. The plane departed *Vnukovo* Airport and headed to France, the rising sun at their backs.

The flight was uneventful and Marie-Claire loved being able to see the countryside from the sky. Far below, people tended to their daily lives, unaware of the plane passengers looking down on them. She wondered whether this is what it felt like to be God, looking down on mankind without their knowledge. Five hours after a refuelling stop at Warsaw, they arrived in Paris. The plane circled the airport before landing and Marie-Claire had her first view of the city. It was beautiful! The Eiffel tower stood out and she could recognise the Notre-Dame Cathedral nestled on an island in the River *Seine*. The plane touched down at *Le Bourget* with a bump and rolled to a stop next to some hangars. A large government sedan, adorned with a pair of French flags, was parked by the building, waiting for the family. A small, nondescript van was parked behind the large sedan, to take delivery of the various diplomatic satchels.

The family stepped off the aircraft and was greeted by a chauffeur. 'Good afternoon Ambassador. Welcome to Paris. I am Georges Rousseau and I have been assigned to be your driver for the duration of you stay. Anywhere you need to travel, you can call on me, day or night. You are booked into the *Bourgogne & Montana* Hotel in the 7th arrondissement. It is conveniently close to parliament.' Mr Le Blanc was pleased with the arrangements.

'Thank you, Georges. I think we should get going, we look forward to getting to the hotel. I can do with a nice walk along the *Seine* to stretch my legs,' he responded as he followed to two ladies into the car.

'Enjoy your trip Ambassador. Enjoy Paris, Marie-Claire! It is a magnificent place to experience for the first time. And every time thereafter! I will see you in Moscow in four weeks,' Jean-Pierre said as he escorted the diplomatic bags, joining the driver in the van.

Once they left the surroundings of the airport, the trip proved magical. Marie-Claire was mesmerised by the beauty of the city. The vibrant street *cafés*; the ornately decorated apartment buildings; the colourful window displays; the green parks and finally, the rows of green *bouquinistes* lining the sides of the *Seine* River were all incredible to see. The green book stands did a roaring trade in the late afternoon with locals and tourists all out in numbers. They had crossed the river at *Pont Neuf* and were now on the left bank. Marie-Claire exclaimed as she saw the Eiffel Tower for the first time from a vantage point on the ground. They passed the *Louvre* on the opposite bank and turned left after passing the *Gare D'Orsay* railway station. The driver weaved through several blocks before arriving at their hotel.

The *Bourgogne & Montana* was a luxurious establishment and their suite was comfortable and very elegant with classic French styling. 'We should go for a walk to stretch our legs. I would like to explore the Latin Quarter. I have not been there since my student days. The left bank of the *Seine* at this time of the afternoon makes for a lovely walk,' Mr Le Blanc suggested. The ladies were in agreement and after putting on more comfortable shoes, they left the hotel and ambled towards the river. Late afternoon in the city was vibrant, with many people opting for walks along the river. They passed the *Pont Neuf* Bridge and could see the Notre-Dame in the distance, on the *Île de la Cité*. When they arrived at *Pont Saint Michel*, Mr Le Blanc turned right and headed into the inner circle of the Latin Quarter. They came across a typical Parisian brasserie with some manner of food related name and Mr Le Blanc suggested that they sit down for a drink and perhaps a bite to eat. They were lucky to find seating amongst the throngs of late-afternoon patrons. Even with the university closed for summer recess, the restaurant was still quite crowded. Mr Le Blanc spotted someone he knew sitting two tables away. *What a coincidence!* He excused himself from the ladies and stepped across.

'Yves, old friend! How are you doing?' Le Blanc greeted Yves Montand.

'Henri, so good to see you! Where on earth has the government gotten you posted nowadays?'

'I'm in Moscow at the moment. You should pop by to do a show there sometime, the Russians love your records. We'd be delighted to host you at the Embassy.'

'What a great idea! I've never been there. I've got some time in my schedule in December, so I'll see if I can set something up,' Montand responded, quite taken by the idea.

'Here is my business card, your agent is welcome to contact me at any time for assistance,' Mr Le Blanc said, handing him a card. They spent several minutes catching up before Mr Le Blanc excused himself and joined the seated ladies. There was a bottle of white wine and three glasses on the table. 'Oh, how I have missed French Wine,' Mrs Le Blanc pronounced as Mr Le Blanc refilled her glass. Marie-Claire got her first taste of wine, French or otherwise. Alcohol consumption by children under fourteen had only been banned in France earlier in the year and there were no questions raised when the fifteen-year-old girl joined her parents for a glass. It was not quite as tasty as she had hoped, but after struggling through the first glass, the second was much more palatable. Her head spun slightly, but it was not an altogether unpleasant experience.

Marie-Claire had never experienced French cuisine as prepared in the heartland of Paris and the meal was somehow more authentic than anything Sister Marcelle or Chef Auguste had ever prepared. *Conceivably, that was the secret to French cooking- not the recipe, but the authenticity of the ingredients.* Marie-Claire was scared that the same perhaps applied to Frenchmen, or women? *Not being brought up French, but having breeding stock from France, which truly makes you of the nation. That would somehow make her identity a hollow shell, devoid of nationality and meaning.* The wine was certainly having its way with her, turning a young woman into a bitter old philosopher.

A full stomach soaked up some of the alcohol and turned her thoughts to a more positive light. The chocolate *mousse* and *soufflé* they had for dessert was scrumptious and they ordered some coffee after the course, which was followed with a small measure of cognac each, as *digestif.* Marie-Claire declined another serving of alcohol, she was still recovering from the effects of two glasses of wine before dinner. Mr Le Blanc settled the bill with some francs which he seemed to have produced from nowhere. As they left the restaurant, he looked back at a "For Sale" sign on an adjacent green doorway. Mr Le Blanc looked down the cobblestoned cross street at the vibrant square opposite and turned back towards the *Boulevard Saint Michel,* seemingly in thought, then appeared to have gotten his bearings. They walked down the road and turned right into the *Boulevard Saint-Germain,* the lights of Paris now there to guide their way to the hotel.

Arm in arm the three strolled down the Boulevard, surrounded by the energy which was only to be found in the Latin Quarter. The cobblestoned sidewalk seemed to give Marie-Claire some trouble, as she intermittently seemed to trip over some of the more uneven stones, only too happy for the supporting arm of her father. The cool evening breeze carried with it the resonance of a hundred lively establishments, bursting with the passionate abandon of the young

Parisians who frequented the area. They turned left into the *Rue de Bourbogne* and followed the road to their hotel.

The Le Blancs retired for the evening, having a quick discussion on their plans for the next day in the sitting area of their suite. Mr Le Blanc had an early appointment with Prime Minister Mollet and would be attending to various other administrative meetings during the day. Mrs Le Blanc proposed that she and Marie-Claire would do some shopping for summer clothes at the boutiques lining the *Rue de Faubourg Saint-Honoré* during the morning. They would also pop by Balmain to have a look at their summer collection. 'I feel poorer already,' was all Mr Le Blanc had to say at the suggestion.

Marie-Claire woke up with a damp pillow the next morning, the Parisian sun streaming in her bedroom window. She was excited by the prospect of a paternally funded spending spree in the premier shopping destination of the world. Her mother was up as well and Mr Le Blanc had already left for his appointment with the French leader. The pair decided to stroll to the *Rue de Faubourg Saint-Honoré*, as it was only a short distance away on the right bank of the *Seine*. On the way, they spent some time in the *Place de la Concorde,* admiring the gorgeous fountains and large Egyptian obelisk adorning the square. Their final destination was the extended collection of *haute couture* suppliers lining the street. Amy Linker, Claude Rivière, Helen Hubert, Hermès, Irmone, and Jacqueline Godard, to name but a few, could all be found there- shiny window displays inviting the avid fashionista inside.

The pair took their time and followed the street at a leisurely pace, entering store after glittering store to view the offerings of summer collections. If they found something to their liking, they requested that it be delivered to their hotel. Once they had finally arrived at the *Rue de Collisée*, they turned left and promptly found a *café* where they could sit down for lunch and refreshments. After the gruelling morning of shopping, the respite in the cool *café* was a welcome one.

'Have you given any thought about what you want to do after school, Marie-Claire?' Mrs Le Blanc enquired during lunch.

'I have thought of maybe doing ballet professionally. If I work hard, I might get accepted into the professional Bolshoi Company. Otherwise, I think I want to come to Paris. It is an amazing city. Perhaps I could study art. What did you do after school, Mother?'

'In my day, one did not have as many choices. My father got me a position as an assistant librarian at the National Library here in Paris. Which is where I met your father. As a young bureaucrat, he seemed to have been given a lot of research to do by his superiors, or perhaps not? It seemed to vary in subject matter depending on where I found myself working in the library on any given day. So I saw a lot of him in the stacks. He finally mustered enough courage to ask me out, after I called his bluff and settled in for a long wait in the ancient Sumerian section one day. He did not read Sanskrit and had no possible business there. The rest, as they say is history. We were married a year later and living in Istanbul, of all places.'

With their energy restored and renewed vigour, they headed to their final destination, now only three blocks away. On the way, they traversed the *Champs-Élysées*, Marie-Claire nearly getting bumped into by several irate pedestrians as she stood staring at the *Arc de Triomphe* in the distance. One block further down, they turned left and arrived at the House of Balmain. They met the man himself inside, running around in preparation for the unveiling of his autumn collection. 'Mrs Le Blanc? Oh, it is such a pleasure to finally meet you in person! I feel like I know you so well already. Figuratively speaking,' Pierre Balmain said in jest as he made a large hourglass gesture with his hands. 'Were you pleased with the designs?'

'Most certainly! The dresses were gorgeous. This is my daughter Marie-Claire. You might also recognise her,' Mrs Le Blanc said, mimicking his hourglass gesture. 'We are not in Paris long so we're looking for some ready-to-wear items for our upcoming holiday in the Riviera.'

'Pleased to make you acquaintance, Marie-Claire. I am sure we can help you. My assistant, Erik, can show you what is available and perhaps make some minor alterations, if required. You will have to excuse me, I have some designs to complete.'

Erik Mortensen assisted them for the remainder of the afternoon and by the time they were done, they ordered delivery to the hotel with additional luggage. Mr Le Blanc was waiting in the suite for them already, along with a stack of boxes and a rail full of couture. He raised an eyebrow as they entered, conveying his lack of amusement at, what was clearly, a spending excursion of epic proportions. 'Been keeping busy, have we...?' he enquired, waving a finger in the direction of the fashion collection.

'Not particularly. Mostly just browsing a bit today. We were thinking of perhaps doing some *real* shopping tomorrow,' Marie-Claire responded feistily.

Mr Le Blanc could only laugh in response. 'Good heavens, please don't! Only museums, art galleries and tourist attractions tomorrow. At least give me the day to find a buyer for the Family Estate, so I can pay for this lot. Let's go out for dinner and then you can tell me what you left behind in the shops today. It will probably prove a shorter list than what you ended up buying.' They laughed heartily as they left the hotel in pursuit of another evening of fine Parisian dining.

A MONTH IN THE RIVIERA, 1956

Their last three days in Paris was spent showing Marie-Claire as much as they could of all the city had to offer, besides shopping. Mr Le Blanc attended a number of official meetings and Mrs Le Blanc spent the time with Marie-Claire, introducing her to all the local sights and sounds. The *Louvre* left a memorable impression on the young girl, the close proximity to the work of so many grand masters inspiring the budding artist in her. They went up the Eiffel tower, visited the *Sacré-Coeur* Basilica and the *Notre Dame* Cathedral and spent an afternoon at the *Père Lachaise* Cemetery.

The cemetery proved an almost surreal experience for the young Marie-Claire. That there could be so much beauty, even in death, changed her outlook on the subject. The exquisitely carved memoires of the dead served as reminders of their lives, forever resting beneath the green trees. It was impossible to believe that everyone there lived perfect lives and yet, there they were, side by side in equal splendour. From the cemetery they went to the *Parc de Buttes-Chaumont*, which lay close by, and spent the remainder of the time before sunset having a picnic in the greenery, next to the lake. The steady fall of water lulled them into a relaxed state. The park was magnificent and the *Temple Sybille,* visible at the top of the hill in the middle of the lake, reminded them of a miniature version of the Acropolis in Athens.

Marie-Claire was equally fascinated by their tour of the Catacombs beneath the city. It was as if the city as she knew it, was built on the bones of millions of the dead. *The cornerstone and foundations of the city, set firmly in the remains of the departed. New life sprouting from the end of the old. Even the City of Light had dark foundations. And those dark foundations were not intimidating or dreadful, they were magnificent.* She could relate to that duality, and it spoke to her on a deep level, with profound realisations. *There was beauty in death and new life grew from it. It was not to be feared and embracing death, meant embracing life.* There was a layer of deeper beauty beneath the upper veneer that was Paris, which not everyone could appreciate. Marie-Claire loved it.

Their time in Paris soon came to a sad end for Marie-Claire, who had fallen deeply in love with the city. She vowed to return for a more extended visit and hoped that she could settle there permanently someday, as she could think of no better place to live out her days. Their afternoon trip from the hotel to *Paris-Orly* Airport in the South of the city avoided most of the beautiful sights, leaving her with an unrequited yearning to see them again. From *Orly*, it took just under 2 hours to fly from Paris to *Nice*.

Their flight arrived in *Nice* in the late afternoon. The airport *Nice Côte d'Azur* was quite unusual, giving the unexpected impression of falling into the Mediterranean when landing. Marie-Claire grabbed the arm-rests of her chair as the illusion transpired, the plane descending into, what appeared to be, the sea. The airport was built on a promontory of land to the west of the city of *Nice*, the runway beginning and ending on the coast. They touched down and the humidity and smell of the sea hit them as they climbed the set of stairs off the plane. Mr Le Blanc was still dressed in a suit and seemed out of place amongst the passengers, all dressed for beach weather.

The family proceeded to the car-rental desk, where they collected the keys to a green *Facel Vega* FV2B convertible, which was reserved in Mr Le Blanc's name. *Good old Jean-Pierre,* he thought. *What a perfect car to explore the Riviera with!* The attendant assisted Mr Le Blanc to put down the top before they left the rental lot and drove west down the coast to *Antibes*. It was a short fifteen-minute trip to reach the picturesque holiday town. Having rounded the *Cape Antibes*, they entered *Juan-les-Pins*, finally arriving at their destination.

The *Le Provençal* Hotel was a ten storey Art Deco building, with magnificent views over the bay and the yacht basin. It had its own private beach club to cater for the affluent residents, who could afford the deluxe lodgings. The hotel stood out as the pinnacle of its surroundings, both in luxury and in height. They pulled up to the hotel entrance, the sound of surf and seagulls greeting them as they exited the car. A manager was standing by the door. He was wearing a white jacket and bowtie, and seemed impervious to the seaside heat and humidity.

'Welcome to *Le Provençal,* Sir. Marc here will assist with your luggage,' he said, pointing to the hotel porter, whose damp forehead testified to being less impervious in his maroon jacket and tie. Their luggage was taken to their suite on the ninth floor as they checked in. The lobby was grand, with red strip carpets laid out over marble flooring, guests in various degrees of summer wear strolled along the velvet pathways to everywhere and nowhere. Such was the nature of *Juan-les-Pins* in season, ending up anywhere was acceptable, as no-one had a schedule or a set destination. 'Let's have some cocktails on the terrace,' Mrs Le Blanc suggested. The sun was setting and the suggestion proved a welcome one.

The rooftop terrace was on the same floor as their room and there were magnificent views of the setting sun to the west over the bay and *Pointe Croisette* beyond it, in the distance. They sat under a yellow umbrella on the roof with dozens of other like-minded guests and lapped up the scenic views. A waiter arrived with their cocktail order, which they slowly sipped as the sun set. It was pure bliss. Mrs Le Blanc seemed happy as she held her husband's hand, staring into the distance. 'Father, this is wonderful!' Marie-Claire observed as she savoured her white wine spritzer. 'However did you come across such a marvellous place?'

'Your mother and I discovered it on our honeymoon. We were driving all along the length of the Riviera and happened to pass here at sunset one day. One could not deny the allure of this view,' he said, accentuating with a sweeping gesture of his arm.

'We ended up staying in the hotel for a week,' Mrs Le Blanc continued, 'we simply cancelled our planned accommodation further down the coast and settled in here. Luckily there were some rooms available due to the shoulder season. Nowadays, one wouldn't find any accommodation without a booking. *Juan-les-Pins* has certainly developed in the decade since we were here last.'

'Is there a lot to do here, father?' Marie-Claire enquired, even though boredom was hardly ever a problem for her.

'Oh yes. The hotel's beach club is wonderful. There are all kinds of water sports to take part in. We can also take a few day trips down the coast. *Cannes* is lovely. I can show you where they hold the annual film festival. There's also the drive down to *Monte Carlo* in the other direction, so you can see where they race in the Grand prix.'

'I'm not a big fan of car races, but I'd love to see where the film festival happens,' Marie-Claire responded.

'Trust me, my dear, you will love *Monte Carlo*! Race or no race, the town is amazing,' Mrs Le Blanc responded in turn. 'Perhaps we can also drive to *Provence* and stay a day or three. The Lavender fields there are so beautiful. And we should drive to the lower Alps and get some wine to stock the cellar at the Embassy, the previous tenants had such dreadful taste in wine.'

'What a splendid idea, my love!' Mr Le Blanc said excitedly, the thought of extensive wine tasting and bespoke orders for the Embassy cellar appealing greatly to the wine connoisseur in him. They would do well to clear out the current cellar contents by giving it away on the sidewalk in front of the Embassy, as free tasting on the next French public holiday.

151

The evening had arrived and brought with it a welcome reprieve from the stifling heat of the late afternoon. They opted for dinner on the terrace and asked for a menu. The dinner was superb and the conversation light, far removed from the troubles of Moscow and the stifling oppression of the Soviet regime. 'Perhaps if the Russians had a coast and food as lovely as this, they might have been less unhappy in Moscow,' Marie-Claire noted.

'Well, technically, parts of the Soviet coast next to the Black Sea are quite lovely and the fish dishes great, but alas, the average Muscovite never gets to go there. When I was stationed in Istanbul, we sailed along the coast of the Black Sea one summer on a small yacht and it was magical,' Mr Le Blanc replied, a far-off, longing look in his eyes. *Father has a romantic soul after all*, she thought.

They retired to their room after dinner, all three displaying the unceremonious stagger of those who had imbibed a little too much. As they entered their suite, they found their luggage unpacked by the hotel staff already. The view from their window was a spectacular one, the glowing lights of *Cannes* visible on the horizon. Marie-Claire's room had a set of twin beds and she chose the one next to the window. Her head was spinning from the wine and as many before her, she now experienced the effects of excessive alcohol consumption. The after effects would come with the sunrise the next morning, a rite of passage that would teach the humble lesson of moderation.

The sunrise over the French Riviera was magnificent. It was the first of many such natural displays of natural beauty they would experience at *Le Provençal*. On this particular occasion, however, they were not experiencing it at all, rather opting to lie in and recover from the night before. Marie-Claire's head was pounding when a stray beam of sunlight woke her up, rudely intruding on a dreamless sleep. She was confronted by nausea and felt ghastly. *Lesson learnt.* After some toast, coffee and apple juice, she felt somewhat better, but in no way capable of spending a day in the sun on the beach. The three opted to rather stroll through town, where shop awnings and trees lining the streets could protect them from the harsh attention of the pounding daylight.

Juan-les-Pins read like a who's who of the celebrity pages in a French tabloid. Everyone was there. Or rather, everyone who featured in French society. Movie stars, both foreign and domestic, mingled with writers, singers and rich industrialists. Marie-Claire was surprised that a fair number of famous people seemed to know her father. He was kind enough to introduce her to many of these celebrities. Even more surprising, was that many of them remembered her when they came across her in town during the following month. As the summer progressed, her tan deepened and gave her skin a rich, glowing appearance, accentuating her natural beauty. She was very popular amongst the males frequenting the seaside promenade, always happy, and lining up, to buy her a beverage when she was around on her own. She had stayed away from alcohol for the rest of the summer, so the drinks were mostly virgin cocktails or lemonade. Being multilingual, she could speak to almost everyone in *Juan-les-Pins*, adding to her rising popularity.

Marie-Claire was somewhat unpopular amongst the socialites, who felt threatened by her charm, good looks and interesting tales. Her saving grace was that she was barely sixteen and when that became common knowledge, they also warmed to her. Someone as young could not really be a threat, even if she was gorgeous. Her parents did not let her go out with the other youngsters after dark, which reflected both common sense and responsible parenting on their part, which helped perpetuate the illusion of her youthfulness. Marie-Claire got numerous invitations to day trips on large yachts, which Mr Le Blanc sometimes allowed, depending on the owner of the vessel. She was well and truly embraced by the prominent vacationing community of *Juan-les-Pins* as one of their own, a young starlet already at home on the high end of the social ladder.

The Le Blancs eventually got around to visiting *Cannes* and *Monte Carlo*, after having spent two weeks mostly relaxing on the sandy private beach of the hotel. They joined the jam-packed ranks of *Le Provençal*'s residents amongst the dozens of brightly coloured umbrellas and matching beach chairs. The young Marie-

Claire was quite an adept water skier, as her trained balance and strong core muscles served her well on the calm waters surrounding *Antibes*. Various day trips proved breath-taking and Marie-Claire enjoyed these jewels that the Riviera offered. The film festival crowds had left *Cannes* weeks ago, only to be replaced by the summer patrons, in search of fine weather and beautiful beaches. Luxury yachts filled the harbour, interspersed with more modest local fishing vessels.

Monte Carlo proved even more extravagant than *Cannes*, *Nice* or *Juan-les-Pins*. Mr Le Blanc parked their car by the Monte Carlo beach and they walked about town from there. 'What are those men doing to the beach, Father?' Marie-Claire enquired, pointing at a group of municipal workers, emptying bags on the beach and spreading the contents around with rakes.

'Oh, they are replenishing the little white beach pebbles. The beach is totally man-made, so they have to keep adding pebbles, lest the whole thing disappear,' he pointed at a restaurant, 'Let's have some refreshments at the *Café de Paris*, it is marvellous.' The famous *café* was situated across the street from the even more famous *Monte Carlo* Casino, which produced enough tourist income to sustain the entire country's financial needs, negating the need for raising taxes. After some coffee and cake, they continued their stroll through the streets of the little town. There was a flag flying at the Royal palace, showing Prince Rainier was in residence. The streets were mostly steep, with either ascending or descending inclines, leaving their legs tired and aching from the exertion. *The thoroughfares were definitely not designed with functionality in mind, but certainly provided scenic views of the surroundings*, Marie-Claire thought. *Perhaps that was the idea all along?*

The Le Blancs spent the afternoon on the white pebbled beach of *Monte Carlo*, adding to their already bronze tans. The water was warm and the beach was packed with tourists, catching some sun before dressing up and spending the evening donating their money to the Casino. Mr Le Blanc had made an amateur mistake by leaving the car roof down, so the seats in the car were blisteringly hot after baking in the French summer sun all afternoon. They had made the unfortunate discovery of the heated seats when first sitting down, smartly followed by exiting the car in a rush. A group of tourists at a café across the road found the spectacle quite comedic, laughing heartily at the impromptu entertainment with their sundowners. The trip home was uncomfortable.

The following day they finally undertook their long awaited road trip to *Provence*. They packed a weekend bag, leaving the rest of their belongings in the hotel suite. The concierge had booked them rooms at the *Ermitage Napoléon* Hotel close to the town of *Digne-le-Bains*, which he described as a lovely sixty room hotel with an excellent restaurant. A leisurely drive brought them into *Provence*, with all its beauty and rural charm. The hotel proved to be a lovely, yellow, three-story affair, with a red tile roof, nestled in the foothills of the French Alps. The *Chateau Rousset* was their first stop and the wine proved delightful. After a comprehensive sampling of the various wines from the cellar, Mr Le Blanc ordered three cases each of the Red and White wines, to be shipped to Moscow. The owner was happy to oblige, after the costs were confirmed.

The meandering tour between wineries continued, some warranting a large consignment for delivery to Moscow, while others simply did not proffer wines of a standard that Mr Le Blanc deemed worthy of a bulk order. Their three days in *Provence* flew by in whirlwind fashion, copious amounts of wine tasting adding to the inexplicable loss of time. At the end of their tour, they had ordered thirty cases of wine from several *chateaus*, all for shipment to the French Embassy in Moscow. The cellars in Moscow would be well stocked until at least their next social function. This inland excursion had been a marvellous addition to their vacation, everyone very pleased with the decision to make the journey.

The vacation slowly wound down, a last couple of days spent relaxing and soaking up all the excitement and delights that *Juan-les-Pins* had to offer. All too soon, they were boarding the plane for Paris, which was followed by the long charter flight back to Moscow. Marie-Claire would always think back fondly of the first experience of her adopted country. France was a wondrous place and she was glad that she could call herself a citizen of such a phenomenal country. Returning was not optional, she would strive to do so on every possible occasion. *What a place!*

GREETINGS FROM RUSSIA

Embassy of France
43 Dimitrov Boulevard
Moscow
USSR
17 October 1957

My dearest Andros

I hope you are keeping well? How is your time in London? Are the business school lecturers teaching you to conquer the business world? I must admit I find commercial talk excessively boring. Sometimes I have to listen to Father carrying on with visiting businessmen and it is very often a completely dull affair. I am not interested in marketing strategies and how the local Chamber of Commerce should become involved in motivating to have the necessary permits issued. Those dinner parties prove utterly dreadful.

I am now at the start of my third year of school at the Bolshoi academy. The classes are really challenging and the teaching standards are world class. I miss the uncomplicated days of your mother's tutoring. It was a simpler time. I simply had to complete a movement, without having to know the history behind it, who wrote the music and who the first performers were, or who choreographed it initially. It is taking the fun out of dancing a little. I sometimes wonder whether I still want to continue along this path, or whether I should re-think where I want to end up one day. There is a girl in my class, Ekaterina

Maximova, who I greatly admire as a dancer. When I see her perform, I realise I will never reach her level of technical skill and grace, no matter how much I train, or what I do. I have resigned myself to this and I am not even trying to compete with her. We became good friends and see each other outside of school as well. Her father's family were distant relations of the Romanovs. They were far enough removed in the family tree to not be targeted by the Bolshevik lynch mobs in 1918, but close enough to have amassed considerable wealth under the protection of the Tsar. They kept a low profile ever since, but are still fabulously wealthy, now in their own right.

Ekaterina will probably be grabbed up by the Bolshoi Ballet Company without having to give it a second thought. She is that good. I am sure I will audition, but I am starting to doubt whether I have what it takes to be accepted. I don't know what I would do if I don't get accepted, I have not really thought that far ahead. It is clear that one thing I do know, is that I want to live in Paris. It is an amazing city and even though I have only been there twice, I definitely know I would want to settle there permanently, someday. Father's career will also come to an end at some stage and I don't know whether I would want to stay in Moscow on my own. The city is cold and the people are even colder. Their demeanour is certainly reflective of the winters here and of the harsh quality of their everyday life. There is a small group of elitists that are living it up, while the rest of the population seems to be keeping to the *Communist Manifesto*, as Marx had envisioned it (except for the parts of overthrowing said elite).

Father has become good friends with Valerian Zorin, the Deputy Minister of Foreign Affairs here. Uncle Val is one of the elite, but cares greatly for the rest of his countrymen and is always trying to treat everyone equally. He seems to have his plate full with trying to keep diplomatic ties going with the rest of the world. He often has to ask father for a diplomatic intervention or to do an introduction to one of his contacts. The Soviet regime seems to be its own worst enemy. They don't play well with others and struggle to make friends. I think Father is also under considerable stress, although he tries to hide it as best he can. This is a tough time to be a Diplomat in Moscow and it seems like we are constantly busy floundering from one crisis to the next. Father is of the opinion that one should never waste a good crisis, but the situation here is sometimes simply ridiculous. I suppose if it has to carry on like this, Father might retire before he is due.

I think the only thing keeping him sane at the moment is the respite he gets when we go on holiday. We have now settled into a summer routine of going to Paris for several days' worth of meetings for Father, while Mother and I explore the marvellous sights the city has to offer. Father seems to be in his element in Paris and de-stresses even before we get to the French Riviera. We have now spent two summers at the *Le Provençal* Hotel in *Juan-les-Pins*. The town itself is really something to see and I quite enjoyed the nightlife there this summer. Mother and Father have started allowing me to go out at night with some of the other young people in the hotel. We often danced until the early morning hours at *Maxim's*, which is the most hip and happening nightspot in *Juan-les-Pins*.

I spent a lot of time this summer with a fellow called Gino Romario. Gino is starting university this year in Milan. He is a dashingly handsome Italian and it is hilarious how we met. It was reaching the end of last summer and I was walking towards my towel on the beach. I passed him and his brother, where they were on their beach mats looking at all the passing people. He told his brother in Italian that this girl walking past is the most beautiful on the beach today. To his great embarrassment, I turned around and responded in Italian that he was not a bad looking specimen himself. I guess he now knows a bit better than to assume everyone on the Riviera are either French or English. Although I must say, the English are easy to spot. They are normally the ones looking like freshly boiled lobsters! They simply do not cope too well in the Mediterranean sunshine. But I digress...

Gino introduced himself and we had a nice chat on the beach. Unfortunately, he had to leave the next day and I resigned myself to never seeing him again, cute as he may be. We agreed to write each other, but as these things go, neither of us seemed to have gotten around to it. Sometimes people just agree these things out of politeness, I think. It's a way of not admitting that you will probably never see each other again, to make farewells a little less painful. Great was my surprise when I stumbled upon Gino next to the hotel pool this past summer. I really enjoyed spending time with him. Father gave him a rather stern look when meeting him and I think the unspoken death threats that all fathers exude to the young men showing interest in their daughters was duly accepted by Gino, with the responding "I am a choirboy in the church" handshake. With those formalities behind us, I had secured Father's somewhat unenthusiastic blessing to spend my time with Gino.

We explored *Juan-Les-Pins* together and spent hours on the Hotel beach discussing life, art and philosophy. One afternoon late, as we were strolling down the beach, the subject of love came up in our conversation. It was a general discussion and not aimed at raising any expectations between us, but as the conversation flowed, we came to a halt on the beach, looking deep into each other's eyes as dusk settled over the water. He took me in his arms and pulled me gently closer, our lips meeting in a warm kiss. It was totally different from when you and I had kissed that one time previously. It started off softly and then it erupted into what I guess might well be the most memorable kiss ever!

The rest of the summer was filled with many more such embraces and we spent almost every waking moment together. Father objected occasionally to my absence, but it seems he and Mother enjoyed the alone time together, re-living the honeymoon they had there many years before. Gino's brother and some of his friends were also there and soon we were a whole crowd of young people who went out together and partied up a storm in the evenings. By the end of the summer, Gino and I had spoken of love for each other and the final parting when our vacation came to an end was heart-breaking. Even though we promised to write and keep in touch, I knew I would not see him again until the following summer, if ever again. Whoever said "better to have loved and lost…" has clearly never loved before, or met Gino. Such cruelty! I will miss him dearly.

I am inspired when I think of Gino and have taken up art again. It is easy to express myself on canvas when the feelings of sadness and missing him come over me. I feel better when I am done, even though some of the works seem a bit dark. I sometimes dream of Gino and see him falling off a height, his face obscured as he endlessly drops downwards, calling me Maria as he descends. It breaks my heart when this happens, as I can almost feel our love dissipating away as the distance between us increases. The feelings of love also seems strange in these dreams, different from when I think of him when I am awake. But enough of my morbid dreams...

My art is really maturing and my art teacher is very impressed with my work. He is talking about hosting an exhibition, but I don't think I want to do that anytime soon, or even at all. I feel my art is personal and that I will share it with the world when the time comes. Father has framed one or two of my better pieces and hung them in the Embassy. Of course, they pale in comparison to all the other exquisite art in the building.

I have to tell you about the amazing ring I got from my parents for my birthday! It all started when I was in the antique district one Saturday morning. I quite like to go there and poke around. Father usually just sends Phillipe along to keep an eye on me and make sure I don't get into trouble. He knows better than to bother me, so he usually dawdles behind me, ready to act if any harm was to come to me. Mother is not really into antiques, so I am left to my own devices. I was walking past the one store and saw the most beautiful jade ring in the window display. It seemed quite old and had a mystical quality about it. I went inside and asked to have a closer look. The shopkeeper told me the most interesting tale about how it had once belonged to a handmaiden of the Romanov household. She was always at the beck and call of the Tsarina and even served as her personal protection. I like to think of myself as a strong-willed girl and the thought of owning such a ring, previously owned by a strong woman serving a powerful monarch, appealed to me on a deep level. One could see the ring was not quite of Royal standard, but it was still very special. It had such a rich history to it, which far outweighed its mere looks. It fit me perfectly and I took it as a sign that I was destined to have it. Of course, it was more expensive than I could possibly hope to afford, so I haggled with the shopkeeper and struck a bargain. I gave him a deposit and in turn, he would keep it safely tucked away until my Father could come around and purchase it for me.

It didn't take a lot of convincing to ensure that Father bought it for me. My birthday was coming up and I assured him that my heart desired nothing more than to own that marvellous ring. He was happy to oblige me and Mother and he duly handed me a neatly wrapped little box on my birthday, containing the ring. The shopkeeper had kept up his side of the deal and I had gotten my glorious, special gift! I wear it all the time now and I often get complimented on the beauty of the handmaiden's ring.

Moscow is a strange city. It has a duality, which extends to all spheres of life here. There is the beauty of the old buildings and the refinement of the contents and then there is the distinctly unrefined local populace who live in the housing projects, which are stark and ugly. In the summer, *Gorky Park* is a lush green oasis and yet in winter, it is covered in snow, white and undiscernible from anything surrounding it. There is the rich elite, living it up on Champagne and Caviar, mingling at the Embassy parties and then the commoners, who live in misery on potatoes and the hope for a better life. The state seems to interfere in every aspect of people's lives, controlling them, keeping them in check. Free thought and free speech are discouraged in a variety of ways and everyone is living in paranoia, constantly looking over their shoulders.

I had to start doing that myself, as we discovered that there are KGB agents following us around whenever we leave the Embassy. I, myself, try and make their lives as miserable as possible when I'm out and about. Many an agent had to stand in the rain up to soaking point as I excessively dawdled in shops or *cafés*. On Saturdays, at the antique markets, I find it particularly easy to make their lives miserable. I would disappear and reappear all over, sometimes behind them. I even bumped into one of them on occasion. This also irritates Philippe endlessly, as he sits with the same problem of having to try and keep track of me. At least we normally make an arrangement to meet somewhere specific at a set time if we get separated, as obviously I would not want to lose my ride home. Father has often raised this issue of the KGB agents with Uncle Val, but it seems that even someone in his position holds no sway over these matters, the KGB is a power unto themselves.

My language skills in Russian are now very good and I can speak like a local. On top of that I am able to speak English, French, Greek, Italian and German. I don't know whether a career as an interpreter would be something I could consider if ballet doesn't work out. Father could easily secure me a position in the diplomatic corps, but I am unsure whether I would be keen to complete formal studies in all these languages, which is often a pre-requisite. It helps quite a bit at the Embassy parties which Father hosts or takes me along to. One never seems to run out of people to talk to when one has a variety of languages to fall back on. We haven't had a Bastille Day party at the Embassy since the first year we came, as we have been on those holidays in the Riviera the last two years. I much prefer *Nice*'s beaches to Moscow's bitches anyway, if you pardon my French.

I suppose secretly Father doesn't think he'll be able to top that first Bastille Day party anyway, so this way, he doesn't even need to try and its legacy can live on in the minds of the Diplomatic community in Moscow. Whenever we host other events at the Embassy, the guests always enquire as to when we will host a Bastille Day event again. We hosted Yves Montand at the Embassy last

December. Father and Yves have apparently known each other for a long time. Yves almost cancelled the performance when the USSR invaded Hungary, but it seems that Father might have been involved in persuading him to come, anyway. He even hosted an event for Yves, who did an impromptu performance at the dinner. I fully understand how someone that can sing like that can be quite popular with the ladies, it was even more telling in the intimate setting if the Embassy dining room. They made a recording of the official performance in Moscow and Yves promised he would sign me a copy of the record once it was released.

Mother doesn't really like it in Moscow. It saddens me to see her like this. She seems like a caged nightingale, stuck in the Embassy. I go out a lot, with my schooling and Saturday visits to the markets, but Mother appears to have pulled into herself here in Moscow. I try to get her to go along with me as much as I can, just to get her out of the house. We sometimes go on walks next to the *Moskva* River and then through *Gorky Park*. I think this helps to improve her mood a bit. The Russian winters can be very harsh and I believe she struggles to cope with them. I suppose she misses her parents in winter, more than any other time of the year. She speaks of them fondly on our walks, when the topic comes up. She revealed for the first time the circumstances around their deaths to me, seated on a bench in *Gorky Park*. Her mother had passed away of cancer and her father struggled to cope with the loss after she was gone, eventually drinking himself into an early grave shortly thereafter. There might have been some pills involved as well. We visited their gravesite the last time we were in Paris. Mother laid a wreath on the graves and cried.

She has been very supportive of my efforts to keep in touch with Gino. I have the suspicion that she had once failed to keep in touch with someone and still regrets it. The "might-have-been" haunting her on the occasions when Father was involved in infidelities. He just blames being French and that it is the French way. I can tell you that French women view the subject a little differently. One day, when the need had arisen soon after we arrived in

Moscow, she had sat me down and explained about men and woman and where babies came from. It clarified a lot of other things I was wondering about.

When she appears to be struggling, I try and cheer her up as much as I can and attempt to get her out of the house. I have explained the situation to the teachers at school, so when Mother comes along to classes to "see my progress", they do not object to her presence. The ballet cheers her up. I don't know if it's the dance or the music, but either way, it does her well. In winter I take her to some of the museums in Moscow as an outing. We have now had to start resorting to some of the more obscure museums, but those have often proved the very best!

We will be going to *St Moritz* in December and I look forward to the ice rink and the ski slopes. I am especially excited at the opportunity to win back my *St Moritz* Town ice-skating title, since I wasn't there last year to defend it successfully, again. Ice-skating is very close to ballet, I discovered. At least the people of *St Moritz* are warmer than the Russians, even if the weather isn't.

I will write you again in the new year and I hope you have a glorious Christmas. Send my regards to your mother.

Best wishes, Marie-Claire

WHEN THE MUSIC DIES IN MOSCOW, 1958

The last of the term was in sight at the Bolshoi School. The end of the school year also meant the end of an era, for those in their final year. A final performance would follow and those who were deemed worthy, would be admitted to the Ballet Company. The triumphant were remembered, their pictures decking the halls, an inspiration for those who were attending and still had hopes which were alive to the thought of success.

Marie-Claire counted herself amongst those numbers. Hope persisted. Acceptance into the Bolshoi Company was just beyond the horizon and currently every moment was spent on perfecting a performance that was remarkable enough to gain access to the prestigious outfit and all the privileges that went along with the honour. Every dancer had to perform a solo act in front of the school faculty and the choreographers of the professional group.

The focused Marie-Claire spent almost every waking moment of her days preparing for the upcoming recital, now only two weeks away. The preparations put an immense amount of pressure on the young woman and she was struggling to cope with the stress. Mrs Le Blanc tried to assist where she could by arranging for a massage therapist to visit the Embassy, trying to help the weary young body to cope with the strain being placed upon it in such a hostile manner. Marie-Claire's only solace was that it would soon be over. She would perform and then it would be all over.

Except if she was successful. Marie-Claire suddenly noted this possibility and what it would mean for her, going forward. Should she be accepted, she would probably be training like this on a much more regular basis. It would not be a once off event, it would be an ongoing process. When one season of performances was over, the next would start. The troupe would travel all across the globe to perform, but were watched like hawks by accompanying state personnel. Marie-Claire wondered if it might be like looking at the world from a gilded cage. 'Mother, do you think I should join the Bolshoi if the opportunity presented itself?' she asked Mrs Le Blanc over breakfast one morning.

'Why would you not want join them? It is such an illustrious opportunity,' was the surprised response.

'I have been thinking about it a lot lately- the long hours of practise, the travels and the quality of life. Would I enjoy a life spent in such a way, commanded and controlled by someone 24 hours a day? I wonder about it now...'

'Perhaps there will be some sort of sign when the time comes, which will help guide you on the right decision to make. These things always seem to work out for the better. My darling, I think you will have absolute clarity when the moment comes to decide. There will be no doubt. You will know what you want, even if you do not know right now.'

The day of reckoning had finally arrived and the excited young woman was in a change room of the Bolshoi theatre. Marie-Claire had the dressing room to herself, the scheduled programme allowing for privacy in the final mental preparations for all the participants. She sat in front of the mirror. The multiple bulbs in the frame lit up her face, accentuating the dark lines of her make-up. She was dressed in the outfit of Odile, the very same costume which had set in motion the events which ultimately brought her to this very point. The Black Swan could once more aim for a performance which would be met with glory and elevate her career to a new level. She thought about the years of hard work at the Bolshoi that were about to culminate in this final performance. The hours were too many to count, the blood, sweat and tears too much to measure. Her parents would be in the theatre, viewing her recital from the back, unobtrusive and unobserved by the judging panel in the front row.

Mr Le Blanc had left his wife in the back of the theatre and made his way backstage, a bouquet of roses resting in his one arm. He would be giving these to Marie-Claire in the change room, a reminder that her mother and him were there to support her, whatever the outcome of the evening may be. Two men intercepted him in the passage, waiting mere yards away from the change room door. The two figures were vaguely familiar to Le Blanc, as if he had seen them many times before, out of the corner of his eye. 'Ambassador Le Blanc, we are so excited to see you here. I am Igor Ivanovic and this is my colleague Ivan Igorovic,' the portly figure addressed him.

'What the devil..?' the surprised Mr Le Blanc stammered, the irony of their names passing him by in his confusion.

'No need to alarm yourself Ambassador. We are simply here to wish you good luck with your daughter's performance. We know that she has put in many, many hours of hard work to get here. It would be such a pity if she ended up failing, so close to success. I know that could be devastating for a young woman. How would she ever recover from such failure..? Of course, there are ways to ensure that she does succeed. Ways to guarantee her acceptance into the Bolshoi. Ways which we can arrange quite easily. But such an intervention on our part, friendly as it may be, would come at a cost. I think we can all agree that Marie-Claire had paid her dues to get here, so it would be patently unfair to tax her further in this endeavour.'

'What do you want?' Le Blanc asked, his controlled anger close to the surface.

'Oh, not much,' Ivan said in a tone that suggested much more than the words themselves indicated. 'We wish to reach an agreement with you. We will arrange for your lovely daughter to be accepted into the Ballet Company. I am sure you can agree that she deserves this placement. In return, you will provide us with some information from time to time. We will let you know when we require this information and it will always be material which you will have at your disposal, or will be able to obtain from some of your friends in the industry. You know, a bit of this and a bit of that.'

'I presume this "information" would be such that you are not able to obtain it yourself, through normal diplomatic channels?' Mr Le Blanc asked, the seriousness of this predicament dawning on him.

'Oh, we would probably be able to source it ourselves, but breaking into diplomatic safes can be such tiring business. I find it plays havoc on my gout. We would much rather prefer that you provide it to us in an amicable manner, so we can spend our nights peacefully sleeping in our beds. As long as you continue to do so, we will ensure that your daughter's career at the Bolshoi flourishes. Do we have an accord..?' Igor asked with a false smile, sticking out his hand, ready to be shaken.

Marie-Claire had been listening to the whole conversation at the door, as she had partially opened it when she was about to leave. She did not have to listen too long before realising what was happening in the passageway. And then she knew. With absolute clarity. She knew that whatever decision she made at this point, she would get her father to accept as the way things would be. That much she had learnt by now. The decision was made. Standing by the door, she waited for the right moment to intervene. She fidgeted with her ring as the conversation played out in the passage. Finally, the moment presented itself and she entered the passage. She was confronted by Fatty and Baldy. Now they had names. 'Do we have an accord, Mr Le Blanc?' Igor asked again, this time with a little less smile and a little more menace in his voice.

'No, you don't!' responded Marie-Claire, slamming the change room door behind her. She was wearing a coat over her ballet outfit and had her bag over her shoulder.

'Come Father, we are leaving,' Marie-Claire said as she bumped Baldy out of the way and grabbed her father by the arm, leading him down the passage. She left the two KGB agents in her wake, Baldy rubbing his ribs and Fatty looking confused at the unexpected turn of events which had just transpired. Mr Le Blanc was equally confused as he was led to where they had parked the car. Phillipe was surprised to see them, but smartly opened the rear door for the pair, none-the-less. 'Go fetch Mother and tell her we are leaving, Father,' she commanded. 'I'll wait here.'

Mr Le Blanc walked around to the front of the theatre and entered, coming out with his wife shortly after. They found Marie-Claire in the car, breathing deeply. 'What happened?' Mrs Le Blanc asked with concern.

'There were some men from the KGB. They offered father a position in the Ballet Company for me, in exchange for his intermittent supply of classified information to them. I could not let that happen, so I walked out. I am done with this!' Marie-Claire responded, now starting to cry.

'Is this true?' she asked her husband, shock reflected on her face.

'Yes, that is what happened.'

'Oh Henri, that is terrible,' Mrs Le Blanc said as she wrapped her arms around her crying daughter.

They drove to the Embassy in silence and when they got there, they settled in the salon. Mr Le Blanc poured everyone, including his daughter, a measure of brandy and settled in to discuss the affair. 'Ok, spill it. Tell me the whole story. How did this come about?' Mrs Le Blanc asked angrily, wanting details on the sordid matter.

'I overheard Father speaking to the two men in the passage. I have seen them around before, they are part of the KGB team that follows us around everywhere. Fatty and Baldy, I call them. Apparently they are called Igor and Ivan. They offered a position in the Ballet Company in return for information. I am sorry, but I cannot let Father betray France for the sake of my ballet career. Once before, Uncle Val interfered to get me into the programme, but I thought that I might have deserved it at that time. I would not be able to live with myself if I had to always wonder whether I could have made it on my own, or whether it was all part of an elaborate arrangement to acquire French government secrets.'

'Oh, Marie-Claire! You had your heart set on this. I am so, so sorry,' Mrs Le Blanc said, hugging her daughter again, struggling to hold back her own tears.

'I have been thinking about this for a while now. I don't know whether I really have my heart set on this anymore. I would be stuck in Moscow, practising ballet eight hours a day until I retire or injure myself beyond recovery, and then what? What do I do when I'm 35 and I can no longer dance..? On top of that, I would only get to see the parts of the world the Russian Government allows me to see, under strict supervision. I would have been a slave, without even knowing it. I am French and I am free! I can do as I like, when I like.'

'We can support any decision you make, as long as you don't make it to please us. I would have to report this incident to the Diplomatic Corps and I am sure that it will have repercussions for our continued stay in Moscow. What *would* you like to do, Marie-Claire?' Mr Le Blanc asked, feeling immensely proud of his daughter.

'I would like to go study art. I enjoy painting and sketching and I feel that I can express myself through the canvas. I enjoy going to museums and appreciating art and I think that I would enjoy learning even more about the history of the great masters and how to perfect my talent.'

'Then we will make it happen. As a French citizen, there could be no better place in the world for you to study art than at the *Sorbonne*. We will send in an application post haste. Some years back, when we took you to Paris the first time, we had an early supper at a brasserie in the Latin Quarter. Do you remember that?'

'Yes, I do! It was the first time I drank wine. I think the place was called *La Bouffe*.'

Mr Le Blanc continued, 'Indeed. On that fateful day I saw a "For Sale" sign on the doorway next to the brasserie. I thought that the building was in an ideal location and went back the next day to have a look at the apartment. It was a spacious penthouse with two bedrooms, which was rather well priced, so I purchased the property. I thought that someday, if you ever did want to go study at the *Sorbonne*, it would be a perfect place for you to live as a student. And now you shall do so.'

'What is going to happen to you with this whole affair, Father? What will the French Government do?'

'I think it is perhaps time for us to move back to Paris as well. I will report on the matter and suggest that they should consider recalling me to France. Your mother and I have been out of the country for too many years now and perhaps it is time to go home. I would like to also start taking a more active hand in managing the family estate in *Chantilly*. It has gone unused for many years and I think if I worked in Paris, we could start using it for weekends. Of course, it would all depend on whether I get recalled or not. In Moscow, these kind of underhanded attempts are par for the course, so it might just be filed and forgotten. If that is the case, you might have to go to Paris alone. Or I can play a trump card and threated to resign if they don't recall me. I would not like to do that, but if it becomes necessary, I can use that avenue.'

'I would have ended up alone in Moscow, eventually. It is unlikely that you would have stayed in this post forever, so if I had joined the Bolshoi, I would have been stuck in Moscow without any family nearby, in the end. Perhaps this turn of events was fortuitous in creating a destiny where I will be much better off. Even if I have to go to Paris alone, you will always have to travel there for work and you will retire to France, perhaps to this family estate in *Chantilly*? Then you will be around. Why have you never mentioned this estate before?' Marie-Claire asked.

'When my parents passed away, they put the estate into a trust. My father never thought that I was a very responsible boy, so they only allowed me to access it when I turned 40. By that age, I was stationed in Italy and enjoying my diplomatic duties, so I did not feel like being burdened with running an estate. I kept it in the trust, which has been maintaining it ever since. Perhaps the time has come to take up the family mantle. I haven't been there in decades.'

'I have only seen this estate once myself. From what I remember, it was a beautiful manor, with sprawling lands,' Mrs Le Blanc added. 'It seems that we have now come to a fork in the road which was most unexpected. We might all end up in Paris soon. I for one, would be happy to move back to France permanently. While it has been nice to see the world, Moscow has not been pleasant. I would fully support requesting a transfer back to Paris and for Marie-Claire to go study art at the *Sorbonne*, staying in the Latin Quarter penthouse. Although I don't doubt she could have looked after herself years ago, it is probably a good time for our little swan to leave the nest and spread her wings.'

'Then it is settled. We will put in an application for Marie-Claire to go study at the *Sorbonne* and I will request a transfer to Paris.' They had spoken late into the evening and everyone was ready to retire. Marie-Claire was still in her ballet outfit. She sat down on her bed and stared at the Degas print that had inspired her to take up ballet so many years ago in Athens. Her feelings were a mixture of relief and anger. *It was over.* She was done with ballet. Like a ball and chain that had come loose, she was now free. But it was not on her terms. She was angry at the KGB which tried to interfere in her life. They had denied her a final recital at the Bolshoi theatre. She had no doubt they would get their just rewards. She took the Degas print off the wall and smashed it over the bedpost.

The school sent someone the next day to enquire what had happened. Mr Le Blanc told them in friendly terms that Marie-Claire had no further wish to be considered for inclusion in the Bolshoi Ballet Company. Her other exams were finished and they were only waiting for her academic record in order to apply at the *Sorbonne*. The school representative was very disappointed by both the decision and the way in which it was communicated. There was a stern rebuke for not informing the panel the previous day at the theatre. Mr Le Blanc accepted full responsibility for the oversight and apologised profusely, also including a case of wine for the panel as part of the act of contrition.

The memo Mr Le Blanc had drafted to the French Diplomatic Corps had been successful. Two days later, a team arrived from Paris to conduct an inquiry. They questioned Mr Le Blanc, as well as Marie-Claire. The team took note of Igor Ivanovic, on his post across the street from the Embassy, still ever the opportunist. Ivan Igorovic was absent during their investigations in Moscow. They had concluded that there was no serious breach of Diplomatic protocol by Mr Le Blanc, but that it would be prudent to replace him in Moscow and acquiesce to his request of a transfer to Paris. They also recommended the posting of additional security personnel to the Embassy, to ensure better cover of the French diplomats when leaving the grounds of the Embassy to enter Moscow. It would, however, take several months to source a replacement for Mr Le Blanc and he would only be able to transfer in January.

A letter of acceptance had arrived from the *Sorbonne* at the end of July. Marie-Claire would be admitted to study Arts. There was a certain finality to the affair when the letter had arrived. The Le Blancs had postponed their annual trip to Paris and the Riviera, until they had more clarity on what the future would hold. They now knew. The family would leave for Paris in two weeks, to settle Marie-Claire in the penthouse apartment off the Boulevard *Saint Michel* in the Latin Quarter. This would give her sufficient time to settle in before the first term started at the end of September. Her time in Moscow was at an end. What might have been a parting of sweet sorrow, had turned into something of an escape. Marie-Claire would never return to Moscow. She was now free to go in search of liberty, equality and fraternity on the banks of the River *Seine*, and live the French dream in Paris.

FINAL SWANSONG IN PARIS, 1958

The customary summer plane trip from Moscow to Paris was different this time around, both because the luggage was considerably more than usual, but mostly because it would be her last. Marie-Claire looked back one last time from the door of the plane at the city which had caused her so much pain and anguish. She left it with a dark heart, harsh lessons learned. Marie-Claire would not need to return again, but would have chosen not to, in any event. She turned her back on the city and its people and boarded the plane, now heading into an uncertain future. The indeterminate nature of what lay ahead was not scary, but rather, exciting.

Marie-Claire arrived in Paris in mid-August, as the summer holidays drew to an end and the Parisian locals returned to their abodes in the city. Upon their arrival, the furniture in the penthouse apartment was covered in sheets, layers of dust coating every surface. It had been unoccupied since Mr Le Blanc purchased it two years prior, and also some time before that. They opened the windows and doors to the patio to air out the stale smelling apartment and to offer an escape to the billowing clouds of dust uprooted with every sheet being pulled off the long unused furniture. Many pieces were antiques or Provençal, but some of it just plain old and in dire need of replacement.

Marie-Claire surveyed the apartment with a critical eye. She relished the opportunity to mould this into a living space that suited her needs and taste. She would, however, probably only have the one chance of doing so with her father's chequebook being readily available to fund the project. Added to this, his guilt about the whole affair in Moscow has created a perfect storm to exploit to the benefit of tasteful, expensive decorations. 'This needs to go,' she said, pointing at a sad looking couch and matching coffee table. 'Would we be able to paint the place out? And I would want to do something decorative with the fireplace, it looks terribly drab at the moment.' The queen was already taking charge of her new domain.

A team of workmen spent a week painting out the apartment and sanding and sealing the floors. Various other bits of long-outstanding maintenance and renovation was performed and burgundy wallpaper added to accentuate the fireplace. Several pieces of furniture arrived from all over the city, completing the look of stylish elegance that Marie-Claire was aiming for. The kitchen remodel was done in the next two weeks, along with the two bathrooms. By the end, it was all stunning. Marie-Claire was pleased with her fancy apartment, a shining tribute to classic good taste.

Mr and Mrs Le Blanc attended the welcoming ceremony for new students at the *Sorbonne*. Their arrival at the University brought back fond memories for Mr Le Blanc, an alumnus from many years before. The couple and their daughter joined hundreds of other parents and first-year students in the Grand Amphitheatre. "Grand" was probably a very apt description of the massive hall, bedecked in shiny wood. Light streamed in through the massive skylight above the stage. The Rector gave a moving welcome speech to all those present, followed by a student representative. The ceremony became dull quite quickly after the Rector finished and Marie-Claire sat staring at the large mural by *Pierre Puvis de Chavannes* behind the stage, getting lost in the colourful characters participating in a ceremony under the trees.

Once the formalities were done they lingered around campus, finalising her registration process. Marie-Claire could feel the influence of hundreds of years of great minds oozing out of every stone of the age-old university. The combined knowledge of many generations of great Frenchmen filled the halls. Her courses for the semester included Art history, Art philosophy, Modern Art, Performing Art and Fine Arts. It was a full programme, but still left room to enjoy herself in the various student social activities.

Her parents left Paris, Moscow bound, for what would be the last time. In January, their relocation back to France would be finalised. Marie-Claire was sad to see them go when she said her farewells at *Le Bourget* airport. They had been in her life for almost ten years now and she would miss their presence. 'Thank you Father. Thank you Mother. I appreciate everything you have done for me over the years. I will miss you dearly and I will look forward to your return to Paris. I love you very much.'

'We love you too, our lovely Marie-Claire. You must enjoy your student days. You are now past the times of having to practise ballet for many hours every day. Live your life! Experience Paris and all the sights and sounds it has to offer!' Their parting words left her in tears on the runway, staring after the government plane, until it disappeared in the distance. She felt alone, but not abandoned. They would return to her.

The government chauffeur drove her back to the apartment. She looked at the city through new eyes, no longer a tourist, but someone living here. The more mundane places, which did not concern tourists, now became of interest-the local green grocer, the laundromat, the stationery shop. She sat down on the new couch in her apartment and gave a deep sigh. It was not a sigh of resignation, but rather a sigh of comfort. Of ownership. The empty space above the fireplace bothered her. It needed something special. She would keep an eye out for a suitable piece.

Two weeks into the semester, she came home after class to find an envelope addressed to her under her door. *What could this possibly be?* She dropped her book bag on the couch and opened the envelope with a practised nail. *An invitation to a party!* "Dear Marie-Claire, you are hereby cordially invited to attend a Halloween Party at my residence on 31 October. Come dressed up and enjoy an evening of foreign fun and frivolity. Best wishes, Yves Montand." His address appeared on the back of the black stationery in silver lettering. *Oh, dear Yves!* Father must have told him she was now studying in Paris. *It's so nice of him to extend the invitation to his party,* Marie-Claire thought. It would offer her a perfect opportunity to make some new acquaintances. Halloween could not come soon enough! She thought of some costume ideas. Weighing up several possibilities, she finally had an epiphany. *It would be brilliant!* The costume might require some interesting footwork to source, but she had no doubt she would be the talk of the party.

Three weeks later, the day had arrived. She donned her costume with some effort and finally left the apartment, approaching the taxi waiting for her on the opposite side of *Boul'Mich*. A cacophony of wolf whistles erupted from the early evening crowd at *La Bouffe* as she passed. She had decided to *own* the outfit, to *be* the character. Strutting past the rows of outside tables, she got into the waiting taxi. The driver did a double take as he glanced at her in the mirror. 'Where to, missy?' She gave him Yves's address and they sped off into the early evening.

She rang the doorbell of the penthouse apartment in *Les Marais*. Yves opened up, dressed as Zorro in a black outfit and sword. 'Oh my! You are going to be popular in that outfit, Ms Kyle. Welcome Marie-Claire! So glad you could join us. Come in, come in.' The almost matching duo entered the living room and a shocked hush fell over the gathered crowd, before everyone returned to some form of discussion again several moments later. She had come as Catwoman and the black, figure-hugging leather outfit and high-heeled boots made quite the impact on the male populace in the living room. A matching leather cat mask and bullwhip completed the outfit perfectly, making for a wicked costume which immediately became the topic of discussion in seventeen conversations around the room.

The host offered her a drink and introduced her to some of the partygoers. 'Marie-Claire, may I introduce you to Sacha Distel and Serge Gainsbourg? Gents, meet Marie-Claire Le Blanc.'

'An absolute pleasure to make your acquaintance,' Sacha responded. He was wearing a toga, with some kind of foliage around his head. Yves grabbed a passing woman by the elbow. She was not wearing a costume of any kind. 'Iris, meet Marie-Claire. She is an art student at the Sorbonne and the daughter of an old friend of mine. This is Iris Clert. She owns a fabulous gallery, definitely make an effort to see it.'

'Lovely to meet you Iris. I'd love to do that! Art always excites me.'

'Come Marie-Claire, walk with me. Excuse us, please,' he nodded to the two gentleman and Iris, now involved in a discussion on antique frames. 'I have some more people for you to meet, my dear. You only get one chance to be accepted by this lot, so make it count!'

Yves took her around the room and introduced her to a veritable who's who of Paris society. She met the fashion icon Gloria Guinness and her husband Thomas; Mrs Daisy Fellowes, the editor of the Parisian version of *Harper's Bazaar*; Charles de Noailles, a nobleman and patron of the arts and his lovely wife Marie-Laure; Jacqueline de Ribes, who was a philanthropist, business women and ballet choreographer; Marie-Hélène de Rothschild, a member of the famous banking family; Francine Weisweiller and her husband, who were also neighbours of the De Noailles, and Jean Cocteau, the famous poet and film producer. Those were only the ones she remembered. After having met fifteen strangers in as many minutes, she was struggling to recall who else she had been introduced to.

It was a whirlwind introduction to the upper end of Parisian society. Everyone was very friendly towards Marie-Claire. The men for more obvious reasons, but even the women, who admired her courage for wearing such a risqué outfit. She had marvellous discussions on art, fashion, cinema, horse racing and every other pastime that the rich and famous indulged in. Towards

179

the end of the night, Yves found her outside on the patio, leaning over the railing with a half filled glass of brandy. 'Thank you very much for inviting me this evening, Yves. It was really a fabulous party. And thanks for introducing me to everyone. It would have taken me years to meet this many people.'

'It's my pleasure, Marie-Claire. It must be hard to be in a new city without knowing anyone, so I am happy I could help. You seem to have made a tremendous impression on everyone, heaven knows why, in that outfit,' he chuckled, 'but nevertheless, they are all glad to have met you. I think you can probably look forward to many more invitations to social functions from everyone in the room. They will not forget meeting you anytime soon. I will pass on your details to people that enquire, with your permission.'

'Permission granted, most certainly.'

The party had slowly started dying down in the late hour, people either going home, or moving on the next affair, which might still be in full swing. Marie-Claire greeted her gracious host and waited for the taxi he ordered downstairs. When she was dropped off, the now drunken students at *La Bouffe* were once again excelling in impropriety towards her, with all kinds of rude suggestions, whistles and gestures. She ignored several invitations to drinks as she passed. Marie-Claire smiled as she entered the green door. *Men are so predictable*, she thought.

The university term sped by with rapid speed. Having now been accepted in the social circles of the high and well-heeled, hardly a weekend passed where Marie-Claire was not invited to some social event. Marie-Claire spent a sad Christmas by herself in Paris. Although she had not celebrated Christmas until she was eight, she had now gotten used to having family around to share it with. At the end of January, Mr and Mrs Le Blanc arrived from Moscow. Marie-Claire was ecstatic to see them again. They rented a duplex apartment close to the *Invalides* in the 7th arrondissement, a mere twenty-minute walk away from her apartment. She might have gotten quite used to living on her own, but she was very glad that her parents were back within easy visiting distance.

Marie-Claire found her studies very stimulating and the atmosphere at university was totally different from what she had experienced at school, either in Greece or in Moscow. The one subject she loathed, was Performing Arts. She had covered the majority of the theory in her time at the Bolshoi School and she simply did not see any point in attending the practical dance classes. Her lecturer called her to stay behind class on a day. 'Marie-Claire, we never see you in the practical classes. Although we do not grade you for attendance, I am afraid that you are unlikely to pass your practical exam if you do not apply yourself and attend class. You seem like a bright girl and it would be a terrible shame if you failed,' the concerned Professor Caville lectured her.

'Thanks for the concern, Professor, but I am quite certain I will be fine in my practical exam. I believe we have to do a dance performance in the style of our choosing?'

'Yes, dear, that is correct. But you have not practised at all! The marking regime is very strict.'

'I am done practising. I will pass,' was the curt response, 'May I be excused now?'

Professor Caville was disappointed that Marie-Claire did not see the need to practise with the rest of the class. Unfortunately, the department policy was to be extremely critical in the marking of students who regularly missed practical classes. Marie-Claire would not pass. No one who attended less than half of their classes ever did. She had done her duty by raising these concerns with the student. If common sense did not prevail, it might do so in the following semester, when she had to redo the course. *C'est la vie.*

At the end of February, the time for practical exams had arrived. The marking panel was seated in the front row of the Grand Amphitheatre at the Sorbonne, the small gathering of students on the course sitting in the block behind them, each having a turn to take to the stage. All the students did their absolute best to impress the faculty staff, which also included an external moderator, *Jacqueline de Ribes*. The eager students followed, one after the other. Some attempts were almost passable, while others barely scraped by. At the end, only Marie-Claire was left to perform. She sat in the back row of the gathered students in a long brown overcoat, seemingly uninterested in even trying to perform. 'Marie-Claire Le Blanc,' she was called to the stage. She walked up the stairs, handing a record to the student responsible for the managing the music score with a nonchalant gesture. 'Marie-Claire has not attended any classes this semester, so I do not expect much from this performance. The critical marking criteria would apply in this case,' Professor Caville whispered to the rest of the judging panel. Jacqueline de Ribes raised an eyebrow when she recognised Marie-Claire. She noticed the young woman's shoes and then vaguely recalled some mention of the Bolshoi in relation to the girl. Her suspicions were that this would not be any ordinary performance.

Marie-Clair took to the centre of the stage. As the music started, she dropped her coat with a flourish, raising her arms above her head and revealing a spectacular black ballet dress studded with glittering crystals. Tchaikovsky sounded over the record player and the dance of the black swan began. Although she had not danced in many months, her muscle memory was faultless. Four years' worth of classes at the Bolshoi School were not forgotten in a couple of months. In a way, it was like her body was a storage vessel for the energy of this one last dance. A dance she prepared for over many months and yet, because of circumstances, simply did not come to pass. The movement flowed out of Marie-Claire like water from the sluice gates of a dam filled beyond its capacity, every drop pushing to exit the unnatural confinement of the enclosing wall. The judging panel sat in amazed silence, the student body equally shocked by the unexpected precision of what they were witnessing.

What was supposed to have been the preconceived task of failing the last, absentee student of the day, had suddenly turned into a technical judging exercise which the panel was simply not qualified to perform with any degree of adequacy. This was above their pay-grade, and the pay-grade above that.

Jacqueline de Ribes was the only panellist who could even start to cast an opinion on the technically complex display with the Russian styling, which they were witnessing on the stage of the Grand Amphitheatre of the *Sorbonne*. The Russian training was not even discernible to anyone else in the room, not being ballet aficionados. Marie-Claire produced a performance unlike any she had ever achieved in the past. The leaps were high and true and the landings pinpoint. Her poses were like sculpted marble and the choreography of it all was breathtaking, everything flowing together in a flawless ballet routine, if ever there was one.

The music finally died away and the performance concluded, the open-mouthed crowd supremely disappointed that the spectacle had to end so soon, for they would have to travel to the Bolshoi Theatre in Moscow to experience such a display of movement again and even then, it might not have measured up to what they had witnessed today. It was the perfect final swansong for Marie-Claire. She had achieved a level of excellence in the art that most could only dream of. And then she was done. Forever. She took a final, lingering bow and ran off the stage, tears streaming down her face. The gathered audience were still silently considering the magnificent episode they had just seen, and then, the cheering erupted with a mad roar, which created great confusion amongst students who entered the hall from outside to observe the source of the commotion. A group of students were apparently giving a standing ovation to an empty stage. But those in the audience could recognise what they had witnessed. They knew. They knew that one of their own had broken the judges, and it was glorious.

A WEEKEND IN THE COUNTRY, 1959

Marie-Claire found herself having lunch at *La Bouffe* on her own, while waiting for her parents to swing by and pick her up. This was not an uncomfortable situation for her, as she often had drinks and meals on her own at the *brasserie*. She had adopted it as her "local" and was a regular client, now well known to all the staff. The seat opposite her contained a leather weekend bag, packed for the outing which lay ahead. The Le Blanc family would make their first exploratory visit to Mr Le Blanc's family manor, in the *Île de France* area near *Chantilly*. He had decided to start using the estate again, as was his birth right. Having not been there for more than two decades, this would both serve as Marie-Claire's introduction to the estate, as well as a reintroduction for Mr Le Blanc and his wife. He had fond memories of growing up on the property and wanted to reconnect to an abandoned part of his life.

It was a lovely spring day and the flowers bloomed all over Paris, as Marie-Claire savoured a glass of white wine with her rabbit stew. She observed the new busboy at the restaurant, who seemed far too noble for such a menial job. He carried the dishes with intense pride and held his head high, not being put down by some of the less flattering comments from the *Maître'd*. His demeanour could probably be explained by being a bit older, and wiser, than the usual busboys. 'Good afternoon, Mademoiselle. May I clear your plate?'

'Good afternoon. Yes, you may. You're new here,' a statement of fact by Marie-Claire. 'I have not seen you around before. What's your name?' she enquired.

'Yes, I started this morning. Brand new to Paris as well. I am Peter. Pleased to meet you.'

'Marie-Claire. Likewise, Peter,' she responded. 'I am sure we'll be seeing plenty of each other here, if you manage to keep the job. Clément can be a bit of a tough task master,' she said, referring to the *Maître'd*.

'All I have to do is keep my head down and outlive him. Old men die eventually,' was the rather unusual response.

'Be sure that you do,' she said, laughing at his candour.

Marie-Claire settled her bill just as her father pulled up across the street from the restaurant. Darting across the two lanes of afternoon traffic, Mr Le Blanc was out of the car when she arrived. The shiny black Delahaye 180 was a new addition. He gave her a quick kiss, loaded her bag in the trunk alongside several others and opened the rear door for her. 'Hello Mother, are you well?' she greeted Mrs Le Blanc in the front as she shifted across the wide back seat, settling partly behind her father and giving her a kiss on the cheek.

'I am well, my dear. How are you? How is school going?' her mother responded, launching into an immediate inquiry, as only a mother can. They continued catching up as Mr Le Blanc wove the stately car through Parisian traffic, which was picking up as the long weekend approached. Friday was a public holiday and people were finishing earlier than usual, to celebrate their Labour Day weekend.

Once they reached the outskirts of Paris, traffic became more manageable, although there was still a steady stream of cars heading to the northern countryside of *Île de France*. The exodus comprised like-minded Parisians who were all looking forward to spending a splendid weekend removed from the urban sprawl to the south. Rural France was dressed in bright green leaves and sunshine for the occasion, a magnificent drive. The trip was not a long one and half an hour later Mr Le Blanc turned off the main road to *Chantilly*, towards the village of *Gouvieux*. A short distance down the road, they turned in at a tall gate on the right, bordered by a high stone wall. An English Tudor style manor house was visible in the distance down the drive. Mr Le Blanc pressed the hooter three times, the pre-arranged signal announcing their arrival.

The elderly groundsman walked down the drive in a red flannel shirt and a flat cap and unlocked the gate, which swung open silently on oiled hinges. 'Good afternoon Mr Le Blanc. Welcome to *Château de Petite Anglaise.* Please proceed through to the manor house, I will be along shortly.' Mr Le Blanc parked in front of the house, everyone exiting the large car, little need to stretch their legs after the short drive in the expansive vehicle. Marie-Claire was very impressed with the property. The house was about the same size as the Embassy in Athens, although probably not large compared to properties in the area, judging by the name. All around the property, the grounds appeared well cared for and everything seemed in its place. The caretaker arrived with a quick shuffle having closed the main gate behind them. 'I am Rémy Bouchard. My family has been looking after the *Château* for as long as your family have owned it. I believe my brother Jean was here when you were a boy. Welcome to your heritage! It is good to have a Le Blanc on the property again, it has been too long.'

'I remember your brother well, Rémy. I spent many an hour hiding from him in the stables as a boy. It was with great sadness that I heard of his passing. Thank you for keeping up the good work here. Everything seems to be in excellent shape. The old house looks just as I remember it.'

Rémy took the Le Blancs on a tour of the estate for the rest of the afternoon, pointing out the various buildings to Marie-Claire, or pieces of maintenance of which he was particularly proud to Mr Le Blanc. The stables stood empty, a sad memory of the thriving stud farm that was once the pride of the Le Blanc family and well known in the area, now long since abandoned in the absence of a landlord. The estate was lush and green, and large trees over-grown, very little open space remaining of what might have previously been paddocks used for horse training. Some painted fencing was still visible in the distance, the last remnants of the horse camps of old.

They returned to the house, their luggage having been moved from the car into their rooms. Mrs Bouchard was waiting for them in the entrance hall. If the house was ever shut down and boarded up, there was now no sign of not having been occupied for two decades. The air smelled fresh and flower arrangements liberally filled the hallways. 'Mr Le Blanc, Mrs Le Blanc, lovely to meet you. And the young lady. There is an invitation that arrived this morning,' she handed over a thick card with golden lettering on it, along with an elaborate crest. It was a dinner invitation from one of the neighbours for the following evening.

'However did anyone know we'd be here?' Mr Le Blanc wondered out loud.

'I'm afraid that the sudden large orders of new linen and consumables drew some attention at the local market in *Chantilly*. It's a small community and everyone knows each other quite well,' Mr Bouchard explained.

'Well, in that case, I guess we better attend, so we can start fitting in,' Mrs Le Blanc said.

They retired to a covered patio on the top floor, indicative of the colonial design of the house, where there was a spread of snacks prepared for them. Mr Bouchard offered everyone beverages, before excusing himself.

'What a lovely way to start the weekend, a dinner party with the neighbours,' Marie-Claire said. 'Do you know them?'

'No, not really. My father used to be good friends with them, but I don't remember that too well.' The sun set over the French countryside as the Le Blancs enjoyed their drinks on the veranda. At eight thirty, Mrs Bouchard rang the dinner bell and they went downstairs to the dining room for an exquisite meal. The inside decorations of the house were an interesting mix of English and French, the house itself quite English, while the decorations and furniture were French. Dark wooden panelling on the walls were contrasted with a French oak dining room table and ornate French chairs. Mrs Bouchard served them a delicious three course meal before retiring for the evening. Mr and Mrs

Le Blanc settled in the main bedroom, while Marie-Claire used a guest room. Her father's childhood room was still there, almost untouched. Her room had the same mix of French and English interior design as the rest of the house. She wondered how a typical English manor house ended up in the French countryside.

Marie-Claire woke up with a damp pillow in the morning. The family enjoyed breakfast on the veranda. 'I want to go into *Chantilly* this morning. I don't think many shops and attractions will be open on a public holiday, but I'd like to see what it looks like nowadays,' Mr Le Blanc suggested. When they opened the garages to get their car, they made a surprising find. There was a 1918 Rolls Royce Silver Ghost parked in the garage, the vintage car apparently still being maintained after all these years. 'Let's take the Rolls to town!' Marie-Claire said excitedly.

The trip to town was not a long one, the Rolls Royce running perfectly along the country lanes into the little hamlet of *Chantilly*. To their great delight, most shops were open for business on the public holiday, the locals realising the value that weekend tourists bring to the local economy. They spent the morning exploring the famous *Château* of *Chantilly* and the *Musée Condé* housed therein. The *château* was housed on two islands in a lake joined together, the small and large island housing the respective parts of the buildings. The *Petit Château* dated from the 16th century and the *Grand Chateau* from the 19th. There was a wondrous collection of tapestries and medieval artefacts in the museum. They also visited the nearby Grand Stables, which housed 240 horses and twice as many dogs back in the 18th century. Their day trip ended at the race track, considered by many as one of the prettiest in all of Europe. The stables behind the back straight added to the royal looking appearance of the course. There were no races scheduled for the day, but some of the local trainers were putting their charges through their paces on the race track, despite it being a public holiday. Marie-Claire looked at some of the owners in the stands, observing their horses and the appointed trainers. She thought it appeared to be an interesting occupation, owing horses. *Perhaps someday she could do that for a living.*

They drove back to the house in the late afternoon, which did not give them a lot of time to prepare for the dinner they had been invited to. Mr Le Blanc found a dinner jacket amongst the clothes from his late father which he could wear to dinner, although he had to remember not to raise his arms above his head, for fear of the ancient jacket parting at the seams. The two ladies dressed up as elegantly as they could with the wardrobe they had packed. Marie-Claire wore a black cocktail dress, which was probably a little too short for a formal evening function. Being nineteen and having legs shaped to perfection by many years of ballet, this fashion *faux pas* would probably be gladly forgiven if the host was a male. Mrs Le Blanc wore a slightly longer summer skirt and blouse, which was stylishly dressed up with a navy jacket from the forgotten collection of Mr Le Blanc's late mother.

They took the Rolls Royce to the neighbours' event, as it was a pleasant evening and there was no rain predicted. They turned right out of their gate and a mere stone's throw away they turned left off the country lane, into the embellished gate of the neighbouring estate. A guard in a crisp, mid-eastern looking red jacket welcomed them to the estate, pointing out the most direct route to take to the manor house. The *château* looked as typically French as was possible and one half expected Marie-Antoinette to greet them at the door, as the view visible through the open doorway was regal enough to remind of many rooms in the palace of *Versailles*. Their classic Rolls Royce fit perfectly amongst the ranks of the other luxury vehicles parked off the drive in the distance. A valet greeted them and opened the car doors. 'Good evening Ambassador Le Blanc.' Someone had done their homework, although not completely. A second servant, dressed as smartly as the first, announced their entrance to the gathered guests in the large entrance foyer. 'Ambassador Henri Le Blanc, Mrs Josephine Le Blanc and Miss Marie-Claire Le Blanc.'

The gathered guests looked in their direction, some gave a nod of recognition, before carrying on with their muted discussions of business, politics and the affairs of the day. The *château* was splendidly grand and the interiors were reminiscent of a royal palace of some sort. Expensive French art adorned the walls, as well as an inordinate amount of paintings of horses, and finally also Arabic looking men dressed in royal outfits. Marie-Claire could still not figure out who their neighbours were and her father had chosen not to divulge the information either. 'You'll see my dear. You'll see. Good things come to those who wait. Even better things come to those who wait patiently,' was his cryptic response to the line of questioning. A young man came down the stairs in a royal outfit similar to that worn on many of the paintings and when the servant announced his arrival, it was met with applause from those gathered in the room. 'His Royal Highness Prince Shah Karim Al Hussaini, Aga Khan the fourth.' Their host for the evening had arrived.

Marie-Claire observed the Aga Khan as he entered the room filled with guests. He was one of very few of those in her age group attending the event. The prince was a handsome man, who exhibited a bearing beyond his years. He had only very recently finished his final exams at Harvard and accordingly, he welcomed his guests in well-enunciated, formal English. 'I wish to welcome you all to my family Estate. This evening we will be honouring all those industrious workers that make France a great country and all those from around the world that try to emulate them unsuccessfully.' Young, and already an accomplished politician. *Did Father perhaps tutor him at some stage?* Marie-Claire thought, hiding her smile behind a glass of champagne. He continued addressing the gathering for another ten minutes, before everyone migrated to a large patio behind the *château*, overlooking the sprawling rear garden and surrounding forest.

The guests mulled around in the early evening, snacking on *canapés* and sampling the fine French champagne on offer. Mr and Mrs Le Blanc was talking to someone Mr Le Blanc knew from work, a conversation that very quickly bored Marie-Claire. She slipped away and sat on one of the stone railings overlooking the garden. It was a beautiful view in the light of the full moon. 'Good evening. I hope the party is not boring you?' It was the host speaking to her.

'Not at all, your highness! It is actually all the excitement that forced me to take a brief respite here, to compose myself and give my beating heart a chance to settle,' Marie-Claire responded sweetly.

'I don't believe that for a second! I may be young, but I am not that naïve,' he said with a laugh. 'Please call me Karim. I apologise if the party is a little slow.'

'Don't worry about it, one needs to be careful with the older folk, lest we require the services of an ambulance before long. I am Marie-Claire. Pleased to meet you, Karim. You have a beautiful home. You seem to have quite a collection of equestrian art. Are you an avid rider?'

'I dabble a bit. I am more of an owner than a rider. I have inherited two stud farms from my grandfather and there are many years of successful breeding behind the paintings. Do you ride?' The Prince looked slightly ill at ease talking to Marie-Claire, not quite knowing what to do with his hands.

'Oh no, I only appreciate from afar. I am more of an art aficionado, so it's really the rest of your collection that intrigues me.'

'Perhaps I can show you the rest of me at some stage.' The prince suddenly realised his *faux pas* and blushed profusely. '… the rest of my collection. I can show you the rest of my collection! Oh, brother…' Marie-Claire laughed at his Freudian slip. He was just like most of the young men in her class, still a bit awkward around girls.

'That would be lovely! Seeing your collection, I mean,' she responded, eliciting an even deeper shade of red out of the hapless man. 'Don't worry about it, it can happen to the best of us. Besides, I am sure the rest of you will be just as fine as your collection' she repaired the damage with a wink. Marie-Claire continued flirting a little with the young prince as they discussed her art studies, his recently completed Degree in oriental history, and shared tales of their various travels around Europe.

Frustratingly, the dinner bell echoed an end to the conversation. 'It was an absolute pleasure making your acquaintance, Marie-Claire. Will I be able to see you again?'

'Come look me up when you are in Paris. You know how to get hold of my parents, they'll give you my details,' she leaned forward and gave him a peck on the cheek. 'Lovely to meet you, Karim. Perhaps you'll have the pleasure of me again soon.' She strolled towards the dining hall, the young man struggling to keep his knees from buckling in her wake.

She joined her parents at the dinner setting, an incredibly ornate walnut table stretching out to fill the room to capacity, twenty guests comfortably seated on either side. They sat halfway down the one side with the Prince making out the head of the table. 'And what happened to you, young lady? You just disappeared?' Mr Le Blanc enquired, feigning mock indignation.

'Oh, I was just playing outside in the moonlight a bit father, you know how these things go,' she responded with a smile, looking towards the head of the table. The Prince seemed to momentarily choke on his soup, before blushing blood red.

Oh dear, my girl. Whatever have you gotten yourself into now...? Mr Le Blanc pondered, following her gaze.

REFLECTIONS ON PARIS

44 Rue Francisque Gay

Quartier Latin

Paris

75005

12 August 1960

My dearest Ekaterina

I hope that you are well and that your career at the Bolshoi is still a sterling tale of success. It has been two years since I left the stage in Moscow, choosing not to perform. The decision has changed my destiny and although there was an empty hole in my life, reflecting on the unfulfilled opportunity of having my moment on the Bolshoi Theatre stage, the chance eventually came to have my moment in the limelight. Although it was a different stage from the one I imagined, it gave me the closure I needed, by ending my ballet career on a high and allowing me to have my final swansong. One of my courses at the Sorbonne was Performing Arts and for our final exam, we had to do a recital for marks. I knew this would give me the opportunity to give the final performance I was denied in Moscow. It went splendidly!

Both the judges and my classmates were caught totally unawares by my performance and I feel it went off flawlessly. The relief and realisation of finally being able to have my last dance was so intense that I could not contain the tears when I was done. I left the stage in a great hurry, but I was told afterwards

I got a standing ovation which was so loud that students in the corridors entered the university auditorium to see what the great racket was all about. The judges gave me an A+ for the dance routine and the lecturer sheepishly indicated that she was wrong to have thought I would not pass. Of course, she had no reason to believe I wouldn't fail, so it was actually a fair assumption.

The external moderator was Jacqueline de Ribes, who looked me up after the term and offered me the lead role in one of her upcoming ballet productions at the Paris Opera House. She said I could be the next Zizi Jeanmaire. For a moment, I considered it. But only for a moment. I have long felt that my final performance in the Grand Amphitheatre gave me closure and allowed me to bring my dancing career to a graceful conclusion, on my own terms. I therefore courteously declined, although I do not think she understood why I wouldn't want to carry on dancing. Perhaps someday I will tell her of my time in Moscow.

I am enjoying my classes at the Sorbonne immensely. I finished off the academic year with the firm knowledge I made the right choice by abandoning the Bolshoi and seeking my destiny elsewhere. My lectures are fascinating and I feel I am gaining a deeper appreciation for art every day. My artistic talent is also being honed and the new techniques I have learnt really opened up new horizons for me to express my inner feelings through the canvas. I seem to have a recurring theme that almost haunts my work. If I don't choose a specific subject matter, I always end up drawing some version a body, lying on cobbled stones. I cannot understand why this image haunts my art so, but somehow I feel it is probably better not to suppress this, but rather to try and give it substance in my drawings and paintings.

We also do sculptures and pottery, but I do not have the same success of expression in these other art forms. I really feel that painting and drawing is my forte and I am enjoying it much more than I ever enjoyed my dancing in Moscow. The art history classes are fascinating and we have the opportunity to do volunteer work at the *Louvre,* assisting the curating staff in all manner of ways. I have been observing their restoration of some of the older pieces in the museum and the care and effort which goes into each brush stroke of the process really gives new meaning to the concept of patience. Someday, I think I might want to do something like that for a living. And of course, keep painting my own work as well.

There are a lot of artists staying in the Latin Quarter and *Saint Germain des Prés*. When I move around the neighbourhood, there is never a shortage of struggling artists, almost on every corner. Of course, one also comes across some of the not-so-struggling artists from time to time. I once saw Pablo Picasso around the neighbourhood of *Montmartre*. He is an absolute genius and must have been visiting his old haunts from the coast. I vowed to look him up next time I was visiting Cannes to engage him in conversation and pick his artistic mind. There are quite a number of artists' colonies in these parts and the students in my class started embedding themselves in this culture of the area. It does make for very interesting discussions over wine. Some of the artists can be so pretentious, but others are just normal people with immense talent. As my circle of artistic friends expand, it is also morphing into other sectors of the arts. Paris is host to a large number of literary geniuses and their writing can often inspire the art I produce, while my art also occasionally inspires poetry and musing amongst this grouping. It is like everyone drinks from a common pool of inspiration and I don't think something like that exists in any other city in the world. Paris is undoubtedly the centre of the art universe and anyone telling you differently, is a bare-faced liar.

The city is a truly amazing place in which to be an artist. There is simply an abundance of inspiring subject matter. In *Montmartre*, there are whole colonies of artists focusing on drawing and painting Paris for the tourist market. Some of these artists have real talent, but I think some of them are only able to reproduce the same, sad landmarks time and again. It is almost like taking a black-and-white photograph. You get the idea, but the reality of the colours is not there. *Montmartre* is actually vibrant and colourful, so I do not see it as a suitable artistic challenge to reproduce this colourful bouquet on canvas. Personally, I like the challenge presented by the various cemeteries in Paris. The monotone nature of the gravestones means that one has to play with light to elicit any depth of expression and one has to use many shadings of the grey to create the prefect semblance. It also offers amazing opportunities to play with the deep green of the grass, or a single flower left in a pot, against the drab colour of the tombs.

The Eiffel Tower offers another amazing perspective of the city, although it quite the challenge to get one's art materials up the 300 metre height of the building. Looking down on Paris from that height gives one an almost god-like feeling, the people below seem like small, insignificant specs in the greater scheme of things. Smiting one of them from far above would not create a stir that is noticeable at such a height, unless they are a ruler, then one might notice a parade down the *Champs-Élysées* in the aftermath.

Besides the inspirational nature of the city, Paris is truly an amazing place to live, even for those not choosing to do so for inspiration. The Parisians themselves are a friendly people and I think tourists just don't get to see the underlying essence of the city. They see the thin veneer which the city reserves for them to admire, not allowing exploration of the deeper recesses of what the city and its people are really all about. If one delves down deep beneath this superficial façade, one gets to experience the *real* Paris. The Paris of passion and of food that is prepared, not from a recipe book, but from the heart of the chef, with recipes handed down by word of mouth for centuries. It usually takes a journey of at least five blocks outside the main tourist areas to start getting to these *real* establishments. The owners recognise other Parisians and the camaraderie between the locals is something one should write a book about and not simply a few short sentences in a letter.

I have been fortunate enough to have been accepted into the circles of, what could probably be considered, the high society of Paris. I met Yves Montand prior to his concert in Moscow and he was kind enough to introduce me to many of his friends at a party he hosted in Paris. This single introduction has led to many further invitations and there is now hardly a social event that passes without my attendance being requested by the host. Although I enjoy these parties and social occasions, I do not think it is reflective of the *real* Paris. The parties are held to impress the other attendees and very rarely to share with them a genuine experience of enjoyment of the city. It is almost as superficial as the experience that the tourists have of the Paris, which is actually quite sad. Although the superficiality of it all cannot be shifted from the mind, it is, none-the-less, an interesting crowd to mingle with. Édith Piaf, Serge Gainsbourg and Sacha Distel are regulars at the parties, giving one insight into the life of the musicians of Paris. Their trials and tribulations are different for those of the average Parisian, but also often the same. Similarly, artists such as Salvador Dali and Jean Hugo, gives one insight into the soul of the painter, which is often rent into different portions, differences which are reflected in the work they produce, depending on which part is in control at any given time.

There are also great writers, actors and producers at these social events. Although the level of conversations are immensely deep, one still does not get to know anyone very well. Everyone still hides their deepest fears and thoughts. One might be able to make educated guesses, based on their opinions on various topics, but no-one reveals their true selves at these parties. They sometimes come close when they are high on absinthe, but even that is a rare occasion.

In my search for the *real* Paris, I have also discovered an even deeper layer of truth in the city. The layer that many would not talk about and most never get to experience. This is the layer one does not get to explore at the high society gatherings of artists and poets. Perhaps if you ever come to Paris, I will introduce you to this other side. I have found this layer particularly appealing and I feel that here I can really be myself. It was like digging a trench in the street and them stumbling across the Catacombs. It's different from everything else, but beautiful in its complexity.

My parents have now permanently relocated to my Father's ancestral home in *Chantilly*. He initially rented them an apartment close to the parliament buildings where he is working, but they have now made the move to the little hamlet to the north of Paris. The *château* itself has the look of an English manor and the surrounding forests are gorgeous. It is amazing to think such relaxing surroundings can be found so close to the city. I go there at least one weekend a month and find it very easy to unwind from the hustle and bustle of the city. I think one of the neighbours has taken a bit of a fancy to me. He is a couple of years older than me and is of Royal Middle-Eastern descent. He makes every effort to visit me whenever I am there for the weekend.

I try not to encourage him too much, as I think it is very unlikely that it will ever be able to develop onto a relationship of any substance. As much as he is handsome and a pleasant man, I think I would have to convert to Islam if I were ever to consider marrying him. That prospect simply does not appeal to me. In the meantime, I think I should just push such thoughts aside and enjoy his company, which is pleasant enough. He is well educated and an interesting character. He has visited me on occasion in Paris, but I try to avoid him when he comes calling unannounced, even if I am at home. While the impropriety of such a thing could be excused, I do not wish him to think I am constantly sitting alone at home waiting for him to make an appearance, to rescue me from a lonely existence.

I don't quite know whether the countryside is doing mother too well. She seems a bit pale nowadays when I see her, despite the abundant country sun, and I think all the stress of moving from Moscow to France might have finally caught up with her. When we went to the Riviera for our annual summer vacation, she spent a lot of time in the room, lacking the energy to go out and enjoy herself. Father is really worried about her and so am I. He scheduled a visit for her to see a Physician when we got back to Paris.

The trip to *Juan-les-Pins* was even more memorable than usual this time around. With Father staying at Mother's side in the suite at the *Le Provençal* or around the hotel pool, I was left to my own devices. I arranged a day trip to *Cannes*, to make good of my vow to look up Pablo Picasso the next time I was there. By pure luck, I ran into him at a *café* overlooking the harbour. He was amicable enough and I managed to engage him in conversation. His dark eyes seemed to stare into my being, perhaps he could recognise the soul of another artist, although not one as prolific or remarkable as him, or maybe noticing whatever it was that has me waking up in tears every other morning. He invited me to join him for lunch and we spent a wonderful afternoon discussing his art. Picasso was passionate about his paintings and was telling me of a series of paintings he was working on three years ago, based on *Las Meninas* by Diego Velázquez. He decided to reinterpret, analyse and recreate the painting and doing works focusing on only portions of it. I found it fascinating that one can be so single-mindedly tuned in on a particular painting that a whole series of 58 works can flow from this. I guess that is what truly makes him the genius he is.

Mr Picasso is busy looking to move inland and he has identified *Mougins* as one of the places he would want to settle to live out his days. We have a lot of common acquaintances, as I now move in the circles in Paris which he frequented when he was still living in the city. Picasso told me about the *Café Au Lupin Agile* in *Montmartre*, where he once did a painting in order to pay his bar tab. Although I know the place well, I was sad to hear his artwork no longer resides there, as it was sold by the owner in 1912 for a meagre twenty dollars.

Picasso invited me to visit him at his house in *Cannes* the following week and said he would like to do a painting of me. I was very flattered. It is not every day that one of the most famous artists in the world expresses an interest to paint you! Alas, I was not able to visit him at *La Villa California* the next week, as

Mother's condition had worsened, moving her skin tone from pale to yellow, forcing us to cut our vacation short and return to Paris to seek medical attention from a specialist physician. I sent him a note, promising to visit when I was in the area again. Although I was very disappointed at not being able to pose for the genius, my concern for Mother's health far outweighed any artistic opportunity and returning to Paris with her was paramount. There would be other occasions to make an appointment to see him in action behind his easel. At least I got to spend an afternoon in the company of such a magnificent artist and I would have the inside track if we ever had to do a paper on his work in our modern art classes.

It turns out that Mother had somehow contracted *Hepatitis* and although the physician managed to stabilise her, it is a disease that lingers and can often flare up again in future. She was in the hospital for two weeks before being discharged into my father's care. They returned to *Chantilly*, hoping that the fresh country air would do her well in her recovery. I did not feel like spending time in the country either and I stayed behind in Paris, finishing my university vacation break amongst the masses of tourists visiting the city.

Having spent this time with Picasso in *Cannes*, I was inspired to do a great artistic creation myself. Although I did not feel like doing an original piece, I thought to take a page from his book and started working on my own interpretation and analysis of *The creation of Adam* by Michelangelo. It had been one of my first memories of time spent with my mother after they adopted me, staring at the ceiling in the Sistine Chapel as a child in *Rome*. If Picasso could do 58 different interpretations off of a single painting, I could certainly manage to do at least one of my own. Although I could still remember the fresco artwork vividly, I bought a book on the Vatican at the local bookstore, in order to refresh my memory and gain a new perspective of the artist and, in my mind, one of his greatest works. I started off with recreating several elements from the painting – fingers, faces, the angels. Two weeks passed by in a flash and I had progressed from line art drawings to coloured reproductions of different areas of focus in the work. Finally, the day came when I started a full reproduction of the work. It took me almost a full fortnight to complete my own masterpiece, but in the end, I was very pleased with the result. I could almost feel the power of life being transferred into Adam, much as I transferred a piece of myself into this work.

The original idea was to give the piece to my mother once completed, as a get-well gift, but somewhere along the way, it had changed from a mere artwork into something much more all-encompassing. A reflection of my soul, a reflection of my new life, passed on by a higher power giving me new direction in my life, pointing the way with a god-like finger. It was a new direction when I was staring at the Vatican ceiling as a 10-year-old and it was reflective of my new life in Paris, now, 10 years later. Perhaps it is time for the sad parts of the past to return where they occurred in Moscow, or Athens, or somewhere in Italy, and be left behind. Now I look forward to my life in Paris.

I wish you all the best at the Bolshoi, my dearest Katja, and may your future be as bright and prosperous as I am sure mine will be in the City of Lights.

With love from Paris,
Marie-Claire

RETURN TO ST MORITZ, 1960

The beautiful snow covered Swiss Alps were whipping by the windows of the train carriage, speeding on its way through the mountains. The winter vacation of 1960 found Marie-Claire on her way to *St Moritz*. This would be her first vacation alone, without her parents. She had been invited by a group of friends to travel along to Switzerland. Sacha Distel had found an amazing lodge for hire in the small Swiss town and Marie-Claire was amongst those invited to join him for two weeks in the mountains. The lodge, located on the upper edge of town, had amazing views of the lake.

The group had all taken the train from Paris together and were currently huddled in a compartment, admiring the views as the train snaked through the mountains. Illicit brandy was liberally consumed, helping to stave off the cold. Whenever the conductor approached, the drinks were hidden under hats, scarves or behind newspapers. The official suspected that the merriment was beyond the levels reasonably expected of a sober grouping, but was not going to pry. He was a fan of Juliette Gréco and hoping to acquire her signature before the end of the journey. Some of the other occupants of the compartment also seemed vaguely familiar to him, but he could not place them. The ten revellers in the first class carriage would sometimes break into song, which proved remarkably melodic and harmonious, unlike the drunken singing he was used to on some return journeys after intercontinental football games. One of the gentlemen seemed to have some descent skills with a guitar and the elderly conductor thought he did quite good renditions of some of Sacha Distel's songs.

In amongst the singing, there were deep philosophical discussions in the compartment, interspersed with readings of poetry and the occasional joke. The philosophy got progressively deeper as the *Rémy Martin* bottled emptied out. The ten bodies stuffed together on either side of the compartment created a warm atmosphere, fogging up the windows, the views long forgotten in the gaiety. They were still in the midst of their merriment, when the train arrived in *St Moritz* in the mid-afternoon. It was now snowing and the inclement weather made for some difficulty in reaching their transport to the lodge.

Sacha had arranged a minibus shuttle to take them all to their destination and the driver was covered in snow once all the luggage was loaded in the back. The town was barely visible through the thick snow and the driver had a difficult time traversing the winding road. Very little was visible of the town through the windows. Marie-Claire had a rough idea of where they were, through the few landmarks she could recognise from her previous visits. The driver almost slowed down to a crawl as they reached the upper end of the little town, where the snow was now piled wheel high on the roads. Their destination finally appeared out of the heavy snow, a welcome relief.

The lodge was a large wooden cabin with views that would normally show the marvellous spectacle of the valleys and the lake below the town. Currently, one could hardly see the road beyond the driveway. It was conveniently located next to the ski slope, once the weather allowed for skiing. Marie-Claire was interested to see what the sleeping arrangements would entail. The three couples would share rooms, but she was wondering how the rooming arrangements would work for the other four people. In the end, it was sorted out quite easily. Luc and Joseph somehow ended up in the remaining room with a double bed together and seemed quite nonplussed with this. She hadn't met the two previously but found it distinctly odd that they chose the room with the double bed, in the presence of other available options. It took a while for the penny to drop and then she finally realised, *there were four couples in the cabin!* Marie-Claire and Catherine, an aspirant actress, each had their own room with a choice of the upper- or lower bunk. The lodge generally catered for families with children and the two drew the short straws on this. Marie-Claire's room was next to the kitchen and closest to the central boiler, which proved almost uncomfortably warm in the small space. *I can rough it for two weeks, it's still cooler than high summer in Athens*, she thought.

Their evening plans of a night on the town had to be postponed, the weather not being conducive to leaving the cabin. The men got the fireplace in the large lounge going and the room quickly heated up. There was a decorated Christmas tree in the corner, even though they would depart before the holiday arrived. The sunken lounge with its yellow couches made for a cosy and comfortable area for the ten to sit and socialise. The kitchen had a well-stocked larder and they could still make a very adequate dinner for themselves with the available supplies. There was also a substantial collection of wine and spirits, ensuring that they would not go thirsty during their two-week stay.

The first evening turned into a drunken ordeal, with copious amounts of alcohol being consumed by all. It was not a question of rampant misbehaviour, but by the end, everyone struggled to make their way to their rooms, staggering through the various passages when the evening drew to a close. Marie-Claire could admit that it took skill to get the right personalities together for a two-week trip in close quarters such as this, and Sacha had done well. He and Juliette had been dating for a short while, having met through their respective singing careers. Marie-Claire did not think it appeared too serious at this stage, but the couple seemed smitten and could not contain their passion as the evening progressed, eventually excusing themselves to retire to the privacy of their room.

Christian and Kate were in the French Olympic fencing team. Marie-Claire could really admire and appreciate the hard work they had put in over many years to attain elite status in their sporting careers. The two had almost reached a stage where they now had to consider how their careers would culminate. *Would they go quietly into the night, or would they transpose into coaching the next generation?*

Jacques was a mathematician and poet, which was not a common combination of talents. His girlfriend Genevieve was also a student at the *Sorbonne* and although Marie-Claire had not seen her on campus, they have met socially at a dinner hosted by Jean Cocteau on one occasion. Luc and Joseph were both actors, who also knew Sacha through Cocteau. Everyone got along splendidly during the evening.

Marie-Claire collapsed into her bed. *I am going to regret this in the morning,* she thought. It was an interesting group of people which Sacha had brought along and she could see it would be a memorable vacation. *He has such a fascinating social circle.* She had now stripped down to her underwear in the stifling room. Marie-Claire stared at the wooden slats of the top bunk, which were spinning around lazily in circles. Her bedroom door creaked open and Catherine stumbled into the room. 'Oh, it's much better in here! Do you mind if I join you for a while, until I'm warmed up? My room is freezing,' she requested with a bit of a slur. Marie-Claire remembered some cold winters in *Marcigliana*, where she and Arianna often had to huddle together in bed to keep warm. She did not deem it a strange request.

'Sure, I'll make some space,' she said as she shifted to the back of the bed. Despite wearing long johns, Catherine's feet were still icy cold. She gripped Marie-Claire, soaking up her body heat. 'Is it just me, or is your room spinning around?' Catherine asked sheepishly.

'I also noticed that earlier,' Marie-Claire said as they both giggled at the improbability of the suggestion.

'You're so nice and warm. Very cosy,' Catherine remarked.

'I try my best. I guess it comes with experience.'

'You share your bed with girls often?' Catherine asked, surprised.

'Oh, no. I grew up in an orphanage until I was ten. The blankets were very thin and we often ended up sharing beds in winter to keep warm.'

'Oh, that's quite different from what I thought. I'm sorry to hear that. What happened to your parents?'

'I don't actually know. I have no memories of my real parents, or of anything else before I arrived at the orphanage when I was eight.'

'That's really unfortunate. It's like you missed out on half your life. You poor thing,' Catherine said and hugged Marie-Claire tighter for a moment, giving her a peck on her forehead. Catherine stared into her eyes for a moment and then kissed her gently on the lips as well. Marie-Claire didn't quite know what to make of the situation. Her head was still buzzing from all the wine and this beautiful woman was right in her face. Then Catherine kissed her again. This time with a little more vigour. Her lips were warm and her breath still smelled of sweet alcohol. Marie-Claire kissed her back, getting lost in the moment, inhibitions misplaced in her inebriated state.

They kissed gently, tongues touching. The kiss intensified, passion flaring up between them. Then Catherine's hand brushed Marie-Claire's breast, causing a shiver through her skimpily clad body. Marie-Claire pulled away from the embrace, placing a finger on Catherine's lips. 'I don't think this is a good idea.' Some semblance of propriety had waded through her hazy mind, overriding the urge to surrender to the desire she felt at the very moment, a drunken embrace she would regret if left to evolve as nature intended. Catherine rushed to get out of bed, but Marie-Claire grabbed her by the arm. 'Stay. If you leave now, this is going to be very awkward in the morning. Stay, please.'

Catherine stayed. She fell asleep next to Marie-Claire, still holding her for warmth. The moment between them had passed, the briefest instant of exploration of the forbidden unknown. When Marie-Claire woke up the next morning, Catherine was sitting up over the side of the bed. 'Are you all right?' she asked with concern, 'You cried in your sleep.'

'I always do,' Marie-Claire responded. 'I have never known why. I think I have bad dreams, but I can never remember them.' Her head was pounding as she sat up next to Catherine, who also looked like she was feeling under the weather. She kissed her on the lips, a quick peck. 'Thanks for staying. I don't know how I would have been able to face you otherwise.'

Catherine gave her a hug. 'Don't mention it. You are very perceptive, Marie-Claire. Any other way it could have played out would not have worked. I'm sure we will have a great two weeks and become the best of friends. Get dressed and let's go find some coffee.'

They entered the kitchen and was spared inquisitive glances by the absence of everyone else, who were still asleep. The smell of freshly roasted coffee soon wafted through the lodge, causing some stirrings in the other rooms. During the night, the storm had settled and as they opened the French doors, they were greeted by a magnificent sight. The air was a bright blue, without a cloud in sight. Seconds later, the chilly morning breeze hit them. The closed the doors and stared out from inside, the glorious Swiss landscape taking their breath away.

Eventually, the rest of the party joined them in the living room, all looking rather worse for wear after the night before. Their clothing reflected that some of them had not bothered looking out the window yet. Those that have, were dressed in ski-regalia, while the rest were dressed for another lazy day inside. Luc got the fire going again and they all sat around discussing the prospects for the day. Christian, who was slightly older than the rest of them, suggested an acceptable course of action. 'Why don't we all go into town and have a late brunch and then we can decide our further plans for the day.'

'That seems like a perfectly good plan. I think a walk to town in the mountain air would do us all wonders. Personally, I am still looking for the string of horses that ran over my head during the night,' Sacha responded. 'I do hope the town pharmacy will have some aspirin.' They all agreed to reconvene in half an hour for the trip to town.

The walk into the *St Moritz* town centre did not take the group very long, despite their tender constitutions. The town was packed with vacationers, enjoying the festive atmosphere. They selected one of the various restaurants around the central circle in town and got a table which was large enough to accommodate them all. After some coffee arrived and aspirin was passed around, they ordered brunch and were soon feeling normal again. 'Who's up for some skiing?' Sacha enquired.

'We're keen!' Luc and Joseph responded.

'Us too!' said Jacques and Genevieve.

'I'd actually like to do some ice skating at the rink by the Kulm Hotel,' Marie-Claire offered.

'That sounds awesome,' Catherine indicated.

'I'd rather do that too, than ski today,' Juliette piped in.

'Christian and I haven't been here before, so we would like to explore the town on foot,' Kate said. After brunch, the party split up. Five skiers, three ice skaters and the remaining duo exploring town. They all agreed to meet up at the lodge at 5pm to decide on dinner plans.

Marie-Claire and her two companions ambled to the ice-rink at a leisurely pace. They walked through the lavish lobby of the Kulm Hotel to reach the rink behind the hotel. 'Who is *Gunter Dietrich*?' Juliette asked.

'He was a boy that died on the cresta run a couple of years ago. Someone pushed him in and he slid all the way down, breaking his neck. I was actually on vacation here with my parents when it happened. Why do you ask?' Marie-Claire responded.

'Oh, we just passed a copper plaque dedicated to him, back there. What a terrible story!'

'Yes, his parents were quite heartbroken. Ah, there's the ice-rink. Let's get some skates!' Marie-Claire broke up the slightly sombre conversation, eager to get onto the ice.

The three ladies spent the afternoon on the ice. Juliette and Catherine were decent skaters, but they couldn't emulate the graceful talent which Marie-Claire exhibited on the ice. Although she only skated annually at *St Moritz*, the many hours she spent on the ice every vacation and her ballet background made her a very skilled skater. When they handed their skates back in at the winter sports club, the clerk recognised Marie-Claire. 'Ms Le Blanc. Welcome back to *St Moritz*. Will you be participating in the competition this year? I am sure no-one would be able to challenge you. Perhaps you can add your name to the trophy again?'

'No, I will have left by then already. Someone else will have a chance at glory this year. I am just here to enjoy myself with my friends.'

'Of course, Ms Le Blanc. You do that. Enjoy yourself! They are having an informal dance at the Kulm tonight. If you are after having fun, you should attend. It promises to be the most exciting event in town this evening.'

'That sounds like an excellent idea. I'll convince Sacha that we should all go,' Juliette responded.

The small group walked up the hill to the lodge as the sun set over the Swiss Alps. When they arrived, it was dark and the rest of the group was there already. 'There's a party at the hotel this evening. We should go there for dinner and dancing!' Juliette proposed excitedly when everyone was sitting in the lounge, warming up with some cognac. The idea got immediate support from everyone, despite their weary bodies from the day's exercise on the slopes and in town. Two taxis picked them up at 7pm and dropped them off at the Hotel Kulm, where they entered the ballroom to settle at their reserved table. Marie-Claire felt quite at home in the familiar surroundings of the ballroom, having spent many hours there in the past with her parents. It was almost like a vacation home to her. Most of the town joined the event at some stage during the evening and Marie-Claire was surprised to note that she knew a number of the attendees from her social circles in Paris.

The evening was a festive one and the jazz band created a lively atmosphere, interspersed with a disc jockey playing records by Chuck Berry, Elvis Presley and various other famous artists. Guests were surprised when a raucous cheer erupted from the one table when he played a song by Sacha Distel. The group thoroughly enjoyed their evening of dancing and it was well after 12 when they first noticed the time. 'Perhaps we should call it a night?' Kate suggested, to general approval by the rest. Two sleepy local taxi drivers dropped them off at the lodge just after 2 am. The group gathered for a last nightcap in the lounge before all retiring to bed.

The remaining time in *St Moritz* was almost a daily repetition of their first day there. Brunch somewhere in the village was followed by outdoor activities and dinner in town, wherever the prospects for entertainment were the brightest. Catherine moved into Marie-Claire's room. Her room really was very cold and no-one questioned the move. The two girls had become good friends during the time in the mountains. Catherine kept to the top bunk for the remainder of the holiday. The trip drew to an end, to everyone's chagrin. They all saw each other regularly afterwards in Paris. Those who did not know each other before the trip, were now good friends. Marie-Claire, of course, got to know some of them better than the others…

NEW EXPERIENCES IN JUAN-LES-PINS, 1961

Another academic year had ended and Marie-Claire was looking forward to spending her summer vacation in the Riviera with her parents. They had booked the usual suite at the *Le Provençal* in *Juan-les-Pins*, promising a wonderful month of relaxation next to the azure waters of the Mediterranean. It was now a week prior to departure and Marie-Claire came home to find a telegram in her post-box. *This was a decidedly odd occurrence.* She opened the envelope addressed to MARIE-CLAIRE LE BLANC and read the enclosed message. MOTHER FELL ILL STOP PLEASE CONTACT ME POST HASTE STOP HENRI LE BLANC. She had been out all day and they could not reach her by telephone! She called her father in *Chantilly* as soon as she arrived in her apartment. The phone was answered by Mrs Bouchard. 'Can I please speak to my father urgently, Mrs Bouchard?'

'Hello, Marie-Claire. Unfortunately your father is not here. Your mother has been admitted to the hospital in Paris. Mr Le Blanc requested that you contact him there.'

'Thank you, Mrs Bouchard. I will find them there. Good day.'

Marie-Claire grabbed her bag and rushed out of the apartment, hailing a taxi in the *Boul'Mich*. '*Beaujon* Hospital, sir,' she instructed, '… and please hurry.'

'Right away miss!' the taxi driver responded to her obvious unease by duly putting his foot down and speeding off. Despite the driver's concerted effort, the long trip to the 17th *arrondissement* in the north of the city still took 45 minutes to complete in afternoon traffic. The *Beaujon* Hospital was a thirteen storey vertical structure, quite a modern change from the traditional multi-building design for hospitals. Marie-Claire asked for directions at the reception desk and found her mother in a private room in the internal medicine ward. Her skin had a sickly yellow sheen, which was quite a sharp contrast to the pale hand of Mr Le Blanc, holding hers. Marie-Claire realised immediately what had happened. *Her mother's Hepatitis had flared up again!*

'Hello Father. Hello Mother,' she said, kissing them both. 'How are you feeling Mother?'

'I'm still feeling quite weak and nauseous, my dear. The doctors have started treatment and at least the nausea is improving a bit. It was much worse previously,' Mrs Le Blanc responded.

'I'm so sorry to see you like this, Mother.'

Marie-Claire spent an hour at the hospital, catching up and getting feedback on the treatment plan from the visiting Physician, before the nursing staff kicked her and Mr Le Blanc out.

'I'm booked into a hotel around the corner. Join me for dinner?' Mr Le Blanc requested. The dinner was a subdued affair, neither having much appetite and only picking at their food. Marie-Claire said goodbye to her father, before she took a taxi back home. Over the next few days, she made daily visits to her mother in hospital. Her condition improved every day, with her normal colour slowly returning. The doctors were finally satisfied with her recovery and discharged her to go home. She was given strict instructions not to travel.

'With your mother's travel ban, we will not be able to go to the Riviera this year. I do, however, think you should still go. Take a friend and use the suite. We've paid for everything in full and will lose our money if we cancel it now anyway, so you might as well go and enjoy yourself. Your mother will be fine now. I will look after her and make sure she gets plenty of rest.'

'But should I not stay with you at the estate?' Marie-Claire asked with concern.

'No, my child. I will be fine. Go to the coast and enjoy your vacation. You had a long year at university and you deserve a nice break,' Mrs Le Blanc insisted. Marie-Claire invited Catherine to travel with her to *Juan-les-Pins*. Because of previous commitments, Catherine could only stay for two weeks. Marie-Claire resolved that she would decide what to do with the rest of her vacation once Catherine had left.

The two young women looked out-of-place in the large rental car that Mr Le Blanc had reserved at the *Nice* airport. Once they put the top down, it looked a little bit more befitting. The weather was lovely as they drove down the coast and crossed the *Antibes* Peninsula. *Juan-les-Pins* already had crowds of tourists on the beaches and walking about in the shopping district. The hotel staff at the *Le Provençal* gave them a warm welcome as they arrived. Catherine had not been to this part of the Riviera before. 'What a lovely hotel! And look at the beach, oh, this is going to be a lot of fun!' she exclaimed excitedly. The bellboy dropped their bags off in the suite on the ninth floor and each one selected a room for the stay. The views of *Cannes* in the distance were still as spectacular as Marie-Claire remembered from previous stays.

'Let's go have some drinks on the terrace,' Marie-Claire suggested, as the sun started to set.

'That sounds like a great idea,' Catherine concurred. The two settled at a table on the hotel roof terrace and ordered a round of drinks. 'What a gorgeous view!' Catherine proclaimed. 'Do you come here regularly?'

'I have been here annually for a couple of years now. There are several really nice places we can go to for dinner this evening. The seafood here is to die for! And we definitely have to go to *Maxim's*. Everyone ends up there at the end of the evening.'

'Brilliant! Put me down for one of everything,' Catherine responded. They had a good laugh. The terrace was now getting very crowded with hotel guests and visiting patrons, all seeking the best view of the setting sun in *Juan-les-Pins*. Soon there was no seating left on the terrace and newly arriving guests were standing around in a throng of bodies between the tables.

Someone bumped into the table, spilling both their drinks. 'This crowd is really getting ridiculous now. Let's get out of here before we get stepped on,' Catherine suggested.

'I agree. Let's move on. I'm getting hungry, anyway. Want to go shower before we find a place for dinner?'

'That sounds like a good suggestion.' The two girls showered and dressed up for the evening. Marie-Claire was finished with her beauty regime first and sat in the lounge sipping a measure of brandy, waiting for Catherine to come out of her bedroom. They went downstairs and headed out for an evening on the town.

The duo strolled over to the Casino, choosing to enjoy dinner at *La Frégate*. A friendly *Maître'd* welcomed them to the restaurant with a flourish and seated them at a table with a view of the oceanfront. The seafood dinner was fantastic and they paired the fresh local line-fish with a bottle of white wine from a vineyard recommended by the sommelier. The meal was completed with dessert and coffee, leaving the two satisfied after a wonderful dinner.

It was now already close to 11 o'clock. They strolled out of the casino towards *Maxim's*. The streets were awash with the after-dinner crowds, most heading in the same direction as them or milling around in small groups. A red neon sign welcomed Marie-Claire and Catherine to the white, double storey nightclub, the jewel of all nightlife in the area. Loud music was audible from the street and revellers were entering *Maxim's* from all directions across town. There was a festive, gay atmosphere in the nightclub, which was quite full already. Chuck Berry blasted over the sound system. The girls bought themselves some drinks, before finding an open table close to the dance-floor. Marie-Claire saw many familiar faces around the room, recognising them from previous trips to

Juan-les-Pins. She didn't know all of them well, but it was definitely not a collection of strangers.

The gorgeous pair were very popular with the young men, offers of drinks pouring in as they were approached in conversation. And then Marie-Claire saw *him.* Gino was there, staring at her from across the room. Although they wrote each other as promised after their previous encounter, they fell out of touch as the letters petered out, each getting caught up in the drama of their own lives. The sudden developments at the Bolshoi changed her life path irrevocably, Gino giving up hope as his letters were eventually returned from Moscow, the addressee no longer residing at the French Embassy. He walked over and the feelings Marie-Claire had for him rushed back with the flood of memories of the moments they shared. He was now four years older and even more dashingly handsome, while Marie-Claire was no longer an innocent teenager.

'Hello Marie-Claire,' he greeted her with a kiss, which lingered slightly longer than socially appropriate.

'Hello, Gino. May I introduce you to my friend Catherine? Catherine, this is Gino Romario.'

'Pleased to meet you Catherine. May I buy you ladies a drink?'

'Yes, thanks. Then come join us,' Marie-Claire responded. He returned a few minutes later and joined them at their table. The nightclub was now jam-packed, as most other places in town had closed down for the night.

'How have you been, Marie-Claire? Where are you living now?' Gino asked.

'I am in Paris. I left Moscow in mid '58 and went to study art at the *Sorbonne.* What are you up to? Your studies must be completed by now?'

'Yes, my studies are finished. I am now doing marketing for my father in his textile factory in Milan. It involves a lot of travel, so I am getting to see all of the major cities in Europe. It's quite exciting. Art..? That's an interesting development. Are you, er... are you seeing anyone at the moment?'

'No, Gino. I am quite happy to find myself right now. You?'

'I am engaged to be married. My fiancé is at home in Italy.'

Marie-Claire experienced utter disappointment at this revelation. Although she did not feel like getting involved with anyone at present, she still had feelings for Gino. She faked sincerity. 'I'm glad you are happy Gino. Let me order a bottle of champagne, so we can toast your love!' *Or rather drown our sorrows,* she thought. A pretty waitress in a short skirt brought the champagne in a bucket with three glasses. 'To Gino and…?' she raised her eyebrows questioningly.

'Juliette.'

'To Gino and Juliette. May there be many happy years.' The three clinked their glasses and Marie-Claire proceeded to promptly down hers in one gulp. Gino filled her glass again. They continued chatting, while she quickly finished her second glass.

'Will you excuse me please, I need to go to the ladies'. Come Marie-Claire,' Catherine grabbed her by the arm and hauled her along to the toilets.

'What's going on? Are you okay?' she asked Marie-Claire as they entered the ladies' room.

'Gino was my first love. We met here one summer. I guess I still have feelings for him from back then. So it's very disappointing for me.'

'But would you want to be involved with him right now?' Catherine asked pointedly as she powdered her nose in front of the mirror.

Marie-Claire thought for a moment. 'Probably not. But I can't control my feelings. I don't want him, but I don't want anyone else to have him either. It's really stupid.'

'Don't worry about it. It happens. Just try and enjoy yourself. Don't dwell on it. Let's go have some more champagne. We're on vacation, after all!'

They re-joined Gino at the table and made short work of the remaining champagne, before ordering another bottle. Marie-Claire seemed more relaxed now.

'When are you going back to Milan?'

'I am leaving tomorrow, actually. I just came for a quick drink after dinner. It's nice to see you again Marie-Claire. You look well.' The conversation flowed naturally as the champagne did its work. When the second bottle was done, Catherine was ready to excuse herself. 'I'm a little drunk and I think I want to go back to the hotel.'

'I'll go with you,' Marie-Claire said. 'It is getting late. It was nice to see you Gino. I wish you all the best.'

'Don't be silly. I'll walk you to your hotel. We can't let you two walk all the way there alone,' Gino insisted.

The three walked the short distance to the *Le Provençal* and Gino escorted them to their room. 'Would you like a nightcap before you go?' Marie-Claire enquired.

'Sure. That sounds like a lovely offer.'

'I'm going to excuse myself, I really am dead tired. It was a pleasure meeting you, Gino. Have a safe trip back to Italy tomorrow.' Catherine retired to her room in the suite, as Marie-Claire poured them some brandy. They sipped it quietly for a moment, seated side by side on the couch. 'It was really nice to see you again tonight, Marie-Claire. You are even more beautiful than when I saw you last.' He brushed a stray hair from her face.

'It was good seeing you too, Gino.' They stared at each other in silence. Gino leaned forward and kissed her. For a moment, she pulled back. *I'm sorry about this Juliette*, she thought and then leaned into him, returning the kiss. It was just as wonderful as she remembered the first time on the beach, not far from here, so many years ago. But now she was no longer a teenager, she was a woman. The passion of the embrace took over her whole being. She wanted him. She did not care that he had a fiancé. It was of no concern right now. She took him by the hand and led him to her bedroom.

She shut the door and kissed him again, unbuttoning his shirt in a frenzy. His hands glided over her body and down the back of her legs. He slid them back up under her dress, gripping her buttocks. Marie-Claire moaned with pleasure.

Then he pushed her dress up. She raised her arms as he lifted it up over her head, freeing her from the fabric. Gino's hands were exploring her body as they stood at the bottom of the bed. Then he unlatched her bra, which dropped to the floor. He kissed her neck, moving slowly downwards towards her naked, heaving breasts. Marie-Claire lifted up her one leg, hooking him closer. He picked her up and dropped her on the bed. They made love, passionately exploring each other. Her thoughts were overwhelmed with the pleasure of the embrace, totally losing herself in the intimacy of the experience. Their intertwined bodies writhed. Marie-Claire's being exploded with an eruption of pleasure, her whole body shaking. It was the first time Marie-Claire had made love to anyone and as they lay holding each other afterwards, her thoughts flitted for a brief moment to his fiancé. There was a momentary pang of guilt, but then it was gone.

The two lay basking in each other's presence for the longest time. Then Marie-Claire broke the silence. 'I really enjoyed that, Gino. Thank you for staying. I don't think this can go anywhere, though. You are engaged and I am not in a place where I am looking for someone to fill my life. I hope you understand?'

'I do. And I think I also know this would never go anywhere further. But it didn't feel wrong. It felt... almost, perfect. Like it has been long overdue. The completion of a thought that was only half expressed previously.'

'I will always remember this Gino. And I will always think of you fondly. You were my first love and I am glad that we had a last opportunity to express our feelings physically, before you left for a life bonded to another.'

When they finally fell asleep, Marie-Claire slept very lightly, constantly being aware of his presence next to her in bed. Gino departed early the next morning to pack for his trip back to Italy. Before he left, they made love again, this time more slowly, extending the embrace, knowing they would never experience each other again. When he left, she kissed him goodbye at the door, closing it behind him. She stared at the door. It had also shut the door on a chapter in her life, a fitting conclusion to an affair that started five years ago on the beach, nine floors below. She sat down on the couch and fell asleep. Catherine woke her up several hours later with a cup of coffee.

'I note a certain whimsical look about you this morning. And why are you sleeping on the couch? Is there anything you need to share with me?'

'Let's just say that I ended up having company for the night and that he would probably have to refrain from telling his fiancé about his evening if he still wishes to marry her someday.'

'Well good for you, Marie-Claire! I trust it was an enjoyable experience?'

'Oh yes, they were!'

'Oh, very good for you!' Catherine smiled at her and sipped her coffee. 'Now that we are finally awake, we should go to the beach, the weather is lovely and we cannot return to Paris without a decent tan!'

The two girls changed into their swimwear in preparation for spending the morning at the hotel's private beach. Marie-Claire's swimsuit was a superbly conceived, strapless design by Balmain, leaving her entire back, neck and shoulders without any visible tan lines from the Mediterranean sun. Catherine wore a dark blue bikini, leaving most of the men on the beach wondering what they would have to do to stand a chance of spending some time with these two beauties. It was the perfect day on the French Riviera and life was good to Marie-Claire.

A TRIP TO MOUGINS, 1961

The two weeks in *Juan-les-Pins* with Catherine had flown by in whirlwind fashion. One glorious day on the beach followed the next, interspersed with day trips to all the surrounding towns and villages. They travelled as far afield as *Marseilles* in the west and journeyed east as far as their French citizenry allowed, a pair of rude border guards sending them the way they had come from at the Italian border. In the evenings, there was revelry of note, always ending up at *Maxim's* towards the end of the night, the call of "last round" usually signalling the end of the frivolities somewhere in the early morning hours. Although the rest of the vacation was spectacular and memorable, none of it could compete with the memories created on the very first night. After Marie-Claire had dropped Catherine off at the *Nice* airport, she had to decide what she wanted to do for the rest of her vacation.

In the short term, she opted to have lunch in *Nice* and sat at a brasserie overlooking the Mediterranean. Marie-Claire was deep in thought. *What to do, what to do?* Staying at the hotel for the remaining two weeks of her booking was an option. She enjoyed *Juan-les-Pins*, but if one was to spend some time alone, it was probably not the place to do that. This was one of the easy decisions to make and one she came upon quite early in her musings. *I think I should spend some time away from people for the next two weeks.* The Riviera did not lend itself particularly well to solitude. *Where does one go for solitude around here? Some people rent those big houses close to one of the towns, overlooking the ocean. It gives you privacy with a marvellous view. And some people flee inland, to some of the little mountain villages. You can still see the ocean in the far distance, but you can't see the tourists on the beach. That's what Picasso did.* And then it hit her. *I missed my arrangement with Picasso the last time I was here! He said he was moving somewhere else, possibly Mougins? I'll find out where and I'll find HIM. We had a sitting scheduled and I plan to make good on that appointment.*

Marie-Claire finished her lunch and drove west. The plan for today was to travel to *Cannes* and do some initial enquiries on the current whereabouts of *Monsieur* Picasso. He was quite a character in the area and it would no doubt be easy to obtain information on where he had moved to. *Perhaps there would be someone at his house, La Villa California, who might point me in the right direction?* The last known residence of Pablo Picasso, nestled in the cliffs around *Cannes,* was unoccupied. Although Marie-Claire could see it was still furnished and clean through a window, there was no-one at home. *Was it abandoned by the owner, or simple uninhabited for the afternoon?* She could not tell which. Marie-Claire drove back into *Cannes,* trying the *café* where she came across Picasso the previous year. *Perhaps he was a regular and would be there, or they would know where he may be.*

Picasso was not in the *café.* Marie-Claire did not feel despondent yet, but was hoping her luck would change when speaking to the manager. 'Good afternoon. I had an invitation from *Monsieur* Picasso to his house last year, but due to illness in my family, I ended up not being able to see him. He was talking of relocation at the time. Is he still living at *La Villa California,* or has he moved on?'

'Good afternoon, Miss,' the portly manager responded quite amicably. 'Yes, *Monsieur* Picasso has moved on. I believe he has bought a house in *Mougins* and is now residing there permanently.' *Third time lucky.* Although *Mougins* was a short drive from *Cannes,* she didn't want to embark on the journey in the mid-afternoon, not knowing how long it would take to find him there. 'Thank you, sir. I will look him up in the morning. May I have some coffee and a piece of your chocolate cake, please?' Marie-Claire finished her mid-afternoon tea break and headed back to the hotel in *Juan-les-Pins.* For the first time in two weeks, she would have an early evening and not go out. She packed an overnight bag to take along the next day. The remainder of her luggage would be left at the hotel.

The next morning after breakfast, she was on her way to explore *Mougins* and find Picasso. She bought a map of the area and then drove westwards. Once she reached *Cannes*, she turned inland towards the tiny mountain village of *Mougins*. The drive was immensely scenic, with the surrounding mountains looking picture perfect and the Mediterranean visible in the rear-view mirror every so often on the turns in the road. She entered the old village centre of *Mougins*. The big car struggled to navigate the narrow turns as she made her way up the winding road through town, until she eventually arrived at the village square.

Mougins was a beautiful, rustic little village, with a fountain in the square, some unrecognisable hero of old placed on top of the water feature. She found a parking spot next to the grassy patch of the village commons. Marie-Claire stood observing her surroundings. She could understand how someone would want to go and live there, it was beautiful. She walked to the closest open restaurant and started her enquiries. 'Good morning. I am looking for *Monsieur* Picasso. Could you perhaps tell me where I can find him?' she asked an idle waiter, polishing a glass.

'He should be in his studio, it's further down the road, last building on the left, before the square,' he pointed down the road past the fountain.

'Thanks kindly,' she said as she walked in the direction he had indicated.

The old town was tiny and she reached Picasso's studio after a very short walk. His door was open and she found the master inside, pondering over a work on an easel. She knocked on the door. 'Good morning Monsieur Picasso. It is nice to see you again.'

'Marie-Claire! We'll I'll be… What a surprise! I was really disappointed when you couldn't make it to my villa last summer. It was your mother, if I remember correctly? She was ill? Has she improved now? I'm so glad to see you. What brings you all the way here to *Mougins*?' he greeted her with a kiss on each cheek.

'My mother is fine now, thanks. I am here for you. I was also disappointed by missing our appointment and I thought that since I was in the Riviera on holiday, I would come find you.'

'Let's go have a cup of coffee. I am having a bit of artist's block this morning. Perhaps some time with you could inspire me.' Five minutes later, they were back at the restaurant she enquired at. The waiter was still busy polishing the same glass.

'Gilbert, if you polish that glass any further, you will melt it down into a paper weight. Bring us some coffee,' Picasso instructed the waiter, who was happy to find some short-term meaning to his existence.

'So you came to find me, Marie-Claire? What were you hoping to achieve once you did?'

'Well, you did invite me to pose for you last year. I hoped I could take you up on your offer, if it still stands?' she asked, slightly embarrassed.

'Splendid! I could do with a muse right now. I am currently busy with a series of nude studies. You wouldn't mind...?' his question trailed off, not quite sure how to finish the sentence.

'Of course I wouldn't mind! You are one of the great masters of all times and being immortalised in one of your famous nude studies would be an absolute honour,' Marie-Claire responded, saving him further discomfort.

'Well, then it is settled. We can retire to my house, once we are done with our coffee. I can really not do proper nudes in my studio in town. The light is just wrong. The villagers are also easily offended at the best of times, even more so when they interrupt unannounced. Absolute Philistines, I tell you. Cannot appreciate the artistic process at all!'

Marie-Claire told him about her analysis of the *Creation of Adam* and the extensive work she did on it. 'You inspired me to do that. It really did wonders for my work.'

'Excellent. Perhaps you can return the favour today and inspire me.' When their coffee was done, they left the restaurant and walked back to Picasso's studio, so he could lock before leaving.

Picasso was about to grab his bicycle, when Marie-Claire stopped him. 'I have a car parked in the square. I can give you a lift home?'

'Thanks for the offer, I think I'll take you up on it.'

The trip to Picasso's house was scenic, following a series of winding back roads. Every so often he'd point up a road and Marie-Claire would follow the directions. Eventually, they reached a gate with a sign that read *Mas de Notre Dame de Vie*. They arrived at a large stone house built on a terraced hill. From the back of the house, the views towards the Mediterranean in the far distance were quite spectacular. Inside, the house was a mass of half-finished paintings, pottery and sculptures. Several rooms served as makeshift studios with art supplies littered around. It would have the feel of a humble cottage, if it wasn't for the thirty-five rooms spread out over the sprawling expanse of the property.

'Make yourself at home. You can use this room for your stay,' Picasso said, putting her case in one of the upstairs bedrooms, with the same spectacular views over *Cannes* in the distance. 'My wife is away on a trip, so we will be able to work undisturbed. But I am going for a swim first. Do join me?' The weather was now sweltering hot, so Marie-Claire conceded without requiring much further persuasion. Picasso was impressed with the design of her swimsuit as they waded around in the pleasant water of the pool. 'What inspires your art, Marie-Claire?' he enquired as they sat on the edge of the pool, legs lazily dangling in the water.

'It varies greatly. Sometimes I will paint when I am angry, but the quality of these pieces are usually not very good. It does help to calm me down, though. Other times, I will sit and meditate for an hour, almost reaching an enlightened state. The art I produce in these instances often has a dark, brooding quality and I have flashes of a body, lying on a cobblestoned street, blood flowing from the head. I have painted this scene on many occasions, but I can never picture the face that goes with the body. I don't know whether it is the angle I am observing from or the absence of a light source. All the colours appear muted and dark, as if only illuminated by a full moon. I have tried versions of the painting in the sunlight, but somehow it just doesn't seem *right*. I also sometimes go to some of the parks in Paris and paint picnic scenes, next to the water, or sitting on a blanket, almost like the impressionists of old. It gives me satisfaction to do this well and people often want to buy these paintings, but it does not feel like I am expressing a deep passion when I do these.'

'It is a great advantage to be inspired by many different things, Marie-Claire. I find that I am able to produce a prodigious amount of art by being inspired by a variety of elements. I think it is too late to start our project today, the light is all wrong. We will start at dawn tomorrow, there is a room in the house that gathers the rays of sunrise perfectly, so we can use it to create a replica of perfection.' The two spent the rest of the day relaxing around the house. An elderly housekeeper arrived early in the evening to prepare supper. Picasso still had a love of his native Spanish food and they had a selection of tapas for dinner, along with a bottle of local wine. Marie-Claire insisted that they not retire too late for the evening, so that Picasso could get some rest before an early start in the morning. Being dead tired herself, so was only too glad to get some rest.

She had set an early alarm clock for before dawn, the persistent ringing waking her from a dark dream. After wiping the tears from her face, she got dressed in a gown, before going to the kitchen. She was making coffee when Picasso joined her, looking wide awake and eager to begin. He led her to a corner room in the house, the first rays of sunlight starting to flood in through the large window. There was a daybed covered with a sheet in the middle of the room, an easel and art supplies standing opposite. Marie-Claire disrobed and lay down on the oversized couch, half supporting her body on the arm rest. Picasso was surprised by her confidence at being naked in front of a relative stranger. It was definitely not typical for first-time models to be so unabashed. *Oh, well...*

'Move your leg a little over. Yes, that's good. Okay, now move your arm there, no, a little back. That's perfect!' Picasso stood, staring at the naked Marie-Claire on the couch. She was indeed perfect. A thing of great beauty, flawless in the early morning light. He walked from side to side slowly, observing her form on the daybed.

Then he started to paint. He used wild, broad strokes creating a vague background, before careful additions of black lines formed windows, the sun shining through. Picasso continued painting for two hours, the nude study reminding more of his earlier work in the 1930s. The artist chose this style because her beauty made him feel like his younger self. It awoke an earlier passion for her immaculate, naked body. Her breasts were firm and the lines of her hips translated to the canvas, an invitation to a heavenly embrace. He was close to being done, when they were interrupted by a loud voice. It was Picasso's wife, Jacqueline. She had returned from her journey and was not impressed by the scene she found upon her return 'Pablo! Who is this woman? What is she doing here? Get her out of this house at once!' she was furious, throwing a vase at the aged artist. 'Get out at once you harlot!' she screamed, before storming out.

She left the room and stomped down the corridor, smashing another vase on her way. 'I am so sorry, Marie-Claire, she can be a bit trying at times,' Picasso apologised, following his wife towards their bedroom at a safe distance. Marie-Claire put her robe on and rushed to her own bedroom, quickly throwing on a summer skirt and dumping her belongings into her suitcase before leaving. On her way out, she took her first look at the painting by Picasso. It was beautiful, even with a lack of the final touches of the foreground. She stood for a moment, admiring the work of art. Then she took it. *I am not leaving this behind.* Marie-Claire carefully gripped the canvas by the frame and hurriedly walked to the car, not wanting to smudge the still-wet paint. She threw her case on the back seat and carefully placed the painting in the trunk of the car. It was the best she could do to protect it, from a transport point of view. Then she sped off in a cloud of dust, glancing backwards one last time at the country house of Pablo Picasso, the genius himself nowhere to be seen.

Driving towards *Cannes*, it took Marie-Claire a while to realise how upset she was due to the whole incident. She had heard rumours that Jacqueline Roque could be quite temperamental, but this incident was more than she cared to experience first-hand. She was beset by a mixture of shock and anger at the rude treatment she received at the hands of the woman. *Surely she must have known her husband does nude studies? How on earth had she coped with this up to now??* As she arrived in *Cannes* a few minutes later, she stopped at a brasserie and ordered some brandy, to settle her nervous state. 'Would the Madame like some breakfast with her drink?' the waiter enquired in a rather snooty fashion.

'No thanks. And you can keep the ice as well,' Marie-Claire responded, referring to his demeanour, rather than the drink. The waiter did not get it. After two stiff measures of brandy, she started feeling better. Her shock had settled down, leaving only anger. *The painting is just reward for the injustice I have suffered today. I hope you will berate her appropriately for what she has done, Pablo. There will be no repeat sitting for completion of this piece. I am sorry Mr Picasso, but you are paying a tax for the boorishness of your wife.* She decided to have breakfast after all.

After a day in the hot French sun, the painting was baked dry in the heat of the trunk. Marie-Claire wrapped it in her beach towel and took it to her room, where she carefully packed it into her luggage. There it stayed for the remainder of the week in *Juan-les-Pins*. The trip to *Mougins* had cured her of the need to be alone in the countryside and she enjoyed the rest of her vacation at the Riviera with sun, sand and cocktails filling her days. The flight back was uneventful and upon returning to her apartment in Paris, she unpacked the Picasso, giving it a place of honour above her fireplace. It would serve as a timeless reminder of days spent with the greatest of the grand masters in tiny *Mougins*.

FESTIVE SEASON IN CHANTILLY, 1962

The Christmas recess had arrived in Paris, the students at the *Sorbonne* scattering across the country to spend the festive season with their families. Marie-Claire was now in the midst of the first year of a Masters' Degree in Fine Arts. The classes took on a much different nature now, small and intimate, with lecturers almost starting to view the students as being worthy of attention. Pre-graduates might have filled the lecture halls of the *Sorbonne*, but government research grants for post-graduate students kept the university finances ticking over. It was freezing cold in Paris and snow had already fallen during the season. Marie-Claire's plans for the academic break was to visit her parents in Chantilly.

The taxi she ordered had arrived and was waiting for her in the *Boul'Mich*, opposite *La Bouffe*. She had a heavy bag in each hand as she crossed the road, with a wrapped parcel under one arm. '*Gare du Nord*, please,' she instructed the taxi driver. The inside of the taxi was hot and stuffy, almost making her sweat in her thick winter coat. The trip to the station was mundane, the surroundings well known to her. She boarded the train to *Chantilly*. The countryside was magical, a scattering of snow covering the local forests to the north of Paris. It gave the trip a surreal quality of being far removed from Paris in the European forests of old. The train headed into a simpler part of France. 40 minutes later, Marie-Claire arrived in the little rural hamlet. The *Gare de Chantilly-Gouvieux* was a small station, but the building was both beautiful and functional.

Henri le Blanc was waiting for his daughter in the station house, seeking refuge from an icy wind that howled around the building. He greeted her and grabbed the two bags, while she carried the parcel herself. They exited the front of station and briskly walked towards the antique Rolls Royce, depositing the luggage in the oversized trunk. Once inside the car, they took a moment to compose themselves and recover from the biting cold outside. Mr Le Blanc started the engine, which spluttered before it took. Even Rolls Royces were not immune to the cold. The heater slowly thawed them out. 'How are you, my dear? How are the studies?' Mr Le Blanc enquired, while he waited for his hands to recover to the point where it was safe to drive.

'I am doing well. The studies are really challenging, but well worth the effort, in the end. I sold a couple of my paintings the other day. Not a lot of money, but it helps to get your name out there. Perhaps I should consider a drawing on the wall of *La Bouffe*. So many other artists in Paris over the years paid their way like that.'

'If you need to draw on walls to make a living, please let me know, I'll be happy to give you some money,' Mr Le Blanc laughed, hoping that she was joking.

By now, his hands were able to open and close with relative ease and he placed the monster of a car in gear and left the station parking lot. The trip to the grounds of *Château de Petite Anglaise* took them 10 minutes, even with icy conditions and slippery roads. Just before turning into their drive, they passed the last gate of the right, a security man hiding from the weather in the guard hut. Marie-Claire stared intently at the gate as they passed. *I wonder if he is in there,* she thought. *Surely he knows I am here for the break? I do hope he doesn't do something even more foolish than the last time. Some people just can't take a hint. That he hasn't given up yet is beyond me.* They were both relieved to arrive at the manor, where Mr Bouchard was manning the gate dressed in a thick coat and accessories. He seemed warm enough, at least. The drive was free of snow, but the yard had a thin layer of either heavy frost, or light snow.

They drove straight into the open garage. Mr Le Blanc grabbed the two bags from the trunk. 'I am leaving the parcel in the car, Father. I do not want mother to see it.' The pair entered the house, which was cosy and pleasant. A roaring fire in the lounge warmed up most of the rooms. They could finally take off their coats. 'Mother, I'm so glad to see you! You look well,' Marie-Claire hugged and kissed her mother, who was dressed in pants and a light sweater. They all settled in the lounge and Mrs Bouchard brought a tray with tea. 'Good afternoon, Miss Marie-Claire. I trust you are well?'

'Yes thanks, Mrs Bouchard. The macarons look gorgeous. Did you bake them yourself?'

'It's an old family recipe. You will love them! Please excuse me, I need to tend to dinner.'

'How is your work going Father? Is the country in a good place? Did it need saving again this month?'

'Things have calmed down a little bit now, I am glad to say. The world was really on a knife's edge in October. Your uncle Valerian played a sterling role to calm things in Cuba down. He kept me updated with the inside scoop of negotiations. It was almost the only news that made it out, so we were certainly better informed than the rest of Europe.'

'It's good that you could count on him for information, Father. Your connections must still make you valuable to the government? It will be awhile before they could afford to put you out to pasture. I think it keeps you out of trouble,' she winked at him, sipping her tea. 'Are you still enjoying the country life, Mother?'

'Yes my darling. It is wonderfully relaxing around here. I have now joined a bridge club and we also do some outrides from one of the racing stables. It is quite sweet, they use the retired race-horses for this. The trainer is a brilliant man with a soft heart for horses and at least this way, his old stalwarts still get to serve a purpose. It's just like your father in government. Old, but not without his uses!' They all had a good laugh at the analogy. 'Is the boy next door still pursuing you?'

'Oh, yes. He pops by the flat every now and again for coffee and invites me to accompany him to the most peculiar collection of events. Who knows whether he's in Paris for legitimate business, or just to see me? I suppose I might have led him on a bit initially, when we met. But now I can't seem to get through to him that nothing is going to come of it. I guess that will teach me a good lesson about applying proper social etiquette at all times! I mean, he is perfectly intelligent, sweet and handsome. And affluent! But the religious thing is just too much. I cannot convert to another religion simply for a man.'

'People do strange things for love, Marie-Claire. Someday, you'll fall in love with someone and then you will not have such doubts. If it is the right man, you will jump off a bridge for him. I followed your father to the farthest reaches of the world during our time together. Luckily for him, his travel demands are much closer to home nowadays, otherwise he might have been in trouble and travelling alone,' she accentuated the last sentence with a playful wink. The wind was howling outside as the three discussed the more mundane elements of their daily existence. Mrs Bouchard announced dinner and they moved to the dining room, a beautiful spread set out for their enjoyment.

The following day was more pleasant and Marie-Claire and Mrs Le Blanc went into town, to join the rest of the crowds for some last minute Christmas shopping. Most shops in town were open, despite it being a Sunday. Mr Le Blanc drove them there and then went on his own way once they arrived in town. 'We'll meet for lunch at 1pm,' he said as they left. The little village of *Chantilly* was packed with warmly dressed shoppers in a festive mood. Christmas trees dotted town and all the brasseries and restaurants were full of patrons, hiding from the weather and on occasion, their money-spending spouses. The two ladies were sitting in a *café*, warming up next to the fireplace. 'I found the most remarkable antique sword at the *Marché Aux Puces* a few weekends ago, which I am going to gift father for Christmas. It belonged to one of Napoleon's generals and it would make a wonderful addition to his study. I am just lucky it fit into my luggage, otherwise it might have proven difficult to hide from him in the trip from the station. What are you getting Father?'

'I managed to acquire a full set of the books by *Alexandre Dumas*, a first print of his collected works. Came across them quite by accident when I attended an estate auction in the area during the year. My biggest challenge has been keeping them hidden from him for all these months. Luckily the old house has plenty of nooks and crannies.'

'This town is really abuzz with activity this morning,' Marie-Claire noted. 'Besides Christmas, is there any other reason?'

'No, it's just the festive season. People come for the break, schools are closed and they try to escape the shopping madness in Paris.'

'I love the festive spirit in Paris. The Christmas markets are delightful! I think I could travel Europe just to see all the incredible markets this time of year. Once my studies are done. I could not even go to *St Moritz* this year because of a project that was due. Catherine said they had a wonderful time out there.'

'I remember when *St Moritz* was just a tiny little village and people only started being enticed to go there in the winter season. Then suddenly it blossomed. Of course I never went there myself until I met your father. By then it was already an expensive trip, which my family could not have afforded. Government wages have never been particularly rewarding. If it wasn't for your father's inheritance, we certainly would not have been going there nowadays either. Oh, look at the time, we have to go meet your father for lunch.' They walked to *Chez Albert*, where Mr Le Blanc was already seated and joined him for an early afternoon meal. Further inclement weather was looming on the horizon by mid-afternoon and everyone in town left, to reach the safety of their homes before more snow hit the area.

The family had no need to be in town on Christmas Eve, so opted to stay at home for the day, enjoying a peaceful day relaxing in the manor. Marie-Claire had found reading material to her liking in the manor library and was curled up on the couch reading a book. Mrs Le Blanc was tinkering around the kitchen with Mrs Bouchard. Mr Le Blanc, however, was called in to an emergency meeting with the Prime Minister regarding some incident in Korea, and had left early in the morning. Affairs of State do not always pay heed to the holiday plans of government employees. The one capitulation which happened, was to rather have the meetings on Christmas Eve. This negated potentially having it on Christmas itself. It would hopefully not take too long, or keep him busy in Paris all day.

The ladies were sitting in the dining room having an informal lunch of soup and sandwiches, which fit in well with the gloomy weather outside. 'I hope father's meeting doesn't keep him busy all day,' Marie-Claire said dejectedly.

'I would think not. From what I gathered, it would have finished up in the morning. He had to action some things, but when he called earlier, he said he would be finished with everything by 2 o'clock.'

'Splendid! We should all go into town for the carol singing in the square at sunset. At least it seems like the weather is settling.' The weather, however, did not settle and by four o'clock the snow was bucketing down. There would be no Christmas service in the town square of *Chantilly* this year, much to Marie-Claire's disappointment.

Marie-Claire woke up on Christmas morning, a childlike excitement filling her whole being. She wiped some tears from her face and walked downstairs in her robe and slippers. *I always seem to be the first one up every morning.* The fire in the lounge had died down to embers, and with a little coaxing she got it going again, soon pleasantly heating the room. She popped into the garage to collect her mother's parcel from the trunk of the Rolls Royce, which she placed under the tree next to the fireplace. She also placed her father's gift wrapped sword amongst the other presents. The next order of business was to get a pot of coffee brewing. The smell of fresh coffee permeated the lounge, wafting upstairs. Fairly soon, activity was audible upstairs, as her parents started stirring. Marie-Claire sat in the lounge, staring at the crackling fire and appreciating the fine cup of coffee. *Life does not get much better than this,* she thought. Her thoughts meandered as she reached an almost meditative state on the couch. *I wonder what they got me for Christmas? Does it really matter? Would it change anything if it was not nice, or was really nice? Where is Sister Marcelle today?* The last thought randomly popped in her head. She had not thought about her kind French tutor and mentor at *Marcigliana* in years, she realised, suddenly feeling saddened by this. *Who else have I forgotten? Christmas is a time to spend with loved ones.* She now also included the ones she left behind over the years in her thoughts. *Karin, Katharina, Arianna. The unfortunate Sofia. Andros and Philippe, Jacques and Jean-Pierre. The Mother Superior and the first gift I can remember ever receiving. Marie-Claire.* Her nostalgia was interrupted by the arrival of her parents, both in their housecoats. 'Merry Christmas, Marie-Claire!'

'Merry Christmas, Father! Merry Christmas, Mother!' They both joined her for coffee by the fire. 'Father, here is something for you,' she said, handing him the gift wrapped sword. He unwrapped it and observed the blade, a striking example of French craftsmanship. 'Thank you Marie-Claire, what a fine blade!'

'It belonged to one of Napoleon's generals. It would make a good talking point in your study.'

'Indeed!'

She handed the parcel to her mother. 'Here is something for you, Mother.' Mrs Le Blanc unwrapped the parcel, revealing a beautiful painting of Auguste Rodin's *The Thinker*, adorned with an elaborate golden frame. 'I spent many hours in Rodin's garden in the sun finishing this. I hope you are pleased?'

'Oh it is simply beautiful, Marie-Claire. Thank you very much for the wonderful effort!'

Their picture perfect family moment was suddenly interrupted by a commotion audible in the distance by the front gate. Mr Bouchard was shouting at someone, who was hooting in return. They stepped onto the landing to see what all the fuss was about. At the gate was a golden Land Rover with a horsebox. 'What the devil?!' Mr Le Blanc remarked, not impressed by the unexpected intrusion on Christmas day. 'Rémy, what in the blazes do they want??'

'They say they have a delivery for Ms Marie-Claire, Mr Le Blanc.'

A delivery for Marie-Claire? 'Well tell them to bring it in quickly and be on their way.' The off-road vehicle parked in front of the house and a foreign-looking gentleman in a turban got out. He opened the horsebox and led out a bay coloured horse, its coat shining in the sun. 'Ms Le Blanc. With the compliments of his Highness, Aga Khan. I present you, *Vaguely Noble*. Merry Christmas!' The magnificent horse had a red bow around its neck and stamped its foot almost in perfectly timed emphasis of the Christmas wish. The Le Blancs stood in stunned silence, not paying the least attention to their apparel, which was not really fitting to receive guests. Finally, Marie-Claire burst out laughing. 'What is the meaning of this then? Are you joking?'

'Not at all, Ms Le Blanc. His highness wants you to have this fine racing colt as a gift. It has a long, illustrious bloodline and he hopes it will bring you lots of joy.'

Mr Le Blanc raised his eyebrows. *This is a bit over the top, even for a love-struck man.* 'Marie-Claire, give the man back his horse and send him on his way. You cannot accept such an extravagant gift.'

'Oh no, sir! You cannot offend his Highness by refusing his offer. He gives it freely and without any expectation.'

'Well thank you very much then, I guess?' Marie-Claire said, still unsure of what to make of the gift. 'I am sure it will prove to be... fun,' she said with a little laugh, at a total loss for a more coherent expression of thought at the present time. The delivery man gave a bow, before driving off with the horsebox in tow. 'I'll go put it up in the stables,' Mr Bouchard volunteered.

'Thanks Rémy. At least until we can figure out what to do with it,' Mr Le Blanc responded.

The Le Blancs went back inside, dazed by the unexpected visit. 'I think this calls for some brandy,' Mr Le Blanc suggested. Everyone agreed, despite the early hour. 'What do you want to do with the horse, Marie-Claire?' Mrs Le Blanc enquired.

'Oh, I'd like to keep it. Perhaps that trainer of yours with the kind heart can make something of it? And if not, it would be good for a laugh next time I visit with Sacha and his friends. Merry Christmas to me…'

GOING UNDERGROUND IN PARIS, 1963

The new academic year started in September at the *Sorbonne*. Marie-Claire's studies continued, with very little difference in course material from the previous year. *A Masters' Degree was a marathon, not a sprint,* she was often reminded. The classes remained informal in nature, with guest lecturers appearing and disappearing without much fanfare. The students were now assisting in the *Louvre* as part of their studies, learning the craft from the professional art restorers employed by the illustrious museum.

One of these restorers was Pietro, a short, stocky Italian. Pietro had a fine eye for colour matching and was unparalleled in his skill within the dark passages of the *Louvre* basement. Marie-Claire was assigned to work with him the first semester. She was not without her reservations of the idea. The man appeared a bit, *greasy,* for lack of a better term. He was slick and patted her bottom much more often than social norms would consider appropriate. As her supervisor, Marie-Claire needed him to sign off on her work hours and she had no choice, other than to accept his uncivilised behaviour.

Some of Pietro's other habits were equally peculiar. The man preferred black coats to the normal white that other personnel wore during the restoration process. The long dark coats were not totally impractical, but did not fit in with the ambiance of the rest of the restoration section and its staff. He also wore black pants, black boots and black shirts to complete his ensemble. A black beret hung on a stand in the corner. *I wonder if his soul is equally dark*, Marie-Claire wondered frequently. Despite his obvious short-comings and occasional lack of social graces, she could respect him as an artist. He was extremely gifted and she was often surprised in the mornings, when it appeared that he must have spent all night working on finishing a specific project.

'Marie-Claire, would you like to come with me to a party on Friday night?'

Marie-Claire was not keen at all, but decided to humour him, none-the-less. 'What are we celebrating? And where is it?'

'Nothing specific. And I can't tell you yet, they only determine the exact venue on Friday afternoon.' This piqued her interest somewhat. *No occasion and last minute venue?* She had heard of such affairs, but had never attended one. It was the stuff of legend.

'Sure, I can join you, Pietro. It sounds mysteriously fabulous.' It was his turn to be curious. *He had hardly said anything and now it sounds fabulous?? Oh well, at least she'd join him, irrespective of her motivations.* 'You'd probably not do too well in your normal party outfits. It is a little bit... eh, darker than the usual. So dress in the female version of my work clothes and you will be fine.'

'Hmm. I think I have *just* the outfit for this event...' Marie-Claire said with a sly look.

'Good. Great. Then it is a... scheduled appointment,' he caught himself just in time. She looked skittish enough as it is and Pietro did not want to repel her by complicating matters and using potentially off-putting phrases, such as *date*. At least he had some commitment from her.

'Any idea in which area it might be?' she asked.

'Indications are, somewhere on the left bank.'

'Excellent. There's a brasserie called *La Bouffe* on the *Boulevard St Michel*, two blocks from the bridge. You will find me outside at 9 o'clock. We'll travel from there.' *At least she could count on home-ground support, in case he tried any funny business.*

Friday night at 9, Marie-Claire was sitting in the outside seating of *La Bouffe*. She was wearing a dark, full-length coat, which hid her clothing as she sipped a pre-paid drink, waiting on Pietro. He came plodding down the Boulevard in clothes that resembled his normal work garments, except for the absence of paint stains. *For an artist, he really has limited imagination,* she thought, looking at his outfit. She was still not even vaguely interested in the man. His art had a lack of originality, giving his work a technically adept, almost mechanical feel. *It was half-art, forever following where others had already been.* Added to that, he was short, fat and always smelled of garlic. His single redeeming quality was his proposal for the evening, which Marie-Claire found extremely alluring. If she had to put up with him until she got to the secret party, she could do so. But she did not see herself leaving with him afterwards.

They took a taxi south, down the length of *Boulevard St Michel* until they crossed the *Boulevard du Montparnasse.* Marie-Claire was feeling comfortable with her surroundings. *This is still my valley.* They passed the entrance to the Catacombs and turned left and after another block, turned right. The taxi dropped them off and Pietro stopped in front of a basement apartment door. Marie-Claire was now slightly ill-at-ease, as the expected sound of revelry was conspicuously absent in the apartment building and surrounds. She fidgeted with her ring as they waited for the door to be answered. *Perhaps I do not know him well enough for this*, she thought.

A tall, heavy set doorman opened the door. At least, she hoped he was the doorman. Pietro gave him two tokens and the bouncer exchanged them for a paper with some hand-drawn lines on it. *A pass, of some kind?* He pointed them to the second room on the right. 'Enjoy!' was the only words he spoke. They entered the appointed room, Marie-Claire now very curious to see what awaited them there. It was empty, except for a ladder in the floor. *Oh my god, it's in a sub-basement*, was all she could think. Pietro gallantly descended the ladder first, although Marie-Claire suspected it was purely because he wanted to look up her coat. *Pervert!* She followed him down the long metal ladder and several floors down they came to an old wooden door. He pushed it open and they entered a wide tunnel. *We are in the Catacombs!* Marie-Claire recognised it from previous visits. There were strings of lights set up and Pietro followed the paper map around twists and turns of the bone filled tunnels. The sound of music reached their ears from a distance. It was heavy rock music with loud guitars and drums. As they got closer, she recognised it as the Rolling Stones. When they rounded the final corner, she was faced with an amazing sight.

There were about 200 partygoers gathered in a large open area in the Catacombs. The cavernous space was lit by floodlights and a disc jockey was manning two turntables on a makeshift stage. Mick Jagger blared over the speaker system, the noisy crowd sometimes singing along. *And what a crowd!* They were all wearing different shades of black clothing, the leather pervaded with metal studs and chains featuring prominently on most of them. Pietro led her to a wooden enclosure set up on the side of the room and checked their coats with the girl behind the table. Marie-Claire's full outfit was visible for the first time. Her tight leather skin suit blended in perfectly with the rest of the revellers. She almost seemed more at home than Pietro did. It was his turn to feel slightly uneasy. 'Shall we get a drink?' she enquired.

He pulled himself together. 'Yes… Yes! There's a bar set up on the far side of the room.' They pushed their way through the throng of bodies moving to the rhythm of the music on the dance floor. The barman had a stud through his ear and also his nose, connected by a tiny length of chain. His scalp was clean shaven end his leather jacket and pants worn out. 'What can I get you?' he shouted over the din of the music. 'Two measures of Absinthe and two glasses of wine,' Marie-Claire shouted back.

The absinthe came with all the necessary paraphernalia to mix it- sugar cubes, teaspoons and some matches. Marie-Claire expertly mixed both drinks, dousing the sugar cube with the liquid and lighting it up, before mixing it into the remaining absinthe. Pietro was quite surprised at how effortlessly this skill seemed to have come to the girl. *Perhaps this was not her first rodeo?* He raised his glass in a toast. 'To the Paris underground!'

'And all the deep, dark secrets it may hold!' she responded, downing the drink effortlessly. Marie-Claire recognised some people from her life up above, but it did not seem the appropriate occasion to loudly call out someone's name across the crowded dance floor. She would speak to them later. Pietro was not troubled by a similar sense of tact and shouted at people in the passing, eager to show Marie-Claire that he was a regular at these events and knew the right people. She was not impressed by this. *The man is a complete boor!* 'Shall we go dance?' he suggested.

'Yes, please!' she shouted back. 'Anything but this,' she muttered under her breath.

They entered the crowded dance floor and danced to a tune by David Bowie. Marie-Claire had always found that dancing to more modern music required some adaptation to her normal ballet, but with enough revision, she could execute moves that had most of the men present swooning over her lithe body, covered in leather and inviting them for a closer connection. She angled away from Pietro and joined some other acquaintances in a group. They all greeted her with friendly shouts, before continuing with their wild gyrations.

The group took a break when the next song started and ambled back to the bar. Another round of Absinthe was in the offing, followed by a second. All around them, the party was getting more rowdy. They switched to a round of wine. 'How are you, Marie-Claire? I didn't expect to see you here on a Friday. Don't you normally have other plans on weekends, with the civilised folk?'

'I'm doing well, Jaime! I like to mix things up from time to time. Nothing like getting stuck in a social rut. I have been hoping to attend one of these things for ages, but have simply not come across the opportunity until now. Some art colleague invited me. The podgy one over there, trying his luck with the cross dresser,' she shouted back pointing out Pietro.

'Are you not going to give him a friendly warning?'

'Nope! We're not *that* friendly. Such a mistake will be a golden learning opportunity for him. He must make his own unwelcome discoveries in that regard.' They all laughed at her response.

Marie-Claire continued the shouted conversation. 'How many of these things have you guys attended? Are they always down here?'

'They are sometimes down here, but not always right at this spot. There are many of these large caverns that are big enough for this kind of event. One always has to be careful with police raids, that's why they keep it clandestine and don't make the venues known until shortly beforehand. They have about one a month. Normally they hold them around the full moon, just to add to the esoteric nature of the affair.'

The disc jockey switched to playing Louie Louie by The Kingsmen. Pietro joined them, seeming rushed.

'You have to all leave right now. I just got a tip off that the police are on their way into the Catacombs. Don't cause a panic before we have our coats.' The group walked to the coat check and recovered their coats, just in time. Suddenly loud shouts rang out. 'Police! The police are on their way! Get out now!' Pandemonium broke out in the cavern below the peaceful streets of Paris. The music stopped abruptly and the crowd scattered in a thousand directions, like a swarm of cockroaches caught in the kitchen light. Pietro grabbed Marie-Claire by the arm and ran into a tunnel. When she looked over her shoulder, she could see the first policemen entering the cavern on the far side, commands over a bullhorn now adding to the overwhelming noise of the evacuation, echoing off the cavern walls. 'This is the Police! Nobody move! Everyone lie flat on the ground now, with your hands behind your head!' The last Marie-Claire saw over her shoulder was that there was minimal compliance with the command.

The lit tunnels were overrun with police. Pietro produced a flashlight from within the folds of his coat and they veered into one of the darker side tunnels, following the beam of light at as fast a pace as they could safely manage. The aim was to get as much distance between themselves and the cavern, as quickly as possible. The direction was not of concern, only the distance. They turned left and right and left as the sounds of the raid started fading in the darkness behind them. Occasionally, they could hear more voices in the tunnels, other revellers hiding in the dark, or trying to find their way out of the maze of tunnels. 'Do you know where you're going?' Marie-Claire asked as they stood to catch their breath in the darkness.

'Not really. But there are exits all over the place. It's just a question of finding one. I don't know where we might end up above, but that does not really matter, as long as we get out.' It was now quiet all around them. They had covered a good distance in their frenzied dash from the Police.

The two were now standing at an intersection in the tunnels. Pietro shone the light down the three possible route choices. They all looked the same. The pair had arrived from the fourth and did not want to go back the way they came. *If it was not for the circumstances, this would have been a marvellous exploration of the Catacombs*, Marie-Claire thought. *I quite like the scenery down here.* 'Switch off the light for a moment, so we can see whether there's any other light,' she suggested.

'Good idea!' The flashlight went off and they stood in the total darkness, their eyes slowly adjusting to the inky blackness.

Marie-Claire could eventually make out the vague outline of the tunnel on the left. *There was light in that direction!* 'We should go left,' she said. 'There is light there.'

'The only light down here this evening is what the party planners supplied. The police will be waiting for us there.' They turned right, heading into the pitch-black tunnel. They passed row upon row of bones, interspersed with stacked skulls and empty chambers. After half an hour, they sat down in a small chamber. 'Switch off the light to save the batteries.' The darkness engulfed them, only their breathing audible in the cavern. Somewhere, there was the sound of dripping water. 'Look! There, in the tunnel on the right. More light!' There was a shuffling sound as Pietro moved. The next moment, he was gripping Marie-Claire and kissing her. *What the hell! Pervert!* First she gave him a slap and then she brought up her knee with a fast swing, smashing it into, what she hoped, was his groin. She could hear the flashlight drop, followed by the dull thud of Pietro himself hitting the ground. From the satisfying groan, she knew she had connected. Marie-Claire ran down the tunnel on the right, following the light. She no longer cared if she got arrested.

The light increased as she moved, making it easier to avoid the tunnel walls and protruding rocks in the floor. She finally reached a tunnel lit with a row of lightbulbs. Everything was dead quiet and she peeked around the corner, observing for any movement. There was none. Her heart was still beating at her chest wall, the shock slowly subsiding. *What was he thinking!* She turned left and made her way down the tunnel with a brisk walk. She noticed that the tunnel now had cement walls, different from the carved limestone of the tunnels before. There were now street names written on the walls. *I must be in a service tunnel of some kind.* The string of lights continued onwards. *If I keep following this, I am bound to reach an exit. And the policemen guarding it.* She saw a ladder in a dark tunnel to her right, leading upwards. Marie-Claire decided to chance the ladder.

Climbing up the ladder slowly in the darkness, she ended up bumping her head against a metal plate. *A manhole cover!* She pushed her shoulder against the cover and heaved. Nothing happened. She heaved again, this time with all her strength. It moved! Two further efforts dislodged the cover and she exited into the fresh evening air, like a bird hatching from an egg. The fresh air was welcoming. Luckily, the street was deserted. She replaced the cover and looked around to see where she was. It was a small quiet street she did not know. She walked to the closest corner and saw a metro station. *She was in Montrouge!* It was now too late to take the metro. There was a public phone against the wall and she called a taxi, which arrived soon after, to take her home.

The uneventful trip back to the Latin Quarter was a welcome reprieve after the hectic evening she had just experienced. As they passed the public entrance to the Catacombs, there were swarms of policemen everywhere. The sidewalk had a row of people lying down with their hands clamped behind their heads, as the law enforcement agencies waited for additional transport to the police station. There were several vans, unfortunate party goers staring out through barred windows. For a fleeting moment, she recognised the face of Jaime peering out from inside one of the vans. The taxi driver left the unhappy scene safely behind as he travelled north.

Marie-Claire was only too relieved when she saw the familiar, welcoming lights of *La Bouffe*. The brasserie was still quite busy and she stepped inside for a drink to calm her frayed nerves. The barman took her order for a triple measure of brandy and raised his eyebrows. 'Interesting evening, Marie-Claire?'

'Oh, I think you could say so…'

RACE DAY IN CHANTILLY, 1964

The summer had arrived and Marie-Claire was pouting. She was seeing off her parents at the *Orly* Airport. The two were booked on a flight to *Nice*, for their annual summer vacation in *Juan-les-Pins*. Unfortunately, or perhaps fortunately, Marie-Claire had responsibilities in *Chantilly* to tend to, so could not join them. Her racehorse, *Vaguely Noble*, was entered into the main curtain raiser before the *Prix de Diane* at the racecourse on one of the coming weekends and as owner, she had to make an appearance and avail herself to the trainer in the week prior to the race. She would be travelling through to *Chantilly* on Monday with a group of her friends.

The horse had been doing well in some minor races the past year and was now finally going to make its debut in a curtain raiser for a major event. Marie-Claire was excited at this prospect and had to delay her summer holiday, until at least after the race. She was feeling disproportionately blue at the boarding gates as she greeted her parents. She would see them again soon, but her emotions were somehow awash with sadness. 'Goodbye Father. I hope you have a wonderful trip. I'll see you in a week or two.' She hugged him. She suddenly struggled to hold back tears as she hugged her mother. 'I'll miss you Mother. Thanks for everything you have done for me over the years and for always treating me like a proper princess. I love you.'

'I love you too, my dear. Don't fret. We'll see you in a fortnight on the Riviera. I'll make sure they keep a cocktail cold for you on the terrace. Goodbye Marie-Claire.'

'Have a safe journey! Goodbye Mother.'

The Le Blancs boarded the plane and waved at Marie-Claire from the boarding stairs.

Marie-Claire took a taxi back to her apartment and decided on lunch at *La Bouffe*. She sat down outside, lucky to find seating at the start of tourist season. 'Good afternoon Marie-Claire,' the head waiter greeted her.

'Hi Peter. I see business is picking up for the season. I'm sure all us locals will begin fleeing Paris for the coast, or anywhere else, soon.'

'I suppose so. Are you going to *Juan-les-Pins* this year?'

'Yes, but I have to be in *Chantilly* next week for the *Prix de Diane*. So will only go to the coast after that. A group of us are leaving for *Chantilly* on Monday. Would you like to come along for the week, we have plenty of room?'

'That sounds great, but work here is a bit hectic at this time of the year. Simply can't get away for a week. I'll join you at the racecourse on Saturday, though?'

'Okay. Here is the number of the house there, you can call and we'll make arrangements to meet up on Saturday,' she said, a little disappointed.

Peter excused himself, the seasonal crowd filling the busy *brasserie* requiring close attention. Her waiter brought her drink, soon followed by her normal order of a *Caprice* salad. She finished lunch and left for her apartment, greeting Peter on the way out. 'Goodbye Peter.'

'Goodbye Marie-Claire. I'll see you on Saturday.'

On Monday Morning, Marie-Claire met up with her group of friends at the *Gare du Nord*. 'Good morning Serge. Morning, Béatrice. How are you? I haven't seen you since your wedding! Did you have a nice honeymoon?'

'Hello Marie-Claire. We are well. The honeymoon was lovely. I can really recommend Polynesia,' Serge responded, as they both kissed her hello. 'Thank you so much for the lovely gift!' They stood chatting a bit, until Catherine arrived with her new boyfriend, Jean-Jacques Marcel. 'Hello, Marie-Claire! Hi Serge.'

'Hi Catherine. I don't know if you've met my wife, Béatrice?'

'No, we have not met. Pleased to meet you. And this is Jean-Jacques,' Catherine introduced the new man in her life.

Serge shook his hand. 'Pleased to meet you. I'm a big fan of your game.'

'Likewise, I am a fan of yours!' the tall football player responded.

'Are we still waiting for anyone else, Marie-Claire?' Catherine asked.

'Yes, we are just short of Annika Walden and her boyfriend. She is one of the art restorers at the *Louvre*. Very talented. You might have seen some of her work hanging on the walls of the museum, without even knowing it. And speak of the devil… Hello Annika!'

'Hello Marie-Claire, lovely to see you. This is Yves Klein,' she said, introducing the man at her side.

'Ah, yes, I am a big fan of your work, Yves. *Leap into the Void* was especially brilliant. Let me introduce everyone. This is Serge and Béatrice, Catherine and Jean-Jacques, and this is Annika.' With introductions made and everyone acquainted, the group walked over to the northern track, to board the train to *Chantilly*.

The trip was of short duration and the station at *Chantilly* provided welcome relief from the sweltering train carriages when they stepped off. 'Would anyone mind if we stop at the racetrack on the way home? My horse is training and I just want to check in with the trainer.' Everyone was happy to approve the request and they took two taxis from the station-house to the *Chantilly* racetrack.

'What a magnificent racecourse!' Béatrice exclaimed. 'Is that a palace in the background?'

'No, those are actually the royal stables. But they are glorious. Would you excuse me for a moment?' There was a cluster of people by the track, Etienne Pollet amongst them, so she walked over. 'Good morning, Etienne!' she greeted the trainer. 'How are you today? How is our boy doing? Is he ready for the weekend?'

'Good morning, Marie-Claire. I think he is doing just fine. I expect that he will give us a good performance in the race. His current times around the track would have secured him a fifth place in the main race last year. I believe that the additional adrenaline on race day, might lead to an even better result than that.'

'Excellent Etienne! I am glad for that. A good showing the weekend will open up many more opportunities for us going forward. I'll leave you to your business. Good luck with the preparations!'

'Thanks, Marie-Claire. Have a pleasant day!'

She re-joined the group, who stood watching the horses on the track. 'Which one is yours, Marie-Claire?'

'The bay coloured one there on the far side. With the jockey in blue.'

They left for the *château* in the waiting taxis, Marie-Claire issuing instructions to the driver. They were listening to a Parisian station on the car radio. The presenter was extremely excited about the glorious weather, before announcing a song by France Gall. 'I like her music, it is really upbeat,' Marie-Claire said to Serge and Béatrice, who were sharing her taxi. 'I'd love to meet her someday.'

'I am sure I can arrange that,' Serge answered. 'I write some of her songs, so I know her quite well. I am certain she'd be happy to meet you too.'

Arriving at the *château* gate, the taxi honked the horn. Mr Bouchard came walking briskly up the driveway and opened the gate for them. Mrs Bouchard greeted them warmly at the house and showed them to their respective guest rooms for the week. 'Mrs Bouchard, we are going into town for lunch, so no preparations necessary,' Marie-Clair informed the housekeeper. The seven had no problems fitting into the large Rolls Royce, although the four ladies and Yves in the backseat was a bit of a squeeze. It was just easier than taking two cars. Serge was driving, with Jean-Jacques next to him in the passenger seat.

It promised to be anything but dull and dreary in *Chantilly* for the next week. The town was already making preparations for a large weekend turn-out. Colourful banting was being put up along the main street and the owners of the *brasseries* were busy stocking up on beer and wine. The group had no problems acquiring a table for lunch at one of the local restaurants and enjoyed a delicious meal. They had a royal time over lunch, with lively conversation lingering into afternoon tea.

The group drove back to the *château,* where they gathered on the patio for cocktails. 'How long have you had your racehorse?' Annika enquired.

Marie-Claire recanted the story of how she got the racehorse. 'Eventually I had to write the prince a letter to inform him that I really don't see any future for the two of us. He seems to have finally accepted this fate in an amicable fashion. I think he is courting someone else now. My mother arranged with a trainer she knew in the area to stable it and it has proven a very interesting two years, indeed. If all goes well the weekend, there might be some major races in his future.'

'A racehorse for Christmas?? How smitten do you have to be to do something like that?' Annika said, to everyone's great amusement.

Marie-Claire woke up on Saturday morning, wiped her teary face and looked at the lovely French summer weather outside her window. She was very excited by everything the day would bring. Having never been to a major race, she was thrilled at the prospect. Everyone gathered for an informal breakfast. 'What time should we be leaving for the track?' Yves asked.

'Let's all meet up outside at 11 o'clock, then we can leave together in one car. They only gave me one parking pass.'

Their arrival at the racetrack was still relatively early, but one could already see people arriving in dribs-and-drabs from all over. Those that came in by train from Paris, where following a footpath through the forest before arriving at the racecourse. Marie-Claire was wearing an elaborate yellow summer dress adorned with sunflowers and a matching hat, both designed by Pierre Balmain. She gave everyone a VIP guest pass which she was eligible for as an owner, and had requested from the racing club. This would give them access to the parade ring and to the VIP lounge at the course. The group stood leaning on the rail next to the track, taking in the view. It was spectacular. The racecourse and surroundings reflected every possible shade of green and there was not a cloud in the sky. The sandstone colour of the grand stables in the background created a perfect contrast to the greenery surrounding it. The pavilions were still fairly empty, but would soon fill up with an explosion of colour as the crowds now arrived in earnest. It was a magnificent affair. 'I have to meet someone at 12 o'clock. Why don't you all go find us a table in the VIP lounge, so we can have lunch? I'll find you there.' Marie-Claire sauntered off to the betting circle, where she arranged to meet Peter.

Peter was already waiting for her when she arrived.

'Hello Marie-Claire. You look radiant in that outfit. Summer personified!' he cheek kissed her.

'Thanks Peter. You look very dashing yourself. Not your first trip to the races, I see. Let's go to the VIP lounge, the rest of our group is there for lunch. Here is your pass.' The two strolled to the middle level of the pavilion and entered the Members' Club. The rest of the party had found a table overlooking the course and there was already wine and platters in the table.

'Everyone, this is Peter. He's a friend of mine from Paris, who works at the brasserie below my apartment. He is also a genius poet and writer in his spare time. Peter, this is Serge and Béatrice, Yves and Annika, and Jean-Jacques and Catherine.'

'Very pleased to meet you all.'

'We ordered some wine and starters, I hope you don't mind?' Serge asked.

'Oh, no. Brilliant. The *Bollinger* is always a good choice,' Marie-Claire answered as they sat down. A smartly dresses sommelier came to fill their glasses. They finished lunch at 2 o'clock, the first race about to start. A large crowd had unobtrusively arrived during their meal. The lawns next to the pavilion were now virtually covered in picnic blankets. The atmosphere was light and festive.

Marie-Claire had to make her official appearance in the parade ring at 4 o'clock with her horse and the trainer. She excused herself and went to the owner's area, where she found Etienne Pollet and *Vaguely Noble*. 'How are you feeling Etienne? Do you fancy our chances?'

'I've instructed the jockey to give it everything he's got. I think we have a reasonable chance of a place and an outside chance of a win.'

'The odds at the bookies seem not to reflect your optimism, Etienne?'

'For once, I think they might have gotten it wrong there. The horse is an unknown in their books. The dark one in the race.'

'Then I'll be sure to place a little wager,' Marie-Claire said with a wink. The time came for them to pose with the horse and jockey, while the press took photographs for the morning papers. The jockey and *Vaguely Noble* looked regal, the colours matching Marie-Claire's outfit, a half yellow and white with yellow spots. If the horse did not perform, the pictures would probably not even be developed. The jockey took the horse for a lap around the parade ring, a loud cheer erupting when it walked past Marie-Claire's group of friends. All formalities observed, Marie-Claire could excuse herself and popped by the betting circle, to lay a wager, before meeting up with her friends in the Members' Club to view the race.

The sixth race at *Chantilly* was the official curtain raiser for the *Prix de Diane*. The track announcer went through the starting line-up. The fifteen horses where champing at the bit in the starting gates, eager for the 1 mile race to get underway. 'And they're off!' *Vaguely Noble* got off to a poor start and was caught in the back of the bunch, several lengths off the pace. The horses progressed down the back straight, Marie-Claire's colt now working its way up the field. She knew the instructions had been to hold the horse back and then let it loose close to the end, but she wondered whether it would have the stamina for the final push if it had to work this hard to catch up on the field during the race.

The horses rounded the bend and entered the final stretch, *Vaguely Noble* now only two lengths off the leader, sitting in fifth place. The announcer was getting quite excited, working the crowd up to a frenzy. 'And *Carry On* is leading by a neck from *Last Siege,* followed by *Almost There, Madame Posey* and *Vaguely Noble. Almost There* seems to be tiring, dropping a half-length to *Madame Posey. Last Siege* stepping up the pace a bit, now a nose behind *Carry On, Madame Posey* still trailing by a length. *Vaguely Noble* is starting to pick up the pace on the outside if the track, now passing *Madame Posey* into third place with *Carry On* and *Last Siege* being neck to neck at the front of the field. As the leaders pass the Quarter pole, *Last Siege* is leading by a nose from *Carry On* and *Vaguely Noble* on the outside, still picking up speed and closing the distance to the leaders. *Madame Posey* sitting in fourth, a length behind with the rest of the field two lengths behind that. The early leader, *Almost There,* is still dropping down the field. *Carry On* and *Last Siege* evenly matched as they approach the finish line with *Vaguely Noble* steaming down the outside, cracking on the pace. *Carry On* and *Last Siege, Vaguely Noble* gaining on the outside. *Vague Noble* is still gaining, now a neck behind the leaders, the finishing line fast approaching.'

At this point, Marie-Claire and her friends were going crazy in the Members' Club. 'Go! Go! Go! *Vaguely Noble*! Go!'

The announcer was equally excited. 'And *Vaguely Noble* now neck and neck with *Carry On* and *Last Siege. Last Siege, Carry On, Vaguely Noble!* And *Vaguely Noble* is now trailing by a nose, still increasing the pace, *Last Siege* and *Carry On* trying to match the newcomer on the outside. The three horses side by side *Last Siege, Carry On* and *Vaguely Noble* as they cross the finish line, *Vaguely Noble* wins it by a nose from *Carry On* and *Last Siege, Madame Posey* coming in fourth ahead of the rest of the field. *Vaguely Noble,* the unknown dark horse has taken the race, sitting at odds of 15-1, with *Carry-On* and *Last Siege* in a photo finish for second place. What a race!'

'Hooray! Hooray for Marie-Claire!' the group shouted in delight, much to the displeasure of the annoyed staff in the Members' Club. Try as they may, they could not control the excitement in the group and were only too glad when they left the area. Serge and Jean-Jacques carried Marie-Claire on their shoulders to the parade ring. They placed her over the fence and Marie-Claire made her way to Etienne Pollet, who she promptly hugged. 'Well done Etienne! Well done!'

'And to you, Marie-Claire. Congratulations!'

The tired jockey and horse made their way into the parade ring, to a great cheer from the gathered crowd. His saddle was removed and the horse was given the winning cover. The horse, owner, trainer and jockey posed for pictures from the press, before a cheque for 5 million Francs was handed over to Marie-Claire, along with a shiny trophy to the jockey and trainer. She hugged the horse and gave it a kiss on the nose. 'Well done boy. Well done!'

Marie-Claire slipped away to the betting circle and handed her stub over to one of the tote agents. His eyes stretched. 'Would the Madame be amendable to a cheque settlement?'

'I would prefer that, actually. You can make it out to *Marie-Claire le Blanc*.'

'An amount of this size, I would just need to get my manager to sign off on it. I'll be back shortly.'

She waited patiently for the agent's return. He finally came back with her cheque, to the value of 16 million francs. A welcome addition to her race winnings. She had trusted her horse and had bet a large sum on the win. It was a good day at the races for Marie-Claire and she hoped it would be the first of many more to follow.

DELIGHT AND DISMAY IN PARIS, 1965

The first course of dinner was about to be served at the Soviet Embassy. Mr Le Blanc and Marie-Claire was seated at one of the tables in the front of the ballroom. It was close to a podium that was set up on an elevated platform, bearing the Soviet insignia of the Hammer and Sickle. From past experience, Marie-Claire knew that they could probably expect a number of exceedingly boring speeches during the course of the evening. The master of ceremonies introduced himself as Matthias Yungski, the head of the Soviet Space Program. 'Quite the high level representative to have here,' Mr Le Blanc whispered, leaning over to Marie-Claire. 'Your uncle Val must have pulled a number of strings before he left Moscow, to manage this.'

Yungski pulled a thick sheaf of papers from his jacket and Marie-Claire dropped her head. *She had seen this coming a mile away.* 'Ladies and gentlemen, on behalf of our illustrious Premier, Comrade Alexei Kosygin, I would like to welcome you all to this glorious celebration of Soviet ingenuity. The rise of the Soviet Space program had its humble beginnings in the late 1920s…' Yungski carried on speaking for fifteen minutes. Marie-Claire was pleasantly surprised that he proved a mesmerising speaker. The man told some interesting anecdotes, some of which must have been declassified before he could dare speak of them in public. He finished off with a toast to Yuri Gagarin and everyone raised their glasses to the Soviet hero. Politics aside, it was quite the accomplishment. When Yungski was done, he received loud applause from the assembled guests. They obviously shared Marie-Claire's perception of fascination with the speech.

A young waiter arrived with a tray, filled to capacity with prawn cocktails. He introduced himself to the table as Yevgeni and started skilfully doling out the starters. Marie-Claire recognised him as the waiter who had served them champagne earlier the evening. *The poor man is really running around tonight*, she thought. Seven other people completed the company at the table, of which Marie-Claire did not know any. There was only one other person of her own age there, a man appearing to accompany his parents. The young man was blond and wearing an ill-fitting tuxedo and a pair of wire-rimmed glasses. He was already plagued by a receding hairline and judging by his father, who had no hair at all, his hairline would probably continue receding quite rapidly. The couple were speaking in German and Marie-Claire discerned that the bald man also worked for the Soviet Space Program. He apparently reported to the man on the podium. She was still deciding whether to indicate that she could speak German, or whether she would keep it to herself and conduct some surreptitious eavesdropping on their conversations through the evening.

One of the other couples knew her father from the diplomatic corps and they were already catching up on old times in the service. The third couple were carefully eating their starters, not speaking much at all. Marie-Claire could not place where they came from and the flower arrangement in the middle of the table blocked the folded name tags by their cutlery. They had tanned complexions with dark hair and she thought they might be Spanish or Portuguese. The gentleman was markedly overweight and balding, and his tuxedo looked like it was borrowed from someone smaller than him. The couple's hands did not have the animated movement typical in Italians, so she discarded that as a potential origin. She introduced herself to the Germans, deciding to do so in Russian. They were Klaus and Ingrid von Hagen and their son Dieter.

'How did you come to be invited her this evening?' she asked, feigning interest.

'We are guests of the ambassador from East-Germany,' they responded. Now Marie-Claire knew they were probably under some kind of instruction to remain *incognito*. She decided to make a little game out of seeing whether she could get them to slip up. *It would add some flavour to an evening that had all the promise of being a thoroughly dull affair.* Klaus indicated he was a Physicist at the University of East-Germany, while his son was an accountant at a firm in East-Berlin. It seemed like a plausible cover story, under the circumstances. 'How do you know Ambassador Zorin?' she enquired. 'Oh, we met him when he was stationed in East-Berlin in the late 50s. Such a lovely man.'

Marie-Claire held her pose, knowing full well that Uncle Valerian was nowhere near East-Germany in the 50s. She decided to push ahead and see where the rabbit hole went. '... Ah! Then you should also know his son, Valentin? The Ambassador always used to insist on pushing his wheelchair around personally, everywhere they went.'

'Oh yes... A fine boy. Such a pity about the wheelchair.' Klaus von Hagen replied, managing to sound melancholic. Marie-Claire pretended to drop her serviette, so she could hide her laughter. She popped up, red in the face. The Von Hagens assumed it was from having her head down and thought nothing of it. She gave a cough to compose herself. Thinking that she had probably played around enough with the poor people and would not want to get them in trouble, so craftily steered the conversation into more innocent waters. Having seen Valentin at a neighbouring table, she would be sure to invite him over and introduce them later, to complete her coup.

Mr Le Blanc drew her attention to the discussion he was having about an upcoming art auction. 'Marie-Claire, Claude indicated they were going to a classic auction at the *Louvre* next week. They are interested in adding some new pieces to their collection. Perhaps you could join them for a pre-viewing?'

'We would love to have an informed opinion on what we should bid on. Heaven forbid we overpay for something worthless, or miss out on a gem,' Claude Lavier piped in.

'That sounds marvellous!' Marie-Claire responded. 'It should prove quite interesting. Some of the pre-grad art students are helping out at the event and they did say there were some glorious pieces up for grabs.'

'It's settled then! We'll see you next Thursday evening at 7. We can meet at the main entrance,' Mrs Lavier declared excitedly.

In the meantime, Ingrid von Hagen was castigating her husband in German for lying to the girl in such an obvious fashion. 'What if his son is here?'

Klaus von Hagen defended his position, a little flustered. 'You know children, he probably wouldn't have remembered meeting me, anyway! Besides, I didn't see anyone here this evening in a wheelchair.'

'What if he recuperated, you dummkopf?' she snapped back. Marie-Claire could barely control her laughter from behind the folds of her napkin, finally having to resort to another fit of coughing as cover. It was at this opportune moment that Valentin Zorin walked past the table.

Marie-Claire grabbed the dashing young Russian by the arm. 'So good to so you again!'

'Always a pleasure to see you, Marie-Claire.'

'You remember Mr Klaus von Hagen? May I introduce his wife Ingrid and son Dieter? This is Valentin Zorin.' Ingrid von Hagen choked on her drink. Her husband turned a dark shade of red in his face.

'Good to see you again, young man. It has been so many years. I am glad to see you are out of your wheelchair,' Von Hagen recovered smartly. Valentin looked perplexed and responded with '… and you too, sir. You too.' He decided not to stick around and rather continue in the direction he was heading in, shaking his head at the oddity of what had just transpired. 'We'll talk a bit later, Marie-Claire,' he said as an afterthought over his shoulder. Marie-Claire excused herself as well, rushing out of the hall. Once outside, she bellowed with laughter, a passing Embassy staffer looking at her with the kind of suspicious look normally reserved for the mentally unstable.

When her laughter had abated, she overheard another speech kicking off in the ballroom. Having already suffered through two sets of ideological rhetoric this evening, Marie-Claire decided to skip the next one and stepped outside for some fresh air. There was still some champagne on the table beneath the mezzanine overhang, so she grabbed a flute before strolling out the French doors and onto the patio. A solitary blonde girl sat at one of the tables, her back to the doors. The parts of the park closest to the back fence and the Embassy grounds were lit with bright floodlights and the greenery took on a magical quality in the artificial light.

Marie-Claire settled at one of the sets of *café* furniture, neighbouring that of the sole figure and gazed over the park, the city lights visible in the distance. The occupant at the next table, was France Gall. The seventeen-year-old singer was nursing a cocktail and a cigarette. She had very recently returned to Paris from her success in Naples. The singer looked over at the new arrival with surprise. 'Marie-Claire, so good to see you! I did not think I would know anyone here this evening.' Serge Gainsbourg had kept his promise of an introduction. He had written her hit *Poupée de cire, poupée de son*, which won her the Eurovision title three weeks prior. 'Nice to see you, Isabelle! Congratulations on your roaring success in Naples,' she commended the singer by her given name. 'Will I see you at Serge's dinner party on Friday evening?'

'Oh yes, I'll be there. I also look forward to seeing Sacha again. I haven't seen him since I opened for his show in Belgium.' They spent some time catching up and when their drinks were done, they went back inside. By now, the speech was finished and the main course was being served. Marie-Claire bid the singer goodbye and returned to her seat, as Isabelle headed to a table on the far side of the dance floor.

The Von Hagen's seemed to have regained their composure and were tending to their dinner in silence. The Spanish couple were absent. Mr Le Blanc and the Laviers were still deep in conversation, the topic now having turned to the newly signed agreement with the USSR on the format of colour television in France. Marie-Claire was not particularly excited with the prospect of colour television in any format, as she had not even found the need to acquire a black-and-white set yet. She thought it a waste of time, frankly. Her father's interest in the subject was probably based on his hope for improved quality of television coverage of the annual French Open tennis. Yevgeni brought her plated vegetables and the chef passed with a trolley containing a pig stuffed with buckwheat, enquiring which cut Marie-Claire would like. The appearance of the poor beast splayed out on a silver platter, put her off this as her choice of mains and she rather opted for the sturgeon, which was on the next trolley to pass by.

The fish was overcooked and dry, and Marie-Claire now regretted not having the pork. The rest of the table had already finished their meals by the time she took her last bite. The Spaniards had also returned somewhere between the head and the tail of her sturgeon and ordered the pork. Yevgeni was waiting in the wings to clear the plate and did so promptly when she was done. A magnificent glass of white wine was the saving grace of the main course, proving the sommelier had more talent than the chef. She now turned her attention to the Spaniards, who seemed momentarily interested in their surroundings.

'Good evening! We seemed to have missed each other at the table. I am Marie-Claire,' she greeted them in Italian, not being aware of what else they might understand and knowing there were some common wording in the Mediterranean languages.

'A good evening to you,' they responded in Russian, which was rather surprising. 'I am Emilio Aragonés and this is Marlena.' Marie-Claire established that he was, in fact, Cuban and that he was the Secretary of the United Party of the Socialist Revolution of Cuba. It appeared that Marlena was only there to accompany him for the evening, which explained their long silences during their meal. The Cuban was travelling and in transit in Paris, *en route* to the Congo, to meet up with one of his compatriots from the resistance. He had met ambassador Zorin during the negotiations in 1962 and they had remained in touch ever since. *Uncle Valerian must have been delighted in the opportunity to include his old acquaintance in the festivities this evening.* Suddenly, Marie-Claire realised the prominence of the table they were at.

'Father, may I introduce you to General Emilio Aragonés, from Cuba?'

Mr Le Blanc was taken aback by the importance of plain looking Latino in the ill-fitting tuxedo. He was well aware of the General's position in the new leadership of Cuba and his role during the Cuban revolution and the Cuban missile crisis negotiation.

'Pleased to meet you, General. Welcome to Paris! I hope you will have time to appreciate some of the finer offerings the city has?'

'Unfortunately not, I am just passing through on my way to the Congo, so I will only have an overnight stop before continuing my journey,' the Cuban responded.

'Such a pity,' Mr Le Blanc said, genuinely disappointed. He had always hoped that exposure to western culture, and everything capitalism had to offer, would moderate the communists from Cuba and Moscow. From his diplomatic perspective, their moderation made the gap to bridge just a little bit narrower.

'With the revolution over, are you going to consider a change in the name of your Party, at some stage? *United Party of the Cuban Socialist Revolution* seems such a long-winded name,' Marie-Claire suggested. 'Something simpler, perhaps? Like the *Communist Party of Cuba*?' Mr Le Blanc's eyes stretched at the brazenness of his daughter.

'We have been discussing the idea of changing the name, to show the progressive nature of the movement,' Aragonés replied. '*Communist Party of Cuba..?* That would be a good title to use. Perhaps I shall borrow it from you,' he joked.

Their conversation was interrupted by the arrival of Yevgeni with a dessert trolley. The trolley was filled with a variety of Russian and French desserts, cakes, fruit selections and cheeses, giving a wide range of choices to finish off the meal. Marie-Claire selected a slice of Kiev cake with some macarons. As the trolley did the rounds at the table, everyone helped themselves to some sweets, satisfying the last remaining needs of their appetites. The dessert course was shortly followed by the coffee trolley, serving strong, dark roast coffee along with a variety of teas from the east. The conversation continued unabated, on a variety of topics. General Aragonés apparently realised that his consort for the evening was not the most eloquent of conversationalists and started engaging with the rest of the table guests, much to the delight of the German scientist.

Ambassador Zorin approached the podium to reflect on the evening and thank all the attendees and the Embassy staff for making the event such a splendid success. 'Ladies and gentlemen, we have offered you some glorious dishes from the Soviet Union this evening, in honour of Comrade Gagarin.' There was some applause from the guests. 'We have, however, saved the best for last.' An almost audible groan came from the assembled guests, who clearly did not have further appetite for any more food. 'The final *coup de grâce* for the evening, will be a serving of the finest in culture my country has to offer. We have the privilege this evening of having a troupe of dancers from the Bolshoi Ballet Company in our midst, who will be performing an act from *Cinderella* to the music composed by our illustrious comrade Sergei Prokofiev.' The guests broke out into thunderous applause. This was indeed an unexpected treat!

Five young dancers in a variety of costumes entered the ballroom and gracefully glided to the central dance floor. The hall went dark and the string quartet began playing. A loud cheer emanated from the audience as the lights on the dancers slowly turned up. The ballerinas started dancing, a marvellous performance of artistic flair. The troupe performed the version of the ballet made famous by choreographer Rostislav Zakharov, which depicted the step sisters in quite a comedic fashion. For twenty minutes the ballet dancers had the audience in rapture. At the end of the performance, the audience gave a standing ovation with roars of appreciation by all those in attendance. It was a magnificent display of talent, appreciated by all present. All, but one.

Halfway through the performance, Marie-Claire had leaned over to her father and asked to be excused. She was looking visibly upset and Mr Le Blanc fully understood her distress at the sight of the dancers from the Bolshoi. He knew her time in the Bolshoi School did not end on her own terms and the memories of it all were still troubling her. The elderly diplomat walked her out of the hall to the reception area. 'Ask Emile to take you home and return to pick me up after,' he instructed her. 'Thanks for escorting me this evening, it was joyful being in your company. Goodbye Marie-Claire.'

'Goodbye Father.' Marie-Claire walked through the reception area and entrance hall with fast steps, tears now flowing down her cheeks. She appreciated the fresh air as she exited the building through the front door. Emile saw her at the door and hurried over, leaving a gathering of other drivers and security staff off to the one side. 'Are you all right, miss?' he asked, which clearly she wasn't. 'I'll be fine Emile. Please take me home.' He opened the rear door to the car for her and they left the Embassy grounds, back to the reality of Paris. A distraught Marie-Claire was staring out of the car window, disappointed with the way the evening had ended.

ILLUMINATING THE DARKNESS, 1965

The trip home was uneventful, but still too long. The late hour made for quiet roads and most Parisians have long since retired for the evening. A light mist was settling over the city, giving each lamppost and eerie quality as the light bravely tried to break through the surrounding fog, creating a series of halos on the route home. Marie-Claire was still upset and had the occasional tear rolling down her cheeks, an imprecise mixture of pain and loathing. The party at the Embassy had started as a delightful occasion, despite some of the more drab speeches.

And then came the dancers. It was not meant in the least to be a personal attack on her dignity, but she could never experience the Bolshoi again with anything but contempt. *Were the dancers there because they had a wealth of talent, or because their fathers had wealth? What strings were pulled in the puppet show that was Soviet politics in order to be part of the dance company?* The image of an elite dance troupe had been shattered in her mind, forever. *They had talent, no doubt, but were they the cream of the dancing crop? She would never be certain of this again.*

Her departure from the dressing room in Moscow had been a sombre part of her life, sometimes mirrored by the brooding quality of her art. There had always been the adage of life imitating art, but she had the constant experience of the irrevocable influence of life on her art. It was a dark influence and she was haunted by the visions of pooling blood on cobblestones. She had always tried to gain inspiration from the darkness, rather than letting it overwhelm her. The beauty of Paris in the evening mist was lost on Marie-Claire. The hopeful radiance of each passing lamppost in the tide of white gloom did nothing to lighten her mood.

They were approaching the Latin Quarter, an end to the journey of darkness for the melancholy beauty. The approaching lights of *La Bouffe* spilled on to the surrounding sidewalk, chasing away the mist and darkness, a hospitable citadel of illumination. Marie-Claire decided to visit the brasserie for a nightcap. There was only a small collection of patrons, usual for the late hour on a Monday night. The car stopped and Emile opened to door for her. 'Goodnight Emile, no need to walk me home, I am going for a drink first.'

'Goodnight miss. I trust you will be all right?'

'I'll be fine, Emile. Just as all good things must come to an end, so too misery does not last forever. Have a safe trip back.' The cold mist washed over her, chilling her to the bone. She entered *La Bouffe*, opting for the welcoming warmth of the seating inside.

All of the waiters greeted her warmly, recognising her status as a regular patron. She picked a table in one of the more quiet corners, of which there were plenty at this hour. Peter came past and greeted her. He obviously had a long day behind him, as he was looking a bit frayed around the edges. 'May I get you a drink?' he offered politely to Marie-Claire.

'Can I have a bottle of the *Château Lafite*? Bring two glasses and join me? You look like you could use a drink.'

'Thanks! Things are winding down and I've been on since this morning.' He disappeared and returned shortly after with the red wine and two glasses. He pulled the cork and put the bottle down to breathe, before settling in the chair opposite.

'Are you all right? What happened at the party?' he enquired, having noticed the unmistakable trails of mascara down her cheeks.

'It all went well until the dancing started,' she responded.

'Did you have a tumble?'

'No, I wasn't dancing. Although in a different life, I might have been.' Peter raised an eyebrow, looking puzzled at the response.

'It's a long story…'

'We have a bottle of fine wine and some time on our hands. Why don't you regale me with your tale?' He poured the wine, raised his glass to Marie-Claire and took a gulp. Not the characteristic way to enjoy fine wine, but he needed some fortification after a long day.

'It started like every other Embassy party – drinks, speeches and an obscenely elaborate meal. Some parts of the food were better than others and we had some interesting characters at our table. All in all, it was not bad affair, initially. The evening was rounded off by a troupe of dancers from the Bolshoi Ballet Company, who did a performance of Cinderella.'

'Yes, that sounds truly horrid. The Bolshoi?? How could the cretins punish such a fine gathering of people in such an inhumane way?' he said in jest, trying to lighten her mood. 'Did someone fall and break a leg? Why did the Bolshoi ruin your evening??'

'Have I ever told you about my time in Moscow?'

'I think you mentioned having lived there once, but I can't remember that you gave any details.'

Marie-Claire continued her narrative. 'My father was stationed at the Embassy in Moscow in the late 50s. It was a trying time in world politics and the government wanted him to keep communication channels open with the Soviets. He was apparently an expert at that kind of thing. I had done ballet when we were in Greece, before that. I had an excellent teacher and I was quite adept by the time we arrived in Moscow. My father held a Bastille Day celebration at the Embassy and I was part of the entertainment programme, doing a ballet performance. The Soviet Premier was in attendance. I trained for weeks and when the show finally came, it was a perfect performance. The Premier recommended me for the summer scholarship programme the Bolshoi ran for talented young dancers. I fit in very well and eventually got invited to the full-time programme. By the year I turned eighteen, I was ready to audition for a place in the professional Bolshoi Ballet Company.' Her hands were shaking slightly as she spoke. It was now her turn to take a gulp of wine, finishing her glass. Peter refilled it before she continued.

'On the day of my audition, I was in the change room, the door slightly ajar. My father was approaching the change room and about to come in to wish me luck. Some men intercepted him in the passage, I later learnt that they were with the KGB. I overheard them advising him they would guarantee my place in the Bolshoi for as long as he was willing to provide them with some information when called upon. I could not bear to place my father in such a compromising position for the sake of my dancing career. Then I confronted the men and left without auditioning. I have despised the Bolshoi ever since.'

Peter looked at her, speechless. It was quite different from what he expected to hear. He actually didn't know what he expected, but this was not it. He suddenly regretted having made a joke about it. It was obvious that she was very hurt by the whole incident and would probably always harbour feelings of animosity towards the dance company and all that it represented in her life.

'I am sorry, Marie-Claire. You were dealt a cruel hand in this instance. However, you do have many other things to be thankful for in life. Were you not better off having moved away from Moscow? You are living in Paris, after all, the cultural capital of the world! You spend your days studying the great Masters of art, you create masterpieces of your own, you own a fabulous racehorse, and you live a contented life. You can come and go as you please, every day. If you joined the Bolshoi, you might have been training twelve hours a day and you would have had little choice in where you went or what you did. Your life would have been theirs to use as they saw fit.'

Marie-Claire realised he reflected her exact reservations at that time. She took another mouthful of wine. She nodded her head slowly. 'You are right. It was probably for the best and I am most probably better off. I enjoy my life here. I did not envy the dancers I saw tonight, but I was hurt by them. I should let it go, once and for all.' She finished the rest of the wine in her glass. The bottle had emptied out as they were talking and her mood had lifted. Peter somehow always understood her and always knew the right thing to say. *He was a good friend. She wondered if he could ever be more than that.*

'I think we need some more wine,' Peter said as he stood up and walked over to the bar. He returned with a bottle of 1960 *Renaudin Bollinger* champagne and two fresh glasses. 'This will help to brighten your mood further. One cannot make enlightened journeys of self-discovery on red wine alone, one needs some sparkle.'

'Indeed! How did you end up in Paris, Peter?' she enquired.

'It might take more than an evening to share my life story, but I'll do the condensed version. I was born in the city of Naples before the war started. My parents had been visiting lecturers from Germany at the local University. My father taught Literature and Writing, while my mother was a Dance and Drama professor. They had settled in Italy before there was any talk of war. Towards the end of the war, they died and my sister and I spent some years living on our own, hiding out in our house. We scrounged whatever we could to eat and stay alive. Eventually we were discovered, and ended up in a local orphanage. We coped under the circumstances and everything went as well as could be expected, until our German ancestry came to light one day. It was not a good time to be German in Italy. I decided we were in danger and needed to escape the orphanage. There was an accident during the attempted escape and when I woke up in hospital some days later, my sister was gone.' His hand reached for the scar on his temple and he had a sad look in his eyes. 'This will always be a stark reminder of the loss of my sister and I cannot look in the mirror without being reminded.'

'I have never been able to discover what had happened to her that night. From my hospital bed, I had asked the police to look for her. There was a kind sergeant who was in charge of finding her. He went to great lengths and visited all the orphanages and scoured the streets, but to no avail. In the end, they had to close the file. She had disappeared that evening, without a trace. The only thing that kept a glimmer of hope alive was that they did not find her body in any of the morgues. She might still be somewhere out there...' He drank some of the champagne, which suddenly did not seem as fitting for the occasion anymore.

Peter continued with the story. 'From the hospital, they moved me to a different orphanage in Naples, as I could not go back to the one I escaped from. I spent another two years there, before the orphanage was closed down by the government. Large numbers of orphans were sent to the South of Italy, but somehow, a bunch of us were shipped to a children's home on Corsica. I learnt French while I was there and I was placed with a foster family on the island, who later officially adopted me. We did not stay there for very long after that. My father was in shipping and his company moved him from Corsica to Malta. After finishing my schooling, I attended the University in Malta and obtained a degree in Literature. By that time I had been living on islands for a good many years and wanted to tour the continent. I think it was partially inspired by the Maltese tradition of young men touring the continent to collect their household goods in the earlier days.'

'I left Malta and travelled back to Italy by way of Sicily. My first stop in Italy was Naples, where I spent a month looking for any sign of my sister. The sergeant who was in charge of her case all those years ago was a Captain by then and he assisted me as much as he could. As a career policeman, he did not like unsolved cases. I travelled to several of the surrounding towns and orphanages in the province, but I ultimately had to give up my search. By then, Child Services had also been centralised, so I had permission to check their files, looking for her. I was not able to find any trace of my sister. I had, however, also not found her grave.' Marie-Claire found the tale captivating. *She was surprised to learn that Peter was an orphan too!*

269

'I spent a year traversing Italy, keeping a diary and doing some travel writing in the process, always enquiring at orphanages as I went along, never losing the slim hope I might find my sister.'

'Did you ever visit *Marcigliana* outside Rome?' Marie-Claire enquired.

'When I passed through Rome, I had heard from my enquiries that it was a Catholic orphanage once, but when I arrived, it was being used as a mental asylum and the nuns were no longer there,' Peter responded. 'Why do you ask?'

'I was an orphan myself. I was adopted from there by my parents, before we moved to Greece. How did you end up in France?' she asked, engrossed by his story.

Peter did not dwell on this interesting revelation, his day had been too long to appreciate the implications. 'My tour of Italy continued, moving further north. I loved Venice and spent a month there, exploring the city's maze of passages. My father's company also had offices there. He always sent me messages to the different branches, so I could keep in touch and keep them informed of my progress. From Venice, I crossed the country to the west coast and entered France. I followed the coastline through France, spending time in the various towns on the French Riviera. It was the closest I have ever come to a vacation. My travels continued into Spain, where I spent time in Barcelona and also travelled inland to Madrid. I then followed the coast of Portugal north, all the way back into Spain and eventually, France. When I reached Biarritz, there was sad news waiting for me at the shipping company offices. My parents had passed away in a car accident two weeks prior.' Marie-Claire held his hand.

'Oh no, Peter! What a horrible turn of events,' she said, shocked. 'Did you return to Malta?'

'I briefly returned, but I was delayed and too late to attend the funeral. My parents had lived in a company house, so I would not have been able to stay on at the property in any event. After settling the estate, there was not much left for me in Malta. I had arrived at a cross-roads in my life, having to decide where I wanted to go next. All the travelling had left me weary and I felt a need to settle down somewhere. With nothing for me in Malta and having a French passport, I decided to pursue a dream I had always had of living in Paris. I flew there to explore and the city proved amazing, leading to my decision to stay. I used my inheritance to buy a small flat in *Saint Germain* and I began working here as a busboy, while continuing to write. The rest, as they say, is history.'

'That is a very interesting tale, Peter. You should write a book about it.'

'Maybe someday I will,' he said pensively. The brasserie had long since emptied out around them and the last waiter had left an hour ago. Marie-Claire looked at the wall clock. 'Oh dear, look at the time! I think I need to call it a night and get to bed.'

'Indeed! I am working the morning shift again, tomo… later today,' Peter responded. Marie-Claire left some money for the wine, Peter rejecting her offer to pay for the champagne. He locked up *La Bouffe* and they kissed goodnight, a slightly lingering peck on each cheek. Peter walked in the direction of *Saint Germain* and she walked next door to her apartment.

Marie-Claire was tired. It had been a very long day. She had a glass of water from the fridge and spent some time contemplating the life story Peter had told her, realising they had probably both been orphans in Italy at the same time. *Life is full of surprises, sometimes.* Parts of his story seemed somehow familiar, as if she had come across it before. She thought about his advice on the ballet company. Maybe it was time to move on. Maybe it was time to make the mind shift and forgive the past. She went to bed, thinking about Italy and one poor boy's search for his lost sister.

A HISTORY IN NAPLES

Like almost every other night, Marie-Claire was dreaming. The conversation with Peter somehow triggered her mind to transpose her consciousness to an earlier time, before any of her living memories, which began on that cold night in Rome seventeen years ago. She was a young girl. There was an orphanage in Naples. Peter was there. Marie-Claire woke up with a start and suddenly, she remembered everything! She remembered the time before Rome. She remembered a time filled with sadness and she knew why she had repressed it from ever coming back after the accident, leaving it to haunt her dreams.

The memories washed over her in waves, some larger and more vivid than others. The memories of her parents were incomplete and fragmented, as memories from decades ago often were. There were fuzzy images of their faces and feelings of love, but not much more. She knew they were German. It was during the time of the war. One day, they were simply no longer there. She vaguely recalled playing in the backyard with her older brother Peter, and the loud wailing of klaxons. On this occasion, the air raid sirens in Naples were late. The bombers had come from inland, not over the sea like they used to in previous years. Her father looked out from an upstairs window, concern swiftly registering on his face. The back door opened, showing her mother's silhouette in the doorway. Suddenly, she heard a deafening explosion and the house collapsed. Her parents disappeared from sight in a cloud of dust. She would never see them again. Peter grabbed her arm and they ran into the streets, away from the dust and flames, looking for the entrance to the nearest bomb shelter.

The shock of what they had witnessed disorientated the pair and while they roamed the streets purposefully, they were lost, valiantly attempting to find an elusive bomb shelter. Eventually, they found a staircase leading to one. By then, the air raid had almost been over. The mood in the shelter was sombre and it was packed with a host of people, everyone crammed in a huddled mass. An eerie silence prevailed in the old stone cave. The girl started crying. Peter held her and tried to comfort the youngster. The consolations in German were met with unfriendly stares from the surrounding people. The bombings in 1944 were mostly inflicted by the retreating German forces and the invasion of Italy by their erstwhile allies in 1943, left the Italian populace with an intense dislike of Germans.

Peter could appreciate that they should not linger any longer than necessary amongst the hostile crowd. After an appropriate lull in noise of the bombings, he decided to take a chance and leave the shelter, before harm befell his sister. He exited the cave up the stairs and they scurried through the streets, into a sheltered alleyway. They sat down behind a dumpster, the smell of rotting tomatoes permeating the surrounding air. Their one consolation was that they were dressed warmly for their play outside. They were thankful that it wasn't raining today, or they would have been indoors in the home with their parents. Maria was sobbing. After the stressful events in the bomb shelter, Peter broke down and cried too. It had finally dawned on him that his parents were gone and that they were alone in the world.

He did not know what to do. Their house was gone, their parents were gone and they didn't have any relatives they knew of in Italy, or anywhere else, for that matter. They had the clothes on their backs and only each other in the entire world. Peter knew he would have to look after them, but he didn't know how to start doing that. The alley offered shelter, so he decided they should spend the night there. The boy checked the dumpster for anything that could be of use. There was some mouldy bread and the rotting tomatoes, responsible for the smell in the alley. He gave the bread to his sister, but the tomatoes smelled too vile to be considered edible, even in their extreme situation. They also found a tattered woman's coat. The coat could cover them for the evening, so he grabbed it. The children spent their first night alone. They were without parents, in an alley in Naples, huddled under an old coat. In the morning, they would go home to see what they could salvage there.

The dawn found them still clinging to each other for warmth under the coat. The sun's rays brought some light to the alley. 'We should get going,' Peter encouraged Maria.

'Can we not lie five more minutes, Peter?' she pleaded with him, feeling the cold as she poked her arms out from under the coat.

'No, we have to head to the house. We have to see what is there.' He took her hand in his and led her out of the alley. Peter didn't know exactly where they were, but if he headed to the harbour, he could find his bearings from there. They walked towards the west, with the sunrise on their backs. A more miserable pair was hard to imagine, cold and dirty. A while later, they reached Harbour road and followed it to the *Piazza Vittoria*. As they walked, the normally azure waters of the Mediterranean was a depressing shade of grey. The greenery of the plaza was a beacon of hope in the darkness, as it would be easy enough to find their way to the neighbourhood close to *Castel Sant Elmo* from there.

'Come Maria, we are almost there now,' he kept encouraging his younger sister as they plodded up the hill past the Spanish quarter. The city came to life, with smoke still rising from some of the buildings that were struck by the German bombing run the previous afternoon. Naples was a miserable city. The damage from a multitude of air raids was widespread and some families lived in the bomb shelters almost permanently. Once a family's home was destroyed, they had nowhere else to go. The Allied advance fuelled hatred of the retreating German occupants. Peter and Maria's parents dared not live in the shelters permanently and they were forced to sit in silence when they sought refuge there during the recent raids, lest they gave away their origins. Misfortune had caught up with them during one of the last air raids of the war.

The children continued up the winding roads towards the fort, Peter sometimes carrying his younger sister on his back. Once, they encountered a policeman, who stopped to question them. 'What are you kids doing in the street all alone? Where are your parents?' he enquired.

'We got separated from them in the shelter yesterday,' Peter lied. 'We are heading home now to meet up with them, it is just around the corner, up there.' He pointed in the general direction up the hill. He did not want the policeman to pay them too much attention, as he would take them to the station and when failing to locate their parents, to one of the local orphanages.

Peter felt they would take their chances in the streets and was hopeful to see what could be salvaged from their house. 'Thanks for your assistance officer, but we are almost home, our parents will be worried and we do not want to delay any further.' The policeman had an overwhelming job at the moment and was not going to bother any further. 'Hurry home now, don't dally any further!' he instructed them.

'Yes, sir,' he responded and continued up the hill.

Their trek ended at around 10 o'clock, when they reached the remains of their house. Firemen must have been there to douse the flames, as there was little burn damage to the collapsed ruin. Maria cried and Peter comforted her, sobbing himself. 'It will be all right. It will be all right,' he kept repeating, almost like a mantra. They stood in the back garden, surveying the rubble which remained of their family home. Some of the rubble had been shifted where the kitchen used to be. When Peter had calmed a bit, he saw the cellar window and decided to investigate whether he could climb in. 'Stay here and keep out of sight,' he instructed his sister, before entering the house though the window, descending into the dark bowels of the collapsed building.

Once inside, Peter knew his way around, or at least he used to. The damage to the building caused chaos in the cellar, even though the ceiling was intact. The contents of the shelves and cupboards were strewn all over and some of the metal shelving units had fallen over in the pandemonium upstairs. He carefully felt his way to the cupboard under the stairs, where they kept a torch. Peter shone the light around the cellar, gauging the damage which the explosive impact upstairs had on the contents. Everything was mostly intact, although nothing was where it used to be. As Peter looked around, an idea formed in his mind- *They could clean this up and they could live here! If they shifted the dustbin outside in front of the window after entering, no-one would even know they were there.* He tried the light switch, but nothing happened. The tap in the old stone basin produced water when he tested it, much to his delight. He walked to the window and called Maria. He helped her climb inside to safety.

They spent the next two days cleaning up the cellar and taking stock of everything useful in the room. The cellar was dark, but well-ventilated. They found a box of blankets, which proved quite handy to make beds with. There were also various tools and pieces of hardware. These were a valuable commodity which they could sell for food money in the future. The one critical missing item was clothing. They did not find any clothes and were confined to the outfits they were wearing. At least there was water and soap, so they could wash the clothes from time to time, and also themselves. Peter made a marvellous discovery when examining the contents of a coffee can. There were several thousand *Lira* in small notes, which would help to buy food for them. By the end of the second day, they had the cellar up to a standard of living in line with other survivors in the bomb shelters of Naples.

Peter made regular outings from the cellar to inspect the surrounding area and to buy food. He did not want to buy anything directly in the neighbourhood, as he was afraid the shopkeepers might know what had happened to his parents. *This could lead to questions, which he did not want to answer.* He therefore made sure to travel to the Spanish quarter to buy his food. The neighbourhood was packed with people and visiting strangers, so another new face did not raise any suspicion. Peter was born in Italy, so he could speak passable Italian, although his accent was a bit odd. He always tried to keep conversations short, so that people did not catch on to it. He got to know the Spanish quarter well, as he did not want to take the same route home too often. After a few weeks, he could find his way home from almost any point in the maze of streets. While he was out, Maria stayed in the cellar, out of sight. Peter took some effort to teach her Italian, as conversing in German in the streets of Naples would only get them in trouble. Maria was a fast learner and apparently had a good ear for languages. The days passed slowly but surely and they fell into a routine which kept them out of the way of the authorities and living undisturbed in the cellar, with only each other as company.

By the time Maria was six, she could speak passable Italian and Peter didn't need to tell people in the streets that she was a mute anymore. The war was over and people moved about more freely in the city, while rebuilding the ruins of Naples. This was also the time where circumstances got harder still for the children. They had used up the money in the coffee can and had sold everything of value in the cellar to pay for food and replacement clothing, once their own got too small or too ragtag to wear outside. Peter and Maria had reached the point where they had to resort to begging to stay alive. October was approaching and their clothing was inadequate to stave off the coming winter cold. The two children were begging in the streets of Naples, clothed only in rags. They often had to resort to travelling in the back streets, to avoid police attention in the main thoroughfares of Naples.

One night, as they lay hungry in the cellar, Peter was telling a story. He often tried to cheer Maria up, by making up tales of different places and of better times. Peter was a gifted story teller and had a naturally active imagination, he could often entertain Maria for hours and make her escape their squalid surroundings. 'Someday we'll be rich, you and I,' he said. 'We'll have a mansion with servants. It will be filled with fine furniture and we'll each have a separate wing to live in.'

'Will we have enough food?' Maria asked.

'We'll have more than we can ever eat. I'll be a writer and sell thousands of books and we'll never be hungry again. We'll live the good life, in Paris!'

'I'll be famous too,' Maria piped in. 'I'll be an artist, like Mama, and my paintings will sell for Millions. People will stand in queues to buy them. They'll hang them in museums. Let's make a promise, Peter? We'll promise to be rich someday, no matter what it takes.'

Peter stuck out his hand and they pinkie swore. 'To being rich and famous in Paris.'

'To being rich and famous!' Maria echoed. The children fell asleep, dreaming of better lives in far-off places.

THE ORIGINS OF TRAGEDY

They were woken up by voices the next morning, as a torch was shone into the cellar, playing over their makeshift bedding. It was the city engineers, inspecting the house. Naples was being restored to its pre-war glory and the damaged buildings were being inspected for repair or demolition. They spotted the children in the darkness of the cellar. 'You in there, come outside!' the elderly engineer commanded. Peter helped Maria out of the window and they stood facing the team of engineers.

'Is this your house?'

The children nodded.

'Where are your parents?'

The children remained silent, staring at the shoes of the interrogator. He opened a file and checked the address. 'Oh!' he whispered sorrowfully, as the file revealed the tragedy of the former occupants of the house. 'They're gone... We'll have to take you to Social Services, so they can look after you.'

'We can look after ourselves,' Peter recanted. 'We'll be fine here, don't worry about us.'

'But we will be demolishing this block next week. You won't have anywhere to live.' The engineer showed genuine concern about the welfare of the children, as they were looking quite bedraggled in their current state. They were dusty and dreary, only half-awake and trying to comprehend what was happening to them. 'Lucio, take the children to social services and see how they can help them,' he instructed one of his juniors. 'Is there anything you want to get before you go?'

'No sir, we have nothing left,' Peter responded. Maria took a last, lingering look at a pile of rocks in the corner of the yard as they followed Lucio to his van.

Lucio drove the children to the Social Services office in the municipal engineering van. Upon arrival, the receptionist pointed them to an office in the back corner with her pencil, before returning to her cross-word puzzle. Lucio tapped on the glass panel of the door. The gentleman behind the desk introduced himself as Alfonso Benetti. He had a kind manner about him and his wire-rimmed glasses and wild grey hair created an almost comical caricature, putting the children at ease. After Lucio updated the social worker with the tale of the two unfortunate youngsters as he knew it, he shook their hands and left the office. 'Good luck, young master Peter. Look after yourself and your sister.'

Mister Benetti tended to the case of the two children in front of him. It was a difficult time in post-war Naples and there were, sadly, still many children in their unfortunate position. Benetti questioned Peter and Maria and filled in some blue forms, which were being copied in triplicate through charcoal paper sheets. After obtaining as much if their history as he could, he knew the likelihood of finding any family of theirs in Italy was very low. Their German origins also made it unlikely that he would be able to find a foster family for them with any great haste either. The sad conclusion was that they would have to be placed in an orphanage in Naples and it was not going to be easy for them.

After checking a clipboard which was updated on a daily basis, he determined which local orphanage had any beds available, or was the least overcrowded. He knew that separating the children would be cruel and he would have to make every effort to keep them together. *Santissima Annunziata Maggiore* had been involved in housing orphans from the early seventeenth century in some form or another and would look after the two children until some other solution presented itself. Benetti called one of his juniors from the telephone on his desk. 'Roberto, please come to my office and fetch two children for *Annunziata?*' There was a reply and he hung up. 'Peter, you will need to keep an eye on Maria. I know you have been doing so for a long time, but you cannot let up now at the orphanage. It is also important that you stick to speaking Italian. Don't let on that you are German, as it will only create problems,' he advised them in a sympathetic tone.

Roberto arrived at the office and mister Benetti handed him an envelope with a copy of the blue form he had completed for each child. 'Take these children to Father Guglielmetti and deliver their papers to him safely.'

'Goodbye Peter. Goodbye Maria. Good luck and God bless.' Roberto led the two outside and they climbed into an old green Fiat parked in a lot next to the offices. The drive to the orphanage was short, as it was not located far from the government offices.

Santissima Annunziata Maggiore was a magnificent church, with tall grey pillars adorning its yellow front facade. A huge dome was visible at the rear of the basilica and there stood a tower to the left of the building. The windows of the orphanage itself faced the grand ancient church across a courtyard separating the two buildings. Roberto led them past the main doors of the church and accompanied them through the entrance under the bell tower. They walked through the entrance hall and continued to the office of father Guglielmetti, who was in charge of the orphanage. His office looked more like a library than an office and probably served that purpose in the distant past. Huge, book filled shelves lined the walls from floor to ceiling. In the middle of the room was a desk with a melancholy looking priest sitting behind it, studying a leather-bound text with some interest.

The entry of Roberto and the two children disrupted his thought process and the priest was visibly irritated with the interruption. 'Yes, Roberto..? May I help you with something?' he asked the intruders with questioning eyebrows.

'Father, I have brought these two children. They need to be accommodated. Here are their papers.'

'I thought as much. You never grace us with social calls, Roberto.' Father Guglielmetti seemed to have recovered from his initial irritation and took the envelope from him. His eyes softened somewhat as he read the papers, despite a stern expression appearing almost permanently etched into his ageing face. 'I will take it from here, Roberto. Please inform Alfonso of the new numbers?' He handed Roberto a sheet of paper. 'Goodbye young man.' Roberto took his leave, closing the door behind him as he exited the study.

Father Guglielmetti observed the two children in silence for a few moments. They were still in their ragged clothes and looked like they could use a bath. Their hair was unkempt and required some pruning, to say the least. 'Welcome to *Annunziata,* children.' They stood silently, waiting for the priest to continue. 'We run a tight ship here, no slacking in your schoolwork or you chores. Breakfast is at seven every morning. I expect any ill-treatment by the staff or the other children to be reported to me, immediately.' He continued reciting a list of the general rules of the orphanage and how the day programme worked. The children stood still, attentively listening. 'Do you understand?' They nodded. 'Do you have any questions?' Peter and Maria shook their heads.

The priest took them to the bath house to get cleaned up. This included a haircut for both Peter and Maria. They received a set of clothes at the laundry. The pair were now looking much more presentable and could almost pass for any normal school-aged child. The other children at the orphanage had already finished their lunch and Father Guglielmetti took them to the kitchen for a meal. Not having eaten since a meagre meal of some dry bread the previous evening, the children were both ravenous. They sat at the kitchen table and were served bread and soup, which they eagerly devoured. Their introduction to the orphanage continued and they were taken to their respective dormitories and assigned beds. Each was showed where the other would stay, so they could find one another. The other orphans were still attending afternoon classes and the two large sleeping halls were quiet. Father Guglielmetti used the rest of the afternoon to finish their tour of the facility. By suppertime, the priest took them to the dining hall, where he introduced them the all the other orphans. 'This is Peter and Maria, they will join us here from today. Treat them kindly.' The other orphans paid them scant attention, as they were much more focused on their meal.

Their stay at the orphanage was rather uneventful and the weeks and months passed without much distinction between one day and the next. Marie-Claire's memories of the time had the days as a never-ending blur of routine. It was a mundane existence, based on endless repetition. There was breakfast, followed by school, followed by lunch, more school, chores and supper. After supper was a bit of freedom and in the summer, it provided for some playtime before sunset. The seasons flowed into each other and her outfits adapted to the passing of time. The monotonous situation abruptly changed on New Years' day in 1948.

There was no school between Christmas and New Years' and the children were roaming the orphanage, keeping themselves busy with leisure activities. Maria sat in the lounge with some girls, listening to a radio show. *Auld Lang Syne* started playing and everyone joined in singing along. Maria recognised the melody and could remember she loved singing the song with her mother. It was a happy memory of a time she had almost forgotten. '*Sollte denn alte Bekanntschaft vegessen sein...*' Maria sang joyfully. The other girls stopped singing by the third line, staring silently at Maria, who then stopped as well, as she realised what had happened. Maria got up and walked out, leaving as the excited sound of chatter erupted in the room behind her.

Maria had run to find Peter in the garden and told him about the incident. He knew it was not good. They had seen German children having a torrid time at *Annunziata* in the past. News of the incident had spread like wildfire through the orphanage and by supper time, Peter and Maria found themselves in a hostile environment. They struggled to find seating for supper, with open spaces suddenly closing up as children shifted positions when they approached. When they eventually sat down at a half filled table, the seated children got up and moved to other tables. This was only the start of their woes.

The next three months proved really tough on Peter and Maria. Although they weren't initially harmed physically, they were shunned and ostracised by the other orphans. By March, it had gotten to the point where the other children started bullying them as well. Peter found Maria outside one day, with a bloody nose. She was quietly crying on a bench. He realised that they had to escape this place, or Maria was bound to suffer a much worse fate in the coming months. The arrival of summer would mean more unsupervised time outside and create endless opportunity for them to be mistreated. Peter was plotting their escape in the ever lengthening period of free time after their daily supper.

The day of their escape had arrived. It was March 28 and although the nights were still cold in Naples, they were not deathly so. The sun was setting as Peter and Maria stealthily moved to the back wall of the orphanage. There was a large oak tree growing close to it, which they climbed, making their way to the top of the high boundary wall. As they rested on the stone wall for a moment, Peter spoke to Maria. 'We'll be ok. We're going to head to Rome. The road at the front of the church heads in that direction if you turn left. We'll follow that out of town.' He gave her a hug. 'I love you Maria.'

'I love you too Peter.'

He lowered her down the wall, using a sheet he brought along for the purpose. Her hands tired quickly and she dropped the last bit, scuffing her shoes and tearing her yellow dress in the process. Peter tied the sheet to branch in the tree and repelled down. The strain was too much for the worn out orphanage sheet and it suddenly tore, dropping Peter backwards from halfway up the stone wall. He landed on his side with a resounding crunch and cracked his head on the cobblestone pavement. He lay still as blood flowed from his temple, pooling between the cobblestones. Maria shook him and tried to wake him up, but Peter was not responding. For the longest time, Maria kept shaking Peter, crying for him to wake up. Eventually, it became too much for her and she ran away, heading to the front street in the darkness. She lost her last remaining relative in the world that evening, in the street behind a Naples Basilica. The lead glass angels silently watched over the boy as the spreading pool of blood created a red halo around his head.

As Maria entered the main road and headed to the left, a truck engine sputtered to life on the side of the road. In an instant, she climbed onto the back of the truck, just before it pulled off. She sat crying between the crates filling up the truck bed and eventually fell asleep, the engine droning in the night. She slept fitfully for many hours, having a temporary reprieve from the tragedy she experienced. Maria was startled awake as the truck slowed down at an intersection. She looked through the canvas covering and saw a sign reading *Rome*. She hurriedly started getting off the back of the truck as it slowed down to a crawl. As she was about the let go, the unseen driver accelerated, jarring her grip loose and spilling her off the back of the truck. Maria hit her head as she landed and rolled to the side of the road, where she blacked out.

She woke up in a strange city, not knowing how she got there or who she was, chilled to the bone. She stood up slowly, dusted herself off and started walking down the road, heading off into the unknown...

THE MORNING AFTER, 1965

Themselves intense returning flood of forgotten memories had abated, leaving Marie-Claire with a blinding headache. She had a racing heart and her head was spinning with the sheer weight of what she had now realised for the first time in her life- *she had a brother!* Peter's presence a mere four stories below her, was the most amazing of coincidences. For years they had both migrated extensively across Europe and had somehow settled in the same city, having almost daily interaction, after Marie-Claire had left him for dead a thousand miles away in a different country, almost two decades ago.

She went to the bathroom cabinet and took two aspirins with a large glass of water. Marie-Claire was feeling a little dizzy and lay down on the couch, a cold compress on her forehead. She thought back to the basement in Naples. 'We'll live the good life, in Paris!' Peter had said. They both ended up here, spending their lives mere minutes apart. *Was it the deeper subconscious which drove them to Paris, or was it some higher purpose?* She lay on the couch and stared at the half-finished painting on the easel, visible in the next room. It made sense now. It was the cobble stone street behind the *Annunziata* orphanage. The sight of Peter's body lying bleeding in the street unknowingly haunted her dreams for decades. She had painted a multitude of variations of the scene over the years, trying to make sense of the brief flashes of recall she had, lingering afterthoughts of a bad dream. And now the nightmare was over. He was alive.

A half an hour later, her thoughts were still racing, but the headache subsided and she had composed herself. Sitting up, she was no longer dizzy. She drank another glass of water and chased it down with a small measure of brandy. Her body would now withstand a trip downstairs. She could no longer contain the urge to leave the apartment and go to *La Bouffe* to find Peter. Marie-Claire dressed in a hurry, throwing on a simple dress and pulling her hair up in a bun. Now was not the time to waste on vanity. Rushing out, she impatiently tapped her foot while waiting for the lift to arrive. The elevator eventually made an appearance. The twenty second trip to the ground floor felt like an eternity in the enclosed space. She almost fell out of the lift doors when they finally opened and hurriedly left the building.

Marie-Claire was almost running by the time she arrived at *La Bouffe*. It was a different shift of waiters from the night before, but she knew their faces from her many years of patronage. 'Is Peter here?' she asked the first available busboy. 'No miss, he went to the market, he should be back in a bit.' Marie-Claire was disappointed beyond belief. She had waited her whole life for this moment, unknowingly. *The empty space of not having blood family would finally be filled.* But not just this minute. She sat down at the closest table, visibly shaking. 'Are you all right, miss?' a nearby waiter enquired.

'I'll be fine. Can I have a double espresso please?' She gazed into the street, unseeing. Then she rested her head in her hands, staring at the table top for the longest time. Her coffee arrived and was placed on the table. She thanked the waiter and looked up. It was Peter. She didn't know whether to laugh or cry.

'I didn't think we drank *that* much last night,' Peter said, looking at her slightly dishevelled appearance. It was definitely not normal for her to appear at *La Bouffe* in such an unkempt state, even on the morning after a party. 'Are you all right?'

She stood up slowly from the table. 'I am Maria,' she said. Peter looked confused. 'I am Maria,' she repeated. 'I am your sister, Peter!'

'Why would..? What makes..? How..?' he stammered for words, even more confused.

'I remembered, Peter! I remember the air raid and the bomb shelter. I remember the backstreets of Naples. I remember the basement and the day the city engineers came. I remember Father Guglielmetti at *Annunziata*. I remember *Auld Lang Syne*. I remember your fall. I remember everything!'

Peter stood staring at her, dazed and reeling. He had told her his story the night before. *But he had not told her all of this. She could not have known. Unless she was there. Unless she was Maria. Unless she was his sister.* Tears welled up in his eyes. 'Maria…' He embraced her.

The exceptional circumstances had warranted Peter being given the day off. After Marie-Claire had eaten something, they walked off together. As they strolled the streets of Paris, Marie-Claire filled Peter in on her own life story, starting at the beginning in Rome. She told him all about her time in *Marcigliana*, about Sister Cecile and learning French. As she got to her adoption by the Le Blancs, they were sitting on a bench in the park behind the *Notre Dame* Cathedral. Her brief stay in Rome was recounted as they walked up the right bank of the river and her inspirational vision of *The Creation of Adam* fittingly came up as they passed the *Louvre*.

They crossed the river at *Pont Royal* and their stroll continued on the left bank, past the *Gare D'Orsay*. Her tale shifted to her time in Athens as they passed under the *Eiffel Tower* and up the stairs of the *Trocadero* Gardens. Marie-Claire told Peter of her first introduction to ballet, the Degas print still fresh in her memory. She also spoke further of her art classes and the origins of her interest in art.

The siblings turned toward the *Arc de Triomphe*, strolling down the *Champs-Élysées*. As they passed the boutiques lining the avenue, Marie-Claire was telling Peter of the fateful *Bastille Day* event in Moscow that changed her life so radically. By the time they reached the Paris Opera house, her story had advanced to the end of her time in the Bolshoi, the last details of her exit from the school now being told in greater detail than the night before.

The pair enjoyed a late lunch at a café overlooking the *Parc D'Belville*. During their lunchtime conversation, Marie-Claire was telling Peter of her first trip to *St Moritz* and her first trip to the Riviera. He was quite surprised to hear the story of her posing for Picasso and the stolen painting, even though he had never seen it himself. After lunch, the pair ambled towards the *Montmartre* area, passing the *Moulin Rouge* and heading up the steep steps into the artists quarter. Peter was very interested to hear of the numerous painting she had unknowingly painted of him over the years, inspired by the mysterious vision of Peter's body, lying bleeding on the street behind *Annunziata*.

When the sun started setting over Paris the two found themselves on the steps of the *Sacré Coeur*, overlooking the city, with the magnificent Basilica at their backs. They were two people in a large crowd, all enjoying the view of the setting sun over the City of Light. Marie-Claire reached the end of the abridged account of the wondrous life she had lived the past 17 years. The sun set on the day they spent getting re-acquainted, like the past sinking behind the horizon, no longer unknown. 'You had an amazing life, Marie-Claire,' Peter remarked. 'It could not have turned out any better for an orphan from Naples.' When dusk settled, they took a taxi back to the Latin Quarter. The siblings parted ways. 'Tomorrow, you must tell me your life story in more detail, Peter. I want to hear all about your travels though Corsica and Malta and Italy and Spain. We can meet up for breakfast and go from there?'

'Agreed! Goodnight Marie-Claire. I hope you will finally have sweet dreams.'

Marie-Claire went to bed, exhausted from the day, but with a previously unknown feeling of tranquillity, unlike anything she experienced before. She drifted off to sleep. The next morning Marie-Claire woke up, her pillow dry.

THE END

EPILOGUE – PARIS, 1969

After the fairy tale reunion, Marie-Claire and Peter had decided to move in together, sharing the penthouse property Mr Le Blanc had bought in the 7th arrondissement for use during his time in Parliament. Although President De Gaulle was re-elected in 1965, the political landscape in France was changing and Mr Le Blanc decided to not avail himself for another term as MP in the French Parliament. He considered it time for a younger generation of Frenchmen, and women, to take over the running of France. Widespread upheaval amongst students and workers in 1968 proved that his views on this were right and President De Gaulle admitted as much when he had to resign in 1969. The property was therefore unused, as the Le Blancs moved back to *Chantilly* to enjoy retirement in the quiet of the countryside.

The siblings shared the three-bedroom penthouse overlooking the *Seine* River. The apartment was lavishly furnished and expensive art adorned the walls. Their pinky promise of becoming rich, made all those years ago in a run-down basement in Naples, had been kept. Marie-Claire's race-horse, *Vaguely Noble*, had won the *Prix de l'Arc de Triomphe* in 1968. This was one of the richest horse races in the world and added to her other winnings, she was now independently wealthy. She continued travelling the world, exploring the Americas, Africa and Asia. She remained unattached.

Peter succeeded in becoming a well-respected writer. In 1968, he published a biopic based on his travels and the search for his missing sister. *Looking for Maria* became a bestseller. He also wrote a song based on Marie-Claire's telling of her life story. This became a number one hit on the UK charts and it won a 1969 *Ivor Novello* award for best song, musically and lyrically. The song was called "Where do you go to (My lovely)?"

Made in the USA
Coppell, TX
16 April 2020